"You know what you want . . . now . . ."

He put his arms around her so suddenly that she had no opportunity to try to move away. He drew her against him as hard as he could, pressing her against him. His demanding lips closed down on hers and held. One hand moved slowly up and down her spine, making her quiver with excitement. She reached up to encircle his neck but dropped her hand just in time . . . she had almost let him know how she felt and how much she wanted him.

"Good night, my love," he said as he released her. "I'll give you notice when I'll be back. Think about me. You'll be on my mind until I see you again."

Then he stepped back and disappeared into the gloom.

Books by
Dorothy Daniels

Conover's Folly

Diablo Manor

The Duncan Dynasty

The Lanier Riddle

The Magic Ring

The Marble Hills

The Sisters of Valcour

For Love and Valcour

Published by
WARNER BOOKS

FOR LOVE AND VALCOUR

DOROTHY DANIELS

WARNER BOOKS

A Warner Communications Company

WARNER BOOKS EDITION

Copyright © 1983 by Dorothy Daniels
All rights reserved.

Cover art by Paul Brian Bachem

Warner Books, Inc.,
666 Fifth Avenue,
New York, N.Y. 10103

 A Warner Communications Company

Printed in the United States of America

First Printing: February, 1983

10 9 8 7 6 5 4 3 2 1

FOR LOVE AND VALCOUR

one

Though the two women who occupied the rowboat bore little resemblance to each other, they were mother and daughter. The younger, Virginia Hammond Birch, shipped the oars, rested her lower arms on her thighs and leaned forward to relieve the strain on her shoulder and arm muscles. Her breathing was labored, and the glare of the sun on the water had made her dizzy. She closed her eyes until her head cleared, ignoring the perspiration that formed rivulets of moisture down her face, dropping onto the skirt of her dress.

"Virginia, are you all right?" Lenore Hammond asked.

"I'm resting, Mama."

"I don't see why you can't get one of the slaves to row—"

"Mama," Virginia interrupted her, "you know perfectly well there are no more slaves. The blacks are as free as we are. We can't take them to the whipping sheds anymore. Things have changed."

"You're right about that." Lenore's voice registered her disapproval. "To think of having to pay one hundred dollars for dinner as we did in Charleston last night. It's outrageous."

Virginia replied with a patience borne more from weariness than tolerance. "Just be thankful we had the money to buy a dinner."

"'Thankful'!" Lenore exclaimed bitterly. "I wanted to buy a supply of coffee to take back to the island, but at forty dollars a pound—and flour a thousand dollars a barrel—it's downright thievery, that's what it is."

Virginia compressed her lips to hold back the angry retort, straightened, dipped the oars again and began rowing. Her hands no longer blistered, for they were well-calloused, but every muscle of her young body was outraged to the point where she felt like screaming from the pain. Yet if she did, she told herself, she'd be like her mother who had never been able to withstand adversity of any kind. Yet, she couldn't blame her mother too much. They'd lived a life of pleasure on Valcour. Growing fine cotton by the sweat of more than a hundred slaves had provided ample funds for the balls, soirees, hunts, picnics and frequent trips to Charleston on the mainland.

Even the beginning of the war had little effect on the islanders until one day Yankee forces stormed ashore unexpectedly and everyone had to flee on a moment's notice, leaving all their possessions behind.

Besides the shock of this, Virginia's mother had lost her husband to the war. Virginia also learned her first husband had been killed in battle, though in her case she felt only relief, for he'd been cruel, unfaithful and had finally turned thief.

To shut out the pain of her protesting muscles, she occupied her mind with memories of that golden time when she was eighteen and her days and nights were filled with laughter, romance and a keen enjoyment of the pleasures of life.

Four slaves would row a barge piled high with her extravagant purchases. At the landing, there would be more slaves waiting to carry the boxes to the mansion. She recalled the thrill of trying on her newly acquired wardrobe, pirouetting before the mirror, then tossing the garments onto the bed where Phoebe would carefully place them on a hanger and manage to arrange them in an orderly fashion in her already jammed closets.

Today no one would be at the small dock. Her father was dead, her sister Nanine, slowly recovering from a serious illness, was still too weak to be fully active. Virginia's brother, Martin, remained in Charleston, as he had done since the end of the war, drinking heavily in an attempt to forget that the war had ended in defeat for the South. Phoebe, Virginia's half-sister, was now married and living in New York City with Tom Sprague, who'd been a lieutenant in the Northern army. Virginia's features softened slightly as she thought of Elias Birch to whom she was now married. He'd been a major in the Northern army and was now trying to make order out of chaos with the plantation. She never believed she would ever marry a Northerner, much less an officer in their army, any more than she ever believed she would accept Phoebe as her sister.

Now she found herself apprehensive about Phoebe who was the result of an affair between Virginia's father and a nearly white slave. Phoebe was, perhaps, one-eighth Negro, but she could pass anywhere as white. And that was exactly what she intended to do when she and Tom departed for the North. Though Tom knew the truth about her origin, he swore it would never make the slightest difference.

Virginia wished Elias could have been at the dock to meet her, but her common sense told her he was far too busy in the fields.

The boat touched the dock and she quickly tied up, helped her mother out of the craft and then unloaded their scanty purchases. She turned one gunnysack over to her mother.

"I think you can manage this," she said, steeling herself for the reply she knew was coming.

"Well, I'll try." Lenore, still unused to any kind of physical labor, accepted it reluctantly. "I'm very angry at the man who sold us back our own silver. He ought to be ashamed of himself, charging more than it cost thirty years ago."

"Mama," Virginia said patiently, "think back to how desperate we were when we sold it to him. He held it for us and he's entitled to a profit."

"Still, I'll see to it that he never gets any more of our business, nor that of my friends."

Virginia made no comment, for the statement was ridiculous. Her mother's friends were on the verge of bankruptcy. They were not as fortunate as Virginia, whose father had been careful to bury gold before the war began so that now his family, though not rich, was by no means destitute.

As she almost always did, Virginia paused, both to get her breath again and to study this island and, particularly, the mansion where she had been born and raised. It wasn't large compared with the plantation house on the mainland, but it always sent a thrill through Virginia when her eyes caught sight of it after a trip to the mainland. The pillared porch that surrounded three sides was impressive. Until the war, the house and blinds had always gleamed with fresh paint. Its whiteness stood out even more, surrounded as it was with old and flourishing elms, magnolias, poplars and maples. There was a formal garden, which grew every kind of rose imaginable, and scattered about the house were lilacs, laurels, japonica, honeysuckle and gardenias.

It pained her now to see the house badly in need of a coat of paint. In fact, there were places where some of it had peeled off. She remembered her father telling her that the house hadn't always been this large. When he'd inherited it from his father, he'd added two wings and a kitchen separate from the house itself, though connected by a sheltered walkway. The interior had suffered also when the slaves ransacked it. They'd stolen clothing, curtains, rugs and draperies and had even carted off furniture to their quarters. Elias had managed to salvage some of the furniture, though it had been badly scratched.

Her two rooms, which had been tastefully furnished, were now mostly barren of furniture, just as her closet was devoid of shelves and the clothes racks were empty. She wondered how long it would take her to restore it to its former glory. Not the remainder of her life, she hoped.

The island called Valcour was part of the Seaward Islands, off the North Carolina coast. It was, perhaps, the most beautiful of them all, if not the largest. It was here that her father's slaves, a hundred or more, worked the fields to produce some of the finest cotton. Far better than that raised on her father's huge mainland plantation where almost a thousand slaves had worked. Today, the cotton was grown on small farms, now owned by the men who had once been slaves. The crop was not going to be very good.

The island had been invaded by Yankees soon after the war began. Its white population, consisting of the occupants of twenty-four large homes, had fled barely in time to escape the Northern soldiers who came ashore so unexpectedly.

Lenore grasped the sack and lifted it, only to let it drop. She burst into tears, turning away to hide her agony.

"Mama," Virginia said calmly, "stop it!"

"How can you ask me not to weep?" Lenore raised a hand and waved it in the direction of the mansion. "Don't you remember how it used to be? Can't you recall anything about the lovely life we had here? Haven't you even a trace of sympathy for my situation?"

"Mama, please shut up." Virginia sharpened her tone. "We've no time for weeping. Or feeling sorry for ourselves."

"How wrong you are. All we have anymore is time, and no way of using it for our enjoyment."

Virginia made no attempt to conceal the exasperation she felt. "Mama, we can't waste a moment. Over and over I've told you I intend to bring back to this island and especially to Willowbrook—our part of the island—the beauty and glory it had before the war. And more! Nothing in the world is going to stop me. Nothing! And we're not alone now. I've Elias to help."

"Elias is a Yankee. He was one of their officers." Lenore's tone was still desolate. "How can you depend on him?"

"You were mighty grateful to him when Phoebe and I brought you back here before the war ended," Virginia retorted, her patience at an end. "I don't know what we'd have done or where we'd have gone if he'd thrown us back in the boat. Especially with Nanine so ill."

"I haven't forgotten," Lenore said. "Still, he is a Yankee."

"The war is over, Mama. Can't you remember that?"

"No, I can't," Lenore said, giving no quarter. "The North is to blame for all our troubles."

"Mama, I love Elias. Certainly you expressed no objection when I married him."

"Would it have done me any good?"

"Absolutely none." Virginia gave a defiant nod of her head.

"That's why I kept quiet," Lenore said, still giving no ground. "However, I'll admit this much: I'm pleased we have a man in the house. I think you displayed good sense in marrying him, especially since there are so many Yankees on the island."

Virginia eyed her mother with disbelief. "Mama, I married Elias because I love him. And he loves me. Have you forgotten how beautiful love between a man and a woman can be?"

"How can you be so unkind?" Lenore's voice broke as she spoke, and she dabbed at her eyes with a handkerchief.

Virginia gave an impatient shake of her head, picked up the box of groceries and started up the slope toward the mansion. Halfway there, she saw Elias coming on horseback. Her features softened at sight of him. She forgot her fatigue, conscious of her quickened heartbeat as he neared her. He sat a horse well and he looked magnificent despite his sweat-soaked shirt and straw-colored hair damp against his brow. His light blue eyes seemed to pierce her heart each time he looked at her. She set the box down, removed her hat, tossing it onto the box and waited until he dismounted. His arms raised to receive her and a smile touched his mouth as he studied her.

"Even covered with sweat your face is beautiful," he said.

Before she could reply, his lips touched hers, lightly at first, then more ardently. She returned the embrace, heedless of her wet face and disheveled appearance. They broke the embrace as Lenore, standing a short distance away, coughed delicately.

"I missed you, darling," he said, pushing the moist strands of blond hair back from her face. "The twenty-four hours you were gone seemed a lifetime."

"For me also," Virginia replied happily. "It's a blessing to be back."

He embraced her with his eyes, then turned to Lenore. "Nice to have you back too, Mother Hammond. I'll relieve you of the sack."

"Thank you, Elias, but be careful of it," she warned. "It contains some of our silver. I had to buy it back and I was terribly overcharged. It's disgusting. And that isn't all."

"You can tell him all about our trip later, Mama," Virginia said. "I want to get out of these clothes. I declare, rowing back and forth is as hard as working the fields."

Lenore followed them at a slower pace. She was beginning to feel her years, though nothing on earth could have dragged such an admission out of her. She watched the two of them walking swiftly up the sloping path. Two tall, slender people, so well matched in looks. The only distraction was Elias's limp from a bullet wound suffered soon after the war began.

Virginia had blossomed during the war, privations or not, for she'd been compelled to lead the way and take upon herself such responsibilities that she had grown into womanhood in a matter of a few weeks. Before the war she also had been a leader, but in the social swirl of the pre-war days when soirees, picnics, elaborate dances, had been her life. From an empty-headed round of nothing but pleasure the war had changed her into a calculating, practical woman. Lenore wasn't sure she liked that part of her daughter, but she silently agreed it had been necessary, though she resented the sharp tone Virginia used to indicate her impatience with her mother. Lenore continued her inspection, noting there wasn't an excess ounce of flesh on Virginia. Her hair was still the same golden color, her eyes just as violet and as enticing as when she'd been an outrageous flirt. Even though long strands of hair had escaped the pins and might be considered in disarray by some, it enhanced Virginia's feminine appeal. She had too much of that, Lenore thought, her brow furrowing worriedly.

A pity Nanine was so devoid of that compelling charm. Not that she wasn't good-looking. She was, but men didn't surround her as they did her younger sister. Lenore felt a trace of resentment as she eyed Virginia walking ahead, her posture beautiful, tired as she was. A gentle breeze blew in their direction and it pressed Virginia's skirt against her form, revealing its shapeliness and allure.

Lenore's hands touched her thickened waistline and her lips compressed in annoyance, then she gave an apathetic shrug. What difference did it make? James Hammond, the only man she'd ever loved, was gone. She wished she'd given more of herself to him, but she couldn't bear the thought of bearing another child. And James, well—he'd wanted more from a woman than she could ever give. Lenore was certain he got it. She remembered his handsomeness and his fierce passion. The thought made her color slightly, knowing she'd matched it in the early years of their marriage. But becoming pregnant removed the pleasure for her, so she began making excuses. James never forced his attentions on her and, after awhile, he let her alone.

Lenore's glance switched to Elias Birch. Major Elias Birch had led the invasion of the island, and became its military commander. To think he'd fallen in love with Virginia, even before he met her. He'd even told them how it happened. He'd occupied the rooms that had been hers, and the scent of her perfume, which was still evident in it, had set fire to his imagination. During the administration of the island, he'd managed the ex-slaves very well and had learned how to raise cotton.

Certainly Virginia needed him to restore the glory of Valcour. Lenore had an idea he would be as capable of doing that as he'd been at commanding the island. She wanted him to succeed, but there were times when she resented the fact he was a Yankee. Once, Virginia had resented it even more. Yet she'd married him. Strange what love does, Lenore mused. Her daughter's hatred for the despised Yankee officer had turned to love. Lenore hoped it would work out. She wanted the old days back. They wouldn't have slaves, but they'd have servants and parties and beautiful gowns, and along with all of that, music and laughter once again. God knows they'd done without it long enough.

Once in the house, Lenore stood patiently until Elias had removed the silver from the gunnysack and placed it on a table in the hall. She nodded with satisfaction and headed for the stairs.

Virginia picked up the box of groceries, but Elias took it from her. "I know where these go. You run along and take your bath."

"I want to see Nanine first," Virginia said. "I'm surprised she didn't meet us."

"She's probably resting," Lenore said, already ascending the staircase. "And I'm going to do the same. I have a wretched headache. But at least we got our silver back. Except for what that horrible Wade LeGarue stole. How you ever married such a man."

"He's dead, Mama," Virginia said quietly. "Killed in the war. He died bravely. Let him rest in peace."

Virginia had followed her mother upstairs and they'd reached the landing. Lenore made a half-turn to face her daughter. Virginia had to admit the dark circles under her mother's eyes attested to the fact the woman wasn't exaggerating her physical fatigue. Also, her dark hair was now generously streaked with gray and the lines around her eyes and mouth had deepened. A wave of compassion swept through Virginia and she embraced her mother.

"I'm sorry I spoke harshly to you," she said. "I know you're tired. A rest will help relax you."

Lenore responded to Virginia's kindness. "I don't mean to be so contrary. I just can't forget what we went through and what we've lost."

"Remember what I said," Virginia replied, her voice still gentle. "I'm going to bring it all back. I swear I will. You wait and see."

Lenore nodded. "You're strong. Like your papa. Thank God I have you to lean on. Now, go see how Nanine is."

Virginia obeyed, tossing her hat on a small table. She opened Nanine's door softly. Her fears evaporated when she saw her sister sleeping peacefully. She bent down and kissed Nanine's cheek. Nanine opened her eyes. A smile of apology touched her mouth when she saw Virginia.

"Oh, you're back. I'm sorry I didn't waken in time to be downstairs to welcome you," Nanine said.

"You need your rest." Virginia eased herself down on the side of the bed. "Didn't you sleep last night?"

"Beautifully," Nanine admitted. "But that weariness has a habit of coming back. I only intended to rest, but I must have drifted off."

"I'm glad you did," Virginia replied, smiling at her sister. "Don't forget, you were ill for a long time and rest is most important for you. The doctor said your recovery would be long and slow."

"I know. How did things go?"

"Charleston is horrible. It's so crowded. Farmers have come into town to live because they can't afford to get their farms going. Negroes are all over the place, mostly loafing or trying to beg their way along. I don't know what's going to happen. Prices are outrageous. You'll hear about that from Mama. She's complaining about everything."

"I know. We must bear it, Virgie. She's not accustomed to living as we are forced to do now. She can't abide it."

"There was no mail. I was hoping we'd have a letter from Phoebe."

"I'm sure she can handle herself well, and she has Tom. It's still strange to think her name is now Mrs. Thomas Sprague. I only hope things are going well for her. I do worry about her."

"You sound like Mama," Virginia said, though her voice was kind. "What do you mean?"

"I'm wondering if she'll pass as white." Nanine spoke with a seriousness that was so much a part of her.

"Of course she will," Virginia said laughingly. "She's as white as you or I."

"Not quite," Nanine mused. "But she's beautiful and kind and loving."

Virginia patted Nanine's hand resting on the coverlet, reassuringly. "You and she have the same qualities. I don't, and I suppose I can't change any more than Mama can with her constant whining."

"You're strong, Virginia, like Papa. I'm the weak sister."

"You're not," Virginia spoke firmly. "And if Phoebe were here, she'd be the first to dispute that."

"What I mean is that all through the war, you and Phoebe were resourceful and saw to it that Mama and I were safe and well fed. I couldn't help with that part. I'll never be able to figure the best way out for us as you and Phoebe did."

"You won't need to," Virginia said. "I've set that goal for myself. Elias will help me attain it."

"Don't be too ambitious," Nanine cautioned.

"Nothing you can say will hold me back. I'm sure if Phoebe were here, she'd agree with me."

"I'm glad you changed your feelings toward her," Nanine said.

"She's my sister," Virginia said staunchly. "I love her."

"I can recall when you didn't," Nanine said with a smile.

Virginia stood up and loosened the bow on her dress. "I was ready to kill her, or at least sell her off to some faraway plantation. I was a different Virginia Hammond then. It almost drove me mad when I discovered she was my half-sister. A slave half-sister because Papa had been indiscreet."

"Papa had a reputation for it," Nanine said reflectively. "But he took good care of his family. Before you left for the mainland, you were going to talk to me about our plans."

"Yes, there's much to talk about. I had hoped Marty might join in, but . . ."

"What's happened to him, Virgie?"

"The same as happened to many of our young men when the war ended. Marty was a fine soldier. You know he was a brigadier and ready for his second star when the war ended. He grew used to being respected and saluted, and he stood on a high pedestal. No more of that. Nobody salutes him now and they respect him only when he manages to find enough cash to pay for their drinks. I think he lives in the saloons."

"Can't we do something to bring him back to the island?"

"I tried. Mama doesn't realize how the war affected him. She's convinced herself he stays on the mainland to find a buyer for the big plantation. Marty knows as well as you and I that there are no buyers. He stays in Charleston because it's what he wants to do and he drinks to shut out reality. He was a brilliant and resourceful general, yet despite that, his side lost. He's bitter and bears a powerful hatred for Yankees."

"All we can do is pray he'll come to his senses and return to the island." Nanine spoke in her quiet way. "I know you want your bath. Your dress is soaked with perspiration. I'll freshen up and see you downstairs."

"I want to talk with Elias first, so don't hurry."

Virginia's rooms were next to her sister's. They were large, airy rooms with a bath. She knew there'd be a large kettle of water on the kitchen stove for her bath, and it should be hot enough by now. She undressed, put on an old wrapper and went downstairs. The kitchen was a building apart from the main house and reached by a short, vine-covered walkway. In the kitchen, Belle, the cook, was seated on a high stool. Ordinary chairs were difficult for her to manage with her bulk. She was engaged in eating what was left of a drumstick. She looked up as Virginia entered, but she made no attempt to rise. This defiance was not lost on Virginia.

"Yo' watah gittin' set to boil, Missy. Took yo' long 'nuff to come down fo' it."

"You could have brought it up for me, Belle."

"No, ma'am." Belle flashed a wide smile. "Ah ain't yo' niggah no mo'. Ah does whut Ah pleases an' when Ah pleases. Ah's free."

"You may be free, but you still work for me and I pay you in silver. I can also fire you if I like and I'm half inclined to do so."

"Cain't fiah me, Missy. No, ma'am, 'cause yo' does an' my man leaves with me an' yo' sho' cain't do 'thout him. Cain't leave runnin' this heah fahm 'thout Moses."

Virginia shrugged, lifted the heavy kettle from the stove and walked out of the kitchen, followed by Belle's soft humming and her big smile. Belle, Virginia decided, was going to be trouble. But she was right in that her husband was indispensable to the restoration of the plantation.

Soaking in the tub, Virginia reflected on all of this. On the abrupt and painful changes that had taken place from the moment she awakened one morning to the sound of guns and the advent of the Yankee invasion. She thought back to the time when she, her mother, Nanine and her father were on the verge of starvation. When she and Phoebe concocted a scheme to slip back on to the occupied island and under the noses of the Yankee invaders recover the valuable silver that her father had buried.

They'd been caught, but it was a most fortunate capture, for, because of it, she met and fell in love with Elias and Phoebe fell in love with Lieutenant Tom Sprague.

She chuckled a bit at the memory, but the recovery of the silver had its light moments only until the time when her first husband had returned on leave and stolen the silver. She'd never seen him again, for he was finally killed in action.

Choosing a dress was a simple matter. The oversize wardrobe, once crammed with all manner of clothing, now stood almost empty. There was a ball gown, miraculously saved by Phoebe when they fled the island. An old, elbow-patched riding outfit was still service-able. There was a tea gown, silky thin and utterly impractical in this new post war era. The other two dresses, one brown, the second a deep violet, were the base of her wardrobe. Today she selected the brown one for no particular reason other than it was nearest.

Freshly bathed, mildly scented with toilet water—used sparingly, for there was no more—she at least felt feminine and ready to have her talk with Elias. She knew he was as strong-willed as she, but sensed she'd encounter no opposition on his part. He was no longer in the army, and as her husband she was certain he wanted Valcour to return to its former glory as much as she.

She left the house and walked toward the old service buildings, the long row of slave quarters and the small, badly run acres now owned by the slaves.

The twenty acres they had been able to retain was growing far better cotton, but certainly not up to the standards this plantation was once famous for. Elias, wielding a hoe, dropped it and joined her. His arm enclosed her waist as they moved to a shady spot beneath an ancient elm and sat down.

She rested her head on his shoulder and regarded his somber features. "Don't look so glum."

"It's just that this seems almost like a waste of time." He kissed her brow. "Forgive me, my love. I shouldn't be glum. Not when I have such a beautiful wife who smells very alluring. I love your fragrance. Whenever I catch a scent of it—no matter where I am—I shall think of you."

"Thank you, darling," Virginia said, reveling in his closeness. "But don't spoil your compliment by telling me the plantation isn't going to work. I'll make it work."

"You know as well as I that twenty acres can't produce enough to make it worthwhile."

"Very true. But before I'm done, I shall have every section now owned by the ex-slaves. Every single one. As well as every plantation now owned by those Yankee carpetbaggers."

Elias released his hold on her and shifted his position so that he faced her. The lines around his mouth hardened.

"Is this a joint venture or am I working for you?" he asked coldly.

"Of course it's a joint venture," Virginia exclaimed hurriedly. "I'm sorry, darling. It's just that I was alone in Charleston when the idea came to me and I'm still thinking that way. I'll need your help. I couldn't do it without you."

"I'm not so sure," he replied. "You managed quite well during the war."

"Oh, Elias, please don't be angry. If you hadn't allowed Nanine, Phoebe and me to stay on the island, Nanine would be dead by now."

"The war is over and what you just mentioned is part of that past. I want to forget it. I also want you to know I'm my own man."

"You made that quite clear when you commanded this island," Virginia said softly. "For me, you stand taller than any other man on this earth. Surely you must know that."

His tone was noncommittal. "I like hearing you say it. What I'm wondering is, do you mean it? You're as strong-willed as I. And as stubborn."

"And I'm also as much woman as you are man." Her voice softened as she spoke. "My love for you knows no bounds. I believe you feel the same way toward me."

He nodded, but his features didn't soften. "Suppose you tell me what your scheme is."

"It's not a scheme," she contradicted. "It's a plan. And a good one."

"I'd like to hear it."

She leaned forward and spoke with enthusiasm. "In the first place, the small acreage the slaves have isn't enough to make it worthwhile for them either. They don't know that yet and probably won't for a long time. They have no understanding of what has to be done to warehouse, bale and sell the cotton. However, I have an idea that will bring every acre of land back to us."

"I'm listening," he said, still somber-faced. He placed his hands behind his neck, stretched out on the soft grass and relaxed.

"What I intend to do is quite simple. I shall buy a large amount of food, clothing, even whiskey, which the blacks will want. I'll start a store in the old hospital, set my merchandise in the open to tempt them. I won't ask for cash. I'll give them all the credit they wish—until it's time to demand payment. They haven't any idea how to save money, how to buy. They'll be head over heels in debt to me and I'll make an offer. I'll cancel their indebtedness if they agree to sign over their land. And I'll guarantee I will employ and pay them to work the land."

Elias sat up, impressed. "It's almost bound to work. I know from experience in running the whole island that they're too inexperienced to handle any ordinary business deal. I don't say they're stupid. No, you'll never convince me of that."

"What makes you think they aren't stupid?"

"We started schools here. The children have been doing quite well, but what surprised me, and also the teachers, was the way some of the adult blacks went to school. Without any semblance of having been taught anything before. They did well, Virgie. Very well, indeed. It's not stupidity that makes them the way they are. It's lack of education and worldly experience."

"Be that as it may, darling, I think they'll be overjoyed to be able, for the first time in their life, to buy whatever they wish. It will be like taking candy from a baby."

"Exactly. A real dirty trick," Elias observed.

"Oh, come now. They'll have a lot more fun making purchases than working their paltry few acres."

"I won't deny that," he said soberly. "It's just not ethical."

"Perhaps," she agreed. "But it's not dishonest either. The way things are going now, none of us are going to make out."

"You talk of the few acres given the ex-slaves. What of the other plantations? Those abandoned by the original owners and now owned by Northerners? There are more than twenty of them and just one grows more cotton than all the patches granted the Negroes."

"I haven't forgotten them," Virginia said. "It's only that getting the acres away from the blacks is easier. Before I'm done, every plantation will be back in the hands of the original owners. It wouldn't be possible to restore Valcour without that."

"And what scheme do you have to accomplish ridding the island of the Northerners?"

"I've a few ideas and, believe me, Elias, I've no compassion for those scalawags who came down here to buy these estates for back taxes. Some paid a few hundred dollars for property worth thousands."

Elias nodded. "I've little sympathy for them. They did take advantage of the conditions at the end of the war. They're not doing very well, you know. They try to raise cotton without knowing a damned thing about it. They hired the ex-slaves to work the fields, without the slightest idea of how to handle the blacks any more than they know how to raise cotton. Their crops are poor, the quality is worse. But—you'll have to come up with something very big to force them off the island."

"Believe me, darling, I will. Once we get control of those plantations, we can really begin to prosper. There's going to be a great market for cotton. The Northern mills are starving for it. England is offering the highest prices ever. We can't delay in this."

"I can see that, but isn't buying all that food very expensive?"

"Very. Good prices are wild, but it's the only way. Even if we spend to a point where most of our assets are used up, it will still be worthwhile. We have no other choice."

They stopped talking for a moment while they both watched the burly black man amble their way. Moses was the most important black on the island now. He'd once been the Hammond driver. The man who ran the cotton fields and kept the slaves working. Who administered the whippings when they were called for and who answered only to the white marse.

"I wonder what's on his mind," Elias said.

"He's a good man, Elias. You can trust him."

"I know. During the years I controlled the island, he was my right-hand man. If we succeeded in anything, it was at least in part due to him."

Virginia smiled slyly. "What was accomplished? I'm a Johnny Reb asking a Yankee."

"I don't know," Elias replied. "It all began when Lincoln worried about what would happen when four million slaves were granted freedom and turned loose to shift for themselves. His idea was to experiment on this island by granting the one-time slaves acres taken from the original owners. That was my assignment—to conquer the island and keep it under Union control until we could find out if the ex-slaves were able to fend for themselves."

"You know it didn't work."

"I admit it didn't work as well as we'd hoped. Even though we gave them tools and paid them for the cotton they raised."

"At the expense of every white who owned an acre." She spoke with quiet bitterness.

"As I said, darling Rebel, it was an experiment. Lincoln even had the idea of giving grants to every slave on condition they'd go back to Africa. Nothing came of it, of course, after he was murdered."

"But land was appropriated and given to the slaves only on the islands. That wasn't fair, Elias. Surely you'll admit that."

"I do. Do you think it's fair to cheat the slaves as you intend doing?"

"I don't consider it cheating. Working for me, they'll do better in every way than trying to run their own small farms. Cotton has to be grown on big plantations to make it worthwhile."

"True," he agreed, eyeing her curiously.

"The slaves raised their cotton and turned it over to you," Virginia reasoned. "Did you have any trouble selling it?"

"None," he said, wondering what she meant.

"You would have in a normal market. The cotton they raised, and are still raising, is inferior. In a market starved for cotton, you can sell anything, but let a year or so go by and nobody would agree to pay for this terrible quality. I'm doing the ex-slaves a favor."

Elias's eyes revealed reluctant admiration. "You're a pretty good salesman. Especially with ideas and plans. Moses looks a bit worried. I wonder what's happened now."

Moses removed his brim-torn and battered straw hat and bowed, as he had always done.

"Glad yo' back, Missy," he said. "Yo' mama feelin' fit?"

"She's fine, Moses. Your wife isn't. I'm going to have to do something about her. She sloths and she's impertinent."

"Knows that, Missy. Knows it fo' sho'. Reckon Ah gots to whup her some fo' she changes. Massa 'Lias, suh, Ah gots trouble with one buck. Say he ain' goin' to wuk no mo' an' he goin' to draw his pay anyhow. He too big fo' me to whup, suh, but he sho' ain' goin' to do no good an' he bioun' to make trouble."

"Can't you fire him?" Elias asked.

"No, suh. Tries that, but he pays no mind. Say he free now an' he don' have to do wuk no mo'."

"I'll see about that." Elias stood up. "Take me to him and we'll settle this now."

"Elias," Virginia warned. "Be careful. Some of these bucks are awfully strong. And mighty independent since they were freed."

"I'll handle him," Elias said confidently. "His arrogance makes it even more important for us to get rid of him, before he demoralizes all of the men working for us."

"I'm going along." Virginia was already on her feet.

"I'd rather you didn't. You might get hurt, darling."

Virginia smiled reassurance. "I'll be careful. I want to stop by the house for a minute. I'll join you two. Moses, I beg the use of your horse."

"Missy, yo' sho' is welcome, seein' it belonged to yo' once."

She knew how to mount an animal without trouble despite her long, voluminous dress. She kicked the horse into a trot because she wanted to waste no time. She ran into the house and took the rifle from the gun case her father had once used. All the guns had vanished after the invasion, but this one belonged to Elias. A Yankee automatic weapon.

Nanine must still be upstairs, Mama was asleep, no doubt, so Virginia came and left with no loss of time for explanations. She rode down to the fields to see Elias wrestling with a mountain of a man. The workers had stopped to watch. Moses was trying to move in, but he was no match for this black either.

Suddenly, as Virginia dismounted, Elias was picked up and hurled to the ground. The big buck drew back a foot for a savage kick.

Virginia pointed the rifle at him. "Step back or I'll shoot," she said coldly. "Step back, I say!"

The black hesitated. Before the war he would have given in with no trouble, but he realized he was now a free man and he no longer had any reason to fear a white, especially a girl.

"Ain't no white gal got guts 'nuff to shoot anythin'," he said. "I goin' to kick this heah white bastahd's face in so he don' fo'git Tobal."

"Tobal, I'm warning you." Virginia spoke harshly, keeping the rifle trained on him.

He showed a row of very large teeth. "Reckon yo' ain't shootin' nobody."

"Get yourself down to the dock," she ordered. "Take a boat. Anybody's boat except mine. It's your last chance."

Elias was on his feet, maneuvering to get in close. He was winded and reeled slightly. He was still no match for this man.

The brawny Negro opened his arms as if to welcome his opponent, but actually he meant to embrace and squeeze him into insensibility. Something he was easily capable of doing.

"Elias," Virginia called out. "No! Elias, please . . ."

"Stay out of this," Elias called back.

He was almost within reach of those powerful arms as Virginia fired. The bullet whistled close to the black's ear and it frightened him into stepping back. Elias looked around, startled as much as the Negro.

Virginia said, "The next one won't miss. Elias, get out of the way. I want a clear shot."

Elias hesitated, but recognized the wisdom of such a move. He drew back and to one side. Tobal regained his courage. In his mind he reasoned that if this white woman really meant to shoot him, she wouldn't have missed the first time. He came forward slowly.

"Get off this island," Virginia said. "Go down to the dock and steal a boat belonging to one of the Yankee families. However you do it, get off this island."

Tobal said, "If Ah goes, an' ain't sayin' Ah will, Ah sho' comes back an' has yo'. Goin' to have yo' fo' Ah kills yo' good!"

"I shot a man for saying that to me," Virginia said quietly. "I can kill you just as easily."

"Yo' kills a man! Yo' talkin' big fo' a white woman."

"She ain' lyin'," Moses called out. "She sho' did!"

"Keep outen this, ol' man," Tobal warned, "or Ah breaks yo' neck."

Virginia fired. The bullet hit Tobal high in the shoulder. He was whirled back while an expression of utter bewilderment blossomed over his wide face. He raised a hand to the wound, removed it, and looked with awe at the blood on his hand.

"The next one will hit you right between the eyes," Virginia said calmly. "If you don't believe me, take one step in my direction. Now get off this island as I told you to. Get off right now!"

Tobal backed away, turned and began walking toward the waterfront. Virginia followed him, the rifle still aimed. Elias hurried to her side.

"Give me the rifle," he said.

"I can handle it, Elias."

He hesitated, and then dropped back a pace, still following. At one of the docks, Tobal climbed into a rowboat. Elias hurried forward to pick up the oars lying on the dock. He threw them, one by one, into the boat. Tobal rowed, mostly with one hand. As the blood on his shoulder spread, his defiance changed to fear. Also, his features revealed he was beginning to feel pain. Virginia remained on the dock until he was well on his way. Then she turned and handed the gun to Elias.

"I'm sorry, darling. About the gun. I thought to keep it so that man wouldn't see the slightest weakness on my part."

"Thanks," he said quietly. "I suppose I thought I could handle him as I used to do when I was in uniform. I realize now he could have killed me."

"I know," she said. She linked her hand under his arm and moved closer to him as they walked back to the big house. "I was sure who Moses meant. Tobal's been a troublemaker for a long time. We're well rid of him."

"All I hope," Elias said, "is that he's not going to make more trouble."

"How can he make trouble now?"

"There's the Freedmen's Bureau. He's almost bound to go there and swear he was shot for no reason."

"Elias." She looked up at him in surprise. "Do you think for one moment they'll believe him? Or if they do, not take our word I had to shoot him?"

"It's possible in any normal case, but not in this one. You see, Ben Bowman, who used to be civil administrator on this island, was transferred to the Freedmen's Bureau and he is in full charge. He's not exactly friendly. I had many an argument with him while the war was on and he's a hidebound Northerner who hates all Rebels. Also, there's still another point. He wanted to buy your home for taxes, just as the other Northerners bought homes, paying a few hundred dollars so they could sell at a big profit later. You outbid Bowman and he's not apt to have forgotten it. He always wanted this house."

"I gave no thought to that," Virginia said. "But even if I had," she added, "I would still have wounded that man. There was nothing else to do."

two

Nanine had heard the shots and was on the veranda, anxiously awaiting them. Her mother was peering out of her bedroom window, concern etching her features. Virginia waved a reassuring hand and managed a smile.

Nanine came down the steps and Virginia explained in an undertone exactly what had happened.

Nanine also kept her voice low. "Tobal gave us trouble before."

Virginia nodded. "We should have sold him long before the war began."

"Did he hurt you, Elias?" Nanine asked.

"No, but he would have if Virginia hadn't had the gun and the courage to use it," he replied.

Nanine's eyes admired her sister. "Yes, she had courage."

"Maybe I gave that impression," Virginia said wryly, "but I'm still shaking inside. It's Elias who deserves praise for standing up to that giant."

"I didn't do so well," Elias said brusquely. He kissed Virginia's brow lightly, then turned to Moses. "Let's get back to the fields before some of the others get ideas. They're not easy to handle these days."

Virginia and Nanine went up the stairs and entered the house. Virginia put the rifle back in the rack, then turned to her sister.

"Let's not tell Mama I shot Tobal."

Nanine looked dubious. "We heard the shots."

Virginia's brow furrowed in thought. "I'll tell her I fired to frighten him and it worked. I'm still too shaken myself to listen to her whining."

"She can't help it." Nanine spoke with her usual tolerance. "She's lived in a constant state of fear since the slaves were freed."

"That's understandable," Virginia replied calmly. "She was very demanding of them."

"So were you," Nanine chided.

"I'm aware of that," Virginia replied. "I'm also aware of the chaotic conditions in which we live. We must be on guard every moment, but we can't live in constant fear that we're going to be struck down, shot or raped any day."

"I realize that," Nanine said. "But that's what Mama lives with and we must feel some compassion for her."

Lenore Hammond's descending steps shut off further conversation. She spoke as she approached her daughters, who were still in the hall.

"What happened, Virginia?" she asked nervously. "I heard shots. Have the slaves rebelled?"

Virginia sighed. "How many times must you be reminded, Mama, that there are no more slaves?"

"Then what happened?" she asked irritably. "Certainly there was trouble of some kind."

"Just a little. We sent the troublemaker packing."

Lenore looked alarmed. "Where to?"

"God knows," Virginia replied, still trying to keep her irritation in check. "One thing's for sure. He won't be back. He knows we're armed."

"With one gun," Lenore said caustically.

"*They* have *no* guns, Mama," Virginia said firmly. "Now stop fussing. You're quite safe."

"The way things have changed, I'll never feel safe," Lenore disputed. "Did you tell Nanine how much everything costs?"

"I'm sure she's aware of it."

"We're lucky we can eat, Mama," Nanine said kindly. "Just try not to upset yourself. You'll bring on one of your headaches."

"The sun did that in the boat," Lenore said plaintively. "And just when I was dozing off, I heard a gun being fired. It's as bad as having the war start over again.''

"God forbid," Virginia said emphatically.

"Do you suppose Belle would bake a cake for dinner?" Lenore asked hopefully. "I know it's an extravagance, but I certainly would enjoy it.''

"I'll ask her," Nanine said. "Now go back upstairs and try to get some sleep.''

"Thank you, dear." Lenore managed a smile. "Belle is so rude to me, I don't dare ask anything of her.''

"She is to me too," Virginia said calmly.

"I can understand her being rude to you," Lenore scolded. "You were always so bossy.''

Virginia eyed her mother with astonishment. Lenore had been as overbearing and arrogant with the servants as she.

"Well, you were," Lenore insisted.

"Yes, Mama," Virginia agreed, smiling despite herself. "I was. And so were you. Now go upstairs and get some rest.''

"I declare, Virginia," Lenore said coldly, "sometimes you're impossible.''

"Mama," Nanine spoke quickly, forestalling any retort from Virginia, "Virgie's tired. You know she had no one to help her row.''

"You wouldn't expect me to, would you, child?" Lenore asked indignantly.

"No, Mama," Nanine said, her manner still placating. "It's just that she's still upset over what happened.''

"So am I," Lenore replied testily. "I'm also upset at the thought that flour costs a thousand dollars a barrel. Did you ever hear of such an outrageous price?''

"It's dreadful," Nanine agreed. "But be thankful we have food to put on the table. So many haven't.''

"True," Lenore agreed. "It's all that terrible Mr. Lincoln's fault. Well, I'm going to try once again to get some rest. Don't forget to ask Belle to bake a cake.''

"No, Mama." Nanine was already heading for the kitchen. "Right away.''

Lenore started up the stairs, then paused and regarded Virginia, leaning against the newel post, her arms hanging limply by her sides. She was a picture of complete exhaustion.

"Are you all right, daughter?"

"Fine, Mama," Virginia said, forcing a smile. "And don't you worry. Elias will see to it that we're safe."

Lenore looked dubious. "I hope so. Certainly we can't defend ourselves."

Virginia compressed her lips tightly to hold back a retort. It seemed as if all she and her mother did was bicker. She didn't move until she heard the bedroom door close.

Nanine returned from the kitchen carrying a tray on which rested two tall glasses and a pitcher filled with lemonade. The very sight of the beverage lifted Virginia's spirits.

"How thoughtful of you," she said.

"You've had an exhausting day," Nanine said. "Belle sent the houseboy to the fields with some for Elias."

Virginia took her glass from the tray and drank half of the beverage before she spoke.

"Any problem about her baking a cake?" she asked.

"None," Nanine replied serenely.

"Good. Let's go to Papa's study. I want to talk."

They moved along the wide hall to what had once been their father's study. The large desk and the high-backed leather chair were gone. An old kitchen table had taken the place of the desk, and two hard chairs composed the rest of the furniture. This room was far more sparsely furnished than any in the rest of the house. Someone among the rampaging slaves must have used everything for a bonfire, probably reasoning that this study was the source of all their woes and pain.

"I've been afraid of this," Nanine said. "I know Tobal was a real troublemaker. He might have inspired others."

"I don't think he did." Virginia spoke with a confidence she honestly felt. "On the island, our slaves were older and less apt to make trouble. Most of them were dispersed over the rest of the island and work for the Yankees or on their own forty acres. The ones who stayed with us were among the most trustworthy and couldn't be lured away. Besides, they know there's nowhere for them to go if we send them packing too."

Nanine placed the tray on a table and refilled Virginia's already empty glass. They sat on soiled upholstered chairs, facing each other. Elias had retrieved several pieces from the slaves' cottages. Virginia rested her head against the high back, heedless of the soiled fabric. She still felt weak and shaken.

Nanine glanced at her in concern, then let her eyes wander sadly around the room, over the faded wallpaper, the holes in the rug, the gouges and scratches on the tables.

"Do you see any way out of this situation?" she asked.

"I do," Virginia replied. Her hands gripped the arms of the chair as she tried to hold her enthusiasm in check.

Nanine leaned forward. "Please tell me. I'm thankful Papa never saw the island. He'd have been desolate."

"He'd have been damn angry," Virginia replied. "And damn determined to bring it back to what it once was."

"You really believe such a thing would be possible?" Nanine asked in awe.

"I'm going to make it possible. Valcour will once again be the envy of all who visit here."

"How soon?" Nanine asked hopefully.

"I can't answer that," Virginia replied. "But I'll tell you *what* I propose to do."

"I hope your plans include our brother."

"Martin would be no help in the shape he's in."

"Don't hate him, Virgie," Nanine begged.

"I don't. I'm just revolted by what he's turned into. A drunken sot."

"Perhaps if he had something to occupy his mind, he'd forget his hatred of the Yankees and the fact we lost the war."

"There's no doubting his presence here would help us," Virginia mused. "But not with a bottle in his hand."

"He was so handsome," Nanine said.

"He still is. Except for the hatred shining in his eyes."

"I know," Nanine agreed quietly. "Just what do you propose to do?"

"First of all, get our land back. I'm talking about the acres given to the slaves when the Yankees came. The Yanks didn't give away any acres on the mainland, only here because this was supposed to be a part of an experiment. Which didn't work, by the way. It's not fair that we should have lost everything when no one else was affected the same way."

Nanine looked dubious. "How do you propose to get the land back?"

"I've already told Elias what my plans are. We'll buy a great deal of food and clothing, plus gewgaws and the like. We'll let the blacks buy on credit and fall in debt. When they owe us more than they can pay, we'll settle for deeds, returning their acres to us."

"The Freedmen's Bureau might not like that," Nanine warned.

"Like it or not, if we get the land back legally, they can't do anything about it. I feel it's worth the risk."

"It's dishonest. I can't imagine Elias agreeing to such a plan."

"He didn't at first," Virginia admitted. "But when I reminded him of how the land was taken away from us, he came around. If he can, you should."

"I don't want you to get in trouble," Nanine said worriedly. "Besides, it's an enormous undertaking. I don't see how you can possibly succeed."

"I can! I will!" Virginia spoke with quiet determination. "I made up my mind while we were hungry and trying to find a place to live that I would devote my life to restoring Willowbrook and Valcour. That sustained me over those difficult war years. Without that hope and determination, I think I'd have given up."

"How does Mama feel about this?" Nanine asked.

Virginia gave Nanine a chiding look. "You know Mama. She doesn't want to hear anything unpleasant. But she wants Willowbrook restored as much as I. She'll not let how it's done concern her, so long as she doesn't have to undergo any unpleasantness in the process."

"I fear we'll have a lot of it," Nanine said worriedly.

"Just let me handle it. All I want for you is to get well. But you may as well know if it takes chicanery, fraud, criminal doing of any kind, I'll risk them. I'll lie. I'll even cheat."

"The way you look," Nanine said sadly, "I think you'd even kill."

"I hope I won't have to," Virginia said calmly.

"What does that mean?" Nanine asked anxiously.

"Make of it what you wish. Just stop worrying. I assure you that I'll be too busy to have time for it."

"I'm frightened, Virgie. I really am."

"Don't be, Nan," Virginia said kindly. "I've managed so far. Trust me."

Worry furrowed Nanine's brow. "I wish Phoebe were here. She's strong like you, but in a different way."

"I wish she were too," Virginia agreed. "Valcour is as important to her as it is to us. It's important to our family. And she's a part of our family. We are the island. Valcour and the Hammonds are synonymous. I want it back exactly as it used to be. So do you."

"Not through stealth, Virgie. And don't forget, Phoebe is part Negro."

"Not enough to matter," Virginia argued. She touched a handkerchief to her damp brow. Despite the cool drink and the closed blinds, which dimmed the room, the sun's heat seeped through. "Nanine, if you're trying to talk me out of this, you're wasting your time."

"I know better than to attempt to dissuade you from something once your mind is made up."

"Good. Just don't worry." Virginia looked about the bare room. "I still remember the day I discovered Phoebe was my sister. She'd modeled a ball gown for me. She unconsciously changed her hairdo so it resembled mine and suddenly she looked exactly like me. The resemblance was so uncanny that even she knew I was suddenly aware of what she'd sensed long before. I was horrible to her. Then I came down here and cursed Papa. All he did was mock me and tell me how it happened, and that Phoebe's mother had also been almost white. He manumitted her and set her up in New Orleans. In the business of running a whorehouse. That's the word he used. He also admitted he wasn't above going down there to see her now and then. I hated him and I hated Phoebe even more."

"You had a right to be unsettled," Nanine admitted. "But not to vent your anger on Phoebe."

"I was a fool! It took the war to straighten me out and to show, to my embarrassment, that in many ways Phoebe was a damn sight better than me."

"The war made a woman of you, Virgie," Nanine said. "A strong one."

"Much as I hate to admit it," Virginia said, her smile reminiscent, "Phoebe helped. It was she who suggested we return to the island to get the silver. At first, I believed her idea as mad as you believe mine in getting back our land. But then I knew it was our only hope." She shrugged. "For all we went through, we failed."

"That was because Wade proved to be less than honorable," Nanine said. "But in the end it turned out well. You met Elias and Phoebe met Tom. I was hoping you'd bring back a letter from Phoebe."

"So was I. But the mails are terrible."

"Virgie, do you believe the North and South can ever be reconciled?"

"Yes. Once we admit we were soundly licked—if we ever do. We have to be part of the Union again. There's nowhere else to go and I firmly believe it's best for us and for the North too. Have you read anything about how it's to be done?"

"Very little. President Johnson is inclined to accept any state back into the Union if ten percent of the voters take an oath to support the Constitution."

"There will be many a hard head on that point, though it sounds fair enough to me."

"I suppose it is, but even in the North, in Congress, there's a great deal of opposition to the idea. Oh, I don't know what's going to happen. But whatever is," Nanine added sensibly, "won't happen tomorrow."

Virginia stood up. "I'm going to my room. I want to pretty myself up for Elias."

Nanine went to her side and rested a hand lightly on Virginia's shoulder. "Why don't you lie down for a while? There's still time. You must be very upset after what happened."

Virginia touched her cheek to Nanine's. "I'd completely forgotten about it."

In the privacy of her room, Virginia slipped out of her dress and went to the bureau, where she regarded her reflection in the mirror. Her hair was mussed again and she raised her arms to take the pins down, wincing at her protesting and weary muscles. She brushed it upward, catching it with combs that were concealed, when the ends fell, reaching to below her shoulders. She separated the strands with a comb and made curls, using the brush and a short, round, smoothened stick around which she brushed the strands. Since her hair had a natural curl, the result was pleasing. She took out the violet dress, but before donning it, she laid out Elias's clothes and put a fresh towel out for him. Despite his weariness when he came in from the fields, he bathed and changed his apparel before coming downstairs to supper.

The violet dress enhanced her eyes, which were the identical color. She wanted to look her best for him. He had gone along with her plan, though for a few moments she feared he'd reject it out of hand. It was daring, she admitted, and could be termed dishonest, except that it was just as fraudulent of the Yankees to deprive them of their land. So she had no feelings of guilt on that score.

Once again her thoughts turned to Elias. He was stubborn and strong-willed, just as she was. She smiled thoughtfully, knowing that in her second marriage she'd been lucky enough to acquire a man. Wade LeGarue, her first husband, was not only a rogue and coward, but a thief as well, stealing the silver, except for what had been brought to Mama's room. Despite what he'd done, things had turned out well. She shut the unpleasantness from her mind and went downstairs. Though the table was set, no one was about. She returned to her father's study and half reclined on a settee that was pushed against a wall. Fatigue finally took over and she fell asleep to be awakened by the sound of voices.

"So there you are." Elias greeted her as she entered the hall. He was perfectly groomed, his tanned skin set off by a white shirt and trousers. "Your mother and Nanine are already at the table."

Virginia kissed him, then said, "You look quite handsome."

"And you're beautiful as always." He took her arm and led her to the dining room, where her mother and Nanine were already seated. Elias wasn't really handsome, but he gave that impression. Possibly because of his confident manner and the proud tilt of his head. Despite the limp, which was the result of a wound suffered in the war, he walked with a measured step. She knew she was lucky. She also knew she didn't want to lose him. Lenore broke into Virginia's thoughts.

"Come, daughter," Lenore spoke impatiently. "We're famished. Where were you?"

"Stealing a nap," Virginia replied. "I'm sorry."

"Don't be," Elias said. "You earned it."

"I was just about to ask Nanine if Belle baked a cake," Lenore said.

"She did, Mama," Nanine said.

Lenore brightened. "Good. I shall enjoy my dinner."

Elias sliced the broiled steak thin, for it wasn't very large. "I think Belle would stand on her head for Nanine," he said good-naturedly.

"That would be a sight to see," Virginia said, unable to restrain her laughter. Even Nanine joined in, but not Lenore.

"She's impertinent and should be fired."

"That's impossible, Mother Hammond." Elias spoke as he served each of them. "We need Moses."

"I suppose so," she replied irritably. "But couldn't she be put to work in the fields?"

"No, Mama," Virginia said firmly. "She's good in the kitchen when she wants to be. But when things change—and you may be assured they will—if she wants to run the kitchen, she'll have to revert to her former ways."

"She was always impudent," Lenore said. "I don't know why James put up with her."

"I do," Virginia replied. "Papa knew a good servant. I haven't forgotten when Phoebe and I came to the island for the silver, she could have given us away."

"She kept silent because of Phoebe, not you," Lenore said matter-of-factly.

"No matter," Virginia said calmly. "The fact remains she kept her mouth shut. Now, enough of bickering. I have more important things on my mind."

"What's more important than flour at a thousand dollars a barrel?" Lenore demanded. "Or coffee at forty dollars a pound."

"Don't carry on so, Mama," Nanine said, smiling. "We're having coffee for dinner. A special occasion."

"I wasn't aware of any," Lenore looked miffed.

"We fired Tobal," Virginia said lightly.

"He was a bad influence on the other men," Elias said. "Much as we need help, we're lucky to be rid of him."

"True," Virginia agreed. "I'm sure he did nothing but sloth."

Nanine addressed Elias. "I notice your limp seems more pronounced. Are you in pain?"

"A little," Elias admitted. "Happens when I'm on my feet too much."

"Or having a wrestling match with Tobal," Virginia said. "He's a giant of a man. He could have killed you. Enough of that. Here comes our dessert. Your favorite, Mama."

Belle set the heavily frosted cake before Nanine. "Yo' cuts an' serves it, honey," she said, her smile reserved for Nanine.

"Oh, that's beautiful," Lenore exclaimed, forgetting for the moment her dislike of Belle.

"Taste jes' as good as it look, Mist'ess." Belle, pleased with the compliment, switched her smile to the older woman. "Made coffee too."

They all thanked her, except for Virginia. She wasn't taken in by Belle, knowing whatever cake and coffee was left would be consumed by her and Moses in the kitchen. Nonetheless, it was a relief not to have to listen to Mama make a fuss. She and Elias even had a second helping of cake and more coffee from Mama's precious sterling silver pot. After Belle had left the room, Virginia sat in silence until Lenore and Elias had finished eating. Then she sprang her surprise.

"I'm going to give a ball," she said quietly.

Elias looked amused. Nanine and Lenore regarded Virginia as if she'd lost her senses.

When she made no further statement, Nanine asked, "Are you serious?"

"Completely," Virginia said firmly.

Lenore, having recovered her composure, smiled. "When, daughter? And who will come?"

"Leave that to me," Virginia said.

"Can't I even issue the invitations?" Lenore asked querulously.

"Yes, Mama."

"We can't get flour, or sugar, or coffee, or wine, and bourbon is hard to come by. What will we give the ball with, even if we can find anyone who can afford to come?" Nanine asked.

"We'll finance the whole thing," Virginia said.

"What kind of magic will you use?" Elias asked, still looking amused.

"No magic," Virginia said calmly. "I learned the Yankee settlers on this island are going to give a picnic next Saturday. I decided we'll give a ball on the same night."

"A picnic!" Lenore exclaimed indignantly.

"Who told you?" Elias asked quietly.

"One of our old slaves who works for the Yankees. He said he thought we'd be invited."

"How dare they?" Lenore asked indignantly. "It's an insult."

"I disagree," Elias said thoughtfully.

"Why?" Virginia asked in surprise.

"I think it's neighborly," he replied, smiling at her sober features. "And if we're invited, I'm sure that will be the reason."

"I agree with Elias," Nanine said in her sensible manner. "We must forget our past prejudices and make friends with our former enemies."

"You're right, Nan," Elias said. "Also, Virginia, if you intend to carry out the plan you outlined to me today, you'd better start making friends, not enemies. Otherwise, you'll never succeed."

"I'll succeed," Virginia said boldly. "Nothing will stop me. As for the picnic, I'll not go. Nor will you. You're one of us now."

"I'm an American," Elias said, his voice hardening. "I suggest you start being one."

"I will be," she replied, "after I get every damn Yankee off this

40

island. They're only here because the owners were forced to abandon their homes and the military said they would be sold for back taxes. I've not forgotten that Ben Bowman tried to buy Willowbrook for two thousand dollars.''

"I thought you weren't going to waste your time hating,'' Elias said.

"I'm not,'' she replied. "I'll apply my time diligently, but with one goal in mind. To outsmart the Yankees every chance I get. I did it during the war. I'll do it now. I don't want to quarrel with you, Elias. I'm only asking that you try to see my side of this.''

"I see one thing,'' he replied. "You want life as it was. It won't be. No matter what you do.''

"What Elias says makes sense, Virginia,'' Nanine said.

"I'll never believe that,'' Virginia replied crisply.

"I don't know what to believe,'' Lenore said mournfully. "I'd like to think Virginia is capable of changing things. At least to a semblance of what they once were. But I don't see how she can.''

"I will, Mama.'' Virginia smiled at Lenore. "Trust me.''

"You said Elias would help you,'' Lenore's glance shifted to her son-in-law. "Will you, Elias?''

"Yes,'' he replied. "Though I'm not as certain of success as Virginia.''

Lenore brightened. "In that case, I'll sleep better, having heard you say it.''

"We'd better not sit around the table any longer,'' Nanine said. "Belle will start fussing.''

"I'm tired, anyway.'' Lenore eyed the cake longingly, but resisted temptation. "I suppose we'll have to do without desserts for a bit, after having used up so much sugar.''

"Coffee also,'' Nanine said, laughing. "It was worth it, though. Good night, Virgie and Elias. Sleep well.''

Elias, already standing, eyed Virginia, who was still seated, her brow furrowed in thought. He doubted she was even aware that Lenore and Nanine had left the room.

"You must be exhausted,'' he said kindly. "You've had a trying day.''

41

"Not that bad. Let's sit on the veranda for a while. You can smoke a cigar."

"I'd like that," he said.

His arm enclosed her waist as they left the house. They chose chairs on the side of the veranda that faced the water. There was a full moon, which made the area as bright as day, and the air was sweet with the fragrance of honeysuckle. Virginia breathed deeply, savoring its perfume. Elias lit his cigar and settled back in the spacious wicker chair.

"Isn't this beautiful?" Her sigh was one of contentment. "Do you wonder I want things as they were?"

"No," he replied after he lit his cigar, puffed deeply on it and blew out the smoke. "What I don't like is that it's become an obsession with you. I'm beginning to believe you think more of the island than you do of me."

She shifted her position to face him. His head rested against the back of the chair and he appeared completely relaxed. He always did when he smoked.

"Do you mean that?" she asked.

"Every word," he said quietly.

"I thought you wanted Valcour to be restored as much as I."

"I want anything that will make you happy, Virgie. What I don't want is to see you destroy people in the process of getting what you want."

"I won't, my love," she said softly. "Please believe me. And believe also that you come first. You always will."

He puffed again on his cigar and exhaled the smoke slowly. Only then did he turn to regard her.

"I'd like to believe that."

"You must." She waved an extended arm to encompass the front of the estate, which sloped down to the water. It had not been divided into plots, thanks to the influence Elias had carried as commandant of the island.

"I know we wouldn't have that if it weren't for you."

"It was little enough," he said. "You know I love you madly."

She relaxed. "It's good hearing you say it. When you've finished with your cigar, I'd like proof of it."

"Aren't you too tired?"

"Never too tired to make love with you." Her tone was low and breathless, almost impatient.

"Then let's not waste more time." He pressed the lighted end of the cigar into the ashtray on the table, got up, and they joined hands. Inside, he released her, patting her bottom.

"I'll lock up. You go upstairs. I can be a very impatient man on occasion."

Virginia laughed gaily and headed for the stairs. She was halfway up when she heard him say, "Damn!"

"What is it?" she called down.

"You didn't close the door of the gun case."

"I'm sorry," she replied. "And don't get angry about such a foolish thing."

"I don't like to be reminded of the fact that I couldn't best Tobal." The resentment in his voice attested to the fact that the softness of his mood was gone. "I don't like being rescued by a woman. I like it less when that woman is my wife."

"You were winded and weakened by Tobal. I thought of only one thing—your safety. I don't want to hear any more about it."

Before Elias could reply, she turned and ran up the stairs, not slowing her pace until she entered their room. Sobs escaped her as she threw herself on the bed. They were brought on partly by the quarrel and partly by exhaustion. It had, as Elias said, been an exhausting day.

She didn't even hear the door open and close. Not until Elias's voice, now contrite, spoke her name. When she paid him no mind, his hands enclosed her arms to turn her on her back. When she stiffened, he used force, not brutal, but firm. He dried her tears with his handkerchief and covered her face with kisses. He was on the bed now, his body securing her firmly. She relaxed and opened her eyes to look up at him.

"Forgive me, Virgie," he said. "I love you. I'll do anything for you. I'm an ungrateful bastard."

Despite her hurt, she had to smile. "Just remember, I also love you madly."

"There's only one way you can prove it." His hands were already fumbling with the buttons on her dress.

"Let me," she chided. "It will take you forever."

He undressed as quickly as she and they made passionate love. Afterward, while he still held her close, she said, "Let's not quarrel ever again. Not about what happened today, not about Valcour, not about anything."

"I swear." His hands were already fondling her. He pressed her body against his and felt another surge of passion. She sought his mouth and gave him kiss for kiss, their bodies moving gently against each other until their emotions reached a pitch, making them both cry out.

Afterward, she lay contentedly in his arms. His hand lightly stroked her head and he murmured endearments as he swore his undying love.

"I know now I must do everything to help you restore Valcour," he said. "I just thought of a reason that's more important than you or I."

"What, darling?" she asked, moving her fingertips lightly along his shoulder and down his arm while she covered his chest with kisses.

"Children," he said. "We're going to have children. So we must acquire a decent legacy to leave them."

For a moment she was too stunned to reply. Then she propped herself up so that her head was above his and regarded him with disbelief.

"Surely you're not serious," she said.

"Of course I'm serious. Why do you want to go to all the work of restoring the house, regaining possession of the grounds and driving the Yankees from the island if you're not going to have heirs to leave it to?"

"My dear man, much as I want children—and I do want them—I have no time to start a family now. When I do, I wish to devote myself completely to them. Just now, Valcour will need every moment I can give it. Nothing is more important than Valcour."

"Nothing and no one," Elias said grimly.

"Oh, God, Elias, don't start that again," she pleaded. "You know you're more important than Valcour."

"That's the hell of it—I don't," he replied bitterly.

"I think you're jealous of the island," she said petulantly.

"I'm beginning to think that one day I'll hate the goddamn place so much I'll wish I'd never heard of it."

"Elias, I want children. I want babies by you, but not yet."

"Do you think you can wait till you're forty?" he demanded. "You know Nanine will never marry. She's already an old maid."

"That's unkind," Virginia said bitterly.

"I'm sorry," he said contritely. "I love Nanine and shouldn't have said that. But you know she'll never marry. Your brother Marty is a sorry excuse of his former self. As for Phoebe . . ." He didn't finish the sentence.

"What about her?" Virginia's voice was touched with sarcasm.

"Tom told me he'd not hesitate to have children. Somehow I have my doubts."

"So do I," Virginia agreed. "Even though Phoebe would love her child regardless of its color."

"Tom's family is so damned conservative, so . . . so . . . well, if Phoebe ever produced a child with even a little color, they'd be devastated and Tom knows it. I think, no matter what he said—he was hopelessly in love when he said it—it would destroy him."

"Even if the child was black, it would still be his," Virginia reasoned.

"That's not the point. What I'm trying to say is what if we don't have a family, what the hell are you bringing Valcour back for? We'll be grandparents—or should be—by the time you restore the island. If you ever do."

"Damn you for doubting me." She sat up. "You talk like a Yankee too much. You seem to regard me as a Reb to make war against."

"Now you're talking nonsense . . ."

"Am I? I'm going to restore this island. Children must wait until I say we're ready to have them. If that displeases you, then you can sleep in one of the other bedrooms."

"Go to hell," he said and turned on his side, moving so that their bodies didn't touch.

She lay quietly, holding her fingers in hard fists, pressing her eyelids tight to keep the tears from coming. Virginia was hurt and angry.

In the morning she was at the breakfast table alone when Elias came down.

"You're early," he said.

"Couldn't sleep well. I reckon you know why."

"I'm sorry, Virgie. Forgive me. I didn't mean to hurt you. I agree Valcour should be restored. No matter how it is done. No matter at what sacrifice."

She bent her head back, reached up and touched his face. "Darling, you've no idea how much I wanted you to say that. I'm sorry too. We should be able to talk things out without shouting at one another."

He bent down and kissed her. "I guess if we can make love as we did last night, then fight, and make up in the morning, we're in love. And by God don't you dare tell me that our lovemaking is of less importance than Valcour."

"Sit down, dear Elias. Belle is making pancakes."

"Well, what do you know! How did you get her to do that?"

"I told her I'd whip her big behind if she didn't."

He pulled out a chair and sat down laughing. "I'll bet she had something to say."

"Oh, yes. She told me to kiss her ass. An old and well-favored expression of hers."

Elias was still chuckling when Belle waddled in with a tray piled high with pancakes.

"These better be good," Virginia said.

"Yo' ain't satisfied, yo' makes 'em yo'se'f," Belle said.

The cakes were light and fluffy. Even the well-diluted molasses tasted good. Virginia said so and Belle beamed.

"One of these days, though," Virginia said, "I'm going to kick Belle where she said."

"Whut yo' talkin' 'bout?" Belle asked.

"Moses or no Moses, one of these days I'll do it." Virginia ignored Belle, directing her reply to Elias.

"She's just talking," Elias said. "Pay no mind, Belle."

"Reckon, suh."

"Just go back to the kitchen and get some more cakes going," Virginia told her. "They're good. I hate to admit it, but they're good and I take back what I said."

"Don' knows whut yo' said. Crazy talk. Gots to make mo' battah. Yo' goin' to have to wait a bit fo' mo'."

Elias poured molasses on a stack of cakes and looked across the table as he put down the pitcher. "You know, I think Valcour is beginning to come back already."

"Didn't I tell you?" she exclaimed happily.

Their laughter mingled, erasing the bitterness of their quarrel.

three

Virginia and Nanine shaded their eyes against the bright sunlight as they tried to identify the occupant of the boat approaching the island.

"I hope it's Marty," Nanine said. "It would be a relief to have him here."

"It would also be a help," Virginia said.

A few moments later they registered their disappointment. "It's that awful Mr. Bowman," Nanine said.

"Means trouble, I'm afraid."

"What sort of trouble? We've had no doings with him since you bought the house from under his nose."

"Yesterday," Virginia said, "I shot Tobal. Elias was afraid Tobal would go to the Freedmen's Bureau and complain. You know Mr. Bowman is head of the Freedmen's Bureau."

"Even if he is, you were certainly justified."

"I doubt a hardheaded Yankee like him will see our side. Nan, please go to the fields and tell Elias I need him. Then go to the house."

"Why can't I come back here?" she asked. "Otherwise, I won't know why Mr. Bowman came."

"I'll see that you do." Virginia spoke with a sense of urgency. "I don't want Mama to come out here and see this man. You may be assured he means trouble. Don't waste another second."

Nanine hurried off. Virginia walked down to the small dock and when Bowman threw her a rope, she tied up for him. He came ashore, a burly, ill-tempered man with no liking for anything about the South.

"I'm taking you in," he began the conversation.

"Taking me in, sir?" Virginia asked innocently, as if she didn't know what he was talking about.

"Nobody, not even a Southern lady like you, can go about shooting people. Not even a nigger."

"Oh, that." She nodded as if in sudden remembrance, then smiled winningly. "Thank you, Mr. Bowman, for calling me a Southern lady."

He eyed her belligerently. "I regard you as a Rebel who talks too much and one who cheated me. You're going to face the court for what you did. That nigger is willing to testify against you."

"Are you referring to Tobal?"

"You know I am."

"If he does, I hope he'll tell the truth about what he said he was going to do to me."

"Know nothin' about that. He said you shot him to make him leave the island 'cause you just didn't want him around anymore. I tell you, ma'am, you Rebs still think the niggers are slaves. Well, they ain't."

"If you say so, Mr. Bowman, they ain't slaves," she said demurely, her mockery lost on the man.

She could see Elias coming at a fast walk, followed by Nanine, unable to keep up with him.

Bowman saw him too and sniffed contemptuously. "If you think he's going to help you, think again. He may have run this island and been a Northern major, but when he married you, he just got to be a plain Johnny Reb and he'll be treated that way."

Virginia addressed Elias as he came to a puffing halt. "Mr. Bowman says you've become a Rebel and you won't be able to do anything about his taking me to the mainland for trial because I shot Tobal."

"Who ordered the arrest?" Elias addressed Bowman.

"Captain Delaney. He says bring her in."

"Which means you're now a law officer and you have a warrant for my wife's arrest."

"He just said bring her in. Anybody can do that."

"If you're certain of it, take her by the arm in a gesture of arresting her and I'll break your goddamn head."

"Now hold on," Bowman said uneasily. "I got no argument with you. But your wife just can't go around shooting people and not expect to find herself in trouble. If she's wise—and you, too—you'll let me take her back. If I don't, our troops will come for her."

"You take me back," Elias said.

"No, Elias, neither of us are going with him," Virginia said.

"You're sure high and mighty," Bowman said. "You're one of these proud Southerners. You think the whole world revolves about you and your family. Well, let me tell you, your family ain't much to be proud of."

Elias said, "What you're saying can get you a bloody nose. The Hammond family is now my family."

"Ain't nothin' to brag about," Bowman sneered. "'Specially since your brother-in-law happens to be in jail."

Before Elias could answer, Virginia spoke. "In that case, I'll go with you."

She started toward the dock, but Elias reached out, caught her arm and eased her back beside him.

"If my wife goes," Elias said firmly, "she'll go with me. Now get the hell off this island. Another word out of you and I'll smash your face. Come on, Virginia."

He cast a disdainful glance at Bowman and urged Virginia into a brisk walk. Bowman, aware that Elias meant what he said, got in his boat, mouthed a profanity under his breath as he manned the oars and began to row.

"So long as I'm going back to the house, I'll change before we leave," Virginia said.

"You're not going," Elias ordered, his tone identical to that which he used on Bowman.

"Elias," she pleaded, "you heard Bowman say Martin is in jail."

"Oh, no," Nanine exclaimed in dismay from the top of the stairs. She came down quickly. "I was watching from the window and when I saw Mr. Bowman rowing away, I thought everything was all right."

"It's not," Elias said. "Bowman placed Virgie under arrest for the shooting. I expected that and I'm sure I can handle it. I'm not so certain Virgie thinks I can."

"I trust you completely," she exclaimed.

"I thought you did when you sent Nanine to the fields to get me," he replied coldly. "But once you learned Martin was in jail, you were quite content to go back to Charleston with Bowman without even consulting me."

"I'm sorry," Virginia's tone was contrite, "I was alarmed at the news and felt I should see what I could do."

"If I can get you out of this mess, and I'm sure I can, I can get Martin out also. It so happens I know the officer in charge of the Charleston barracks. Just let me handle this—in my way. Not yours."

"Of course, Elias," she said, her smile uncertain.

"Do you think you can keep them from putting Virgie in jail?" Nanine asked worriedly.

"Virgie's not going with me," he replied. "There'd be no way of explaining her absence to your mother. She can think up some reason to explain mine."

"Why do you suppose they put Martin in jail?" Nanine asked, her concern still evident. "He wasn't even here when Virgie shot Tobal."

"I suppose he got drunk and started a fight," Elias said. "Whatever it is, I'm sure I can get him out of it. Just don't worry—either of you. I'll change out of my work clothes and row to the mainland. I won't be gone long."

After he went upstairs, the women occupied chairs in the hall. Nanine reached over and patted Virginia's shoulder reassuringly.

"You're concerned because you antagonized Elias," Nanine said.

"I'm trying very hard to hold back my anger," Virginia said testily. "He doesn't seem to think I have any intelligence."

"You're wrong, Virgie," Nanine said kindly. "He loves you, but he resents you wanting to take things into your own hands when he happens to be present to do it."

"I've never been a shrinking violet and I'll not start now," she argued. "He's got to understand that."

"Please don't make an issue of it when he comes down," Nanine urged. "He has too much on his mind. And he does have friends in the military. Which we don't."

Virginia relented, though reluctantly. "You're right, of course. I just wish he wasn't so quick to anger."

"You're the same," Nanine said softly. "But just now, wish him luck, embrace him warmly before he departs and make certain he knows you have absolute confidence in his ability to straighten things out."

Virginia accompanied Elias to the dock and followed Nanine's advice to the letter.

"Are you sure you have friends there?" she asked with genuine concern.

"Trust me," he said.

"I do, my darling," she replied. "Just be careful—and remember I love you."

"Thank you, my beautiful wife." He spoke as he took her in his arms. Their kiss, though brief, was passionate.

"Hurry back," she called after he started rowing.

He nodded assurance, his smile warm. She waved a farewell and returned to the house.

Nanine had the door open for her. "How did it go?"

"I did everything you told me." Virginia's smile was further assurance she had. "You were right. I must exercise care with Elias."

"You must also remember he's surrounded by women," Nanine said wisely. "He has to assert himself. And in this case, he knows what he's talking about. You might have gone to the mainland alone and ended up in that horrible jail. We have run into a lot of bad luck."

"What bad luck? Certainly we had our share while the war was on, but it's over now. We've regained ownership of the mansion, plus the opportunity of putting the island back on its feet."

"You're so sure of yourself, Virgie. I'm not at all convinced that business of a store will work."

"The only thing that concerns me more is getting the right hands to work the fields when I get them back."

"I know what you mean," Nanine reasoned. "They'll resent your

53

taking their lands from them so much they'll refuse to work for you."

"I mean no such thing," Virginia replied indignantly. "They'll work because they'll go hungry if they don't. Even if they should resent me, it will be short-lived."

"And if you fail?"

"I told you I won't. Elias is convinced the plan will work."

"Speaking of Elias, please be careful not to lord it over him."

"I don't," Virginia exclaimed impatiently.

"You do, Virgie," Nanine said calmly. "You must remember he didn't have to remain in the South. He did it for you."

"He'll be far better off once we've attained our goal than if he went North."

"That wouldn't keep him here if he felt you insisted on being the boss. Making all the plans and decisions. One other thing. I suppose I shouldn't mention it, but since you're my sister, I'm going to. I was restless last night and went downstairs for a book. In passing your door, both coming and going, your voices were raised in anger."

"Oh, that." Virginia dismissed it with a shrug. "It concerned our raising a family."

"What a splendid idea," Nanine exclaimed. "Though not entirely original. I'm very happy and I'm sure it will do more than anything to appease Elias. Assure him he's the head of the family."

Virginia made no attempt to conceal her exasperation. "You talk the same nonsense he does. How can I raise a child while trying to regain this island? It would slow me down and do the child not one whit of good."

"And you told Elias that," Nanine reasoned.

"Of course. When I have my family, I want to devote my complete attention to it. How can I do that and work to get the scalawags and carpetbaggers off the island? There's no place in my life for a child until I get Valcour back to where it once was."

"You're as strong-willed as Papa," Nanine said. "I admire you for trying to do the impossible. But I fear that, in the process, Elias's patience may be strained to the breaking point."

Virginia smiled, thinking of their passionate lovemaking the night before. "I'm just as certain I can handle him as I am that I can regain the island and bring back the families who once lived here,"

"Sometimes I think you're the stronger," Nanine said quietly. "And possibly—more intelligent. Though I'd never admit that to Elias."

"What makes you say that?" Virginia asked, her puzzlement evident in her face and her voice.

"Take yesterday, for instance. You had enough presence of mind to return to the house for the gun. Elias went directly to the fields, never thinking a former slave would attack him." She paused, then added reflectively, "I hope Elias doesn't run into any trouble in Charleston."

"So do I," Virginia spoke with open concern. "He's right about that horrible Mr. Bowman. He hates me and will make all the trouble he can."

"He hates all Southerners," Nanine said complacently. "Let's put him out of our minds. I suggest we pay Belle a visit. See what she's planning for supper and hope it will be sufficiently appetizing to keep Mama from asking questions about Elias's absence."

"The best tonic for Mama would be Martin's return. Though I fear it's too much to hope for."

Elias, once on the mainland, made his way straight to the garrison of Northern troops in charge of running the city of Charleston. He knew it was a benevolent control, for Washington had given orders that only the lightest pressure should be exerted, and encouragement to set up a city government be given priority over enforcing laws.

Captain Delaney, only a few years older than Elias, seemed more so because of his prematurely white hair. He was as tall as Elias and made a commanding figure in his uniform. His craggy features broke into a smile when Elias entered his office.

They greeted each other with a hearty handshake and exchanged a few words of small talk as the captain motioned Elias to a chair beside his desk and resumed his own.

"Major," Captain Delaney said, his manner still friendly, "you look fit. Obviously, marriage to a Rebel has done you a world of good."

"I've never been happier," Elias replied, "and never had more problems."

"As for the first part of your statement, having seen your beautiful wife, I know what you mean. As for the problems, I assume one of those concerns Bowman's charge that she shot a nigger."

"That and other reasons. The truth of the shooting is that this big buck was doing his very best to break my back. Virginia warned him, he turned on her and mentioned the fact that he'd come back and rape her before he killed her. For a second I thought he was going to try and rape her on the spot, but when he moved in her direction, she plugged him in the shoulder. She could have put a bullet between his eyes. She's a sharpshooter."

"Forget the whole thing. The buck disappeared, anyway, and you know they never show up to prosecute. They're always making trouble. What else is on your mind?"

"My wife's brother, General Martin Hammond," Elias said. "He's in the stockade."

"Good God, is he your brother-in-law?"

"That he is. I want to get him out."

"I can understand why. But he's been a nuisance for weeks now. He drinks too much and he fights anyone who says a good word about Yanks. I don't have much sympathy for him."

Elias handed the captain a cigar. They lit up and relaxed while Elias explained his cause. "I can see why, but put yourself in his place. He was a very proud man, a typical Reb. He raised hell when he was young, but when the war began, he changed. He worked himself up to the rank of brigadier and was ready for his second star when the war ended. In fact, we thought he was a major general. Even as a brigadier he was saluted, looked up to. He was a fine officer too. Then it ended and everything crashed. All he stood for and fought for was gone. His family was destitute. Marty couldn't accept that and he took refuge in drink."

"I agree he deserves some consideration. But if I let him go, can you guarantee he won't give us any more trouble?"

"I hope to take him back to the island. I won't swear he'll go, but I'll do my best. We have plans he doesn't know about. Once he hears about them, I believe he'll pitch in and help. Straightened out, he'll be a fine man. He rates the chance."

"I'll order his release in your custody. How are things on the island?" Captain Delaney asked.

"Middling, I'd say. The Northerners don't know how to grow cotton, they don't understand the blacks and I don't think they're in love with the climate. The ex-slaves piddle around with the acres given them, but they're not getting anywhere either. And we've been held back because we don't have enough land to run a big plantation. Small ones don't make it."

"Come to think of it, Elias, I've got some good news for you. Washington just issued orders that all lands confiscated from their former owners and turned over to ex-slaves are now to be returned. The blacks can't handle it. We need cotton and the former planters are the ones to grow it right. So every acre owned by the family you married into is now turned back. The only provision is that you allow as many of the ex-slaves to work as sharecroppers as you can."

Elias whistled in elation. "Now that's news to carry back. My wife is going to be delighted. Our situation seemed hopeless. I'm glad Washington woke up. A big plantation runs best and produces a better crop. I've seen that—during my conversion from Yankee to Reb."

"I'll send for your brother-in-law. You can meet him outside. I'll give him a lecture first. He needs it. And as a captain, I've always wanted to lecture a general. Good luck, Elias."

Captain Delaney accompanied Elias to the door. There, they shook hands and bade each other a farewell. Elias puffed serenely on his cheroot as he made his way to the gate. He was so elated he almost broke into a dance. The plantation was theirs again. He could visualize Virginia's beautiful face lighting up as he broke the news that the plantation was once again in the hands of the Hammonds.

He was secretly pleased that she'd not have to open the store to carry out her wild scheme. He'd have gone along with it, though he hated the idea of cheating the Negroes out of what had been given them. Seducing was a better word. He'd wanted no part of it, but he loved Virginia too much to refuse. Now he could forget it.

God knows what she'd think up as her next step now that she had the land back, but whatever it was, he knew he'd give in to her. He was madly in love with her. If only she didn't have that way of making him feel her inferior. It was that damn Southern pride. He knew she secretly hated the Yankees, though she never made her contempt for them evident in their presence. At least, not when they could be of use to her.

She was clever and she was a Hammond. She'd always be that. He wished he could feel that he was part owner of what was now a large plantation, but he would always think of it as belonging to the Hammonds. At times he even felt like an intruder. He knew he could go North and resume his career in engineering, which had been interrupted during the war, but he wanted Virginia to have things as they once were. At least, as near to that as possible. He hoped that didn't make him a weakling. Was it possible he was using her as an excuse for not going back? He thrust the worrisome thought from his mind when he heard footsteps behind him and turned to see Marty coming down the walk escorted by a soldier who promptly retreated once he'd turned his charge over to Elias.

Marty had the Hammond good looks, resembling Nanine more than Virginia. His face still didn't show the ravages of dissipation from the amount of spirits he was consuming. His eyes, like Nanine's, were deep-set and dark brown, almost velvety. A woman could have used them to good advantage. Just now they were bloodshot and filled with resentment. His dark hair was unruly, though tendrils of it framed his face, giving him an almost boyish look. But there was nothing boyish about his manner.

His smile was bitter as he spoke. "What are you—Virgie's errand boy?"

"Come off it, Marty," Elias said good-naturedly. "I'm not your enemy any more. I'm your brother-in-law."

"You're a goddamn Yank," Marty said matter-of-factly, though his tone had softened.

"Would you object to this goddamn Yank buying you a drink?"

Marty softened further, even managing a chuckle. "Now you're talking like a brother-in-law. Can you loan me a hundred or so? Since the war, booze is terribly expensive."

58

"We're well aware of the price of everything," Elias said, keeping his manner casual.

"It's all your fault. You won the war. That's what made whiskey so expensive."

"Wars make everything expensive," Elias replied, "and nobody really wins."

Marty bristled. "I just got a lecture from the captain. I don't want another."

"Let's go someplace where we can talk."

"I know a place. A good one."

"Fine. Lead the way."

It turned out to be a cheap, malodorous saloon, but it did have small round tables, one of them in a dismal corner where they could sit and talk without being overheard. Elias went to the bar, bought a bottle of alleged bourbon and carried it back to the table along with glasses. Marty poured a long drink, gulped it down and refilled the glass. He gave a sigh of contentment and settled back.

"What's going on these days?" he asked.

Elias smiled. "Something that'll surprise you. I just learned that a ruling came through from Washington that all confiscated land be returned to the former owners. That means the family will get the whole plantation back."

"I'll be damned. I didn't think Washington had sense enough to do a thing like that. I hate them a little less now. About this much."

With two fingers he indicated a tiny space between them. "They're still a bunch of bastards, including you."

"Marty, you're being childish. The war is over. Our side lost hundreds of thousands of men."

"And you think we didn't?"

"Of course you did. It was a hell of a war, fought for not one damn thing. If it never happened, slavery would have ultimately been abolished and you know it."

"Maybe so, but under our terms."

"We never regarded you as traitors, Marty. Now that it's over, we want you back in the Union. Together we can make a great country. From what I hear in the North, things are booming."

"Of course. You won. Down here we starve. Let me tell you

something, Yank. We lost, but no man can ever be prouder than me about how we fought and survived. I commanded a brigade from South Carolina. While you Yanks had to resort to the draft and face up to draft riots, and all kinds of trouble, South Carolina had forty-four thousand and forty-six men under arms. Of that number forty thousand were volunteers. Can you give me any figures like that on your side?''

"I can't answer that because I have no way of knowing. But dammit, Marty, nobody on my side ever thought of you Rebs as cowards. You whaled the hell out of us too many times. We respected you for your courage and fighting ability.''

"Bullshit!" Marty said and reached for the bottle.

"Marty, listen to me. When there were wars like this in Europe or anywhere else on earth, the victors came upon the vanquished like a swarm of hungry locusts. They raped and stole and killed. The leaders they had vanquished were executed.''

"Don't you suppose I ever read history?'' Marty retorted.

"You don't sound as if you have,'' Elias replied.

"Well, I have, dammit.'' He reached for the bottle to fill his glass again, but Elias was quicker and snatched it.

"How many Rebs did the North execute?'' he asked.

Instead of answering, Marty glared, extended his arm, hand open to grip the bottle. Elias eyed him with disgust as he handed it to him.

"I'll tell you, anyway.'' Elias spoke as Marty filled his glass and drank most of it. "They hanged one man, named Wirz. He was commandant of Andersonville Prison and he deserved what he got. And let us not forget General Grant. He ordered all Rebel soldiers to retain their guns and horses. There were reviews held at points of surrender and at every one Union soldiers lined up and presented arms when the Rebs marched in.''

"Now wasn't that nice of them?''

"There were hatreds on both sides. Hell, there was plenty of that before the war. There are people in Maine who hate people in Massachusetts. Hatred didn't begin with this war and it won't end with it. But it's a stupid emotion. And the most destructive one on this earth. You're destroying yourself with your hate.''

"So be it," Marty said matter-of-factly, eyeing the half-empty bottle. "I'll enjoy my hating just as I enjoy my bottle. I admit I'm getting a little drunk, but that's because I haven't eaten in a couple of days. I refused the army swill in the stockade just to show them I was still a Reb."

"Why didn't you tell me? Do they serve anything in here?"

"All they serve is bad booze. It makes you damn good and drunk and ruins your stomach and softens your brain. There are restaurants."

"I know, but you look like something that just crawled out of a primordial ditch, if you don't mind my saying so. Do you know a place where they won't turn us away at the door?"

"Those kind are my specialty. There's one just down the street. Did you pay for the whole bottle?"

"Yes, it's ours."

Marty tucked it under his arm. "You didn't think I was going to leave it, did you? But I expect in this fancy place where I'm taking you—they don't have tablecloths and they don't serve filet mignon—the booze is a little better and of course you're buying another bottle."

"We'll talk about that after you eat."

As Marty had said, it wasn't much of a place and there wasn't much in the way of food—some fatty ham and some eggs. Marty bolted his food and ate enough bread to soak up some of the alcohol. He seemed less belligerent when he leaned back and patted his stomach.

"Very, very good, my friend. Now—a fresh bottle."

"After we talk," Elias said quietly. "You don't make sense when you drink too much. Virginia, Nanine and your mother want you to come back. We need you there. We need all the help we can get."

"Then hire it. I'm still fighting the war. I'm not going back."

"Never?" Elias asked mildly.

"Well," Marty said grandly, "not until after I've sold the big plantation."

"When's that going to be?"

"How the hell do I know? No Southerner has enough money to buy the place. It's worth half a million or more. In all the South there's not that much money. But, I keep trying. What I'm really looking for is some smart Yankee I can trim good and proper. Now that would be soul-satisfying to me."

"I told your family I'd try to persuade you to come back. Despite your ornery nature, I like you, but you're destroying yourself with all this drinking."

"I thought it was hate that was destroying me." Marty spoke with mock seriousness.

"That too," Elias replied. He knew there was no argument he could use to change Marty's mind. In his sardonic mood, helped by the alcohol, nothing could move him.

"Whoring too. The most beautiful destruction," Marty said, his smile reflective. "Of course I come by that naturally, inherited from Papa. Now there was a man who had his women. Poor Phoebe was one result and damned if Papa wasn't proud of her."

"He should have been. I don't know about you, but the rest of the family is."

"Damn it, so am I. She's gorgeous, but stupid for marrying a Yank lieutenant. Heard from her?"

"No, and we're a bit worried. I'll stop by the post office before I go back. Why not come with me?"

"Not on your tintype. How can I face my family looking the way I do?"

"That's merely an excuse. They'd love seeing you even as you look now and, believe me, it takes a strong stomach to do it."

"I may be back someday. First I'll get a haircut and a shave, but not now. I've got too much forgetting to do, Elias. Much too much. Until I finally do get over it, I'm not good for anything. Tell Mama I love her. Tell her you found me well and handsome and clean, not stinking of booze. Tell her I'm spending all my time trying to sell the plantation. What you tell Virgie and Nanine is your business. Virgie wouldn't believe a story like that, anyway, but Mama will."

To Elias's surprise, Marty was serious. Elias drew out his wallet and removed fifty dollars. "Drink the damn war out of your system, Marty. Then come back to us before the booze, the hate and the whoring kills you. You'll still be Brigadier Martin Hammond, Confederate army, to your family, and that includes me."

"Elias, I'm glad Virgie married you. You'll be the savior of the family. The name won't be the same, but the blood will. It'll be up to you—and Virgie. Nanine's—well—she's sick all the time. Phoebe may be a Hammond, in a way, but how can she have any kids? If I were her husband, I'd never be willing to take that chance. I wonder what would happen if she did have a mahogany-colored baby? The North would probably declare war over again."

Elias stood up. He'd wasted enough time and he wanted to get back before dark. He offered his hand. Marty rose, swayed slightly and took it in a limp grip.

"You're all right, Elias, except for one thing. You never bought me that second bottle of rare bourbon out of yesterday's still someplace in an alley."

They stopped by the bar and Elias made the purchase. On the street they shook hands again and then Marty, somewhat uncertainly, from too much food and whiskey, weaved his way back to the bar where they first talked.

Elias felt a sense of defeat as he watched. Marty had none of Virginia's determination or Nanine's steadfastness. Yet he was a Hammond. There had to be good in him somewhere. Whatever it was, Elias knew he'd failed to penetrate Marty's armor of bitterness.

He turned and walked briskly to the post office. It was on the opposite side of the city and he moved at a brisk pace, hoping to get home before dark. There was mail, but from the looks of it, mostly bills. He walked to the window to better scan the envelopes. To his delight, there was a letter from Phoebe. His spirits lifted. He'd not succeeded in convincing Marty to return, but at least he was returning with something. In fact, a great deal really. The land! He smiled as he visualized the effect the news would have on them, but especially on Virginia.

Nanine and Virginia were at the dock, awaiting him. Virginia gave him a fierce embrace and a hard kiss. It served to further raise his spirits.

"Darling," Virginia said, eyeing him carefully, "something good must have happened. You have a gleam in your eyes."

He laughed. "You always have that effect on me. But let's be serious. First of all, you need have no further worries concerning Tobal or Bowman."

"You settled that," Virginia said, relief flooding her voice. "Thanks, my love."

"I really didn't have anything to settle," he said honestly. "Tobal disappeared. Captain Delaney told me they usually do."

"What about Marty?" Nanine asked.

"As you can see," Elias placed an arm around the shoulders of each and the three of them started toward the house, "I failed to persuade him to return."

"Is he still in that horrible jail?" Nanine asked.

"No," Elias replied. "But he'd probably be better off there. At least, he couldn't get a bottle and that seems his only interest."

"Is he that far gone?" Virginia asked.

"He's in fairly bad shape, but somehow I have a feeling there's enough family pride buried deep within him that he'll come to his senses. Just now he's still fighting the war—with the help of the bottle."

"It's destroying him," Virginia said sternly.

"It will if he doesn't stop," Elias agreed.

"And if he doesn't," Nanine said in her logical way, "Mama is going to find out. She was so proud of him."

"It's better for him to remain on the mainland," Elias reasoned, "while he's still drinking."

"Thank God he was sober when we were there," Virginia said. "I'll never know how it happened—unless he had a premonition."

Elias smiled, but Nanine was not amused.

"I have good news," he said. "Something that will cheer Nanine especially. I brought back a letter from Phoebe."

Nanine smiled up at him. "That is good news. How is she?"

"I didn't open it. I felt the entire family should be present for that. But let it wait a bit. I have news that is so exciting I'm almost afraid to tell you."

"If you don't tell us immediately," Virginia spoke with mock sternness, "you may return to the mainland and remain with Marty."

"Not that, please," Elias said, laughing. "He's not very good company. Please be quiet till I tell you. Captain Delaney, in command of the stockade, just learned that an executive order from

President Johnson has returned to original owners all lands taken from them.''

"Do you mean,'' Virginia exclaimed in tones of disbelief, "that the land taken from us and given to slaves reverts back to us—the original owners?''

"Exactly,'' Elias said. "The plantation you had before is now yours once more. Wholly and completely. The slaves can be kept on as sharecroppers. You don't have to pay them a cent for the land.''

Virginia reached out, caught his hands in hers and danced him along the path. It took only a moment or two for him to become infected with her high spirits. Nanine gave vent to a surprisingly loud Rebel yell, then followed the other two with her own version of a triumphant dance.

They paused just before they reached the house, breathless but laughing at their foolishness.

"Now!'' Virginia exclaimed, when she finally calmed down enough to speak. "Now we can go! Now we can get things done! It's wonderful! It's a miracle! Yes, I'll believe in them from now on.''

"If only Marty had come, our happiness would be complete.'' Nanine spoke with sudden remembrance.

Elias caught one of her hands and held it between both of his. "Don't worry about him.. Nobody can rise to the rank of general unless he has a good head on his shoulders. Marty proved that. Give him time. He'll come to his senses.''

Virginia's arms extended and raised heavenward. "We're blessed. Heaven has to be on our side.''

"We'd have been doubly blessed if Marty had come back,'' Nanine said. It was as obvious that Elias hadn't convinced her as it was that Virginia hadn't heard him try to reassure her sister.

"And we've a letter from Phoebe,'' Virginia said, her face radiating the happiness that consumed her. "I've a feeling that will contain good news also.''

Elias's arm enclosed Virginia's waist. He said, "We'll never know if we don't go inside and read it.''

Belle opened the door just as they reached it. Her dark eyes observed them closely.

"Soun's like y'all gone crazy,'' she said.

"Crazy with happiness," Virginia exclaimed. "Tell Mama to come downstairs. We have a letter to read to her."

"From Phoebe?" Belle asked, her features brightening hopefully.

"Yes." Virginia's voice registered her disapproval of Belle's boldness.

"Whut she say?" Belle asked. "She lak it up No'th?"

"We haven't read the letter yet." Virginia's eyes flashed with irritation. "Now get upstairs and fetch Mama."

"Sho' will," Belle retorted, already ascending them. "But not fo' yo'. Jes' wants to heah whut's in the lettuh." Her voice raised. "Miz Lenore. Miz Lenore. Comes quick, yo' heah?"

Virginia's mouth opened to chastise Belle verbally, but Elias gripped her arm and guided her into the parlor where Nanine had already seated herself, patient as always, but eager to learn the contents of the letter.

Virginia, seated beside Elias on the settee, held the still-sealed envelope. The three of them were silent, their eyes on the letter. Virginia was surprised to hear her mother's rapid footsteps on the stairs. When she wished to move quickly, she could. In fact, Virginia mused, the woman could do most anything when she wanted to. If only she could get rid of that peevish manner she had always affected. However, Virginia's spirits were too high to let anything bother her now. Not even the fact that she caught a glimpse of Belle hovering in the hall so she could eavesdrop as the letter was read.

"We have some very good news to tell you, Mama," Virginia addressed her mother as she entered the room. "But first we'll learn what Phoebe has to say."

"Please hurry, Virginia," Nanine pleaded. "I've been very concerned about her."

Elias rose and moved a chair closer to the group.

"I'm interested in the letter," Lenore said demurely, seating herself, "though I don't believe it called for the yelling and loud laughter I heard drift through my windows."

Elias chuckled as he resumed his seat. "That concerned good news of another kind, Mother Hammond."

"Then let me hear that news first," she replied testily. "After all, Phoebe is not my daughter."

"Whether you like it or not, Mama," Virginia said with a trace of sternness, "she's your stepdaughter."

"That's true, Mama," Nanine said. "And she's almost as white as us."

"*Almost*," Lenore said balefully, "isn't white."

"Even if she wasn't our sister, we owe her a lot," Virginia said, holding back her anger with difficulty.

"A lifetime of gratitude," Nanine said. "And love."

"There are times when I think neither of my daughters like me."

"We love you, Mama," Virginia said, "but you can be very difficult. And while you're being so petulant, you're delaying my reading of the letter. We were kind enough to wait until you came downstairs so we could all share in the news."

"I apologize," Lenore's tone held an injured air. "I am interested in learning how Phoebe is doing in the North. I hope she'll be as well treated there as she was here."

"She was also very loyal to us, Mama," Virginia said remindfully. "I was under the impression that you had finally accepted her into the family."

"I have," Lenore said complacently. "Otherwise I wouldn't have come down to learn the contents of the letter."

"Then, for God's sake," Elias said testily, "stop the bickering and learn how the newlyweds are doing."

"As well as we will be, I hope." Virginia flashed Elias a grateful smile as she opened the envelope and unfolded the white sheet of paper. She quickly scanned it, then read it aloud.

Dear Family,

How wonderful to be able to begin a letter in such a way. This will be but a brief note, for Tom and I are going out to supper and he is standing impatiently while my pen flies over the paper.

Our journey to New York City was both pleasant and uneventful. For the time being, we're living in a one-room flat, but I don't mind. The city is so exciting. And everything, for me, is so different.

It is both strange and wonderful for me to walk into a restaurant and not be ordered to go to the back door and eat in the kitchen. Today, when I was walking along the street, a gentleman brushed against my arm. He raised his hat and apologized. I was too startled to answer. It is also exciting to walk along the street with the white folks. Of course, I doubt anyone has given a thought that I am not like them. So far, no one has even questioned it. Tom is delighted that I've got away with my little charade. It's our own private joke.

We're very happy except for one dark note. Tom has not yet found work. His position as a teacher was filled when he went into the army and there seem to be no openings at present, but we're certain there will be. I've all the confidence in the world in my husband.

He has promised to take me to meet his parents soon. For now we don't have the money for the journey. But each day my happiness grows, for there is so much of interest here. The shop windows are filled with clothes and items so beautiful they are beyond description.

Tom is growing impatient so I will close now and write more later. I love each one of you dearly. I hope your happiness matches mine and that things are working out well for you.

Please give Belle my love and tell her I'm very happy. Though she is gruff and rude in her ways, remember she has been loyal to all of us.

"I'm sorry Tom hasn't found work," Nanine said. "But Phoebe's happiness leaps right off the page."

"Things will work out for them," Virginia reasoned. "It has for us."

"Just what has changed for us?" Lenore asked.

"Let's forget us for a moment," Elias said somberly. "I don't like to spoil the fact that we finally heard from Phoebe, but I'm concerned Tom hasn't found work. I'd like to send them some money."

"So would I," Nanine said.

"Can we spare it?" Lenore asked.

"Certainly," Virginia said. "After all, she is our sister. Whether you accept her or not, Mama, you must accept that."

"Very well," Lenore said coolly. "Send her money."

"On second thought," Elias mused, "I'm reluctant."

"Why?" Virginia asked.

"If I were Tom, I know I'd resent it," Elias replied. "I got to know him well when he was here. He has a fierce pride."

"Then we'll wait," Virginia said. "I'll write to them and inform them that should things become difficult for them, they're always welcome to come back. And if they need money to tide them over, write immediately."

"Thanks, Virginia," Nanine said gratefully. "I'll write to her also, but I won't mention that."

Elias said, "I'll write to Tom."

"Certainly," Lenore reasoned, "the South would never have done such a thing to him. If he'd been in the Southern army, his job would be waiting for his return."

No one answered. There was no need, since most of the schools in the South still hadn't opened.

"Mama," Virginia said softly, "the North hasn't treated us too badly. We're getting back the land that was taken from us."

For once, Lenore was at a loss for words and looked as if she couldn't believe what she'd heard. "Where did you learn that?"

"Elias went to see his friend Captain Delaney on the mainland. He wanted to learn if there was any news of significance from the North." The lie slipped easily off Virginia's tongue. "He returned immediately to tell us. That was the reason for the shouts and laughter you heard."

"I must say that is good news," Lenore commented. "But do you suppose the slaves will give up the land?"

"They'll have to," Elias replied. "Though they may work as sharecroppers. In any case, as Virginia said, now we can get things going."

"I still believe it's a miracle," Virginia said happily.

"I wouldn't say that," Lenore disputed. "After all, it was our property. We have rightful ownership to it."

Before they could say more, Belle appeared in the doorway. "Suppah's on the table. Gittin' col' a'ready."

Lenore was the first on her feet. Virginia extended the letter to Nanine who took it with a grateful smile and followed her mother. Virginia and Elias paused long enough for a passionate embrace.

four

In the morning Virginia summoned Moses to the house. He entered the study, looked about the bare room and shook his head.

"Used to come heah to see yo' papa, Missy. Sho' looked bettah then."

"Wait a bit," she said. "The whole place will look better than it ever did. Right now I want you to assemble all the field hands in front of the house in one hour. I'm going to tell them something important. It will change everything and for the better, I'm sure."

"Yes, Missy, Ah gets 'em heah."

"I don't know how they'll take it. So I'll tell you first. There's a new law that just came from Washington. The land taken from us and given to the slaves now comes back to us. The Yankee government says so."

Moses sat down on one of the old kitchen chairs. "Missy, sho' ain' goin' to be the same." His voice was that of a worried and surprised man.

"How will they take it, Moses? Can you guess?"

"Don' knows fo' sho'. Ain' much cotton bein' raised, that's fo' sho', but they gots this heah lan' an' it makes 'em feel impohtant. Cain't make no livin' off it, but it's they land."

"Do you think they'll quit when they hear the news?"

"Cain't tell. Nevah figgered on anythin' like this, Missy."

"I want them to stay. As sharecroppers. I'll pay them fifty cents a day and charge it off on the sale of the cotton once a year. They can live in the old quarters rent free. They'll have money, a cabin, credit and a share in the profits. They won't have to pay taxes any longer. Those they owe now I'll pay.''

Moses nodded. ''Reckon that goin' to make 'em think some. Yes, ma'am, thinks they bettah off that way.''

''So do I. Now don't tell them what I'm going to do. I want them surprised so I can see their faces when they realize what this is all about. I want their reactions because this is going to be very important for all of us.''

''Ah jes' gits 'em ready fo' yo', Missy. Aftah yo' gets finished talkin', Ah sho' goin' to do some of it mahse'f.''

''Thank you, Moses. Incidentally, you'll lose your acres too, but I'll pay you double that of the others and add a good bonus as soon as we sell our first big crop.''

''Ah sho' thanks yo', Missy. Goes now an' gits 'em ready.''

''Oh, yes, and tell my husband I want to talk with him.''

Moses nodded, then bowed his head, a habit he would never change. After he left, Virginia settled down to her bookkeeping and decided that from now on she would turn that chore over to Nanine, who was far better equipped mathematically to handle figures. She was pleased that her mother had remained in bed. For Virginia this was going to be a busy day and she had little time to listen to her mother's never-ending complaints.

Elias came promptly and Virginia outlined her plans. He was in full agreement, though he seemed a trifle irritated.

''Elias,'' Virginia said, ''if there is something about this you don't agree with, tell me. It could well be I've gone wrong somewhere.''

''It's not that. Your plan is good. The field hands have nowhere else to go. Besides, every one of them worked on the plantation long before the war and the island is all they know.''

''Well, what then?'' His troubled features warned her something was wrong.

''I'm just wondering what part I play in this. Or if I have a part—other than the role of your overseer.''

72

"You're my husband," Virginia said firmly. "I've never thought of you in any other capacity."

"That's difficult to believe," he said quietly. "Especially when you summon me from the fields to tell me the plans you thought up."

"What difference does it make?" she asked impatiently.

"One hell of a lot—to me," he replied, his voice hardening.

Virginia softened hers. "Elias, be reasonable. The Negroes know us. We're Hammonds."

"I'm not a goddamn Hammond," he replied impatiently. "Marty told me what I was—your errand boy. That's exactly what he said. Virgie's errand boy. I'm beginning to believe he's right."

"Marty's a drunk and a fool," Virginia said impatiently.

"I agree that he's a drunk. But a fool—no." Elias paused, then added bitterly, "I'm the fool."

"Why must we quarrel?" she asked, once again controlling her emotions. "We've been married only a few weeks and it seems that we can't agree on anything."

"I agree on one thing. Your plan is very good. I congratulate you." His smile was sardonic.

"You're being difficult, Elias. Our future is here—the plantation will be run by you."

"I doubt that." He thrust his hands in his pockets and started pacing back and forth in front of the desk.

"Please, Elias," Virginia begged. "You're making me nervous."

"I apologize," he said brusquely and paused to face her. "It's just that I remember when I sat where you're now sitting and when I gave orders that were obeyed. Now you've summoned me and I'm to carry out your orders."

"I'll change places with you," Virginia replied coolly, "if it will make you feel better."

"I'm beginning to wonder if such a thing is possible so long as I'm here."

Virginia got up and walked around the desk to face him. "You're thinking of only yourself. I'm thinking of both of us and the rest of the family. It would be much more pleasant for me if I had a closet filled with beautiful dresses and a calendar marked

73

with multiple social functions. That isn't possible. I can't even buy a dress.''

"There's money for that," Elias contradicted.

"The money must go toward the plantation," Virginia said. "It must be restored to its former glory. Now it can be. We'll make it come true. When it is, we'll have a sumptuous wedding. I always wanted to be married in a beautiful satin gown with a tiara and a veil that would trail behind me. Our wedding was tawdry.''

"You could have had a beautiful wedding if we'd gone North. My parents would have seen that you had one every girl dreams of. My mother even wrote me suggesting it.''

"I couldn't leave Mama and Nanine," Virginia countered.

"Yes, you could," Elias said easily. "In fact, they were included in the invitation.''

"I wouldn't dared have left the plantation. You know what happened when we fled the island.''

"Damn the plantation," Elias said impatiently. "You think of nothing but the plantation.''

"You were as anxious to restore it as I," she countered.

"Because I loved you. I'd have done anything for you." He paused, then added bitterly, "The hell of it is, I still will. But I'll hate doing it because I suddenly realize I'm nothing but your errand boy.''

"Why must you repeat what my drunken brother said? He said it only to rile you. He hates you because you're a Yankee.''

"He's right." Elias shifted his gaze away from Virginia. "I am. I wonder what the hell I'm doing here.''

"You said—" Virginia's voice faltered.

"I know what I said," he broke in. "And because I gave my word I'd work with you—*with* you, Missy—to restore Willowbrook, I'll do it. Now—I had some work I wanted Moses to do, but he told me you also had sent him to summon the help from the fields.''

"Yes." Virginia's tone was still uncertain. She'd not been prepared for Elias's rebelliousness. "I'd like you to speak to them. They're to come to the house.''

"No," Elias said. "I'll stand by your side while you speak to them.''

She searched his face for some sign of sarcasm, but his features were now noncommittal.

"Is that your preference?" she asked.

"Yes. They know you. They'll undoubtedly listen to you with more respect than to me."

"That's not true," she replied. "They respect you. They know you ran this island during the war and ran it well."

Elias allowed himself a smile. "Thank you, ma'am."

"Please be kind." Her voice was an entreaty. "I want us to work together."

"It's worth a try," he replied. "Just one thing, while we're still alone. Don't ever throw in my face the fact that we had a tawdry wedding. I hope Phoebe and Tom don't feel that way, since it was a double wedding. Such a thought never occurred to me."

Virginia smiled. "I'll be honest. I was afraid you'd return to the North. I couldn't bear to have you leave me. I wonder if you really know how madly I love you."

He smiled despite himself, reached out and drew her close. "When we're making love, I wonder how I could ever doubt you. The only thing is—standing here, even with my arms around you, I feel that if you had to make a choice between Valcour and me, it would be Valcour."

"Nonsense," she exclaimed, already stirred by his closeness. "You'll always come first."

"Only time will tell," he replied. His head lowered to kiss her, but the sound of approaching footsteps separated them. It was Nanine.

Her mouth opened to speak, but Virginia immediately launched on the plan and the fact that she wanted Nanine to join them on the veranda to inform the blacks that they must give up the land.

"Do you think they'll accept such news?"

"They have no choice," Virginia replied cheerfully. "Don't you agree, Elias?"

"Yes," he replied. "Certainly they'll not be able to make a living on the mainland. There are ten men for every job."

"We must be certain they understand that," Virginia said. "I'd like one of you on either side of me when I make the announcement."

"Wouldn't it be preferable for Elias to make it?" Nanine asked. "After all, he ran this island and was respected by the slaves."

"Virginia will make the announcement," Elias said quietly. "I'm no longer in uniform and I had no claim on this land before the war."

"That's true," Virginia said. "However, I'll depend on you to handle the changeover to a sharecropping plantation."

"I'll do my best," he said quietly.

"Thank you, darling." Virginia kissed his cheek.

Nanine sensed there had been another quarrel or, at the very least, a disagreement, and knew it was over Virginia's high-handedness.

"I came here," Nanine spoke quickly in an attempt to smooth things over, "because I have news of another sort. We're going to have visitors."

"We're not equipped to have visitors," Virginia said quickly.

"Whether we are or not," Nanine replied, "they'll be here this afternoon."

"Who?" Virginia asked.

"Two Yankee ladies who live on the island. As you know, a picnic is being given by the Yankees. We're to be invited and they've sent word they're coming. I assume they'll issue the invitation."

"We'll not accept," Virginia said flatly.

"Why not?" Elias asked.

"I wouldn't attend a picnic given by Yankees," she replied.

"Then you'd better have a good reason for not attending," he replied.

"Apparently you've forgotten I have, though I don't really need one." Her eyes took on a faraway look.

"What scheme are you cooking up now?" he asked.

"Not a scheme, darling. Just another part of my plan. It will work in beautifully."

Nanine regarded Elias with sympathy and addressed her remark to him, attempting humor. "Something horrifying, no doubt."

Virginia laughed. "Nothing like that. I'm not so stupid. I have to think like a gambler. Be very careful how I play my cards."

"Don't play cat and mouse with me," Elias said curtly. "Tell me what you're up to."

"Don't be angry, my love." Virginia gave him a look of wide-eyed innocence. "I'm going to behave like a perfect Southern lady."

"If your definition of a perfect Southern lady means what I think it means, you'll be most unpleasant." His manner reminded her of the way he behaved when he commanded the island.

She addressed Nanine. "Go upstairs and tell Mama we're having guests. We'll use her beautiful tea service to make them feel comfortable."

"You know she'll refuse." Nanine's voice registered her astonishment.

"She must do it." Virginia spoke quietly but firmly.

"I'll have to tell her why," Nanine said worriedly.

"Do so. And tell her I'll expect her to put on her lace cap and tea gown, worn though it is. Don't waste a moment. Elias and I are going out now to address the Negroes and I'll want you there also."

"You don't even know the names of the ladies," Nanine protested.

"Tell me later," Virginia replied. "There's no time now. I already hear a commotion outside."

Nanine, knowing further argument would be useless, hurried from the room. Virginia followed. When she reached the hall, she realized Elias wasn't with her. She turned and saw him regarding her, his mouth compressed in a thin line.

"Please, Elias," she said, "come with me."

"You don't really need me, Virgie," he said coolly. "You do quite well by yourself."

She returned to face him. "I do need you," she said vehemently. "I may not be able to convince them to stay."

"You will," he replied, his manner softening.

"Elias," she spoke softly, her eyes pleading with him. "Maybe I seem self-assured, but I'm frightened. After all, I am just a woman."

"A very strong one," he said. "But you put on a show I find quite fascinating to watch. Yes, I'll go out there with you. It's something I wouldn't want to miss."

"If things don't work out well," she said, "promise you'll step in."

A cynical smile touched his mouth. "I promise. Though I doubt that will be necessary. Let's go."

They went outside and walked to the edge of the veranda. Virginia wished she'd had time to change, especially with the Northern ladies coming to extend an invitation to their damned picnic. But Mama would look the part of the perfect hostess. Nanine would help her with her gown and her hair.

The blacks were already assembled and standing quietly, their manner one of obedient submission. Moses stood slightly ahead of them. He was facing them, but when Virginia and Elias appeared, he turned and took off his battered hat.

Virginia observed them quietly, noting that they stood four abreast—like in the old days when they were about to be sold—except that now they weren't spanceled.

Elias addressed her under his breath. "They're waiting for you to speak."

"All of you," Virginia addressed the forty-odd ex-slaves, "are going to be affected by what I'm going to say, but it is a law coming down here from Washington. We can't do anything about it. The new law says that every one of you must return the land given you during the war."

There were murmurs of dismay and some louder noises of anger. Elias raised his arms and shouted for quiet. Though Virginia didn't reveal her relief, she was secretly pleased. It meant Elias would continue to lend support to her cause.

"What was done on this island was an experiment," Elias said. "Nobody knew if it would work. Northerners thought small farms would produce as much cotton as big plantations, but all of you know that it can't be done. Your crops are smaller, you don't have the help to take good care of them and the cotton is inferior. We'll pay you fifty cents a day and your share when we sell the cotton."

"But we ain' got no land, Major, suh," one man called out. "Ain' that whut the wah was carried on fo'?"

"No." Elias peered at the speaker and recognized him as a man who had done some preaching on the island. The kind of man who might understand and be able to offer explanations to those who did not.

"The war was fought not for land. It was fought because of you. That is, you were the basic cause of the fighting. There were other reasons too, but it was not a war for profit. It was to set you free."

"We gets a full share o' whut the cotton sells fo'?"

"You'll get fifty percent to be shared among you. Of course, you'll have to pay back the fifty cents a day you'll be getting. However, you'll have your own cabin, good food, and whatever you can afford to buy."

"But you'll have to work six days a week," Virginia added. "There can be no slothing. Those who don't give a full day's work are not going to be paid. You must understand that."

Belle waddled closer, her wide face showing anger. "All Ah understan's is yo' gettin' ev'ythin' back. Ain' right 'cause yo' lost the wah. Yo' got no call to get high an' fancy with us, 'cause we's black. We's free now, an' don' yo' fo'get it."

"You talk too much, Belle," Virginia addressed the squat cook. "In this case you and Moses have to give up the land granted you, but it certainly can't be any sacrifice for you. So far as I know, you've never even set foot on the plot your husband takes care of."

"Ah ain't no field niggah, that's fo' sho'," Belle retorted. "Jes' so yo' don' get high an' mighty with me."

"You certainly are free, Belle, and you may leave the island whenever you wish. Perhaps the sooner the better."

"Moses comin' with me Ah goes," she warned.

"I don't think so. Moses has no intention of leaving, but you seem eager to go, so leave. But I warn you—and everyone else who has ideas about finding work on the mainland, there isn't any. For every job, there are fifty of you. Even white people can't find work, and are as bad off as your race."

There'd been some muttering as Virginia invited Belle to leave.

To Virginia's surprise, Nanine addressed the gathering. Virginia hadn't even been aware of her presence.

"Folks," Nanine said, "I can assure you staying on the island for the time being is best for everyone. You've been here most of your lives. The mainland isn't like Valcour. You would have a difficult time of it there. If you wish to leave after everything quiets down and business and cotton-growing begin to take hold in our state, then you may leave. No one will stop you whenever you wish to take your chances somewhere else."

There was a great deal of muttering going on and the ex-slaves formed small groups to discuss the problem. Moses kept moving among them, giving his advice. Once he passed Belle, who stood with her legs firmly planted, her hands on her hips in a pose that dared anyone to argue with her. He drew back a hand and slapped her backside resoundingly. She squealed, but she didn't strike back at him. He continued on. Belle glared her anger at Virginia.

Elias spoke again. "We'll give you until tomorrow to make up your minds. We'll bring the old barge down to the dock for those who wish to leave. That's all. If you want to stay, just go to work in the fields."

"But once you make up your minds to go," Virginia called out as they began to turn away, "there will be no changing it. You will not be welcomed back."

There were no comments. They were accustomed to being overruled by the white masters. Some didn't even fully understand what had happened and they remained meek and humble, as if that was their birthright. Their freedom was still an uncertain way of life for them. They had long since become too dependent on their masters. Being set free had exhilarated them for a time, granted them the privilege of not taking orders, or sassing back, but in a situation like this, where the choice was limited, they were not apt to take chances. They would accept what was offered, though a few might take advantage of their liberty and leave.

Virginia had little fear that she would have so few hands left that the fields could not be worked. They'd been too docile to rebel now. Freedom was too uneasy and an unfamiliar business to face.

The three reentered the house and went directly to the parlor, where Lenore sat stiffly in a tall-backed chair, her arms gripping the arms tightly, her features grim with disapproval.

"Did you hear what went on outside, Mama?" Virginia said lightly, pretending not to notice her mother's manner.

"Some of it," Lenore replied stiffly. "I'm more concerned with your ordering me to put on my tea gown to receive Yankees."

"Come to think of it," Virginia said, glancing at Nanine, "I don't even know their names or how many are coming."

"Two ladies," Nanine replied, her manner one of quiet resignation, knowing she'd have to listen to a sharp exchange of words between Virginia and their mother. "Their names are Mrs. Pallen and Mrs. Blair."

"I'll not receive them," Lenore replied, eyeing Virginia defiantly.

"You will, Mama," Virginia replied calmly, too relieved at the smooth way things had gone outside to allow her mother to upset her. "And you'll serve them tea and cucumber sandwiches."

"I'll not use my silver service," Lenore said.

"You will, Mama. It's freshly polished and it will impress them."

"Why should I have any need to?" Lenore demanded.

"You may not, but I have." Virginia walked over to the fireplace and leaned against the brick wall. She folded her arms before her and eyed her mother calmly. "We'll show them a little Southern hospitality. After all, we're known all over the South for it."

"How can you stand there and talk about being warm and friendly to the Yankees we hate so deeply?"

"You don't have to be warm and friendly," Virginia replied. "You will be courteous, but coolly aloof."

Elias stood behind a chair, his arms resting on the back of it. He looked highly amused at the verbal byplay.

"I think that would be quite impossible to accomplish," Lenore said.

"You would, Mother Hammond," he said, "but it'll be no problem for Virginia."

"I see no harm in our being sociable," Nanine said. "After all, they are our neighbors. And their reason for coming here is to invite us to a social gathering."

"Which I'll not attend," Lenore said promptly.

"None of us will," Virginia spoke easily. "Apparently you've forgotten I've planned a ball for that very night."

Lenore brightened at the mention of it. "So you did. Then that's settled. All we need do is send word to the ladies. There's no need for them to come here."

"Oh, yes, there is," Virginia said. "I think it would be good to get acquainted with them. I want to see what they're like. It's always good when one has a chance to observe the enemy."

Nanine said, "Why use that word when the war is over?"

"I'm not speaking of the war that's over," Virginia replied with a harsh laugh. "I'm referring to the one that's just begun. We've won the first round. Getting our land back. Now we must get the island back and return the land to its rightful owners. We must rid ourselves of the Yankees. But do it in such a way that before they know it, they've lost everything."

"And serving them tea is part of your plan?" Lenore asked incredulously.

"It is, Mama. Trust me," Virginia replied.

"Victorious Virginia," Elias said softly, his smile admiring. "That's my new name for you. I really believe you're going to accomplish everything you've set out to do."

"I've never had the slightest doubt," she replied.

"Just remember," he cautioned, "you didn't have to raise a finger to get your land back."

Virginia stiffened momentarily, then relaxed and flashed him a smile of apology. "You're right, as usual, Elias. You may call me Victorious Virginia because that's exactly what I'm going to be."

"Good luck," he said. "Now, I'm hungry. Thank God, I won't have to be here to listen to such hypocrisy. Though it might well be I'd enjoy the show. Virgie always puts on a good one."

"You're welcome to stay," she said, ignoring his sarcasm.

"No, thanks. I just want to put some food in my belly, then get back to the fields. You don't want your overseer to sloth on the job now, do you?"

Before Virginia could answer, he shouted a command to Belle to get the food on the table. She bellowed back that it was ready and waiting for them. Lenore was on her feet and the first to reach the table, the others following.

True to her word, Belle already had a light broth at each place setting. It was followed by a lamb roast, vegetables and steaming hot gravy. Each time she set down a platter or dish, she muttered something under her breath. She picked up the large tray and was about to leave when Virginia called to her. Belle turned reluctantly to face her mistress.

Virginia said, "I meant what I told you this morning. If you don't like it here, get off the island. The war that just ended was fought so you could do exactly that. Many men died so you could work where you pleased and if you didn't like where you worked or the people for whom you worked, quit and go elsewhere. You may leave immediately. I will have no difficulty hiring another cook tomorrow and you know it."

"Ain't sayin' Ah'm goin'," Belle said hastily.

"We can also fire you if we like. That is our share of this freedom. Either stop complaining and improve the quality of your cooking or, by heaven, you will be fired. We shall all pray that the dessert is better than the rest of the meal."

Belle stormed out, stamping her big feet to show disapproval. Nanine held out her plate for a second helping, which Elias carved off the roast.

"It seems to me everything is very tasty and well cooked," she observed.

"So it is," Virginia agreed, "but I didn't want her to know that. She's a good cook and we're not going to lose her if I can help it."

Evidently Belle had foreseen this argument and she brought in a three-layer cake covered with chocolate frosting. Lenore's eyes grew wide. She licked her lips in greedy anticipation and was holding out her plate before the cake was set down. Nanine cut and served the dessert.

The Northern women arrived just before two o'clock. Virginia met them at the entrance to the parlor and bowed her head slightly as the two identified themselves as Mrs. Pallen and Mrs. Blair.

Virginia smiled briefly. "I'm Mrs. Elias Birch. Please follow me. I would like you to meet my mother and sister."

Mrs. Pallen was a tall, austere, grim-faced woman who proved, in the course of the visit, to be a lady of surprising charm. Mrs. Blair, round-faced, with small eyes, made more so by a constant squint, made no attempt to conceal her offensive inquisitiveness. Her eyes first inspected the hostess and her two daughters, then shifted their gaze to the makeshift furnishings, faded wallpaper and finally the threadbare carpeting. The smug suggestion of a smile as she settled back in her chair was visible evidence that she realized the occupants of the house had indeed felt the deprivations of war.

Virginia, in turn, while making the introductions, observed the dress of the ladies. Each wore light cotton afternoon dresses, well tailored and in the latest fashion. Virginia couldn't help but admire the flat front of the skirt, made so by the bustle that extended the back of the skirt. She'd read it was pulled into shape by tapes that were sewn under the skirt and tied back. Mrs. Pallen wore it well, but Mrs. Blair, whose curves extended from her rounded cheeks to her over-developed bosom, abdomen and enormous derriere, made more so by the bustle, resembled an inflated balloon.

Virginia seated both ladies close to her mother, since she would pour the tea and Nanine would serve. Virginia would lead the conversation into what she hoped would be social but impersonal channels. Nanine rose and asked if the ladies would enjoy a light repast to relax them. They accepted without pause and Nanine excused herself and went to the kitchen to inform Belle. Virginia was certain Belle was fully aware of the procedure they had planned and would have the tray, complete with teapot and sandwiches, ready.

Mrs. Blair's eyes finally settled on Virginia. The feeling Virginia got while being appraised was that she should be honored to be visited by the victors, who showed compassion in doing so, and also should be appreciative of the invitation that was about to be extended to them. She was also aware that she and her family were supposed to be in ignorance of the invitation.

Nanine returned to the room, followed by Belle who had changed to a fresh uniform and a fresh lace cap held on by black velvet ribbon. Apparently she'd hoarded it, wrapping it carefully and placing it in a drawer where it wouldn't yellow. Belle set the tray down on the table to one side of Lenore, gave a slight bow of her head and quietly withdrew. Virginia could have embraced her. Lenore immediately began to pour while Nanine passed out napkins and small plates for the tray of dainty cucumber sandwiches.

Mrs. Pallen said, "It is kind of you to receive us so graciously. It is further assurance to us that Southern hospitality has a definite meaning."

Lenore, who had for the moment forgotten her hatred of the Yankees in the joy of once again playing the role of hostess, was caught by surprise, nearly dropping her precious sterling teapot.

"Do you mean to say you didn't believe it, Mrs. Pallen?" she asked, her tone as formal as she could make it.

"Oh, no," Mrs. Pallen said, her smile apologetic. "But to be truthful, I didn't expect you would allow us in your home. I've been on the receiving end of extreme rudeness since my family and I moved down here. You've received us very kindly."

"It never occurred to us to do otherwise." Virginia smiled winningly. "Despite the hardships we endured during the war."

"And continue to endure," Lenore added, handing Nanine a cup of tea, which the latter presented to Mrs. Blair.

"I'm sure you do," Mrs. Pallen said sympathetically. "Just as I'm certain our being Northerners means nothing to you."

"I wouldn't go that far," Lenore said stiffly. "The change for us has been very severe and most difficult to adjust to."

Mrs. Blair coughed delicately and took a sip of tea before she spoke. "Your defeat was so complete that it is easy to understand the bitterness you must be consumed with. However, we are neighbors and, as such, we should forgive and forget."

"The forgetting part won't be easy either," Lenore said, pouring herself a cup of the beverage after both Nanine and Virginia declined. "You see, ladies, I lost my husband in the war. My daughter Virginia also lost a husband."

Mrs. Blair switched her gaze to Virginia, her tone slightly disapproving as she spoke. "But you married immediately after the war. A Northern officer. You also had a sister who married a Northern officer. It was a double wedding, performed, I believe, by a Northern minister."

"How did you know?" Virginia asked coolly.

"The hired hands do gossip, you know." Mrs. Blair flashed Virginia a smile that revealed she knew far more than they imagined. Virginia returned the smile, aware that they had no idea the reason for their coming was also known.

"They always knew everything that was going on," Virginia said.

"In many cases, before we did," Lenore said. "Though they never let on they knew and we never let on we knew that they did."

"Being neighborly," Mrs. Pallen spoke in her quiet voice, "has nothing to do with war or who was on which side. It's stupid to carry grudges or hatreds throughout our lifetime."

"Your thinking," Virginia said thoughtfully, "reveals you to be a woman of high intelligence."

"Thank you, Mrs. Birch."

Virginia found, to her dismay, she would have no trouble liking this woman.

"May I also add that on the mainland your family is regarded with great respect."

"Tessa, for goodness' sake," Mrs. Blair said, "will you stop passing out compliments so I may tell the Hammonds our reason for coming? Or do you wish to?"

"No, Margaret," Mrs. Pallen replied. "Coming here and inviting our neighbors was your idea. Therefore, the honor should be yours."

Mrs. Blair set down her teacup, gave another little cough and started to speak. "Our purpose in paying this visit is to invite you to a picnic we shall hold at the grove of elms Saturday afternoon. We shall provide the food. We know how difficult it is to obtain groceries. We, of course, have relatives up North who provide very well for us. We also patronize the military stores, so we are in a position to do something like this."

Mrs. Pallen leaned forward. "Will you, your daughters and your son-in-law attend, Mrs. Hammond? We want very much for you to come."

"It is kind of you to think of us," Virginia said sweetly, speaking before her mother could. "But it's quite impossible."

"Why should it be?" Mrs. Pallen asked, truly puzzled.

"We've already planned a soiree for that evening," Virginia

informed. "It would be too much. And since our entertaining must, of necessity, be limited, we could not return your invitation for some time."

"That's quite all right," Mrs. Pallen said. "You'll not be obligated in the least."

"We would." Lenore spoke as she helped herself to another sandwich and extended the tray to their guests. "Will you have another?"

Mrs. Blair's hand extended. "Yes, thank you. They're very good."

"We have an excellent cook," Lenore said. At the look of covetousness that crossed Mrs. Blair's face briefly, Lenore added, "And a very loyal one. No one could bribe her to leave us."

Virginia moaned inwardly, knowing Belle, as likely as not, was in the hall listening.

"Couldn't you change the date of your soiree?" Mrs. Pallen asked hopefully.

"No more than you could change the date of your picnic," Virginia replied.

"But we could—and we would," Mrs. Pallen said excitedly. "It would be no trouble."

"It would be embarrassing for us to have you do such a thing," Virginia said. "Also, as I told you, our social events will, for some time, be few and far between."

"It's strange," Mrs. Blair mused, eyeing Virginia thoughtfully, "no one on the island mentioned your giving a soiree."

"No one on the island," Virginia said pointedly, "has been invited."

"I understand," Mrs. Pallen said quietly.

"So do I." Mrs. Blair set her cup and saucer down on the tray with such force it almost tipped over.

Before any more could be said, Belle waddled into the room. "Got a boy heah say y'all owes him two bits."

"What are you talking about?" Virginia asked, taking no pains to conceal her irritation.

Nanine spoke for the first time, addressing Virginia. "Let him come in. Then we can find out why he believes you owe him money."

The boy, about ten, in a white shirt and ragged knickers, held out a branch over which a fairly large dead snake dangled.

Virginia gave her sister an inquiring glance, but Nanine had paled in fear at sight of the serpent. Their mother was frozen in her chair, teacup in one hand, a half-eaten sandwich in the other. Their guests were equally upset.

Virginia said, "I'm sorry, Mrs. Pallen and Mrs. Blair. The boy shouldn't have brought the snake farther than the kitchen. I don't know what got into Belle."

"She can be very perverse when she wants to be," Lenore said, finally recovering her composure.

Nanine said, "You can't blame Belle. And I suppose the boy insisted on seeing you, Virgie, since you promised him two bits for any rattlesnake he caught."

"But I . . ." Virginia caught herself in time. "I must confess the fault is mine. And I do apologize to our guests. Please forgive me, both of you."

"I'd be of a far more forgiving nature," Mrs. Blair stated worriedly, her face turned away from the snake, still dangling on the stick, "if you'd order that boy to get the snake out of here."

Virginia motioned with her head to the boy to go. "You may bury it now. I'll see that you get your two bits."

"Ah thanks yo', Missy." The boy backed out of the room. "Ah'll looks fo' mo'."

Mrs. Pallen and Mrs. Blair stood up, both openly unnerved by what they'd just witnessed. Virginia stood up also.

"I'm sorry you were subjected to this. It was most unfortunate."

Mrs. Pallen managed an uncertain smile. "We'll survive. We're just sorry that you won't accept our invitation."

"I explained why," Virginia said. "To be perfectly honest, we need a little more time to adjust to the fact that all our friends lost their homes."

"You mean," Mrs. Blair said pointedly, "that we have usurped what you feel rightfully belongs to them."

"I didn't say that," Virginia protested, though mildly.

"There was no need," Mrs. Blair retorted, making no attempt to conceal her irritation. "Your manner expressed it. In fact, you and your mother find us despicable."

"I think our behavior was exemplary," Virginia protested.

"And you happen to be our guests," Lenore replied gently, though her eyes regarded the women coldly.

Mrs. Blair addressed her friend. "We will not intrude again, will we, Tessa?"

Mrs. Pallen flashed Lenore an apologetic glance, but made no answer.

"Will we, Tessa?" Mrs. Blair demanded.

"No, Margaret," Mrs. Pallen replied mildly. "However, you must admit I was against this from the start. I realize that coming here was like rubbing salt into a wound. These ladies' lives have been badly disrupted because of the war."

"Everyone's was," Mrs. Blair retorted, flashing Virginia an angry look. "We'll not intrude again, Mrs. Birch, and we hope your soiree is as huge a success as I know our picnic will be— even without the presence of the Hammonds."

Nanine stood up. "I'll escort you out."

"No need." Mrs. Blair was already taking short, mincing steps, which caused her to shake like jelly. "We know our way. Come, Tessa."

Virginia and Nanine stood in silence until they heard the closing of the door. Virginia looked thoughtful as she went to the tray, took a fresh cup and saucer and poured herself a cup of tea. Nanine did the same. Only when they heard the wheels of the carriage moving along the dirt drive, did they relax and sit down.

Lenore regarded Virginia with disapproval. "I'll confess I'm glad you got rid of them, but I don't like the way you did it. There's such a thing as going too far and that rattler . . . ugh!"

"I had nothing to do with it, Mama." Virginia eyed Nanine over the rim of her cup. "I thought my sister might have had a part in it, since it was her idea for the boy to be brought in."

"Such a thought never occurred to me," Nanine protested. "Even if it had, I'd never suggest it since I detest snakes. Even the harmless kind," she added, and burst out laughing.

"You are a conniving miss," Virginia said. "You mentioned it was a rattlesnake."

"Perhaps Belle had a hand in it," Lenore mused.

"Perhaps," Nanine said. "If so, she certainly had an innocent look on her face when she announced the boy."

"That wouldn't be difficult for Belle," Virginia observed caustically. "She can put on quite an act when she wants."

"In any case," Lenore observed, "it served to get rid of those two. And frightened them in the bargain. I hope they will like Valcour the less for it."

Virginia finished her tea and stood up. "That was the general idea, Mama. I'm going to write Phoebe. At least I'll have an amusing anecdote to include in the letter."

"I wrote her yesterday," Nanine said. "I hope you don't mind that I told her we recovered our land again."

"Not in the least," Virginia replied. "I want them to know we're available should they be in need of funds. As I'm sure they are."

"Why don't you enclose some cash in the letter?"

Virginia pondered the idea, then rejected it, saying, "Not after what Elias said about Tom being so proud he might well resent it. Come to think of it, Tom couldn't be any more touchy than my husband."

At dinner, Virginia was impatient to learn if Elias had heard any talk among the slaves regarding the property that would now be taken from them.

"A little," Elias replied. "They're bewildered rather than angry and I doubt few, if any, will leave. Also, the thought of not having to pay taxes is a relief to them. When will they be due, Virgie?"

"In eight months," she replied.

"Good," he said. "By the way, how did the afternoon go?"

"Quite smoothly," Virginia replied, "until one of the boys brought in a half-dead snake on a stick. The ladies believed it was a rattlesnake."

"Are you serious?" he asked, his glance switching from Virginia to Nanine and then to their mother.

"Completely," Virginia replied with feigned innocence.

"As scared as I was," Nanine said, "poor Mrs. Pallen and Mrs. Blair were terrified."

"Who do you suppose did it?" he asked.

"Belle, of course," Virginia hazarded a guess.

"Whut yo' talkin' 'bout?" Belle demanded, waddling into the room. She paid no attention to the look of annoyance that crossed Virginia's features at sight of her.

"Since you were listening, as usual," Virginia said mildly, "you know what we're talking about."

"Got no idee," Belle said. "Jes' heerd mah name spoke."

"Did you give the boy two bits, Virgie?" Nanine asked.

"Not yet," she replied. "But I will. It was worth it, though I'll warn him not to do it again or he'll be fired."

"Y'all seems to lak that word 'fiahed'," Belle snorted. "Yo'all is fiahin' me ev'y day."

"I'll fire you permanently one of these days if you don't behave," Virginia replied matter-of-factly. "But it was clever of you—and loyal too —to play that little game with the snake. We certainly got rid of the ladies in a hurry."

"Ah done tol' yo' Ah had nuthin' to do with that duhty snake," she replied huffily.

"Is that the truth?" Virginia demanded.

"Sho' as they's a God in heaven, it's the truf." Belle's eyes went upward as she spoke.

"Then who?" Virginia demanded.

"Ain't got no idee," Belle retorted, "but 'twa'nt me."

"Virginia," Lenore regarded her daughter sternly, "are you sure you weren't a party to this?"

"Of course I wasn't, Mama," Virginia said indignantly.

"I can't see Nanine doing it," Lenore said, but shifted her gaze to Nanine.

Nanine smiled. "I doubt I'd be ingenious enough to think of it. That still doesn't explain who put the boy up to bringing that snake in."

"Guess Ah bettah tell Moses to fin' out effen he kin." Belle spoke as she brought the coffee pot around the table to Elias and refilled his cup.

"No need," Elias said. "I've already paid him the two bits."

"You!" Virginia exclaimed in astonishment.

He laughed heartily at her surprise and that of Nanine and Lenore.

"You devil!" Virginia's laughter mingled with his. She jumped up, ran around the table and kissed him soundly on the mouth.

"It was worth it to receive a reward like that," Elias said happily when she released him. "Let it be a reminder to you that you're not the only resourceful one in the family."

Virginia walked around the table slowly to resume her seat, never taking her eyes off Elias. "Why did you do it?"

"Two reasons," he said, sobering. "First, I knew you detested them and I thought the shorter their visit, the less your ire would be aroused. The second reason was that I thought it might be a good idea for you to be reassured about me. I do want to help you, Virgie. I'm not certain I'm doing the wise thing in remaining here, but I don't want to lose you either. I've a feeling that if I issued an ultimatum to the effect that unless you came North with me, I'd leave, you'd tell me to go —alone. And for me, life without you would be unbearable."

"It would be the same for me without you," she replied worriedly. "Please don't ever issue such an ultimatum, my love. I need you—I want you. We have no one else to help us."

Elias's smile was tinged with bitterness. "Sometimes I feel the plantation is my worst rival."

"That's foolish," Virginia said, her smile flirtatious. "And not true. Even if it was, you'd never need worry. A hunk of dirt couldn't make love to me. And there's not another man on this earth who interests me."

"I hope there never will be," Elias said quietly. "That I couldn't endure. I'm very jealous, you know."

"I didn't," she replied. "But I'm glad to know you are. I remember the first time I came to this island, I thought you hated me."

"I knew you hated me." Elias sipped his coffee and regarded Virginia, marveling at her beauty and poise.

Nanine had been studying the two of them and absorbing their conversation. It was the first time Elias had spoken so openly of his feelings regarding the plantation. She felt a pang of compassion for him and wondered if Virginia realized he felt like an intruder here despite the fact that if it hadn't been for him, they wouldn't be living in this house now. And even she might not be alive.

She decided to voice her thought, wanting Elias to know her gratitude would be never-ending.

"I'm glad the two of you fell in love and you helped us, Elias," she said. "If it hadn't been for that intelligent army doctor, I'd not be alive now. I owe you my life. I'll never forget it."

"You owe me nothing, Nanine," he replied. "Let's talk about how we're going to convert the plantation from about fifty plots into one big farm."

Lenore said, "Please excuse me." She picked up her dessert plate. "I wish to talk to Belle about something."

"Whatever the subject matter is, it won't do your figure any good," Virginia warned.

"I wish to discuss tomorrow's supper, that's all." Lenore spoke as she left the room, flashing Virginia an indignant look.

"I haven't had time to really see how those small plots were worked," Virginia said. "Can we just merge everything?"

"I wouldn't," Elias cautioned. "The cotton they're growing is worthless. You could never mix it with ours. We can afford to pass up that part of the crop and plow the whole thing under—so we can begin again."

"What of our own crop, grown on what was left to us?" Nanine asked.

"It's as fine as cotton can be, a good example of what this plantation can do."

"What it used to do," Virginia corrected him. "And what it will do again. But, darling, we're going to need more field hands. At least a hundred more. We used to use more than a hundred slaves here. Several hundred on the mainland plantation. Should we try to recruit some of those who used to work for Papa?"

"They've scattered," Elias said. "You'd never find them."

Virginia nodded slowly. "I think it's possible to get more hands without going too far, and it fits in well with our plans. We can talk about that later when things settle down. So now let's talk about the ball I'm going to hold."

"You did mention something about a ball. I thought you were reading too many fairy tales," Elias said. "What do we hold a ball with, may I ask?"

"There's still quite a lot of money," Virginia said.

"Enough to risk spending some on a ball?" Nanine asked.

"There are times when we must make sacrifices," Virginia said. "It's for a good cause."

"And it also is a lesson the Northern ladies won't forget," Elias commented. "They surely know now just how unwelcome they are on Valcour. So give your ball. Will it be formal?"

"As formal as we can make it," Virginia replied.

"What should I wear—my uniform? I don't have civilian formal dress."

"Please don't," Virginia entreated. "If they see you in it they'll not get off the boat. Are you sure you won't be angry if we give the ball?"

"I won't be," Elias spoke with certainty. "Though you'll have to be a magician to pull it off. Those people have nothing."

"That's one reason I want to do it. Their clothes won't matter. Just let them forget for a little while. We'll make it as magical as possible. Mama can make up the list and send out the invitations. She'll love that. Nanine and I will help her with the names so no one will be forgotten."

"We've each managed to hold on to a gown and so has Mama. We can thank Phoebe for that. I expect some of our friends did too. If not, what difference does it make? We just want our friends here for a taste and a memory of how it used to be."

Elias said, "I'll have the barge ready to ferry them, make all the trips necessary. Now, if you don't mind, I'll take a little walk and clear my wits. Virgie, I do want you to hold this soiree."

Virginia changed her chair to the one Elias had abandoned, next to Nanine. "We'll have to hire some sort of an orchestra. A small string group, perhaps. And we'll gussy up the place with bunting, streamers and banners. We'll hang Japanese lanterns outside. I want the Northerners to know we're not like them and we have our own ways."

"All I look forward to is bringing our old neighbors back. Like old times. So they'll have something to look forward to once again."

Belle entered to remove the dishes. "Yo' mama sho' goin' to get sick eatin' so much o' mah cake."

"She's trying to compliment you, Belle," Virginia said.

"She tryin' to eat all the cake she kin get, thass whut she doin'." Belle rattled the dishes on her way out.

"Wait," Nanine said gleefully, "until we tell her perhaps sixty or seventy people will be coming to a banquet."

"You tell her," Virginia laughed. "I'm not up to it. Right now I'm going to bed and that's the place for you too, sister Nan, because you're not entirely well yet."

five

On Virginia's last trip to the mainland, she had sought out a secondhand store and made what she felt was not only a wise purchase but rather a good one, considering the times. She'd managed to find a red riding habit, complete to boots and a black derby hat with veil. Neither the hat nor the boots showed much evidence of wear, but the cuffs of the jacket were frayed and the black velvet lapels were devoid of most of the pile. Despite that, when Virginia stood before the full-length mirror, her smile was one of satisfaction. It was almost as if the old days were back and she was ready for the hunt. She'd not told a soul of her purchase, for it was a definite extravagance. It would have been wiser to purchase a dress that was both serviceable and attractive. Yet she didn't feel the slightest pang of regret. In fact, she couldn't wait for Nanine to see it and hoped she'd be downstairs.

She wasn't. But she was outside, holding the brown mare Virginia was to ride.

"Isn't she a beauty?" Nanine had her back to Virginia and was stroking the horse's muzzle affectionately.

"Elias said she was," Virginia replied, already studying the animal.

Nanine turned around and exclaimed in astonishment. "Where did you get that beautiful habit?"

"It's not so beautiful when you get close," Virginia said, pleased at the compliment.

"Where did you get it?" Nanine repeated. "It fits perfectly."

"In a secondhand store in Charleston. I slipped away from Mama while she was in the hotel lobby talking to Marty. I'd intended to get a dress, but I couldn't resist this."

"The mere sight of it makes me wish I could ride again," Nanine said wistfully. "It's been years."

"You'll ride one of these days." Virginia spoke in that assured way of hers. "And when you do, you'll have a spanking new habit."

"I'd settle for that one," Nanine replied, still regarding Virginia with admiration. "And don't tell me what's wrong with it. I don't want my illusions spoiled."

"Very well, I won't." Virginia tucked her riding crop under her arm and drew on her gloves. She gave an impatient shake of her head when one of the seams gave way. As quickly she shrugged. What did she expect? After all, she'd found them in the skirt pocket.

"How's Mama?" Virginia asked.

"Tired but still working."

Virginia looked puzzled. "What do you mean?"

"Mama and I sat up most of the night writing invitations," Nanine said.

Virginia studied her sister more closely. "You shouldn't have done a thing like that. Your eyes are bloodshot and, besides, you need all the rest you can get."

"I'll get it after we finish the invitations," Nanine said. "This is Tuesday and the ball is Saturday. There's very little time. The ladies will have to refurbish their gowns—if they have them. Since hoopskirts are out and the bustle is in, they'll have to improvise."

"Their gowns won't matter that much," Virginia said.

"That's strange coming from you," Nanine observed.

Virginia took the reins from Nanine, but made no move to mount the horse. "It's the spirit that counts. I want our friends to have the proper spirit. A feeling that they're going to be reborn. That things will be as they once were. That, just as before, they will live in the houses they once owned."

Nanine smiled. "I'm beginning to become infected with your confidence."

"Good." Virginia's brow furrowed. "How many of the Yankee houses can we buy at about two thousand apiece?"

Nanine thought a moment. "Most, if not all. However, we could never pay the expenses of the families once they moved in. Nor would they accept it."

"We wouldn't have to," Virginia declared. "As soon as they take over, they'll plant cotton, and with their investment in the land the banks will loan them enough to get a crop started and take care of their personal needs as well."

"If the banks have anything to loan," Nanine said dubiously. "They certainly haven't now."

"Things will change. They must. I already told you I believed in miracles. Perhaps Marty will surprise us by finding a buyer for the mainland plantation. We'll have enough, even if the banks don't."

"I wasn't aware you had the slightest confidence in him."

"I didn't, but Elias has and I respect his judgment."

"Even if Marty should find a buyer, who has that kind of money?"

"We must still have patience. There's talk on the mainland that the North is bending over backward to bring the South back into the Union. I have a strong feeling that things are going to change for the better."

Nanine's smile was dubious. "I'll pray it doesn't take too long."

"When will you have the invitations completed?"

"It shouldn't take more than an hour."

Virginia shook her head. "Mama never ceases to amaze me— when it's something she wants." She mounted the animal gracefully.

"Be careful," Nanine warned as Virginia urged the animal into motion. "You haven't ridden in a long time."

"Don't worry about me."

Nanine watched apprehensively as her sister urged the horse into a trot, but her fear subsided as she observed how well Virginia sat the mare. She wheeled and came galloping back, smiling triumphantly as she passed Nanine, then slowed and at a more sedate speed headed for the road that led to the opposite end of the island.

Passing the fields she could watch the hands at their hoeing. Moses was plainly visible, riding a big farm animal, supervising the workers and making certain none of them slothed. Elias was afoot, with several of the hands grouped around him. Everything seemed to be going so well, with a fine promise for the future.

Her random ride reached the middle part of the island where there were virgin forests and heavy brush, though the trail was open and easy to follow. She had observed that those island houses she saw were surprisingly well kept up. This pleased her. She was enjoying the ride and it served to bring back some of the old days. But it was time to go back. With the ball coming so soon, there was a great deal to be done.

She turned her horse along this shady, tree-lined path and as she headed back she was quite unprepared when a dozen roughly clad men came swarming out of the forest to encircle her and stop the horse. The lustful faces that peered up at her made her shudder in fear and she raised her quirt.

With a shout, a man in a battered Rebel uniform and a gold-braided campaign hat ordered the men away. He pushed back the cap and looked up at her. He was about Marty's age. A man of brawn, hard and sinewy. Tall too, and quite handsome with a definite masculine appeal. His hair was black, thick and unruly. He had deep-set dark brown eyes, a sensuous mouth and a strong jawline.

His lips parted, as he studied her, into a satisfied smile. Somewhere in the back of her mind Virginia thought he was the handsomest man she had ever seen . . . and perhaps the most dangerous.

"Ain't she a beauty?" one of the men shouted. "We sure lucky this heah day, ain't we?"

"We oughta look for more," another added. "One woman ain't enough. We kin wear out this one in no time."

"Shut up!" the man in the faded uniform said harshly. He reached for Virginia's hand and pulled her down off the horse. Before she could even regain her balance he embraced her with strong arms and drew her to him so their bodies were locked tight against each other. She opened her mouth to scream, but he covered it with his own, so hard she was sure her lips would bleed. As his hands reached for more intimate parts of her body she drew back one foot and kicked his ankle hard. With an oddly cheerful curse, he loosened his grip.

"You bastard!" she shouted. "Let go of me or I'll have you horsewhipped."

He threw back his head and howled in glee. "Damn me if you don't sound like a Southern lady. You Yankee women can sure fool a man."

"I am a Southern lady and don't you dare call me a Yankee."

He thrust his head forward as if to examine her closely. "By hell, I think you are one of us."

"I am Virginia Hammond," she said sternly. "Let go of me you . . . foul creature!"

He stepped back, removed the old campaign hat and swept it as part of a low cavalier bow. "I beg your pardon, Miss Hammond."

"My father died for the Cause," she said. "My brother was a brigadier in the Confederate army."

"Ma'am," he said, "I heard of your brother and of your father. I met him once. A remarkable man. I have insulted you in a manner I can never atone for except to say again I am sorry I called you a Yankee."

"Who are you?" she demanded, feeling more secure now. The men gathered about had ceased to look at her with open lust. "What are you doing here?"

"We're raiders, Miss Hammond. I am Bradley Culver, ma'am. Colonel Culver, if you please. I and my command here have decided for ourselves that General Lee's surrender was premature and we are carrying on the war in our own way."

"Why you're nothing but bandits and robbers," she said, still smarting under the arrogance of the man.

"That we are. We also do a bit of raping when we find a pretty Yank, or some misbegotten Southerner who harbors and abets the enemy. We're outlaws and we ride our own paths and take whatever we wish. Does that satisfy you?"

"We heered tell they's nothin' but Yankees on this island, so we come here to teach 'em the war ain't all over," one man said.

"And that," their leader added, "is our reason for coming to Valcour."

"You are cruel and corrupt and worthless," Virginia announced coldly.

"Ah, we accept the compliment." Culver made another of his elaborate bows.

"We're only goin' to pay the Yanks a little visit," another outlaw said. "We ain't in a killin' mood today, ma'am. Just teach 'em the war ain't over."

"Except for Willowbrook, where I and my family live, all others on the island are Northerners," Virginia explained. "Carpetbaggers for whom I have little or no regard but . . . they will leave eventually and I do not want any property on this island destroyed. This is a Southern island and will one day have only Southern families living here again. Those families who were here before the war and whose ancestors, like mine, lived here for generations."

Bradley Culver seemed to agree to this request. "We will take only property of the Yankees. If they do not resist, nobody will be hurt. In an hour's time we shall be gone, much to my regret, for had I known such a lovely lady lived here, I would have sought an invitation and not come as a raider."

"Let me go then," she said. "This very minute."

"At your command," he said. "Shall I help you mount?"

His hands touched her leg and her ankle and she gasped. Then she swung onto the saddle and dug her heels into the horse. The men parted to let her by; all bowed, as low as Bradley Culver was now bowing. She looked back once. He stood in the middle of the path, legs parted, hat tilted back as both arms waved a farewell. She automatically waved back, which drew a loud Rebel yell from him.

She was shaking, but managed to compose herself as she neared the mansion. She knew about these raiders. The most infamous of them had been a young man named Quantrill. His kind, which obviously included Bradley Culver, were regarded, even by the South, as outlaws fit only for hanging. But Virginia felt a genuine satisfaction in their coming. If anything could frighten the Northerners off this island, it would be bands such as these. She wished no one hurt, but . . . of course she should notify the garrison in Charleston. After all, they were renegades and highly dangerous.

She decided, for the moment at least, to do nothing. It would, she thought, be a downright shame to see Bradley Culver at the end of a rope. Besides, he'd once been a colonel and fought for the South.

She returned to the mansion and found Moses waiting near the barn. He stood by while she dismounted and then he ordered a boy to water and cool the horse before returning it to its stall.

"Thank you, Moses," Virginia said. "Is something the matter?"

"Ain' impohtant, Missy, but thinks yo' mayhap likes to know that the niggah yo' stopped with a bullet gone to New Yawk. Sho' won't bring yo' no mo' trouble."

"I'm glad to hear that, Moses. He's a dangerous man."

"Sho' ain' goin' to fuss no mo' heah on this islan'. When yo' wants he'p to get ready fo' the ball? Missy Nan an' Belle tol' me 'bout it."

"Friday afternoon. I'll need four men and half a dozen women. They'll be paid just as if they worked in the fields."

"Yes'm, tells 'em."

"How do they feel about losing their acres?"

"Some likes it fine. Some don't. They say it like wukkin' fo' the ol' marse an' worryin' when they goin' to get led to the whuppin' shed like befo'."

"No more whipping shed, Moses."

"Yes'm. Bettah that way."

Virginia walked slowly toward the mansion, her mind wavering with each step. Should she tell Nanine about this man Culver, or say nothing and pretend surprise when the news came that the Yankees had been visited by marauders? She hoped they wouldn't inflict too much damage or pain.

When Virginia entered the parlor, her sister was mending some slight damage to the ball gown she'd managed to save. Virginia's gown and their mother's were spread carefully across the sofa, she noticed, and invitations were stacked on the table in the hall.

"I take it you finished the invitations," Virginia said.

"Yes. Shortly after you left. Did you enjoy your ride?"

"Yes."

Surprised by Virginia's terse reply, Nanine looked up, regarding her sister more closely. "Do you feel ill, Virgie? You're very flushed."

"Valcour," she said, "is being raided by Southern renegades."

Nanine dropped the gown she was working on. " 'Raided'?" Do you mean they are stealing, killing—like Quantrill?"

"The band is led by a man named Bradley Culver. He told me he used to be a colonel in the Confederate army."

"But shouldn't we do something . . . ?"

"There is nothing we can do. Before we could get word to the mainland, they'll be gone. Besides, they swore they would not come to Willowbrook and we have nothing to fear."

"Virgie, men like that . . ."

"Colonel Culver knew Papa and he knew Marty. I believe his word is good."

"But if he murders and burns . . ."

"I begged him not to harm any property on the island and he promised he would only steal from the Yankees."

"Oh, Virgie, if they come here Mama will have a breakdown."

"They won't."

Nanine looked doubtful. "We must send word to Elias. He'll know how to handle this situation."

"They'll not bother us. Colonel Culver assured me of that."

"And you believed him?" Nanine asked. "Are you that naive? These are outlaws. Their word is worth nothing."

"Nan," Virginia said patiently, "there were more than a dozen of them. Do you think I want Elias to try to stop them? Besides, they may do us more good than harm."

"I don't even know what you mean," Nanine said.

"They are going to frighten the Northerners half to death. This may hurry their departure from Valcour."

"Good heavens," Nanine gasped, "is that why you favor them?"

"I do not favor them. They are here and nobody can stop them. But if there is an advantage for us in their coming, we must accept it if we like or not."

In sheer exasperation, Nanine moved toward the door. "I never realized you could be so callous. I'm going to send for Elias."

Virginia bent her head and covered her eyes with her hands. "Forgive me, Nan. I don't know what I'm talking about. They frightened me until I'm so upset . . . before they knew who I was all of them seemed intent on violating me. They said so."

Nanine turned back and quickly went to her sister's side to

embrace and comfort her. "I'm sorry, Virgie. This must have been an awful experience, but Elias must be told at once."

"I know. But be sure to warn him these are desperate men. If Elias was hurt I'd die."

"I'll go to the fields myself. Please go upstairs and try to rest. I'll be back as soon as I can."

It was almost an hour before Elias entered the bedroom suite. Virginia was seated in a chair near the window, waiting for him, and her fears for him were so great that she came to her feet and clung to him, weeping uncontrollably.

"It's all over," he said. "They've gone, the whole lot of them."

"You're all right . . . ?"

"I never even saw them. They didn't stay long, but they raided seven or eight homes and took what they wished."

"Was anyone hurt?"

"No, and that's strange because Culver isn't noted for being merciful. He's an evil man with a short future that will end with a rope around his neck."

"I'm glad no one was harmed."

"What did he do to you? Nan was vague about that."

"He yanked me off my horse and he kissed me and . . . and . . . fondled me . . ."

"Damn him!" Elias exploded.

"But he became gentlemanly when I told him who I was."

"Now that was nice of him. I swear I'm going to do all I can to see that he hangs. Right now I'm going to the mainland."

"But why? It's all over, darling. I want you close to me . . ."

"I won't be long, but the military command in Charleston must be told about this. These men are not human beings. They're savages."

Elias led the way downstairs where Nanine waited. Virginia suddenly left them and hurried to the library to return with a small sack and the loosely tied bundle of dinner invitations. She stuffed these into the sack.

"What the hell are those?" Elias asked.

"Invitations to the ball. Please mail them, darling."

Elias shook his head, but accepted the sack.

Virginia and Nanine watched Elias walk briskly to the dock. Behind them the door opened and Lenore emerged, wearing a faded wrapper over a nightdress. Her face was still heavy with sleep.

"What's going on here?" she asked. "What's Elias up to now? I was awakened from a perfectly nice nap . . ."

"Mama," Nanine explained, "a band of ruffians came to the island to steal and loot. Now don't get upset . . ."

"They've gone," Virginia added quickly to keep her mother from either screaming or falling into a dead faint. "No one was harmed."

"They stole from us?" Lenore asked fearfully.

"No, Mama," Nanine assured her. "They didn't even come here. They went only to the lower part of the island where the Yankees live."

"But why? Perhaps they're still here, waiting for Elias to go off . . ."

"Mama," Virginia said patiently, "they were Confederate soldiers who are still fighting the war. They do not prey on Southerners. We are safe, and I assure you they have all gone."

"What of the invitations to the ball?" she asked in further alarm.

"Elias will mail them," Nanine said. "Mama, I think you should finish your nap."

"What with all this excitement, how could you suggest such a thing. But, I'll try if you are sure I won't be attacked in my sleep."

"You are perfectly safe," Virginia said.

Lenore nodded, yawned, tapping fingers to her mouth gracefully. She went back upstairs.

Nanine said, "Virgie, I think we ought to find out for ourselves what happened to the Yankees."

"Of course we shouldn't neglect them. They've been through an awful experience. Shall we walk or ride?"

"I'm not quite up to riding. Come along."

The Yankee families were gathered together and in a state of uproar. They regarded the approach of Nanine and Virginia with a mixture of suspicion and dislike. Mrs. Blair took the role of spokeswoman, granted her by the others because she had already been in touch with the Hammonds.

"We were robbed and insulted," she complained, "and scared to death. We certainly found out what Reb soldiers were like. They boasted they had been in the Reb army. Is there no way to protect ourselves from such beasts?''

"Was anyone hurt?'' Virginia asked.

"Got roughed up some,'' a man offered.

"But nothing serious?'' Virginia persisted.

"Can't say they hurt anybody much,'' Mrs. Blair admitted. "What are you going to do about this?''

"My husband has left to warn the garrison in Charleston,'' Virginia told them.

"They come swarming into our houses like a bunch of hyenas,'' one man called out. "They took everything they could lay their hands on.''

"I'm afraid to live here any longer,'' a woman's voice announced. "My family and I can't live in fear.''

"We noticed they didn't rob you,'' Mrs. Blair said sarcastically.

"Mrs. Blair, we were not in control of that band of thieves. They did as they wished and I do not know why we were spared.''

"I think they were frightened off somehow,'' Nanine said.

"Likely they favored you, being Southern and all,'' Mrs. Blair said.

"We came to see if we could be of help,'' Virginia said coldly. "Apparently there is nothing we can do. Please excuse us.''

She grasped Nanine's elbow and they walked quickly away from the still upset, muttering group.

Once they were beyond hearing distance, Nanine said, "You can't blame them.''

"I'm sick of their hatred,'' Virginia said. "That Mrs. Blair is a harridan.''

Nanine couldn't repress a smile. "You'd be one too if you were robbed.''

"We were,'' Virginia retorted. "But we didn't go around screaming at anyone who would listen.''

"We were scarcely in a position to,'' Nanine reasoned, "since it was your husband who robbed us.''

"Oh, Nan,'' Virginia exclaimed impatiently. "How can you even have a kind thought about those Northerners? I came here with you actually wanting to help if they needed it. I'll not offer again. I don't give a damn what happens to them. I don't even care if the raiders come back. I half wish they would."

"Virgie," Nanine exclaimed, "that's dreadful talk. I feel very sorry for those people and I can understand their anger."

"Which they vented on us."

"I didn't like that part any more than you," Nanine admitted. "But it was a terrifying thing for them to go through."

"It's useless trying to reason with you." Virginia spoke more in defeat than anger. "You'll never think as I do and I'll never think as you do. Let's get back to the house. No telling whether Mama is sleeping or hysterical."

"I believe she'll be sleeping," Nanine said. "Especially with Belle in the house. Virgie, would you mind if I asked you some rather personal questions?"

"We are sisters," Virginia said. "You may talk about anything you wish."

Nanine spoke as they walked. "You've grown into a resourceful woman. Perhaps too much so."

"Do you think Elias resents it?"

"I wish I could answer that," Nanine said. "I hope he doesn't. You need him, Virgie. He's a good, steadying influence on you."

"Oh, good heavens," Virginia exclaimed impatiently. "I'm not reckless. Once in a while, of course—like purchasing that riding habit."

"I'm glad you did," Nanine said. "But I'm talking about something far more serious."

"I don't understand," Virginia said, frowning.

"I can't really put it into words." Nanine looked as perplexed as she sounded. "I'm thinking of those renegades. You said you were terrified of them."

"I was," Virginia replied indignantly.

"But you weren't," Nanine reasoned. "You lost your fear and became curious and fascinated. Didn't you? Tell the truth."

"How can you say that?" Virginia asked indignantly.

"I wonder, myself," Nanine replied serenely. "But I know you. You're a very beautiful, spirited woman. One to whom life is a challenge. And a daring man— even a lawless one—presents a greater challenge. You always sought out excitement, Virgie. Somehow, I believe a man senses that in a woman. When he does, she presents the same challenge to him as he does to her.''

"I don't like what you're implying," Virginia said, keeping her voice stern, though it wasn't easy. She'd been shocked by Nanine's keen perception of her character.

"I'm sorry," Nanine said contritely. "I shouldn't have spoken that way. But I become frightened sometimes at your daring."

"I learned to be that way when we had to fend for ourselves," Virginia said, keeping her eyes straight ahead. "That doesn't mean I'm attracted to scalawags or lawbreakers of the opposite sex."

"Let's not talk any more about it," Nanine said. "Try to forget I said what I did. Just remember I love you. Elias loves you. And Mama loves you."

"In her own peculiar way, I suppose she does," Virginia reasoned. Somehow her statement struck a humorous cord in both of them and their laughter mingled, sending a squirrel that had been sitting on a nearby limb scurrying up the tree to a safer spot, where he scolded them vociferously for disturbing his privacy.

Nanine stumbled a couple of times and Virginia caught her arm, preventing her from falling.

"You're exhausted," Virginia said.

"Yes. I'm going to bed as soon as we get home. But it's a relief to know there were no killings on the island."

"Yes," Virginia said simply.

But she didn't look at Nanine as she spoke, for she was afraid she might, in some manner of speech or demeanor, betray the fact that she had been attracted by Bradley Culver. The others were riffraff and not worthy of consideration, for they were bandits and murderers. Likely Brad was too, but somehow, where he was concerned, it didn't matter.

Even in her own mind it seemed strange that she should single him out from his companions, but there had been a certain magnetism about the man. When he had kissed her savagely, a strange feeling came over her. She had almost raised her arms to encircle his shoulders and try to press him even closer. She tried to excuse herself that she'd clung to the man because she hoped he would not harm her. Yet she knew that wasn't true.

She reminded herself that she was a married woman with a husband who adored her and whom she loved with all her being. But comparing these two men, the outlaw and her husband, only served to prove how different they were; Elias, a New Englander, had inherited the provincial manner of his ancestors. Also their staidness and formal ways. Brad, in his wild, ungovernable behavior, inspired adventure, danger, even romance. And his cavalier style enhanced his image.

Suddenly she realized how barren those war years had been. She was a passionate woman, held back by war, distress, poverty and even hunger, but before the war it had been different. She recalled, with a warm feeling, how she had teased one of the young men on the island just before he went off to war. She believed herself a true Southern girl intent on sending off to battle a young man with a memory he could hold dear, and she'd given herself to him that night. Yet, when he was one of the first killed and his body brought back for burial on Valcour, she'd felt sorrow of course, but not deeply, for she'd known he meant little to her.

Nanine, in her wise ways, sensed that Bradley Culver had an indecent effect on Virginia, and she knew her sister was right. She really wanted him to come back—but why? She was married and in love with her husband. She worried her underlip nervously and fought to be rid of that idea. Yet it prevailed. If he came back, she wondered what she would do. How could any woman love a man like Bradley Culver?

And how could she not?

six

Much to their delight, Virginia and Nanine had found three large boxes of bunting under an eave in the attic. Alongside it were other boxes, which contained Japanese lanterns. The eaves were so low that the area was in darkness and when the slaves looted the house, they'd never noticed them. And so, shortly after sunrise on Saturday, Virginia supervised the young girls from the black families in hanging the cloths. Not only did they lend a festive air, but they hid the faded and, in some cases, barren areas where the paper had been torn from the wall, leaving plaster visible.

Outside, Nanine was instructing the girls on how to hang the Japanese lanterns along slender ropes suspended between the trees. Fortunately, the rope had been nested in the boxes with the lanterns. More were hung on the long, wide veranda. The day was going to be a warm one, followed by a sultry evening. Fortunately, though, sea breezes would keep their guests comfortable, not only for dancing, but when they were seated close to one another during the dinner.

The decorations completed, Virginia led the girls to the walk area between the kitchen and house. There, flowering branches from bushes, plus flowers from the garden Nanine nurtured, had been picked and set in large buckets. She started to show the girls how to place the branches in an attractive manner in the urns and vases that were clustered in one area. One girl in particular seemed especially clever at doing the work. Virginia was also impressed by her beauty and grace. She was slender, though not too tall. Her oval face betrayed the fact that someone among her ancestors was white. Her skin was a beautiful shade of light brown and her features were perfect. A soft mouth with curving lips, slender nose and large brown eyes that shone with intelligence made her seem out of place here. She was well-mannered and moved with exceptional grace. Very much like Phoebe, Virginia thought. She wondered momentarily if the girl might have been sired by Papa. No matter. She dismissed the thought quickly, not only because there was too much of importance yet to be done before the arrival of the guests, but she'd been through that once with Phoebe and had no desire to discover she might have another half-sister. In answer to her question, the girl revealed her name was Ivy and she lived with her grandma in one of the cabins. A further question from Virginia elicited the information that her mother was dead.

"Do you think you could supervise these girls?" Virginia asked, "while I check on other matters pertaining to the ball?"

"Yes, Miss Virginia," came the quiet reply. "I would even like to be given permission to place the flowers in the house where I think they would show off the rooms."

"Where did you learn to talk so well?" Virginia asked in stunned surprise.

Ivy smiled. "I went to school during the war. I got special tutoring from the Northern teacher, who said I learned quickly."

Virginia returned the smile. "You speak English beautifully."

"Thank you, miss. I also teach the others."

Virginia nodded approval, though not certain she meant it. If they learned too much, they'd only be trouble and that was something she needed no more of. The Northerners were enough to contend with.

"Very well, Ivy. I'll put you in charge of these girls and let you place the flowers wherever you think best."

"Thank you, Miss Virginia. I'm pleased and proud to help."

Virginia headed for the kitchen. She heard Ivy's soft voice giving orders before she'd entered the kitchen, the heat of which reached well beyond the door. She turned once and saw two girls already picking up an oversize urn that Ivy designated as the one they were to fill. Virginia noted her black hair hung down the length of her back in a thick braid. There wasn't a trace of kink to it. Again, the thought of Papa being responsible for her presence nagged Virginia. She knew she'd have to find out and the one who would be best equipped to inform her was Belle, whose voice was raised shrilly as she bellowed orders to the black women in the kitchen who were helping her with chores ranging from peeling vegetables and basting roasts to making dessert.

Belle turned just as Virginia entered. "Whut y'all doin' in mah kitchen?"

Virginia stifled the irritation Belle always succeeded in raising within her. "I came to see if you had enough help and if everything will be ready on time."

Belle placed her hands on her ample hips and eyed Virginia in disgust. "Did Ah evah let yo' mama an' papa down?"

Virginia couldn't hold back a sigh of exasperation. "Not that I know of. But this is a very important occasion and nothing must go wrong."

"Effen it do, won' be none o' mah doin'." Her glance shifted to the area where the girls were diligently at work following Ivy's instructions.

"Who is that girl?" Virginia asked.

"Name's Ivy," Belle replied. "Mahty smaht she is."

Virginia nodded. "She speaks excellent English. Strange I never noticed her before."

"Nothin' strange 'bout that," Belle said.

"I don't just mean since we returned to the island," Virginia retorted. "I know she's younger than I, but I don't recall seeing her even before the war. She wears her hair differently."

"Ain' got no kink to it." Belle's smile was spiteful. "Ah knows whut y'all thinkin'."

"You know no such thing," Virginia said stiffly.

Belle shifted her glance to the group of women who were working at various tasks in the kitchen. One who was supposed to be peeling onions had paused and was listening to Virginia and Belle.

"Git back to peelin' them onions o' Ah kicks yo' ass back to the fields," Belle bellowed. She turned to Virginia. "Ah ought to lets y'all stew 'bout Ivy, but yo' gots 'nuff on yo' min'. She seventeen an' she ain' yo' papa's chile. She ain' even bohn on this islan'. Comes from the mainlan', she do. Her mama gets buhned up in a house when the wahr goin' on. Her gran'ma heerd 'bout it an' got yo' husban' to bring her heah. Yo' papa sol' her mama long ago, 'cause she didn' have suckuhs.'' Belle snickered. "She sho' had one.''

"How interesting," Virginia said coldly, wondering just how deep Elias's concern might have been for Ivy. Without being aware of it, she had a great sensual attraction.

"Don' get no idees in yo' haid. Yo' husban' true to y'all. Hopes yo' is the same to him.''

"You are impertinent," Virginia said, making no further attempt to hide her anger.

"Oh,'' Belle replied, not in the least concerned with Virginia's anger. "Ah don' means now. Ah means some tahm latuh. Y'all knows Ah watched yo' grows up. Flirtin' an' teasin' evah chance yo' got. Yo' ain' changed that much, Miss Uppity.''

Virginia's eyes flashed angrily, but she compressed her lips. Nothing she could say would intimidate Belle. She left the kitchen, certain the dinner was in good hands despite Belle's rudeness. She had to pass Ivy on her return to the house, but was in no mood to speak to her. She wasn't going to encourage her. However, Virginia's fears were groundless. Ivy didn't even seem aware of her. Ivy was speaking softly to one of the young girls who was rearranging the flowers in a large vase that did not meet with her satisfaction.

Virginia had supervised the removal of much of the drawing room furniture so that the room was now converted into a ballroom. The oak floor had been waxed and it gleamed with polish. Also waiting in the walkway between the kitchen and the mansion were long tables to be set up in the drawing room after the first session of dancing ended. There was a platform for a five-piece orchestra Virginia had managed to round up —at a steep price. It was already shielded by greenery and flower arrangements.

Both Nanine and Virginia were wearing their oldest dresses, which were faded from many washings. They wouldn't bathe and don their ball gowns until noon, just before the first of the guests would arrive and it was almost time. It was going to be a large affair. Less than ten percent of the invitations had been rejected and those on the grounds of illness or previous engagements that could not be broken. Both girls knew the "previous engagements" were, possibly, lack of even one decent garment or, more likely, they were hopefully looking for employment. Or even doing some kind of work so menial they avoided all contact with their former acquaintances. Both girls understood and sympathized. Virginia told herself she would change their lives back to what they once were. She was still certain she could do it, even though she hadn't figured out all the details.

Nanine joined Virginia in the drawing room to admire the decorations. While they were standing there, Ivy entered, carrying a large urn, followed by the other girls, almost concealed by the large bouquets they carried in the heavy vases, urns and even metal pots, which were concealed by cleverly bent branches. With scarcely a glance about the room, Ivy immediately placed the urn she held to one side of the fireplace. A fanlike flower decoration she ordered placed in the fireplace to conceal its charred interior. Nanine stood fascinated by the competent manner in which Ivy spoke to the girls. They followed her instructions willingly and some of her able manner seemed to rub off on them.

Nanine whispered, "Who is she?"

"Her name is Ivy. She lives in one of the cottages with her grandma."

"I never saw her before."

"I have an idea," Virginia said flatly, "Belle told her to stay out of sight lest I see her and question her."

"Her competence and intelligent manner reminds me of Phoebe."

"She also speaks perfect English."

"Like Phoebe?" Nanine queried.

"Exactly like Phoebe."

"Not another of Papa's, I hope." Nanine paused a moment, mentally calculating ages. "She couldn't be. She's just a child and Papa was on in years..."

"Papa," Virginia said, without condemnation, "was never that old. But I agree, she likely is not another sister."

"If she's like Phoebe I wouldn't mind if she were," Nanine commented.

"Well, we're talking nonsense as usual," Virginia said. "Let's get on with this. Our guests will be arriving before we know it."

Virginia climbed onto a chair and adjusted one of the lengths of bunting. She looked down at her sister as she finished tacking the material in place.

"Remember the last ball? So many years ago, when we were so sure there'd never be a war. And how we used to laugh at all the young men from the other islands, gathered on Valcour to train and drill."

"They did look so handsome in their uniforms," Nanine sighed in remembrance. "They took it all as a game."

"Well fortified with champagne and spirits." Virginia reached for Nanine's hand to steady her in getting off the chair. "I did feel bad about poor Jordie Crawford. He was so sure he wasn't going to come back—and how right his prophecy turned out to be."

"When they brought his body back for burial on Valcour, that was when all of us, I dare say, truly realized that this was no game."

"So now it's time to get dressed. In our six-year-old gowns. But they'll do."

"I wonder what our guests will look like," Nanine mused as they walked up the staircase to their mother's rooms on the second floor.

"Maybe we should name this the Hobo Ball," Virginia laughed. She felt happy, gay, full of mischief, so much like the days before the war. She restrained herself from skipping down the corridor.

That feeling vanished when they found their mother in tears, with her ball gown lying across the bed.

"The seam gave way," she said. "I can't fix it. I never did know how to even thread a needle."

"Don't worry, Mama," Nanine reassured her. "I'll let it out. Be ready in ten minutes."

Virginia had walked to the window, where she looked out over the sea. "I'm not sure," she said, "but I think there's a barge, still far out, but we'd better hurry."

Virginia brushed her hair, then bent forward, letting it fall. Using her hands skillfully to manipulate her hair, she placed combs in it.

When she straightened, her gold tresses fell to her shoulders in a soft wave. It looked like spun gold. She'd wanted to make curls, but there just wasn't time. However, she wasn't displeased with the results. She slipped into her undergarments, put on a pair of cotton stockings with a design running up the sides. Her shoes were a pale violet satin to match her gown, but the satin had slit across the instep of each slipper and the white cotton lining was plainly visible. She laughed aloud at sight of it, knowing that once she'd have gone into a rage for having had to be so shabbily shod. Now she felt fortunate to have a pair of dress shoes, even though they should have been discarded long ago.

She picked up her lavender gown. It had been made for a hoop, but, to Virginia's surprise, Nanine had copied the latest fashion from a magazine she'd somehow got her hands on. Considering she'd had only a week to work on it, she'd performed a miracle. Virginia slipped the strings into the loops and tied them in the back. It took a bit of doing, especially with the bustle, but she managed. She slipped a faded silk flower in her hair behind her ear, then regarded her reflection in the mirror. She gave a nod of satisfaction and hastened downstairs to greet the guests. She felt certain Nanine would already be there and she was right. They went out on the veranda, ready to greet the first boatload of guests that had just reached the landing.

Virginia said, "Thanks, sister, for making over my gown. I love the bustle. I had no idea you were doing that."

Nanine smiled. "It looks stunning on you. I felt that, as Mrs. Birch, you should look the best. Mama will have a fit when she sees it. All I did to hers and mine was shorten them. As you know, they should have a hoop underneath the skirts."

"You must have stayed up every night this week to alter mine," Virginia said. "I know better than to scold you. I appreciate it very much."

"I just wish the lavender hadn't faded. Nothing I could do about that."

Virginia laughed. "It matches the faded lavender orchid in my hair."

Their attention was drawn to a couple who came directly up the path and had almost reached the veranda. The others were taking their time, pausing to observe the grounds and obviously making comments or reminiscing about the past.

Virginia concentrated on the two who were now near enough to identify. They were Alice and Lipton Trent. The Trent plantation was on the right side of Willowbrook. Jordie Crawford's mother's plantation was on the left. Virginia remembered that well, for there was a path she and Jordie used when they wished to rendezvous.

Just now her attention was on Alice Trent.

Under her breath, Nanine said, "How ill Mrs. Trent looks."

"And how old," Virginia replied without moving her lips.

Alice Trent had been a close friend of their mother and though both Virginia and Nanine managed to conceal it, they were shocked at the change in the woman. Where once she had been vibrant and endowed with more than average good looks, she was now frail and walked with stooped shoulders. Also, she had aged greatly. Small wonder, Virginia thought. She had lost two sons and a brother in the war that had also left her husband with one arm. Nonetheless, Lipton Trent still had the dashing look that had attracted many of the ladies on the island. He had retained his figure—not difficult, Virginia thought, in lean days such as these—and the thin line of mustache on his upper lip. Other than a goatee, he was clean shaven. He wore a white suit that had seen better days, but it was spotlessly clean. His blond hair had now turned white. It seemed to make him even more handsome.

His smile revealed even white teeth and his gray eyes had a hint of merriment in them.

"How well you look, Mr. Trent," Virginia said graciously, extending her hand.

He took it with his left, bent and kissed her cheek lightly. "And you're as beautiful as ever, my dear. Thank you for inviting us. I hope there will be dancing."

"Indeed, yes," Virginia replied. "With a five-piece orchestra."

"You can't dance with one arm, Lipton," Alice exclaimed in disapproval.

"Like hell I can't. I dance with my feet," Lipton said. "And for God's sake, Alice, try smiling. This is the first event we've been to since the end of the war and though it may be the last, I'm damn well going to enjoy it."

"You do that, Mr. Trent," Virginia said, laughing. She kissed his cheek.

Alice looked shocked at the gesture and Nanine suppressed a smile.

"I haven't forgotten you, my dear Nanine," he said, moving on to Nanine and bestowing a kiss on her cheek also. "You look so much better. It sounds like heresy to say it, but you look as if the war must have helped you in some way."

"What a disgusting thing to say," Alice exclaimed.

"He's right, Mrs. Trent," Nanine said. "A Yankee doctor prescribed the proper medicine for me and I'm practically recovered."

"Too bad he isn't around now," Lipton said. "He might have a nostrum for you, Alice. One that would cheer you up." His voice took on a touch of sternness. "You've got to forget the past. We can't bring our sons back, or your brother. Or put my other arm back on. We have to build a new life for ourselves and stop whining about what happened. We were beaten soundly. And, in fairness, we deserved to be."

"Oh, dear God, that's heresy," Alice exclaimed, her eyes raising heavenward.

"I'm not certain I agree with you," Virginia said. "Perhaps I do regarding the cause. But what happened following the war on this island and other places, I will never forget. The burnings, for one thing."

"Nor will I, my dear," Lipton said. "But I'll not go around raving and ranting, making myself ridiculous."

"You're absolutely right, Mr. Trent," Nanine said. "Those are my sentiments exactly."

"Things aren't so bad for you, my dear," Alice said pointedly. "You're back on Valcour."

"Don't give up hope, Mrs. Trent," Virginia said. "Or may I address you as Alice?"

To Virginia's surprise, Alice Trent brightened. "Of course, my dear. And how kind of you to want to."

"There's a lot more I want to do," Virginia said, her smile mysterious, "and you'll hear about it later."

Lipton eyed her curiously, but made no comment. Alice smiled politely, indicating she believed Virginia was merely making small talk.

Virginia said, "Suppose we go inside. The others are coming up the path now and Mama must be ready to come down. She'll want to head the receiving line."

"As she should," Alice said, her mood seeming to brighten even more as they stepped inside and saw the bunting and flowers and shrubs placed everywhere. She sighed happily. "It really is like old times." She turned then and saw Lenore.

"Oh, my dear," both women exclaimed as they embraced and their eyes filmed tearfully.

"I suppose we'll have a lot of that today," Lipton said in an undertone to Virginia.

"Yes," she agreed. "But I'm hopeful I may dispel much of it."

"Whatever are you talking about, girl?"

Before she could answer, Alice Trent addressed her. "Have the detestable Northerners taken good care of our homes or are they wrecked?"

"What difference does it make, Alice?" Lipton asked. "The house doesn't belong to us now. Forget it."

"I'll never forget it." She began peering about the room. "I haven't met your husband, Virginia."

"He's on the mainland," Virginia explained. "Some of our guests had no way of reaching the Charleston dock, so Elias hired a carriage and brought them there. He'll be back on the last barge."

"He's a Yankee, isn't he?"

"Yes, he's a Yankee."

"Virginia, how could you?" Alice's voice registered her disapproval.

"Marry him? It's very simple, Alice. I love him."

"But a Yankee . . . and your father killed by them . . ."

"I said," Virginia spoke firmly, "I love my husband. Isn't that enough? And I might add that he was commandant of Valcour during the war. He was among the first to invade it. And, it happens Papa died a perfectly natural death."

"And you can see for yourself," Nanine added, "that Elias did his very best to maintain the property. The looting began before he arrived. But, then, you know that."

"He's a fair man," Virginia said, "and for him the war is over."

"It will never be for me," Alice said bitterly.

"Alice," Lipton spoke sharply, "please behave. We're guests."

Alice glared at her husband and turned to face Virginia. "Forgive me, my dear. I know it was improper of me to speak as I did. I shouldn't lose control, but my grief is still much with me."

"Be assured I understand," Virginia said sympathetically. "Each of us still carries a degree of pain inside us."

Alice looked relieved. "You do understand."

"More than you know," Virginia said kindly.

Feeling more at ease, Alice changed the subject. "We don't look our best, but we wore what we had. This gown—the only one I own—I held in reserve for funerals before the war. And of course," she said with a sigh, "I had occasion to wear it during the war. It's not the type one wears to soirees, but it's all I had."

Lipton placed his arm around her. "They understand, my dear, that we do the best with what we have."

"Indeed, yes," Virginia said, smiling mischievously as she lifted her skirt just enough to reveal her frayed satin slippers. "Aren't they scandalous? My one fear is that they'll come apart before the evening ends."

Lipton laughed. "If they do, be assured you won't turn into a pumpkin."

The mood of those gathered around lightened. So much so that Lipton ventured to ask, "Just how are the Yankees doing here?"

He had touched a subject that Virginia immediately warmed to. "They don't know how to handle slaves nor do they have the slightest idea of what it takes to raise good cotton."

"I hope they lose everything they have," Alice Trent said spitefully.

"They just about did," Virginia said. "Raiders came. They didn't kill or molest the women, but they took all their valuables and food and ransacked the houses for whatever they wanted."

"From the Yankees, good!" Mrs. Trent said.

"The slaves, as they were set free, were worse than the outlaws, I expect," Virginia said. "Before my husband and his men controlled the island, the slaves carried off everything they could handle. Such foolish things. Draperies to be made into dresses. But they looted well."

"I had so many wonderful things," Alice Trent said.

"We all did," Nanine commented. "But the houses themselves were not damaged to any degree. They were soundly built and seem intact."

"I wonder, after those scalawags get through with them," Lipton said. "Anyway, the houses belong to them now. Why should we rave and rant?"

"I'm going to talk about that after dinner," Virginia said. "For now we'd best get on the receiving line. Everyone is beginning to arrive."

By late afternoon, when the barge had completed its last trip, Willowbrook was ablaze with candles and lamplight, noisy and gay. Old neighbors were greeting one another, commenting wryly on what was left of their wardrobes. Only seven men had managed to save their formal clothes and, in most cases, they were now too large. But everyone was a victim of the same circumstances so there was no complaining, only good-natured joshing.

Dancing began before the meal was served. It wasn't dark, though dusk was rapidly approaching. Virginia called out for attention.

"I would ask each of you to go back to your own homes and see for yourselves in what condition they are today. I want the Northerners to see you. To realize what these homes meant to you and how sad you are that you lost them."

"I couldn't," Fran Bancroft called out. "I'd rather die than let them see me prowling about."

"I have a plan," Virginia said. "I'll explain it to you after dinner, and visiting your homes is part of it. The Yankees have had a picnic this afternoon. They invited us, but of course we refused. They will likely see you, even approach you."

Nanine waved her hands for attention as Virginia stopped talking and the guests began moving about again.

"Folks," Nanine said, "the Northerners are not vicious folks. They've not lorded it over us..."

"Not yet!" Virginia added, in a voice tinged with sarcasm. "Who cares if they are kind or cruel. All we want is to be rid of them. Nothing else matters. Now let's all walk about the island. You have an hour and a half to dinner and the exercise will do you more good than dancing. We'll have all you want of that later."

Still, four families refused to visit their old homes, certain they could not stand the ordeal. Some others were reluctant but went anyway at Virginia's urging. Most were glad of the opportunity and soon the mansion was mostly emptied and the orchestra ceased playing. Only Lenore was discomfited. She could see no reason to stop the dancing, and resented those who left, if only temporarily.

During the interim Belle began preparations for the banquet, bossing a dozen fearful girls setting up the long tables and putting down the linen.

When Nanine was satisfied that everything was progressing smoothly, she stepped out onto the veranda for some evening air. She discovered Ivy there. The girl was looking pensively out over the sea now becoming covered with a light fog that would soon dissipate. Ivy bent her shoulders and started to edge past Nanine.

"Please don't go, Ivy," Nanine said. "I want to talk to you."

"Yes, Missy," she said obediently.

"My name is Nanine Hammond. Other employees here should call me Miss Hammond, but I want you to call me Nanine."

"Why are you favoring me?" Ivy asked bluntly.

"I like you. You are well spoken, very efficient."

"And not completely black," Ivy added candidly.

"Ivy, don't be resentful. Please don't be. Do you like it here on Valcour?"

"I hope I may die here, Miss Hammond."

"All right, be formal."

Ivy's laugh was light and suddenly gay. "Nanine, I love you for being kind to me. I know you mean everything you say."

"Now, that's better. We'll talk more later. The guests are beginning to come back. Run along now—and I love you too."

She embraced the girl impulsively and was startled to see two large tears emerge from Ivy's eyes as she broke away. Nanine turned to greet the guests on their way back from their inspection of the island. Virginia came out of the house to join her.

"I wonder what's keeping Elias. He should have been on the last barge."

"I'm sure he'll be here soon. The barge did go back to the mainland, so he must have ordered it. He's been delayed for some reason."

"I hope he didn't think he'd be out of place here."

"Well," Nanine commented, "you really couldn't blame him if he did. After all, he was a Yankee officer."

"That's all over for him. There's no one here who'd taunt him or make him feel uncomfortable."

"I still say he'll be here. There's time before the banquet."

The islanders began returning from their walks around much of the island. Some were saddened, almost to tears. Others were angry; a few were tolerant of the Northern invaders, for they found their homes intact and reasonably well cared for. While they exchanged views on conditions, Nanine saw two people slowly approaching the mansion from the dock. They seemed to be having some difficulty. One appeared to be supporting the other.

"Oh, damn!" Virginia said a few moments later. "It's Elias with our drunken brother."

"Good heavens," Nanine said, "it looks to me as if he is wearing his uniform."

"But he's drunk. He's terribly, soddenly drunk. Elias is all but carrying him."

"We'll have to do the best we can with him. I'll try to get him into bed."

"You and ten like you couldn't get him into bed when he's in that condition. All I hope is our guests will understand. Elias should not have brought him here."

"As you say," Nanine commented mildly, "it would also take five of Elias to stop Marty from coming. Drunk or not, he is our brother."

With a shout of exuberance, Marty pushed Elias away and staggered up the veranda steps to greet everyone with a hearty rebel yell.

"He's even wearing his sword," Nanine said ruefully.

"He's a disgrace to that uniform," Virginia said. "But we have to quiet him down. It'll take the two of us. Now look . . . Mama's going to him. Doesn't she realize he's so intoxicated he can't stand up straight?"

"Perhaps," Nanine said, "a mother doesn't notice such things."

"Come on. And when you get a chance circulate among our guests and explain how Marty came into such terrible circumstances. Later, when he sobers a bit, I want to talk to him."

"You won't get him to change," Nanine warned.

"I know that, but I'm going to try and induce him to stay sober long enough to concentrate on selling the big plantation. Even if he has to sell it cheaply. We'll need the money when we begin buying out the Yankees."

Marty and Lenore were now circled by a ring of guests who pretended not to be aware of his condition. Elias joined Virginia and Nanine.

"What a time I had with him," he said. "When I got to the city he knew about it and came to meet me. He demanded I let him return to the island. At the time he was fairly sober and I could see no reason to deny him. This is his home."

"Why did you let him get so drunk?" Virginia demanded.

"Listen, Virgie, I told you he was fairly sober when he met me. He said he'd meet me at the Bar and Whistle. When I met him there he was in uniform. He'd gone to his room and changed. Now, in that uniform —he was a general, you recall— every man who had a dollar was buying him drinks. I had to drag him away."

"I'm sorry," Virginia said. She stood on tiptoe and kissed him on the lips. "I've been so damned upset . . . I'm glad you're back."

"Looks to me," Elias said, "that you've got a mighty fine party going on. By the way, I'm going to hide all the guns. Marty's been talking crazy about shooting all the Yankees on the island."

"Oh, Elias," Nanine said, "please hide them quickly."

"I hope it will work," Elias said, with half a grin. "He's also wearing his sword and I wouldn't want the job of taking that away from him."

"Has he put it on for a purpose?" Virginia asked.

"Well, he did mention that he might cut off a few Yankee heads."

"He can't mean that," Nanine said.

"I wouldn't count on it. Something like that would completely wreck every plan I've made. Elias, stay close to him. Please, for my sake and his. Try to sober him up. Make him drink a lot of coffee and walk the alcohol off him. I want to talk to him later and he must be at least half sober."

"Do the best I can. I'll sit next to him at the table, if you like."

"Please do," Virginia urged.

"Maybe I can keep him from falling out of his chair. You're not serving any spirits or wine...?"

"'Spirits or wine'?" Nanine scoffed. "There's been none here since we came back and I certainly don't think any was hidden."

Virginia glanced into the ballroom. "I've got to go. Belle's raising the devil again. I swear I'll send her packing one of these days. See to our guests, Nan. Elias, thank you. I love you very much."

She hurried to placate Belle, who had just cuffed one of the girls behind the ear and was telling her how incompetent she was, in language she'd have been whipped for in the days of slavery. Virginia quickly took charge, quieted Belle, saw to it the soup course was ready to be brought in. She signaled the orchestra leader, who ordered a riffle of the drums, and Virginia announced that everything was now ready and the banquet was served.

At the head of the table, with Mama between them, Nanine and Virginia looked about and felt elation and comfort in seeing all those familiar and well-loved faces. Dress-wise it was a motley group, but they were all happy now and openly and loudly marveling at the oyster bisque.

Hot rolls were placed on the table; Lenore bowed her head in silent prayer. Then the eating began with a relish on the part of the guests that warmed Nanine's heart and even made Belle, in the doorway, nod in approval and satisfaction.

While the first course was being cleared, Country Captain, sweet potato biscuits and salad were served. Because of food shortages, they'd had to plan carefully, but the oysters were from the bay, the chickens had been grown on the island by the ex-slaves and the vegetables came from the kitchen garden.

"It's all very wonderful," Mrs. Curtis said from near the foot of the table. We haven't had food like this in almost five years. It's beyond me how you did it and you certainly have my heartfelt thanks."

"Where's the bourbon and wine?" Marty called out. "Used to be some mighty fine brandy too."

"As we invaded the island," Elias said, without thinking, "the slaves drank everything in sight."

There was a sudden silence. Nanine covered her face and began to laugh. Virginia bit her lip, but finally she gave way and joined her sister. The atmosphere, gone grim for a few seconds, was now free and easy again.

"I guess I stubbed my toe that time," Elias called out.

"He's a goddamn Yankee!" Marty shouted and began to rise. Elias forced him back into his chair.

Virginia stood up. "If you please, all my good friends, we will finish eating and then I shall have something to say. When I talk, I'll want all windows and doors tightly closed. I do not wish any of the Northerners to hear one word of what I intend to say."

Marty grumbled aloud, but a few moments later his head fell to one side against Elias's shoulder and he snored lightly and peacefully.

Elias said, "General Hammond wishes to be excused, if you don't mind."

He rose, pulled Marty out of his chair, hoisted him over his shoulder and carried him upstairs where he dropped him on a bed, closed the door and rejoined the guests.

Virginia rose to speak. As if they all realized the importance of what she was going to say, conversation ceased and they gave her all of their attention.

"We are all occupants of Valcour. Our forefathers lived here, we spent our lives here until this awful war began. We belong here, and we are going to return to Valcour, every last one of us. To live our lives here exactly as we used to. This I promise you will come true."

"Virginia," Paul Blair said, "we appreciate what you are telling us, and if it comes true we shall be forever indebted to you, but I, for one, cannot see it happen. All of us, except your family, are destitute. We lost everything and we live hand to mouth. I see no way this condition can be relieved for years."

"I will say that all of you will return to the homes that were once yours," Virginia assured them. "I intend to drive the Yankees out of them and to reclaim them for you."

"But where's the money coming from?" Blair asked. "You may drive the Yankees away, but they'll still own the property that was once ours."

"When they leave," Virginia said confidently, "they will not own those homes or estates or plantations. Each one of you will own what was once yours. What has been rightfully yours will be returned to you. I intend to buy out each Yankee family. They came here to profit from our misfortune. We were driven off the island, the homes were declared forfeit and put up for sale. Naturally we'd not paid any taxes during the war, and at its end, the Northerners sold each parcel of property for whatever was due for taxes. That meant plantations worth thirty and forty thousand dollars were purchased for one or two thousand. In some cases even less than that."

"Granted that you may rid us of the Northerners, it still takes cash to buy back the property." Blair remained spokesman. "You say you are going to pay this money?"

"Yes. We were lucky. My father saw to it that what gold he had saved did not get into enemy hands. There is a goodly amount remaining, and we also own one of the largest plantations in the Carolinas. It's just outside of Charleston, as you all know. There's not much left. The Yankee soldiers burned the house and everything else except the old slave hospital, which was intact last I knew. My brother is now trying to sell the plantation. It should bring enough to allow us to buy everything on the island."

"But with your money?" Blair persisted. "Just where do we, your guests now, fit in?"

"As each property is purchased, that family can move back. The Yankees can't make a go of the plantations. They never will. But you can, and in short order you'll be able to repay us. If circumstances make it impossible for you to do so, the debt will be forgiven."

There was a murmur of surprise and approval. Blair spoke again. "That's generous on your part. We appreciate it, but what does your sister, your brother, your mother and . . . forgive me . . . your Yankee husband have to say about it?"

"Let them speak for themselves," Virginia responded.

Nanine spoke quietly, her voice barely reaching the end of the table. "I agree. I too want Valcour restored."

Lenore said, "We can have our dances and balls. We can ride again, have all the fun we used to have."

Elias stood up, looking at his wife with an amused glance. "I came to this island as an invader, and I commanded the Northern forces here for four years. I came to love this island, just as I fell in love with a girl who adores Valcour as much as I do. I want it restored. The war is over, even if all of you don't agree. We are all Americans. This enmity between people may last for a long time, but it has to be tempered with tolerance and forgiveness on both sides. Yes, I will do all I can to restore Valcour and nothing will make me any happier than to have every last one of you move back here and have things exactly as they were before the day I came ashore. Thank you."

Someone applauded lightly, but it was not taken up. Yet it was easy to see that Elias had spoken well and his words were believed and admired.

"Thank you, darling," Virginia said warmly. "Now, all of you have heard what my plans are. If any of you disagree, or for some reason do not wish to return to Valcour, this is the time to say so. Once our plans go into motion there can be no backing out. Is everyone agreed?"

A great shout went up along with raised arms indicating unanimous approval. Virginia sat down, well pleased. Now the guests began talking to one another, talking of dreams that might now come true. Everything else was forgotten. Nobody left the table. The orchestra had returned from another room where a table had been set up for their benefit. They resumed their places on the bandstand and began playing, but no one rose to have the tables cleared away and to begin dancing. The orchestra wisely reverted to chamber music. It was a fitting musical background for awakened hopes and peering into a future that seemed at least a little more bearable.

Virginia was encouraged. She'd been afraid there might be a few dissenters, but she'd put over her theory well and it had been accepted readily and gratefully. Now she had to find the money to put the idea into being, but she anticipated little trouble with that. She had sufficient capital to get the plan started. She could now begin the other phase of her determination. Ways must be found to entice, or even force, the Yankees to relinquish title to the homes. It wasn't going to be easy, it was a distinct challenge and Virginia was not going to let anything stand in the way of accomplishing what she wanted. Not ethics, nor laws.

Lenore was already looking forward to new gowns, new jewelry, new silver, better food, more horses and frequent trips to the mainland. She was still not quite certain how this would come about, but she had faith in this determined daughter of hers.

Nanine was filled with doubts. There were many estates here, all of them large. All coveted by the Northerners who would not easily be dispossessed.

Elias, now entirely at ease in this group, didn't have the slightest doubt but that Virginia was going to succeed. Long ago he'd learned that her determinations were something to behold, and respect. Once, he knew, she'd been a silly, willful girl growing up without care on this island, but the war had turned her into a mature, wise, and almost ruthless woman when it came to getting her ideas into motion.

He was in no way able to change her mind, even if he wished to do so. He had little but his army mustering-out pay and a modest sum he'd saved up during the war years. Compared to what Virginia had, the amount was puny. Virginia was in control. All he could do was stand by and offer his services and his advice, if she would take any of it. Yet he was in full agreement with her and he respected and admired her for what she had proposed.

Marty, sleeping off his jag, had no say in the matter. Elias thought he'd better go upstairs and see how Marty was. Elias rose, stood behind Virginia's chair for a moment to bend and whisper that he was about to try and sober Marty up. He straightened, raised his arms high and called for attention.

"This is a festive occasion. We all have much to be thankful for, and it's time we once again indulged ourselves. There should be music and dancing and joy. I have been told Willowbrook was once well suited to such occasions. Let them begin again, the start of a return to Valcour's greatness."

Virginia rose quickly, put her arms around his neck and kissed him soundly. As she let go of him, a round of genuine applause filled the room. Elias bowed slightly and left, hoping he had reduced his standing as a Yankee, at least to being now accepted.

Upstairs he found Marty on his back, snoring lustily, and looking nothing like a brigadier general in the Confederate army. Elias hung up Marty's jacket, laid his sword across the surface of the bureau and then removed his shoes. He unrolled the blanket at the foot of the bed, lifting Marty's legs to free it, and covered him. He then sat down to wait until Marty showed some sign of a return to consciousness. It might be some time, but Elias didn't mind. He could hear the dance music begin once more. He would prefer not going onto the dance floor except with Virginia or Nanine, for no matter how hard he tried to convince himself that the Rebs gathered in the drawing room would stop thinking of him as an enemy, he had a feeling that no matter how often they assured him this was a fact, it was not entirely true.

There were even times when he wondered if marrying Virginia and not insisting on taking her to the North had been a mistake. Still, it would have been impossible anyway, so he didn't dwell on this for long. Under no circumstances would Virginia have agreed.

Her almost savage determination to restore Valcour worried him too. While he had no doubts she would succeed, in one way or another, he did wonder how it would change her. Marty gave a grunt and turned on his side.

seven

Freshly bathed, shaved and wearing a newly pressed uniform, Marty once more looked like the brigadier general of the Confederate army whose illustrious career was well known. He walked into the study, around the desk and kissed Virginia on the cheek. She showed neither surprise nor anger.

"I apologize for the way I suppose I behaved," he said. "It will happen again and I'll apologize again, but as of now let's call a truce. Elias said you wanted to see me on an important matter."

Virginia spoke quietly. "Please sit down, Marty. I'm not going to lecture you. But are you doing anything about selling the mainland plantation?"

"I've been working on it." At her look of disbelief, he spoke with more fervor. "Honestly. But you must remember that it's one of the largest plantations around this area. Besides, the mansion and outbuildings were destroyed."

"But the land is there. Fertile, fine land."

"I know. Under ordinary conditions it would not be hard to sell, but now—with everyone broke... I've had a few feelers from up North. However, I will never sell it to a Yankee."

"I would never allow you to. That land produced some of the finest cotton grown in this country. That's a well-known fact."

"It is well known," Marty conceded, "but who has the money to buy it? We can't let it go for a cent less than twenty thousand and nobody I know has one-tenth of that."

"Don't you have any leads?"

"Only one man. From New Orleans. I don't know him well, but I'm trying to get closer to him. He's been looking around."

"What's his name?"

"Miles Rutledge. His father was killed at Shiloh. Miles is very wealthy. When the war looked as if it might start, he didn't turn everything over to the Confederacy. He put a lot of cash into Northern banks and he's now beginning to take it out."

"Then what's to prevent him from buying?" Virginia asked, careful to conceal her irritation.

"Nothing that I know of. I haven't talked to him yet."

"Well, get on with it before you lose him."

"I've worked only through intermediaries, but as soon as I get back to the mainland, I'll contact him direct. One thing worries me. I've seen him twice. He looks like a scarecrow. A very pale scarecrow. He's about six feet tall and I doubt he weighs more than a hundred thirty or so. He gets around, but I've an idea he's a sick man."

"Then, for heaven's sake, don't waste any more time. And please, Marty, try to stay sober. We need the money the plantation will bring. We must have it as quickly as possible. We have to depend on you."

He nodded. "After what I did here, I'll behave. I owe it to you. I'll go back today. Tell me, how was the soiree? I recall getting here, but after that, everything is pretty much a blank."

Virginia's tone was businesslike. "We had a good time. Our friends were fed well, much to their astonishment and satisfaction. You made an idiot of yourself at the table. Elias took you in charge after that."

"For a Yankee, he's a pretty good man though I'd never tell him that. You'd do well to hold on to him."

"I intend to."

Marty regarded her thoughtfully. "Just remember he's used to taking charge. He ran the island well enough to have attained an excellent reputation as a manager. Give him his head, Virgie."

Virginia's features revealed her surprise. Her tone held an air of innocence as she spoke. "I always have. We share in everything."

Marty's smile was sardonic. "I have my doubts, but if you say so."

"Just sell the plantation," Virginia responded with a tinge of anger. "I don't care what you have to do to accomplish that, but do it. And keep in touch. Move into a reputable hotel and stay away from those friends of yours who aren't worth the space they occupy. Remember, you're a Hammond. The name commanded respect. Please don't destroy it."

Marty softened. "I'll do as you say though I need money. A hundred or so."

"You'll have it before you leave. One other thing. Have you heard of a renegade named Bradley Culver? He leads a pack of scoundrels who prey on anyone who has anything worth stealing."

"I heard of him. Why?"

"He came here. He raided the Yankees after he accosted me in the forest. I was terrified, but needlessly so. He swore he would never harm a Southern woman or family. He promised he would not burn any of the houses on Valcour, or do material damage to the property."

"If he kept that promise, it'll be the first time. He's an outlaw, Virgie, a highly dangerous man. If he's caught, he'll hang. If the North doesn't hang him, the South will. He's a cheat and a scoundrel. Don't ever take him at his word, for he's a man without honor. That about covers it."

"Completely," she agreed. "I doubt he'll return. Elias reported the raid and brought back guns so we'll be prepared."

"I imagine the Northerners will be also. Did I bring any baggage?"

"Not that I'm aware of."

"Then I'll take a walk down to the fields, say good-bye to Elias and get someone to row me to the mainland. Kiss Mama for me, and Nanine too. Oh—heard from Phoebe?"

"We had one letter. She's fine, she likes New York, but Tom's having some difficulty getting his job back."

"Phoebe's resourceful. It still seems strange to me that we have a sister with Negro blood, even if it doesn't show."

"Just remember, dear brother, that Phoebe shares the same father as we."

Marty laughed aloud. "He was a lusty old boy, wasn't he? And he had a fine sense of humor. One of the funniest things he did was to manumit Phoebe's mother and give her the money to start a whorehouse in New Orleans."

"I don't think it's funny," Virginia replied. "Certainly not for Phoebe."

"Father's ideas were bizarre, I know. Papa used to go there from time to time. I wonder if she charged him for the use of her girls?"

"I don't care to discuss Phoebe's mama. Or any involvement Papa had with her."

Marty's smile mocked her. "If I ever get down that way I'll drop in and check up on her."

"If you do, don't bother to tell me about it. Just get the plantation sold. Please! So much depends on it."

Marty rose. "My word on it."

Virginia also stood. "You look well in that uniform. Why don't you try to honor it by staying sober permanently?"

"What the hell for? The uniform is defunct. It represents nothing but a lost cause and nobody gives a damn for lost causes. That awful moonshine they sell makes me forget. If I drink enough, I'm back in service as a general. I'm planning campaigns and battles. I'm a soldier! Sober, I'm nothing. Whiskey has its uses, dear sister."

Virginia sighed in despair as he left the room. She settled down to study financial problems, partly working on guesswork, for she had no idea how much Marty would get for the mainland plantation—if he could even manage to sell it. If he did, and got a reasonable figure, she could handle everything with enough left over to maintain her family's present status.

Then she leaned back and thought about Bradley Culver. Marty was right in his appraisal of Bradley as a scoundrel, a murderer and a person without a conscience. She closed her eyes and brought back the moment when he held her close and his mouth covered hers. Her breath quickened and a weakness overcame her as she relived the memory of their brief encounter. Despite his evil reputation, she couldn't get him out of her mind. She could think only of the handsome face above hers, his eyes mocking her, his mouth pressed against hers.

It was the morning after the ball. Lenore likely wouldn't get out of bed all day. Nanine, not yet fully recovered, would sleep late. Elias, rising even before Virginia, was already in the fields. The thought warmed her, for she knew he was doing it for her. He worked hard and he handled the blacks well. They, in turn, respected him. Elias had learned to know their ways from his leadership during that interminable period of the war. He had governed the island fairly and wisely.

Virginia was prepared for almost anything, but not the unexpected visit from Henry Tannet. One of the housegirls announced him and Virginia had him brought to the study.

He proved to be a lanky scarecrow of a man, with a lean face and pointed chin. Large ears gave him what Virginia thought was a satanic appearance.

"Good mornin'," he said as he sat down without invitation. "Want to talk to you some, you don't mind."

"What about, Mr. Tannet?"

"Lots of things. Been here goin' on a year and a half now and I never been able to get the hang of this island. Need help. How do you grow cotton that sells? The stuff I grow is rank. And the niggers. They don't pay any attention to me except on the day I pay their wages. Fifty cents a day and they ain't worth half that. Lazy critters!"

"Negroes," Virginia said, "are a different breed of people. They have to be handled firmly, but with tact. In the old days, we whipped them when they misbehaved. If their misdeeds were minor, we made them work harder and longer. But you kind folks from the North seem to think they will work as they used to because you set them free. We in the South know how to handle them. You from the North will never be able to get work out of them. They'll sloth, they'll lie and cheat, but they won't work for you."

"Times I get thinkin' you folks might have been right in the way you handled them. They make me so damned mad I could break their necks."

"I wouldn't advise that, Mr. Tannet."

He eyed her speculatively. "You're not being very cooperative, ma'am."

"I was merely trying to acquaint you with the ways of the Negroes." Virginia's manner was cool but polite.

He looked dubious. "One thing more. I'm goin' busted tryin' to raise cotton. Got me an idea I might take over the sutler's store. Since the army moved out, it's been half empty and we have to bring everything in from the mainland. Takes a lot of rowin' back and forth. Seems to me if I get the store goin' good, I'll make out. What do you think?"

Virginia smiled contentedly. He had just given her plans a mild lift.

"I think it would be to the advantage of everyone on the island, sir. The Negroes will be especially appreciative because they're not able to get to the mainland often. They'd like that."

"Then, by George, I'll do it. Takes my last dime, I'll do it. Never thought about the niggers. More of them than us. My wife says I'd be talkin' to a stone wall comin' here like this, but you talk straight talk. I can take it, bein' a Yankee. From Vermont. Real nice state. Better'n this damn place. My wife talks about hurricanes and rattlesnakes. Been listenin' to a lot o' trash."

"Not exactly," Virginia said calmly. "But nothing you couldn't handle."

He brightened. "Say, comin' here I was able to see the cotton you grow. Looks ten times better'n anythin' I got in the ground."

"Cotton grows best for Southerners, Mr. Tannet," Virginia said modestly. "It's all we know. All we've ever done."

"Makes sense. Well, thankee kindly, ma'am." He paused, then asked, a hint of mockery in his eyes, "You still mad at us for winnin' the war?"

Virginia managed a smile. "Would it do me any good?"

"Not a damn bit. Just asked on accounts you married a Yank."

"My husband is a man without a trace of prejudice," Virginia said quietly.

"No one'll say the same of you, ma'am. Leastwise, that's what the womenfolk say."

"Just what do they say?" Virginia asked, keeping her tone casual.

"That you're stuck-up. You won't be friendly."

"I help to run this plantation, Mr. Tannet. I have no time for idleness. Did you have any more questions?"

He stood up. "If I did, doubt you'd answer. Leastwise, the way I'd want them answered. Ain't got no more time to waste on you. Shoulda' knowed better'n to come."

"I'm sorry, Mr. Tannet. I thought I was being helpful."

His mouth opened to speak, but then he thought better of it, turned on his heel and walked out. Virginia looked thoughtful, then smiled serenely. It was easy to see that Mr. Tannet's financial future would come as a surprise—to him.

Tannet made his way along the path that led to the cotton fields belonging to Willowbrook. He skirted the edge of the fields, pausing now and then to study the large, healthy-looking balls of cotton, more than twice the size of what his plants produced. He wondered if they had a secret method. Wouldn't surprise him. Damn Rebs were full of tricks.

Moses, riding the only mule on the island, watched Tannet for a moment and then rode to intercept him.

"Kin Ah he'p yo', suh?" Moses asked when he reached Tannet.

"Sure can, you a mind to," Tannet said. "You boss the slaves, don't you?"

"Ain' no slaves on this heah island, suh. Ain' no slaves nowhar Ah knows of."

"Didn't mean it that way. Do you boss the Negroes?"

"Yes, suh, sho' does, suh."

"How do you get such a fine crop when none of us Northerners can match it?"

"Don' know, suh, lessen cotton grows bettah fo' us black folks."

"I'm gettin' to the point where I think it does. How'd you like to come an' work for me? Get my crop goin' like it should."

"No, suh. Wuks fo' Miss Virginia an' her fam'ly, suh. Wukked fo' 'em all my life an' sho' ain' fixin' to quit now."

"I'll pay you sixty cents a day."

"Wouldn' come yo' pays me six dollahs a day, suh."

"Humph," Tannet sniffed. "Reckon six or seven years ago I could have bought you for a hundred dollars."

Moses' black face, usually smiling, became a mask, but he could scarcely suppress his anger. "Sees Massa 'Lias comin'. Reckon yo' kin talk to him. Sho' don' knows how to talk to me."

Under a hard prod of Moses' heels the mule ambled away, passing Elias, who continued walking briskly toward Tannet.

"Mornin', Major," Tannet said amiably. "Mighty glad to talk to a Yankee. Yes, sir, been here some time now and I ain't caught on how to understand the niggers. They got a language all their own."

"No doubt," Elias said dryly. "Their ancestors certainly did."

"They don't understand me either. Real stupid. No mind at all."

"They have a mind, Mr. Tannet. Trouble is, they were never allowed to use it. Never taught to read and write. But that will change with time."

"Don't believe it. Nobody as thick-skulled as they are will ever learn anythin'."

"I take it you have no children, Mr. Tannet."

"What's that got to do with it?"

"If you had children, you might know something about the school on this island. We Northerners came here and seized the island. We didn't do it much good, but one of the things that did work is the school. The Negro children study harder than any white ones I've known. Their elders attend too, because they want to learn to read and write. You underestimate them, Mr. Tannet. Go to the school and see for yourself."

"Ain't got time for such shenanigans like visitin' a school. Don't give a damn if they learn anythin' or not."

"You should if you want them to become useful citizens instead of a burden to the community."

"Now, you're a Yank," Tannet said. "A reasonable man. Why can't we get together and see what can be done?"

"Mr. Tannet, the war is over. I'm neither a Yank nor Reb. I'm an American. I don't have to form an alliance with any group. No need to. I intend to live in peace and mind my own business. Was there anything else, Mr. Tannet?"

"Well, not's I know of." Tannet regarded Elias with grudging respect. "Been talkin' to your wife. About takin' over the old sutler's store."

"A risky business, Mr. Tannet."

"That ain't what your wife said."

"Beginning any business these days is a risk."

Tannet shoved the old Panama hat back on his head and studied Elias with little sign of friendliness. "Seems to me, Major, that even if you married a Reb, you ought to stand up for your own people."

"I believe I do, sir. I stand up for my family every time."

"I mean us. We who came down here out of the goodness of our hearts to settle in and make somethin' out o' this godforsaken island."

"Mr. Tannet, pardon me for saying so, but you and the others who came here from the North did so to speculate in real estate. You bought large homes and mansions for back taxes. You intend to hang on to these places until the aftermath of the war fades and you can then sell at a fat profit. I don't like what you did and intend to do. You've been called scalawags and carpetbaggers and I think either or both terms apply."

"By damn," Tannet made no attempt to hide his anger. "They turned you into a Reb!"

"Good morning, sir."

Tannet didn't intend to let him off so easily. "Your wife sure can boss a man around. Yes, sir, she still thinks she's a rich woman in the South that used to be, and everybody she meets is a slave she can order around. Like she orders you."

"Mr. Tannet," Elias said politely, "would you like a punch in the nose?"

Tannet backed away a step. "You lay a hand on me and I'll have the law on you. I'm ashamed of you. You, a major in the Union army, turned yellow an' Reb. You're a traitor . . . an' . . . don't you raise a fist to me. I'm older'n you. Too old to fight a buck like you, an' I swear I'll have the law on you."

"You are standing on Willowbrook property. Get the hell off it, or I will do something. And you can make all the damn trouble you want."

Tannet turned away. Elias exhaled sharply, releasing some of the anger within him. These people couldn't get over the fact that they were victors in a war that should never have been fought. They believed what they had paid for on Valcour were actually spoils of war. Elias angrily resumed his walk to the mansion. He'd taken no more than a dozen steps when he saw two men walking from the vicinity of the dock. One of them was tall; the other, who carried a large sack over his shoulder, was wiry-looking even while bent under the weight of his burden.

"Oh, damn!" Elias said aloud.

The tall man was Bradley Culver, the outlaw feared by both the North and the South. Even from this distance he looked flamboyant, cocksure, a man without fear. But to be feared, because he made trouble wherever he went. Elias turned around. Tannet had stopped, shaded his eyes with his hand and certainly would have no trouble recognizing Bradley Culver. As Elias watched, he turned around and began running back to his part of the island at a speed certainly induced by fear.

Elias broke into a run himself, wanting to intercept Culver before he reached the house, but Culver had too much of a start and by the time Elias mounted the veranda stairs, passing the shorter man with the sack, Culver was already inside.

He was bowing over Virginia's hand when Elias entered. Virginia gave a gasp of surprise and, perhaps, consternation, blushing slightly as if the situation embarrassed her.

Culver bowed and extended his hand toward Elias, who accepted it automatically, thinking a second later he should have refused to shake hands with this outlaw.

"I've come in peace," Culver said. Virginia admired his low, easy voice. "When I was here before, I spared the homes of Southerners and took only from the Yankees."

"We were grateful for that," Virginia said, "since we're the only Southerners on the island."

"Taking from anybody by force is robbery," Elias said coldly. "There's no difference."

Culver smiled. "I disagree, sir, but I grant that you are entitled to your say. In fact, because of my reputation—well deserved I admit—I should not be allowed to express an opinion either way on the subject of what is fair and what is not."

"What do you want?" Elias demanded.

"Now, Elias," Virginia spoke before Culver could reply, "at least we owe this man the right to explain why he came. Most certainly it is not to harm us."

"I merely asked him what he wanted," Elias said, not taking his eyes off Culver.

"Please," Culver said. "There is no sense in fighting over my purpose in returning to the island. Let me explain. I did no harm to anyone during my visit. Nor did my men. I didn't even loot the homes as thoroughly as I am accustomed to do. I felt that those who lived on the island, be they Yankees or Rebs, must look to you folks for protection and advice."

"Poppycock," Elias said, making no attempt to hide his dislike for Culver.

"Depends on how you regard the matter." Culver's tone was casual, as if totally unaware of Elias's antagonism. "I got thinking it over after I returned to the mainland and I confess I felt ashamed of myself for attacking this island. I've never had that feeling before, but I learned what a stalwart and staunch Confederate lady your wife is, sir. I regard her and her entire family to be among the finest people the South is blessed with. So I returned to bring back every scrap of loot I took from the Yankees. I ask that it be given to them with my apologies."

"Thank you," Virginia said softly.

"I don't understand this," Elias admitted, relaxing slightly, but still suspicious. "You came here and robbed a number of Yankee families. You've been doing this for weeks on the mainland, and I never heard that you returned anything you stole."

"Quite true. It's against my nature to return articles I—ah—took. But in this case I feel I must because of the Hammond family. Because of Mrs. Hammond, her daughters, her illustrious son and martyred father. And because of you, sir."

"I'm a Yankee. I was a major in the Union army. So why the hell include me?"

"What you were before the cease-firing is one thing. What you are now, married to your lovely wife, is something else. I admire you, sir, and I compliment you for the reputation for fairness you built for yourself here. I envy you because, in all truth, I have never met a lovelier woman than Mrs. Birch, sir."

"Thank you, sir," Virginia said modestly.

Elias shook his head. "I don't know how to take you, Culver. From what I have been told, you spare no one and your methods of robbery are violent. It is said you and your renegades have murdered a great many people."

"Murdered? It depends on how you look at it. If the victims we select do not stand aside while we take possession of their property and if they defy us by force, then we use force."

"It's still murder," Elias reminded him. "You're nothing but an outlaw."

Culver shrugged, but retained his easy manner. "As I said, it depends on how you look at it."

"Also," Elias said, "you must be aware that there's a bounty on your head and when you're caught—I don't say *if*—I say *when* you are caught, you'll hang."

"Fully aware of it," Culver said cheerfully.

Virginia entered the conversation, her voice subdued, her manner one of maidenly innocence. "Why do you pursue such a life, Mr. Culver, if you know how it will end?"

He turned to her and, for a brief moment, his eyes held a hint of intimacy. Virginia felt color flood her face, but managed to keep her expression formal.

He said, "I too fought in this war brought upon us by the stupidity of the North. I lost many fine years of my life and I am a man who feels that any such loss should be paid for. So I visit Yankee sympathizers, Yankee carpetbaggers. I take what I want, for that is the one and only way I can exact the payment I feel that I deserve."

Elias said, "What if everyone in the South maintained such an attitude? We'd be at war again."

"My dear Major, I have always been at war. I shall always fight the North. Lee's surrender did not end the fighting for me. It goes on until I am certain that I have, at least, won something, even if it costs me my life."

"You should reconsider, sir," Virginia said. "If you are truly repentant, mercy will most certainly be extended to you."

"Not a chance," Elias said bluntly. "Your life was sacrificed long ago and for good reason."

Culver smiled cynically, walked over to Virginia and took her hand. It trembled in his as he bent forward and kissed the back of it in his most chivalrous manner. He offered his hand to Elias, who spurned it. His eyes, appraising Elias, revealed respect.

"I shall leave your island, sir. Please do not regard me as your enemy, even if you won't regard me as a friend. The articles stolen from the Yankees are in that large sack on your veranda. Good day, sir, madam."

He turned and walked with military precision out of the house. After a few moments, Virginia and Elias followed. They stood on the veranda and watched him reach the dock where a rowboat and his aide waited for him.

"What a strange man," Virginia said, her eyes on the departing boat. "What a wasted life!"

"'Strange' isn't the proper word, Virgie." Elias's tone evidenced his disapproval.

"Be fair, Elias. There must be some good in him. He brought back everything he stole."

"I don't pretend to understand his motive for doing that. But it doesn't change my opinion of him. Up to now I never heard of him respecting anyone's heritage, family or rights. He has always been a thief and a murderer. He's a brutal, vicious man."

"He did bring back what he stole," Virginia repeated.

"Virgie, do you honestly believe that gesture did us any good? When he arrived, I had just left Tannet. He saw Culver on his way to the house. Of course he recognized him. Culver robbed his house along with the rest of them. And Tannet is bound to do something about it."

"Oh, damn!" Virginia exclaimed angrily. "Tannet will report this to someone, I suppose. Can they do anything to us because Culver visited us?"

"It's the law that anyone who comes across Culver must at once notify the authorities. Anyone who harbors him shall suffer the same fate as he will someday suffer."

"They can't say we harbored him."

"Perhaps not, but they could say we invited him, we tolerated him, we did not notify the authorities. Tannet is going to do that, I know."

"Then we should immediately go to the mainland and explain that Culver returned with the loot. We can simply repeat what he told us, that he believed we were responsible for everyone on Valcour and he felt he was insulting Southern patriots by coming here even if his actual victims were Yankees."

"They'll believe that as much as I believe Culver's motives were honorable." Elias smiled sardonically. "That he was repentant."

"But we have no other explanation. Elias, I want to go to the mainland at once, before Tannet can send word. If we act first, there will be less reason to hold us responsible."

"Perhaps," Elias said, but with considerable doubt.

"Culver left us only moments ago. How could we report his presence here? There's no one on Valcour to report to. We have to go to the mainland and inform the authorities that Culver has been in the vicinity. If we do this now, without waiting another moment, we cannot be held responsible, since we reported his presence as quickly as we possibly could."

"Get your hat," Elias said. "I won't even bother to change. Come down to the dock. I'll be waiting. I agree you should accompany me. It will mean you have the same regard for him as I."

Virginia hurried into the house, ascending the stairs noisily in her haste. She ran along the corridor, awakening Nanine, who opened her bedroom door and peered out.

"I can't stop but a second," Virginia explained. "Culver came back with everything he stole from the Yankees. I'll explain later, but right now Elias and I have to report to the mainland authorities so we won't get into trouble by holding back information about him."

Nanine looked puzzled. "What are you talking about? I was sound asleep and I'm still groggy."

"Later. I'll tell you about it when I get back. Don't let Mama know we've had a visitor."

Virginia drew a light shawl over her shoulders, brushed up a few stray hairs, and got a bonnet from the closet. She tied the bow firmly under her chin so it wouldn't blow off during the journey over the water. She paused to give Nanine a fleeting kiss and then left the house, running all the way down to the dock. Elias helped her aboard, manned the oars and began rowing the moment she cast off.

"I hope the authorities will believe us," Virginia said, still breathless from her exertions.

"So do I. While I waited for you, I saw a boat leave the island. Two men were in it, rowing as fast as they could. Tannet is losing no time."

"He's very disagreeable."

"He'll be more so now," Elias said. "He'll make all the trouble he can. However, this time I think we can counter any charges he tries to make."

"Whom shall we report this to?"

"Tannet is going to tell Bowman at the Freedmen's Bureau. We'll report it to my friend at the occupation headquarters. He's in charge of law enforcement and he should know first. As soon as Bowman hears what Tannet has to say, he'll be coming after us. We've made an enemy of him also and he does wield a certain amount of authority."

"I know," Virginia said worriedly.

"Not as much as the Union army, though, and that's where we're going first."

Virginia sighed. "We've so much to do and we must take time out for something we had nothing to do with."

"If we don't spend this amount of time clearing things up now, we may spend much more later trying to explain. If I run across Culver again, I swear I'll take him in—unless he has a gun pointed at me."

"Such a strange man," Virginia said.

"Damn it, Virgie, why do you keep saying he's strange?" Elias's voice held a hint of irritation. "He's a scoundrel. Committed every known crime in the books. Contemptuous of law and order. A respecter of no one or nothing."

"You're forgetting one thing," Virginia said, a hint of a smile touching her lips. "He returned everything he stole."

"I wish to hell I knew why," Elias said bitterly. "But be assured, he has a reason. Sooner or later, it'll surface."

"He stated why," Virginia replied. "He didn't know there were any Southerners on the island."

"What the hell are you defending him for?" Elias demanded.

"I'm not," she said quickly. "Please, Elias, let's not quarrel over him. He's not worth it."

"You're right about that," Elias agreed. "Now, no more talking. I have to concentrate on rowing. We'd better get there as fast as we can."

Virginia nodded and lowered her eyes, fearing they might give away her feelings. Not that she had any about Culver, she told herself righteously. Yet she wondered why her hand had trembled at his touch. In fact, she'd felt a wave of weakness overcome her when he walked into the room. She gripped the sides of the boat more tightly in order to calm herself. She was frightened at the thoughts that were running through her brain. She didn't find him evil, despite everything she knew about him. She couldn't forget that single embrace. It had sent her blood racing.

She was glad Elias's attention was on getting the boat to the mainland as quickly as possible. He was in such excellent physical condition the boat seemed almost to fly through the water each time he dipped the oars. She forced herself to watch him, letting her eyes travel the length of his body. She knew she still loved him and desired him as much as he did her. If only she could get that handsome devil Bradley Culver out of her mind.

eight

At the waterfront in Charleston, they hired a carriage. Elias gave orders to be driven to the Union army headquarters located in the center of the city.

The carriage meandered its way over streets still littered with the result of the fires, explosions and the falling walls as the war ended. Virginia dabbed at her eyes with a handkerchief at sight of it.

"I used to love coming here and riding around in a carriage. Everything was so beautiful and exciting. You should have seen it in those days before the war. There were trees everywhere, no yard was without flowers. Everyone was happy and content. It was a wonderful life and a fascinating city."

"A wonderful life for white folks," Elias said sardonically. "If you'd been black and a slave..."

"Even so, there was no reason for all this destruction," she said petulantly.

"I agree. But remember this, the Union army didn't do it. The people of Charleston did. The fires they set to destroy property they believed the Yankees might want got out of hand. And when it happened, no one attempted to fight the fires. They were too busy trying to get out of the city. There was confusion and panic, which happens whenever people act without thinking."

"I know, Elias. Don't rub it in."

"I'm not trying to. I hate this as much as you do. War does

nothing but destroy. And that's the trouble now. Men returning home don't know how to renew their lives. Only about one-quarter of the farm animals are alive. Any farm machinery was destroyed. The blacks haven't had their freedom long enough to want to go back to work. Nothing was gained by this war and now we have Bradley Culver on our minds. He's still fighting and he's not fussy whom he fights.''

"Do you really think he's as bad as his reputation?''

"Worse. I believe half his crimes aren't even known. His men live to kill and rape and destroy. After they loot. That comes first, for there must be a profit in what they do. Right now, I'm worried.''

"About Culver?'' she asked.

"About those two men who rowed away from the island before we did. Without doubt they're to carry word of Culver's presence with me. And he docked his boat at our landing. If Bowman gets moving before we can, there's going to be trouble.'' Under his breath, he added, "It's already here.''

Elias's carriage pulled up before army headquarters. Four men, wearing no uniforms, were waiting in front of the building. Elias pretended not to notice as he helped Virginia out of the carriage. He took her arm, but their path was blocked by two of the men.

Elias tried to brazen it out. "Will you please move? You're standing in our way.''

The spokesman for the quartet said, "You're Major Birch. Don't try to deny it. And this is your wife. I place both of you under arrest.''

"By whose authority?'' Elias asked bluntly.

"The Freedmen's Bureau, sir.''

"In other words, by the order of Ben Bowman.''

"He's in command, yes.''

"What's the charge?'' Virginia asked stiffly.

"Harboring a known murderer and fugitive, ma'am.''

"What do you think we're doing here? We were about to report this to the military. We do not harbor renegades, sir. We came to advise as to his presence in this area.''

"There will be a court hearing, ma'am.''

"May I make a formal report to the Union army?'' Elias asked.

"You may not, sir. You will come with us right now. The Freedmen's Bureau is close by."

Elias addressed Virginia. "I could break through them and reach the captain to whom we were to report, but I can't take the chance with you beside me, darling. The men we face are Bowman's toughs. They enjoy a fight and you'd be in the middle of it."

"But we must defend ourselves in some way, Elias," Virginia protested.

"We will. At a hearing, which I'll insist must be held immediately."

"I'm afraid," she admitted. "There's no telling what a court will believe."

"Virgie, for a Southern Rebel you are not well versed in the ways of the South. Anyway, it's better than fighting." He raised his voice, shouting to the pair of sentries on duty at the head-quarter's gate.

"Tell Captain Delaney that Major Birch is being held at the Freedmen's Bureau."

The spokesman for the four signaled and his men closed in on Elias. For a moment he bristled and set himself for a fight, but one of the sentries hurried off to notify the captain and the other moved to join Elias.

"Elias," Virginia said shakily, "we'd best do as they say."

He nodded, the soldier backed off uncertainly, and the strange procession made its way three blocks to the office of the Freedmen's Bureau. Elias marched in the center of the four men, who kept crowding him as if they courted resistance. Virginia trailed behind.

In the outer office of the bureau, several ex-slaves eyed the arrival with some astonishment at the sight of an obviously white matron being taken by the elbows and marched into the private office.

Bowman sat behind his littered oak desk with the attitude of an emperor casting judgment on some lowly evil-doer. There was a glint of satisfaction in his eyes.

"Well, now, what have we here?" he asked pompously. He consulted papers on his desk, then looked up at them. "Mr. and Mrs. Birch of Valcour, hobnobbing with a murderer and rebel outlaw."

"If we're to be tried, get it over with." Elias spoke with quiet firmness.

"Why should we be in such a hurry," Bowman asked innocently. "We've accommodations. They ain't the best, but they'll do for folks like you who entertain a murderer."

"By whose authority will you hold us?" Elias demanded.

"Mine, of course," Bowman replied blandly. "I'm in charge here."

Elias led Virginia to a chair and sat down beside her. "We'll wait," he said.

Bowman stood up, tired of the cat-and-mouse game he was playing. "You'll do like I say. I'm going to lock both of you up till we get a judge."

"If you lay a hand on my wife," Elias said, "I'll likely kill you. If you call for help, I'll beat your brains out before anyone can reach you. We're going to wait for Captain Delaney. He is the recognized authority here, not you."

Bowman sat down, saying nothing, but slyly trying to open a desk drawer. His hand closed around a pistol but hastily let go of it when two Union soldiers appeared in the room, followed by Captain Delaney.

"Elias, how are you?" he said. He bowed to Virginia, "You're looking very well, Mrs. Birch. I understand you were forcibly brought here. I want to know why. Bowman, I've warned you before not to exert authority you do not have."

"They took in Bradley Culver. Made no bones about it. Just had him on their island. Like he was regular folks and not the bloody-handed murderer he is."

Delaney said seriously, "If what you say is true, Bowman, I'm very surprised."

"We all know there's a price on the head of that outlaw," Bowman went on. "And anybody who aids or hides him is guilty of a serious crime."

"That's true," Delaney agreed. "What have you to say, Elias?"

"We came to the mainland as soon as Culver left, to report he had been in our home, but Bowman had men waiting outside army headquarters to arrest us."

"Arrest you?" Delaney turned to face Bowman. "By what right did you assume such authority?"

"I'm in charge of the Freedmen's Bureau. That gives me some right, don't it?"

"The Freedmen's Bureau was established to help the Negroes who were set free. That's all it's supposed to do. Now how do you connect Mr. and Mrs. Birch, Bradley Culver, or anyone else with helping the blacks?"

"I got authority," Bowman insisted.

"Show me the papers that grant you this authority."

"They don't give no papers . . ."

Captain Delaney said, "Elias, I'm taking formal notice of the fact that you and your wife have reported that an outlaw named Bradley Culver was in your home. Will you tell me for what purpose?"

Elias said, "He raided the island, as I reported to you some days ago. He came back to return the loot he'd stolen."

"They're in cahoots with Culver," Bowman said loudly. "What kind of crazy story is that?"

"They returned what they had stolen," Virginia said, "because they felt that anyone on Valcour looked to me and my family for protection. Mr. Culver stated that, under those circumstances, he could not keep what he had stolen."

"Why not?" Delaney asked.

"I am a Hammond, Captain. My family has lived on the island for many, many years. We are of the old South, something Mr. Bowman cannot understand. Mr. Culver claims he does not prey on Southerners, so he returned what he had taken, even though the booty came from the homes of the Northerners."

"I've been here long enough to know how you Southerners respect and honor one another," Delaney said. "In my opinion, it's a trait to be envied and might well be adopted by the Northerners who've come down here."

"Thank you, Captain," Virginia said graciously, warmed by the compliment.

Elias rose. "Captain, my wife and I would be delighted to offer you supper at the hotel."

"Accepted," Delaney said. "We'd best get over there if we want a good table."

Bowman came to his feet. "Now see here, you can't just walk out o' here like you ain't done nothin'."

"Well, what have they done?" Delaney asked. "They came to report Culver's visit, they have done so. Do you have any further accusations to make?"

Bowman sat down, red-faced with anger, knowing he'd been bested. Captain Delaney turned to Virginia. "Since Mr. Bowman has nothing more to say, we may as well leave."

Outside, Elias extended a hand. "Thanks, Doug."

Captain Delaney said, "Thanks for the supper invitation. I accepted it to give Bowman something to think about. Actually, I can't leave my office that long. Watch out for that man. He could be dangerous and he seems to have it in for you."

"We're aware of that." Virginia's smile was one of relief. "Thank you, Captain."

"We'll be careful," Elias said gratefully. "We know Bowman's out to get us. He tried to buy the Hammond plantation, but Virginia outbid him."

"So that's it."

Elias nodded. "We'll hold you to that supper invitation for another time. And in case Bowman should make any more charges against us, Virginia and I will stay over night at the hotel. You can reach us there. is that all right with you, Virgie?"

"Wonderful. I don't like being on the water after dark."

Their farewells completed, they headed for the hotel. There, they registered and were given a room that was clean and spacious. After freshening up, they went immediately to the dining room and had an early supper, surprisingly good, even to a bottle of wine.

"Where do you suppose they had this hoarded?" Elias held up his glass, regarding the amber liquid appreciatively.

Virginia laughed. "Who cares?" The lilt in her voice revealed she was already stimulated from the beverage.

Afterward, Virginia purchased a nightgown and a comb and by ten they were in bed. Elias had grown more and more somber as the evening progressed—sometimes to a point where his preoccupation was so intense he didn't even hear Virginia speak.

She lay on her back, completely relaxed. The bedside lamp was still burning. She turned on her side to face him.

"Elias, what's wrong?"

"Nothing's wrong."

"Something is. We enjoyed the first part of the evening. Now, all of a sudden, you've grown so quiet, so reserved. You didn't even hear me talking to you."

"Maybe I'm just plain tired."

"Are you homesick? For the North and your own people?"

"No. I can say that without reservation. My folks had their lives and I have mine. As for business, I didn't get far enough to make that count before the war broke out."

"There's something bothering you," she insisted.

"Do you really want to know?"

"Certainly," she replied. "We share our happiness and our worries."

"Very well. I want a family. Now."

She said, "Oh," in a small voice.

"You're putting Valcour ahead of a family. That's not right."

"I'd rather not talk about it."

"We must. Unless you're determined never to have children."

"You know better than that," she said somewhat sharply.

He turned on his side to face her and he drew her closer in a tender yet possessive embrace. "Darling, no man ever loved a woman more than I love you. I want living proof of that love we have for one another. I want a family and in the next few minutes we might even conceive one. There are things more important than getting the damn island away from the Yankees."

She pushed him away and sat up. "No, Elias. I told you before. No! And I told you why. I can't bring up a family and restore Valcour at the same time."

"Is there no way I can convince you?" His voice pleaded with her for understanding.

"There's no need to tell you how I feel about you. But we're still young. I'm in my twenties and you've just turned thirty. What's the hurry?''

"Because, my beautiful, ambitious wife, we will wait and we will wait. Until one day it will be too late because the restoration of Valcour is not going to be done in three or four years. Nor in ten or twenty years. It will take a lifetime and more. For years you'll not be satisfied with it and you'll look for more improvements. Valcour is an island, nothing more.''

"How wrong you are." She spoke without rancor. "Valcour is family and it's tradition. It's a way of life. The kind I grew up with and learned to love. It's happiness beyond description. It's the South as it once was and as it will be again. At least on Valcour. Can't you understand this?''

"No," he said flatly. "It's just a lot of dirt. What are you bringing it back for? What the hell good will it be after we die? You'll have preserved the island for nothing, as far as the Hammond family is concerned. Because there'll be no Hammond family.''

"I told you," her voice now held a hint of irritation, "I do want a family, but not now.''

"I'm half inclined to take you right now. And without any preliminary lovemaking.''

"I would hate you for the rest of my life if you did." She paused and when she spoke again, her tone had softened. "I know it's difficult for you to understand. You'd have had to grow up here, been a part of the life on Valcour as it was. Then, with the war, you'd have to find yourself suddenly poor, without hope, without even a home, while all around you the world you once knew and loved was falling into ruin. You'd have to be hungry and desperate, trying to figure out how to get food—and shelter. And all the time you went through that, in the back of your mind would be stored the memories of the life you once lived. They'd keep nagging at you until you would make a solemn oath that one day you'd bring it back. That's my dream and I'm determined to make it a reality.''

"It's a goddamn obsession.''

"Then it's my obsession," she said breathlessly.

He looked up at her face. Her eyes sparkled and her cheeks were flushed. It always happened when she spoke of her plans for

Valcour. He almost wished the army had set a torch to the damn island. Try as he might, he couldn't share her love for the place. It was his love for her that made him drive himself the way he did.

"I have a little news for you. It's almost too good to be true."

"What is it?"

"You recall that I once planned to buy the sutler's store on the island? When Washington gave us back our land, that became unnecessary. But today Mr. Tannet came and asked my opinion on his buying out the sutler."

"He mentioned that to me. Is he out of his mind?"

"Quite the contrary. He admitted he and the other Northerners were unable to grow cotton profitably, or handle the blacks well. So he got this idea of making a living by selling to the blacks."

"He'd have to. There's certainly not enough whites on the island to make a living."

"But he thinks there are enough blacks. He'll have to grant them credit, and you know as well as I that they'll never be able to pay up. Tannet will go broke. The only asset he'll have left is the house he bought for a pittance. He'll have to put it up for sale, or have it taken away by those he owes money to. So I'll buy it and we're rid of one Yankee family. We'll bring back one Valcour family. That's how it will work."

"That's just one house," Elias said, unimpressed.

"It'll be a start," she said, then sighed dismally. "If only we could sell the mainland plantation. Darling, will you find Marty tomorrow and light a fire under him?"

"My God, he just left the island today," Elias said impatiently.

"I know, but he has a prospect. It sounds good. He's supposed to have a lot of money."

"Then let Marty do business with him. Besides, there's no love lost between your brother and me."

"He has tremendous respect for you," Virginia said.

"He has one hell of a way of showing it," Elias said.

"Oh, darling, please try to find him. He felt very contrite when he left this morning, because of his behavior at the ball."

"I should think he would," Elias said.

"I really believe he's going to make an effort to contact this gentleman. Tell Marty how the Yankees came to Bowman and reported us. That'll make him angry. Tell him it's urgent he raise money for us by finding a buyer for the plantation.''

"I suppose I won't get any sleep unless I do," he said, turning on his side away from her.

"Aren't you going to kiss me good night?" she asked petulantly.

"No. You wouldn't even be aware of my lips against yours. You'd be planning how to get the damn Yankees off your precious Valcour."

Virginia laughed gaily. "Now you're beginning to understand."

"You're wrong. I'll never understand, but it doesn't seem to matter anymore, does it?" He pulled the blanket higher until only the top of his head was uncovered.

Her hand extended to touch him, but she drew it back. He was right. She was too excited about Valcour to think of making love. There'd be plenty of time for that. But they must work fast to fulfill her plans. She had so many they were crowding her mind.

She slept very little, but she didn't change her mind. Whatever the consequences, she was going to bring Valcour back. She told herself it would take but another two or three years and then she'd be ready to begin a family. She consoled herself with this thought, but she also realized it was an uncertain prediction. Still, it would have to do.

It was late morning when she awoke, for it had taken a long time to fall asleep. She discovered Elias already gone. He must have dressed quietly out of consideration for her, and she liked that. He was a dear man.

She felt actually lighthearted this morning with the sun streaming through the lace curtains. If only Elias understood, accepted her reasoning, so there'd be no more arguments on that score. She began making plans for her morning of shopping.

Elias didn't have to hunt for Marty. As he guessed, Marty could be found in any of two or three malodorous saloons where he usually drank himself into a state of what he termed forgetfulness. Evidently he had slept in this saloon, for he was unshaved, dirty and seated with his head resting on one arm on the table. There were others in the same sorry state. Drifters, with no home, who slept wherever they could find a place; and the saloons never closed, so most spent their sleeping time in one of them at a cost of a few drinks.

Marty blinked and shook his head vigorously as Elias shook him awake. He peered at Elias through bloodshot eyes, at first without any trace of recognition.

Then he grunted in annoyance. "Goddamn Yankee," he said.

"Wake up." Elias shook him again. "We've got to talk."

"What day is it? What time . . . ?"

"What difference does it make to you? Your sister's here. She asked me to find you."

"I need a drink. I'll even drink with a Yankee bastard like you. If you'll buy," he added slyly. "I suppose you mean Virginia."

Elias summoned the man behind the bar and paid for a bottle of whiskey, or what passed for it. Marty poured a stiff portion and drank it like a hungry man bolts his food. He settled back and felt better. Or so he claimed.

"What brought you to the mainland?" he asked.

"Bradley Culver."

"The outlaw?"

"He visited us on the island and some of the Northerners saw him. Virginia and I came to Charleston to report Culver's visit before they did, so we couldn't be accused of harboring him."

"What the devil would cause a man like Culver to come back to the island?" Marty asked.

"We can't figure it out, but that's beside the point, anyhow. We also came to find out what you've been doing about selling the big plantation."

"I could have guessed that," Marty said with more than a trace of sarcasm. "She thinks of nothing else but restoring that damn island. Well, I do have a man lined up. I'll either sell the place to him today—or never. I got to work on it yesterday when I returned."

"Then, for God's sake, get cleaned up and sober. In your present state, any decent buyer would shy away from being next to you."

"I was clean yesterday, so I won't even take offense," Marty grinned. "I've got a scheme cooked up. It'll take some doing and be a bit expensive."

"How much?"

"A hundred . . ." Marty studied Elias for a moment, " . . . and fifty."

"All right, but you'll get no more money if you miss this one."

"I'm going to hook him. Just as you would a fish. I'll have him in my pocket before sundown."

"Good. Once you've accomplished that, you're coming back to the island and lend us a hand. I've been working like hell and I'm damn tired. Just forget the damn war. It's over."

"I'm going to try. My word on it, Elias. I'm really going to try hard. If I make the deal, I'll come back at once. I'm beginning to know what I've turned into and why."

"Virginia will be delighted to hear that." Elias handed over a hundred and fifty dollars. "Good luck. I'll leave now so you can get yourself cleaned up and put this scheme of yours into operation."

On the way back to the hotel, Elias stopped by military headquarters to thank Captain Delaney again. He found the captain in a somewhat different mood.

"I'm glad you stopped by," he told Elias. "Are you sure, Major, that you or your wife do not have some sort of—well—collaboration or liaison with this man Culver?"

"What the devil do you mean by that? We've no reason to help or befriend that man. What's happened?"

"Bowman's house was burned down last night. He and his family barely escaped with their lives, and that fire was not an accident."

"Culver, eh? Damn that man!"

"Some of his men were seen around the neighborhood just before the fire. Seems to me Culver knew of your run-in with Bowman and that was his way of warning him not to repeat that arrogant business of yesterday. Now why would Culver do that if you've no connection with him?"

"I don't know the answer to that any more than I know why he returned the booty. I don't understand the man and I don't even want to try."

"All right, Elias. I'll accept your word on that, but there'll be talk. Culver never befriended anyone before."

"Next time he shows up, if he ever does, I'll do my best to turn him over to you, Doug. Should that day come, I hope you hang him from the nearest tree."

"That's how he's going to end up. Have you contacted your brother-in-law?"

"I just left him. Has he been in trouble again?"

"No, but courting trouble. I wish you could help him. Sooner or later, he'll get himself into a serious mess."

"I just had a talk with him. He's coming back to Valcour and once there we'll straighten him out. Anyway, we'll do our best. He may be too far gone, yet he rates a chance."

"Good. Keep your eyes peeled for Culver. I don't believe anyone would take offense if you killed him."

"I'd rather leave that to you. Thanks again, Captain."

Captain Delaney gave a wink and a nod of understanding. "We Yanks have to stick together. Especially in enemy country. Drop by anytime."

Virginia was excited and happy when they began the row back to Valcour. "One for me, Mama and Nan. Before the war I wouldn't have even looked at them, but right now they're beautiful. And so expensive," she added ruefully.

"Good. It's a sign things are going to change. I'm pleased to inform you that Marty swears he is too. He thinks he'll sell the property today, after which he's coming back to Valcour."

Virginia gave a whoop of joy. "That's the best news I've heard yet. I'd hug and kiss you right now, but I'm afraid I'll upset the boat."

"I'll remind you later. I've something else to tell you. It's rather mysterious. At least I thought so. Though maybe you can think of an answer."

Virginia sobered at his change of expression. "An answer to what?"

"Last night Bradley Culver burned down Ben Bowman's house. Bowman and his family had a narrow escape. Fortunately for them and for us."

Virginia didn't get the significance. "That's horrible, but what has that to do with us?"

"I don't know," Elias said flatly. "Delaney doesn't know either. I was wondering if you had any answers."

"Of course I don't," she exclaimed indignantly. "How could you even ask me such a question?"

"Only because I can't figure Culver out. His returning the stolen loot doesn't make sense. He never went in for gallantry before. He's no Robin Hood."

"He certainly is not," Virginia agreed. "I regard him as a dangerous man."

nine

Marty thought the location a suitable one for an auction. He stood atop a large concrete slab in the middle of what had once been a slave auction yard. On this platform slaves were exhibited and bid upon.

In those days the yard would be crowded. With a few serious buyers, but mainly with riffraff who came mainly to watch, as slaves, especially female ones, were stripped and fingered for examination.

The people here today were also riffraff, with but one or two present for the legitimate reason of bidding on the once prosperous and still very large plantation operated by the Hammond family.

One of the serious viewers was a tall, very thin, almost emaciated man. His long legs and slim torso gave him the appearance of a well-dressed scarecrow. For he was fashionably dressed in gray trousers, white shoes, an ice-cream-colored frock coat of fine material, excellently tailored. He wore a broad-brimmed straw hat and a white scarf around his neck. His pale eyes held a sad look and were sunk deep in a gaunt face. His hair was light brown and thin. Miles Rutledge looked like a very sick man, and he was.

"Six thousand." He lifted his cane to draw Marty's attention. As auctioneer, Marty kept up a chant, urging more and more bidding.

"Six five," someone in the crowd called out.

"Six seventy-five," another cried out.

"Seven," Miles Rutledge bid promptly.

It went on and on, the bidding topping thirty thousand before it weakened. One man bid thirty-two and Rutledge quickly made it thirty-three. Marty raised his arm high.

"Thirty-three thousand," he said loudly—and joyfully. "Once, twice . . . sold to the gentleman in the white coat."

The crowd began to disperse with surprising speed until only Rutledge and Marty were left. Marty, clean shaven, hair cut neatly, and dressed in a worn but serviceable and clean suit, held out his hand.

"You've made a wise purchase, my friend. I know, because my father once owned and ran this plantation. At times a thousand slaves were required, sir, to operate it at its peak and no finer cotton was ever grown anywhere. You've done well to make this buy, if I do say so."

"I rather believe I paid an excessive price for it, sir," Rutledge observed.

"My dear sir," Marty was at his best now, cold sober and eager to get this over with, the papers properly signed and registered and the payment made in full. Marty was getting thirsty.

"The plantation," he went on, "would have brought twice that sum before the war."

"I have no doubt of it, but this is after the war. Money is scarce and property is going cheaply."

"Well, sir, why, then, did you bid so high?"

"I don't know. I suppose I wanted it. I've always wanted a going plantation. I was brought up in New Orleans and I doubt I was ever on any kind of plantation until I was well along in years. I'm a city man, born and raised. Worse luck, for I believe I might have been in better health if I'd lived more in the open air."

"You do look a bit unwell," Marty observed. "I pray it is not serious. Of course it isn't," he added quickly. "You wouldn't have invested in the plantation if you did not think you were capable of running it. Now, shall we make our way to City Hall and complete these arrangements?"

"Of course. It surprised me the way the bidding went."

"This plantation is well known in these parts," Marty explained.

"Everyone is aware of its potential. You will not be disappointed, sir. I swear to that."

"Charleston must be in better circumstances than I anticipated, Mr. Hammond."

"Well . . . we did suffer great losses."

"What I meant is that there seemed to be more money about than I believed."

"Oh! Oh, yes, there are a number of folks who wisely invested their money before the war began. And over the course of the war, the money accumulated interest. It was in gold too—Yankee notes."

"I see. When we've completed the paperwork, I shall arrange that a draft be sent. Where should I send it and to what name, please?"

Marty hesitated. Thirty-three thousand coming into his hands would be a windfall that would never again be repeated. But if he laid claim to it, was able to use any part of it, he knew what might happen.

"I would suggest it be sent to my sister Mrs. Virginia Hammond Birch on Valcour Island."

Rutledge made a note of this in a small book he produced from his pocket. "I've heard of Valcour. The Yankees had possession of it during the war, didn't they?"

"Yes, they invaded us right after the war began and held it until the surrender. It was used as a sort of experimental place. They were trying to find out if the ex-slaves could become self-supporting."

"Ah, yes," Rutledge recalled. "It failed, didn't it?"

"Completely. A disaster. We only got it back a short time ago. That is, the part we owned. The other homes and plantations were bought up by greedy carpetbaggers for back taxes. The whole business was an abominable affair, sir."

They reached City Hall and the papers were promptly executed. Marty accompanied Rutledge to the telegraph station, where he sent a message to his New Orleans bank authorizing payment for the plantation. Outside, the two men shook hands and Marty promptly made his way back to his favorite saloon now crowded with his cronies, all lined up at the bar and already in various stages of intoxication. Marty's entrance was greeted with loud cheers and a great deal of laughter.

"We surely took the stranger this time," one man chortled.

"Drink up," Marty said. "And then line up. Five dollars for each of you."

"I was sweatin' some, Marty, when I bid it up to thirty thousand," another man said. "What if the sucker didn't bid it up some more?"

"That was a chance we had to take," Marty said. "We agreed if it got that high to make one more small raise and then stop. The sucker was bound to add a little more and he did. Yes, sir, he surely did."

"Maybe you oughta pay us twenty dollars 'stead o' five, Marty," a wizen-faced man named Curly said.

"Five. We agreed to five," Marty insisted.

"Yes, but twenty ain't too much. I say you pay us twenty."

"Go to hell," Marty said. "You keep talking that way, I'll wring your scrawny neck. Five was what I said and you all agreed that was fine. Now you got some of the others thinking maybe you can get a little more out of me. But you're wrong. Five it is and no more."

"Twenty," Curly insisted. "You don't give me twenty, you'll be damn sorry. I'm warnin' you. We made you rich and all we get is five dollars. Ain't right an' you know it, suh."

Marty bolted the drink before him, elbowed his way through the crowd at the bar and seized the smaller man by the throat. He shook him until Curly stopped trying to fight.

"For that," Marty said, "you get nothing. An agreement is an agreement and you violated it. So you get the hell out of here and if you open your mouth, I'll take you apart. Do you understand?"

He pushed the man away, sending him reeling backward. Curly opened his mouth to make a shrill, blasphemous protest. Marty raised his fist. Curly closed his mouth and slunk out of the saloon. Marty turned to the bar and began doling out five-dollar bills. Nobody else protested. In short order, Marty had almost exhausted his bankroll, provided by Elias, but Marty was also on the threshold of a good-size drunk. Before he succumbed to the cheap whiskey, he wrote a note on a bit of paper provided by the barkeep.

Virginia, I sold the place for thirty-three thousand cash on the line. Bank draft from Miles Rutledge ordered sent to you. I'm

going on one last spree and then I'll come back to Valcour and
help you restore it to its former grandeur.

He signed it with a flourish, looked about for a man he knew and
summoned him with a curt gesture.

"Claude," he said, "you get an extra five right now if you'll
deliver this note to Valcour. To my sister. You can swipe a boat or
pay somebody four bits for the use of one, but get this note to my
sister as quickly as you can."

"Sure, Marty, sure." Claude greedily extended his hand for the
note and the extra five dollars.

Marty had now completed the transaction entrusted to him. He felt
quite proud of himself and it was time now to get seriously busy on
that spree. He had almost forty dollars left. He called for a full
bottle.

But there was one thing Marty didn't know, or couldn't have acted
upon anyway, for he was already at a stage where he'd soon not even
know his own identity.

The man named Curly, still smarting over being roughed up by
Marty, had entered the best hotel in town and inquired at the desk for
Miles Rutledge. He was told to wait. Rutledge would be asked first
if he wished to see this unsavory character. Curly sat down in one of
the big lobby chairs and nervously tapped the arms with his fingertips. Ten minutes went by and Curly was on the verge of exiting in a
fast retreat when he saw Rutledge approaching him, a question in his
eyes.

Marty stopped drinking late in the afternoon. The success of his
mission had inspired him to reform. To sober up, return to Valcour
and stand beside his sisters and brother-in-law while they worked to
restore the island to its former glory.

He had imbibed enough to be sleepy, so he tumbled into bed still
dressed and lay on his back studying the water-spotted ceiling of the
cheap hotel room. Now his mind swirled with plans, hopes and an
ambition suddenly renewed. He'd wasted enough time feeling sorry
for himself. The war was over. His side had lost; so be it. One side
had to lose. Now the wounds must heal and the South get back on its
feet. Taking part in that endeavor was better than killing himself

with bad whiskey. He was, after all, a general in the Confederate army and he had served with distinction. It was time he lived up to the reputation he'd gained during the war.

What had carried him along for these terrible weeks since the surrender was the lavishness of the praise rendered to him. But on more sober contemplation of this praise he knew that it was false. The tributes came from men for whom he had bought drinks. Men who wanted to bask in the shadow of a general officer in the army. But Marty realized that there were no genuine plaudits for an officer on the losing side. Everything up to now had been a fraud, a game to bolster his badly shattered ego.

For the first time since the war ended, Marty had taken hold of himself and forced the truth to take the place of shallow praise and a faded gray uniform.

He began to doze after awhile, lulled by a fresh feeling of responsibility and the desire to get back to Valcour. And, as he slowly sobered, he felt no need for whiskey. Virginia and Nanine were going to be proud of him yet. There was so much to be done. Someone had to step into his father's place. Elias could do it, but that would not be the same. It was Marty's heritage and he must now preserve it.

He mused, in his half-wakeful, half-dreaming state, that he'd never even been really in love. He'd do something about that too. Then he fell into a deeper sleep.

Ordinarily, after a serious drinking bout, the insistent knocking on his door wouldn't have awakened him, but on the verge of sobriety, he came awake quickly and sat up, wondering if he'd dreamed all that racket. He already had a violent headache and his vision was still blurred as he got out of bed and unlocked and opened the door.

Three men stood before him in the hallway. The one who moved into the room without invitation was Miles Rutledge. His thin face was glowing with a pink blush of anger. When Marty remained fixed in position, Rutledge pushed him back until he fell onto the bed.

"What the hell do you think you're doing?" Marty suddenly came awake. He tensed to make a lunge at the man but hesitated. The two who accompanied Rutledge moved quickly to Rutledge's side. Marty was no match for the three of them and he knew it. He also knew, with a sinking sensation, the deal was about to blow up.

Rutledge said, "You're a drunken slob, which makes it all the worse as far as I'm concerned."

Marty had a horrible feeling that all his thoughts about reforming and becoming a useful member of the family were coming apart, but he had to brazen it out.

"Maybe," he said, "if you'd tell me what this is all about, it might make sense to me."

"Being bamboozled, tricked and cheated by a drunk makes me ten times as angry. And don't ask for an explanation. You know very well why I'm here."

Marty nodded. "Someone talked, I suppose."

"Yes, someone talked and I verified it. Getting the truth out of your unsavory associates is quite easy and costs only the price of a drink. That whole auction was set up to raise the price. I know now I could have bought your plantation for less than half the sum I paid."

Marty fought off the still-growing hollow feeling in his stomach. "I will turn your draft back to you, sir."

"That's not enough. I've sufficient money that it doesn't matter to me, but being cheated by scum like you hurts, and I intend to do something about it."

One of the men accompanying him took Rutledge by the elbow and dragged him back a step. "Miles, don't do it," he urged.

"Please," the second man implored. "This is no answer to what happened."

"Let go of me," Rutledge said angrily and pulled himself free. He took a step closer to Marty and suddenly slapped him across the face as hard as he could.

"That," Rutledge said coldly, "gives you the right to demand satisfaction. If you do not, then I shall demand it. You're not getting out of this one, sir. Not alive."

Marty looked his astonishment. "Are you challenging me to a duel?"

"How else do you repay a slap in the face? Unless you're a rank, miserable coward."

"I think you're crazy," Marty said.

"If you do not give me the satisfaction I wish, I shall brand you a complete coward, sir."

"Miles," the first man implored, "you can't do this."

"I'm doing it," Rutledge said. "What's your answer, General?" He spoke the appellation with open sarcasm.

"Miles," his companion pleaded, "you're a sick man."

"General Hammond is a trained soldier," the second man observed. "Quite likely, he's an expert with a pistol."

"What do you know about guns?" the first man asked.

"Enough. And as for being ill, I'll regain my strength when I see this scoundrel either go down with a bullet through his heart, or he shows me his heels. Mr. Hammond, I'm waiting for an answer."

Marty said, "You gentlemen with Mr. Rutledge, take heed of this. I do not wish to fight a duel with Mr. Rutledge. For two reasons: I intend to return his money and call the deal off."

"And the other reason?" Rutledge asked.

"I can put a bullet through your right eye at a hundred yards."

"Miles, I told you," one of the men said.

"Keep out of this. Mr. Hammond, give me an answer now."

"If you insist, there's nothing else I can do, but it will be on my terms. If you kill me, naturally there will be no deal and you have your money back. But if I kill you, the deal stands."

"Agreed," Rutledge said with astonishing promptness.

"Name the time and place," Marty said.

Rutledge drew out a gold watch and snapped open the case. "It's now one o'clock in the afternoon. Have you heard of a place called Miller's Field?"

Marty nodded. "It's a burned-out mill a mile beyond town. Is that the place you have in mind?"

"It is, sir. I shall be there at four. My friends will take up the matter of any other provisions. Good day, sir."

He turned, pushed his companions aside and stalked out. Marty sat down on the bed.

"I say he's crazy. Talk him out of this. I'm a crack shot. I was raised with guns and I don't think Rutledge even knows which end the bullet comes out of."

"General Hammond," the taller of the pair said, "my name is

James Warren. My friend is Anton Boyle. With Miles, we came here from New Orleans and that is a city favoring duels. A day doesn't go by but that there are two or three. And Miles is a proud man, from a family of proud men."

"Mr. Hammond, by deliberately cheating him as you did, you have violated his honor and he will have his satisfaction," Boyle said earnestly. "While we do not condone what you did, we do not wish our friend to be killed. Neither of us can give you as much money as Miles paid for the plantation, but I for one can provide a thousand dollars."

"I might be able to double that," Warren added.

"You're asking me to take money, and crawfish?" Marty demanded.

"That's about it. Mr. Rutledge is a very sick man."

"What difference does that make?" Marty asked. "I've some degree of pride too. If I don't fight him, he'll make it known all over town that I'm a coward. He said that. I don't mind being called a cheat, but I defy anyone to brand me a coward. If your friend persists in this, I'll honor him. I'll likely kill him too."

Warren said, "Then there's nothing further to say. We shall expect you at the old mill at four. We shall find pistols somewhere. Come with your seconds and we'll get this miserable business over with."

"I'll be there," Marty said. "Without seconds. I don't need them."

"Thank you, sir," Warren told him. They bowed slightly and went out. Marty kicked the door shut and sat down on the bed again. For a moment he buried his face in both his hands and then shook his head violently. For the first time, he began to develop doubts. He was an expert gun shot, but his head ached worse than ever. When he held out his arm full length, the hand trembled badly. He'd let himself into something serious this time. He could only console himself with the fact that Rutledge was a sick man and perhaps barely able to aim a heavy pistol.

"Got to get more sober," Marty said aloud. "Got to get hold of myself."

He stepped over to the sink attached to the bedroom wall. There he poured water from the large pitcher into a bowl and doused his face with it until his wits cleared somewhat. He dried his face and then made his way to the hotel lobby, where he asked the desk clerk for paper and an envelope. He carried these over to a writing table, sat down and composed a quick letter to Virginia.

Dear Virgie,

Something has come up. By now you know I sold the plantation to a man named Miles Rutledge. His draft is on the way. However, I resorted to a few small tricks to raise the selling price to three times more than I expected to get. Rutledge got wind of it and just now left me with no option but to fight a duel he insists upon to soothe his pride. The man is so ill he can barely stand up, but he is insistent and I could do nothing but agree to his terms. I am to meet him on this so-called field of honor today at four. At a place called Miller's Field. I'm not afraid of him. I don't believe he could hit the walls of a room he was enclosed in. But I can't let him kill me, so I will fight him and I pray I will only wound the man. Yet, if he is wounded, he will probably die. That's how ill he is. So the man is actually committing suicide and I only regret that I am the instrument he has chosen.

Yet, there is always a chance he might, by sheer luck, put a bullet where it won't do me any good, so I have made an agreement with him which I'm sure he will carry out. If he gets killed, the deal for the sale of the plantation remains as agreed upon and the draft from his bank will be honored. If I lose, the deal is off.

It's a crazy business, but I can't say I'm afraid because Miles Rutledge couldn't inspire fear in a mouse. As soon as the damn thing is over, I'll come back to stay. I realize now what an idiot I have been. Don't worry about me. I can handle a pistol better than I can handle myself.

Marty

He wrote Virginia's name on the envelope, sealed the letter and carried it out on to the street. There he looked about for someone he knew, one of his old companions. Finding no one, he made his way to one of the saloons he frequented and there he discovered Claude, the man whom he had paid to deliver his first note to the island.

"Claude," Marty greeted him. "I'm glad to see you. Did you deliver my note as I paid you to do?"

"Sure did, Marty. Handed it to your sister, I did. Right in her hand."

"Good. I want you to deliver another one. It's worth ten dollars."

"You goin' to give me ten more? Say, that's mighty nice o' you, Gen'ral. Mighty nice. I lost the money you gave me before. Made a crazy bet and lost. Drive a man to drink only I didn't have any money to get drunk on."

"Well, you have now," Marty gave him a ten-dollar bill. "But don't get drunk until after you deliver this letter. It's very important."

"Sure, Marty. I'll do like you say." He tucked the note into the breast pocket of a soiled shirt, slipped the bill into his trouser pocket.

"Get on it right away," Marty said. "The letter must be delivered within an hour."

"I'll row as fast as I can, Marty. Yes, sir . . . fast as I can."

He left the saloon at a slightly weaving trot. He'd been drinking despite what he had said, but Marty trusted him because he had delivered the first note and there was no reason why he wouldn't deliver this one right away. Maybe, Marty thought as he headed for the bar, Virginia might come to the mainland in time to do something about this sorry and impossible situation.

He poured a drink, raised the glass to his lips and then firmly set it down. He slid the glass along the bar to the nearest patron, who promptly disposed of it without asking a question. Marty left the saloon and returned to his hotel room. There he opened the ancient carpetbag he'd been using as a wardrobe, removed most of the clothing until he came upon the big service pistol he'd kept. There were bullets too and he dumped a handful into his pocket. He stuck the gun under his belt, buttoned his coat over it and went out to the street. There he hailed a carriage.

"Know where Miller's Field is?" he asked.

"Cost you a dollah an' a half, suh," the driver said.

"Take me there," Marty ordered. He climbed into the carriage and it moved off along the fairly busy street. After several blocks Marty called to the driver to pull up in front of a saloon he knew.

"You pay me now," the driver said, "if you want me to wait."

Marty gave him a dollar. "The rest when you get me there. I won't be but a few minutes."

He hurried into the saloon and was greeted by a dozen men he knew and had drunk with, but this time he had no wish to either buy or be treated to whiskey. He stepped up to the bar, and placed a dollar bill on it.

"Yes, sir," the bartender said. "What'll it be, General?"

"I want a dozen bottles. Empty ones."

"Empty bottles? General, you don't look that drunk to me."

"I'm cold sober. I want a dozen empty whiskey bottles, or as many as you have. In a sack."

The mystified barkeep had nine bottles and placed them in a sack that he handed to Marty and then swept the dollar bill off the bar. Marty returned to the carriage, got in and ordered the driver to go directly to Miller's Field.

There he dismissed the carriage and, holding the sack of empty bottles in one hand, he surveyed the cleared area. He recalled now that just prior to the beginning of the war, the city fathers of Charleston had planned to turn this area into a public park. The land had been cleared, leaving a stand of magnolias to ring most of the field. It was grown over but not badly.

Marty walked about until he found an old log. On this he placed the empty bottles, lining them up. Then he withdrew to a respectable distance, drew the pistol from under his coat, cocked it and aimed. He missed the first bottle, then the second. The third one was shattered, but the fourth and fifth came through.

Marty sat down on the grass and worried some. Then he reloaded the pistol and tried again. This time he was more successful, but he knew, despite that, his hand was not steady. When he aimed the gun with his arm at full length, it trembled like a man with malaria. He began to hope that Virginia would get there in time to stop this nonsense. Rutledge wouldn't listen to him, but he might reason with Virginia, for she possessed a powerful degree of persuasion.

Marty reloaded, set about more target practice and made up his mind not to worry. He might have, however, if he had been able to follow the man he'd entrusted with the note to Virginia.

Claude had started for the harbor promptly, but halfway there he recalled rowing all that distance was tiring and he needed a drink before he tackled a task as hard as that. He entered a saloon with the ten dollars clutched in a sweaty hand.

In ten minutes he was gloriously drunk and half asleep at one of the tables.

ten

In the study at the mansion on Valcour, Virginia read Marty's letter aloud for the third time.

Nanine, seated facing the desk, leaned forward. "I find it so hard to believe. He actually sold the plantation and for an incredible sum. How in the world did he manage that?"

"I don't know. He told me that he had a buyer. He also said he'd stay sober. He had to be when he handled this deal. Perhaps now he'll give up that wasteful life and come home. He told Elias he would. I'm hoping he finally came to his senses."

"I'll pray he has," Nanine said wistfully.

Virginia placed the letter on the desk and smoothened it out carefully. "You know what this means, Nan. We've sufficient money to buy out everybody on Valcour—when they grow desperate enough to sell—and we'll see to that in good time. But the fact remains, we can do it. And have enough money left to rebuild the island. To buy machinery, horses and mules. To bring more blacks in from the mainland if we need them. *Everything is absolutely perfect.*" She slowly emphasized every syllable of the last sentence.

"What does Elias think of it?"

Virginia laughed happily. "He's as proud of Marty as we. Elias says it justifies his faith in our brother. He always said Marty would come to his senses one of these days."

"Now if only he comes back. The four of us can work on the project. Though I can't help but feel sympathy for the Yankees."

"Not too much, please," Virginia said sternly. "They're nothing but carpetbaggers who came down to make a profit on the misery of others."

"They won't," Nanine said soberly.

"You're right. Their crop is doing poorly. It will sell, but they'll not make any money on it. They're fully aware now that they don't know how to raise cotton. They won't stay long."

"They can't handle the blacks, either," Nanine said. "I saw one of them slap a Negro boy when he slothed some in carrying out an errand. That Yankee is going to find himself in a lot of trouble if he persists in physical abuse."

"He may even find his throat cut," Virginia said. "Now, let's begin with this list of Yankee invaders. Let's see if we can determine which are the weakest and the most likely to fail soon."

"I'd say the Hagers are weakening. They had the old Murtha place and it was run-down to begin with. They've not improved it and they have seven children to feed. I don't see how they can hold out much longer."

"Then we'll bide our time and keep watching for signs. They'll try to borrow money and you know how impossible that is. When they do that, they'll be ripe for an offer. My records show they paid seven hundred dollars for that plantation. Seven hundred! It's worth fifty times that much. Honestly, Nan, I don't feel one whit sorry for those folks. They took advantage of the invasion and our defeat. They came down here to make easy money at our expense. They've no business here. Valcour is no ordinary island. It's too good for the likes of them."

"Well," Nanine said thoughtfully, "I'm not as vindictive as you, Virgie, but I feel it would be best for the Yankees if they went back home. They might make a go of it there, but certainly they won't on Valcour."

"Know what I think?" Virginia asked dreamily. "I think by next summer we'll be rid of these people. Our old neighbors and friends will be back and then we can restore the island. If it takes every goldback we have to accomplish this, it'll be a bargain."

"Talk it over with Elias," Nanine suggested. "He's a man of sound judgment. We must spend our money judiciously."

"I'll talk to him," Virginia promised. "Right now, get yourself to the kitchen and tell Belle to prepare something special. The occasion calls for it."

Nanine nodded as she rose. "I certainly agree with that."

Virginia read Marty's letter again and smiled as she tucked it into the desk drawer. She meant to keep it, for it represented the turning point in her determination to bring Valcour back. She believed it would benefit Marty too. It was just as well he had come to the ball and made a fool of himself. It had brought him to his senses.

She was impatient to sit down with Elias and Nanine after supper and begin putting their plans into motion. Her mind was swimming with ideas. It had been a long and awful ordeal, those war years. She'd lost her faith many times, but it had always come back when she thought about Valcour and how it once had been. The dreams of the island had actually carried her through many a lonely and woebegone day. When there'd been no hope whatsoever, or so it seemed, she'd braced herself with the determination that there had to be some way to make her dreams come true.

Now she was on the threshold of success. Before, the lack of money was their greatest drawback, but thanks to Marty that was no longer a problem. Sounds drifting in from the dining room indicated the serving girls were setting the table. Virginia had told Belle to get two girls and supervise them in their household chores. The girls were pleased to escape the hot fields, and became diligent workers.

She'd even given orders that flowers were to grace the table each evening. Lenore missed her sterling silver footed dish to display them in, but fortunately she was more interested in what was on her plate. She was eating ravenously and gaining weight because she was so sedentary.

When Virginia had relayed the news of the sale of the plantation to her mother, she'd burst into tears and gone to her room. Her reaction came as a shock to Virginia at first, then she realized she'd probably have done the same thing. The loss of the plantation was a blow. Virginia knew her parents had developed it and done a remarkably good job. They'd also been leaders in Charleston's social and civic affairs. To Lenore, the loss of the plantation was another symbol of what the war had cost them.

Virginia made a mental note as she left the study to freshen up for dinner that she must devote more attention to Elias. She wasn't entirely at fault, for he was bone-weary when he came in at night. His fair skin was burned from the sun and his hair had been bleached almost white by it.

In the hall, her attention was attracted to a black boy who was standing before the open front door, shading his eyes as he looked seaward. She stepped on the veranda and shaded hers, trying to see what had caught his attention, but the sun was such a glare on the water, she couldn't.

"What is it?" she asked the boy.

"Don' knows fo' sho', Missy, but thinks they's a man comin' an' he rowin' like he crazy."

Now Virginia could see the rowboat. It was heading for the island, was actually just off it, but the craft seemed to waver and change course every few feet. She thought at once of Marty. Fear coursed through her. She wondered if he might be hurt, or ill, or . . . drunk again. God forbid. Whoever it was she had to know. She ran down to the dock, heedless of the heat.

As the boat neared shore, she realized that it was not Marty, but the man did seem familiar and she realized then that it was the same man who had delivered Marty's letter. Now Virginia waited impatiently, for the man must be arriving with more news and she prayed that it did not concern a cancellation of the sale.

The man threw her a rope and she pulled the boat close to the dock. He stood up, swaying as the boat rocked. He took an envelope from his shirt pocket and handed it to Virginia. Then, without a word he sat down, pushed an oar against the dock and began to row back to the mainland. Virginia had seen that he was more than a little drunk.

She opened the envelope and tilted the paper to read better in the bright sunlight. Then she gasped in horror and began running back to the house, screaming at the top of her lungs for Nanine and Elias. She waved the letter aloft as if it could be read that way. Her mind was in a turmoil of terror and dismay. Nanine hurried out to the porch as Virginia neared it.

"Marty!" Virginia cried out. "Nanine, he's going to fight a duel."

Nanine paled. "'Duel'! Oh, no!"

"It's in his letter. He must have cheated the man who bought the plantation and that man found out and challenged Marty to a duel."

"When? Where?" Nanine was trembling and trying not to lose control.

Virginia scanned the letter again. Its contents sent fresh terror through her. "This afternoon. In an hour. At a place called Miller's Field. . . . Oh, God! What'll we do, Nan? What can we do? There's no time."

"Send for Elias," Nanine said in her practical way. "Maybe we can get there in time to put a stop to this. A duel! What madness."

Elias, on his way back to the mansion, had heard Virginia's hysterical voice calling his name. He was already running toward them. Virginia handed him the letter with no explanation.

"We must leave at once," she said fearfully. "We can't waste time. Try to think of something we can do."

Elias scanned the letter and with a loud, vehement curse, he ran down to the dock to get the boat ready. Nanine and Virginia followed. He was at the oars when they boarded. Nanine was trembling visibly from the shock of what was about to take place. Virginia's hands were tightly clasped in her lap, and her face showed strain.

Elias kept his face impassive as he began rowing, but he was as fearful as he knew both girls were. He was muscular, he rowed well and they were making good time, but it would take them an hour to reach the scene. They could well be too late.

"I know where that field is," Elias said between deep breaths of air. "Not too far if we can find a carriage quickly. What the devil got into Marty to create such a mess?".

Virginia gave a despairing shake of her head. "Possibly overeagerness to sell the plantation."

"He may be killed," Nanine said.

"And the sale of the plantation may be canceled," Virginia added.

"To hell with the plantation," Elias said. "We've got to stop this crazy business. If only we're in time . . ."

"How can we hope to stop it even if we are in time?" Nanine asked apprehensively.

"Pray, Nanine," Elias said kindly.

"Perhaps I pushed Marty too hard," Virginia reasoned.

"Shut up!" Elias said harshly. "Let me save my breath for rowing."

He made the trip in record time, helped both women ashore, then ran ahead of them to find a carriage. He spent a few precious minutes trying to attract the attention of a driver who seemed to be asleep in his carriage. Elias ran to it, reached in and shook the man awake as he jumped into the carriage.

"See those two women?" he pointed to where Virginia and Nanine stood. "Stop to pick them up, then head for Miller's Field as fast as you can whip these horses. And whip them. A man's life hangs in the balance."

"Yes, suh," the driver declared sleepily, as if saving a man's life were an hourly occurrence.

Virginia and Nanine got aboard. The driver did use his whip, but it seemed to his three passengers that the horse was either lazy or ancient, even though the animal set up a good pace.

"We're too late," Virginia wept. "I know we're too late."

"Then we do whatever we can," Nanine said, now in command of her emotions. "Just now your prayers might also help."

When the carriage pulled up, they saw two figures on the ground and two men bending over one of them. Virginia screamed and leaped out of the carriage to run toward the scene. Nanine followed. Elias was moving away from the carriage. He looked back. "Wait!" he yelled at the driver.

"Not me," the driver said. "It's against Yankee laws for duelin'. The Yankees say so an' Ah ain't gettin' mixed up . . ."

Elias turned and ran back to the carriage. He reached up, grasped the driver and pulled him off the seat.

"You wait here and be ready to move fast or I'll break your goddamn neck. Do you understand?"

The man couldn't reply because of the choking grip around his throat, but he nodded assent. Elias released him and ran as fast as he could toward the spot where Virginia and Nanine knelt on each side of one of the prone figures. It was Marty. Nanine's hand rested lightly on his brow. Virginia held one of his hands between both of hers.

She looked up at Elias. "Marty's been shot."

"What do you know about this?" Elias demanded of the two men who stood over the other prone figure.

"My name's James Warren," the first replied. "My friend Anton Boyle and I were seconds for this gentleman on the ground."

"I assume he's Miles Rutledge," Elias said, eyeing the gaunt figure.

"Yes," Anton Boyle replied. He was holding both pistols.

"Now that you've introduced yourself," Elias said curtly, "suppose you tell me about this."

"Our friend Mr. Rutledge challenged Mr. Hammond to a duel. Mr. Hammond had no choice other than to comply," Boyle said.

"Is Mr. Rutledge dead?" Elias asked.

"No. He fainted."

Elias couldn't believe his ears. " 'Fainted'? What the hell's going on here? Your friend Mr. Rutledge must be arrested. If my brother-in-law dies, Rutledge will hang."

"I can understand your anger," Warren said, taking a step toward Elias. "I suggest you get Mr. Hammond to a hospital before wasting more time on explanations. The ball hit him in the chest and he's bleeding."

Elias nodded agreement, identified himself and shouted to the driver to bring up the carriage. The driver obeyed and Elias ordered Nanine and Virginia to get to their feet and step aside. He bent to lift Marty, who was now conscious and had complete awareness.

"I ducked in the wrong direction," he managed to say. His voice was weak, and as he spoke, blood seeped out of the corner of his mouth.

"We're taking you to a hospital," Elias said, then looked up at the driver. "Do you know where the military hospital is?"

"Yassuh," the driver replied. He was still too frightened to protest.

"The Yankee hospital?" Marty tried to sit up. "I won't go. I'm

183

"The Yankee hospital?" Marty tried to sit up. "I won't go. I'm not submitting myself to the mercies of some Northern doctor . . ." His voice trailed off. His breathing became labored.

"He means it," Virginia said. "There are doctors . . . the Charleston hospital was burned to the ground. Please get him to a doctor quickly. Please, Elias."

Warren said, "Let me help you. I'll go along too. The authorities have to be told. Anton, stay here and do what you can for Miles. Ladies, don't be too harsh on him. There are facts you don't know."

Elias addressed Virginia and Nanine. "I'll be back as soon as possible. The lady by my side is Mrs. Birch. The other lady is Miss Hammond."

"I'll look after them, Mr. Birch," Anton Boyle said.

"A good idea," Warren said. "Keep an eye on Miles also."

No one spoke as Elias and James Warren lifted Marty slowly and carefully placed him in the carriage. The three standing nearby watched the carriage move away. Marty leaned against Elias in back, making no further protest. Warren sat in front. Virginia bit her lip and turned to regard the figure on the ground with distaste.

Anton noticed and said, "Please don't prejudge my friend, Mrs. Birch. I'm sure you won't when you learn the facts."

"The only fact that concerns me, sir, is that Mr. Rutledge murdered my brother."

"The duel was conducted according to the rules," Boyle said. "Your brother disdained seconds."

"Your friend didn't," Virginia said scornfully.

Nanine, who had been quiet up until now, said, "Mr. Rutledge looks very ill."

"He is," Boyle said quietly. "That's part of it."

Nanine seemed not to have heard. She moved slowly toward Rutledge, still lying motionless on the ground.

"Come back, Nan!" Virginia ordered sternly. "Don't you dare go near that man."

Nanine seemed not to have heard. Or if she did, she chose to ignore her sister, for she continued to walk slowly toward Rutledge. It was as if something drew her to him.

"Ma'am, will you please let me explain?" Anton Boyle took a step toward Virginia.

"How do you explain the bullet in my brother?"

"It's difficult, I know," he replied.

"Do you know how serious his wound is?" she asked, with less rancor in her tone.

"Very, I'm afraid. There's a lot of damage done inside the man. He's bleeding."

She shifted her gaze to Rutledge and was astonished to see Nanine kneeling beside him.

Boyle said, "If you would just let me tell you about this tragic incident. First of all, your brother began it. He cheated Miles, got him to pay much more than the plantation was worth. One of your brother's drinking companions got angry with him and came to Miles. Informed him of the trick your brother had staged to get Miles to bid higher for the property."

Virginia, despite her anger, knew Marty wouldn't be above such chicanery. She knew also she'd nagged him to get a buyer. He did it in the only way he knew. Was she as guilty of her brother's death as the man lying on the ground? Or was she more so? She thrust the ugly thought from her mind. Even so, she couldn't find an excuse for herself.

"Who is this Miles Rutledge?" she asked.

"He comes of a fine New Orleans family."

"One that specializes in duels, I suppose," Virginia said sarcastically.

"No, miss. He happens to be a man who hates violence."

"You could never convince me of that."

"Perhaps if I told you I believe he's dying, I could."

"You don't make sense."

"He has some kind of blood disease. He's wasting away."

Virginia's eyes scanned the form lying on the ground. He was so thin he resembled a scarecrow and his face was a pasty white. Her resentment toward this man outweighed any sympathy.

"I hope his illness does not take him too quickly," Virginia said vehemently.

"Lady, you're not in any mood to listen to reason."

"I can listen, if you have anything worthwhile to say, which I doubt."

"Well, I'll say it. We found your brother here when we arrived. We had dueling pistols and we gave one to each man. They walked apart to a designated distance and turned to fire. Your brother fired first—and missed."

"Then what's he doing lying on the ground?" She pointed toward the prone man..

"I told you, he's a very sick man. After he fired and saw your brother go down, he fainted."

Virginia looked her disgust. "I can't believe it."

"It's the truth. He didn't kill your brother, ma'am, and I say that even in the full knowledge that you'll never believe me. Maybe nobody other than James Warren will, but it's the truth."

"You said 'killed.' Do you believe my brother is that seriously wounded? Tell me the truth."

"Ma'am, only God can tell you if he'll live or die. I said 'killed,' but it's not the proper word. He may live. But, as I said, Miles didn't deliberately shoot him."

"How can you say such a stupid thing?" She pointed a finger at Miles. "That man is lying there, unhurt—you said that—and my brother is on his way to a hospital, seriously wounded. You don't make sense."

"That's because you're not listening."

"Listen to drivel such as that?"

"It was an accident," Boyle said earnestly. "Your brother being shot."

"You're mad, sir. There are no accidents in duels."

"Granted, in an ordinary duel."

"What are you saying?"

"Miles had the second shot. He aimed his pistol away from your brother. Your brother moved, trying to avoid being shot—and stepped right into the line of fire. Miles was deliberately trying to miss."

"If you expect me to believe that—" Virginia began hotly.

He interrupted her impatiently. "Not only that. Miles sought this duel because he wanted to die. He wanted your brother to kill him."

Virginia regarded him as if he were a madman, then she turned abruptly away from him and walked toward the spot where Nanine was now helping Miles sit up.

"Get away from him, Nan," Virginia's voice revealed her disgust. "Get away from that murderer."

"Please, Virgie," Nanine implored with her voice and her eyes as she looked up at her sister.

"I said let him lie there. Marty may die. How can you comfort this murderer?"

"Mr. Rutledge is a very sick man."

"So is our brother." Virginia spoke with rising anger. "Get away from him."

"No, Virgie."

"Are you mad?"

Nanine was as calm as Virginia was emotional. "This man is ill and needs help."

"So does your brother and this man is responsible. He's not hurt. He's shamming. He's frightened at what he's done. He's afraid to get up. He's a coward."

"Please go away and calm down," Nanine said quietly. "I know what I'm doing."

"You don't. You're treating this man the way you always treat a stray dog or cat. Your sympathy has overcome your common sense. That man is a murderer. You shouldn't soil yourself by touching him."

Nanine stood up, facing her sister. In a hushed voice, she spoke with a firmness unusual for Nanine.

"This was a duel and duels do not result in murder. If Marty is killed, then he knew that might happen beforehand. Until I know the circumstances that preceded this, I am concerned only that this man at my feet is in need of help. He is very ill and I know what that is. Please don't annoy me or upset this man."

"Oh, you stupid woman," Virginia cried out in frustration.

She strode away, but there was nowhere to go. Not back to Boyle, who hadn't moved, but who was regarding her thoughtfully. She knew her terror at what had happened was partly responsible for her rage. She also knew there'd been no need to ask Anton Boyle if her brother's wound was serious. She was well aware of what that wound was like and what it portended. She'd spent time in military hospitals during the war and she was no stranger to wounds.

She sat down on the grass and began to weep. Boyle began walking toward her, but changed his mind. He'd had enough of her tongue-lashing, yet he felt sympathy for her too. Nanine, seated beside Miles, was fanning his sweat-streaked face with her hand.

"Don't try to do any explaining now," she said gently. "Let it wait until you feel a little stronger."

"I . . . killed him, didn't I?"

"I don't know. You may have."

"I aimed to miss him. Honestly, I did. I had the second shot, but I didn't mean to hurt him. I fired to the side of him just as he moved to that same side Oh, why couldn't he have put a bullet through my carcass the first time?"

"Be quiet," Nanine urged. "There's help coming soon. We'll get you back. Where do you belong?"

"I'm at the hotel . . . the biggest one. I can't even think of the name."

"Don't you worry. We'll get you there. Are you certain you're not injured?"

"I wish I were. I wish I were dead."

"Don't say that. You've no right to say that, especially if what you just told me is true."

"It's true. Won't make any difference. I'm finished anyway. I've been told I haven't much longer to live, but I didn't have the courage to take my own life."

"Is that why you wanted this duel?"

"I insisted on it. Your brother wanted no part of it. I wanted him to kill me, to put an end to me, but without branding me a cowardly suicide. What I could not do myself, I wanted him to do for me."

"That's enough. Be quiet now. Just rest. We'll go into this whole situation when you feel better and when I know how my brother is."

"I'm sorry I'm such a coward."

"You're not. You're ill and discouraged. Now, please don't talk. Just rest. Soon now we'll be able to really help you."

"There's no help for me," he said morosely.

"I used to believe that about myself, but a Yankee doctor proved me wrong."

"One thing more I must say. Your brother negotiated a business deal and I will adhere to the terms of it. I shall not stop payment of the draft."

"That's of no consequence now," Nanine told him, though she was pleased to hear it because she now had a way of making Virginia listen to reason. If what Nanine intended really was reason. She wasn't sure of that, but she did know she was attracted to this strange man.

"I'll be quiet," he said.

"Good. I'll do the talking. My name is Nanine Hammond. My sister over there is Virginia Birch. Our family has lived on Valcour Island for generations. That's what made it so important to Marty to sell the mainland plantation. We needed the money from the sale of the mainland plantation to buy back the island. It's not easy to explain in a few words, but Marty was, very likely, desperate. I don't fully know the circumstances but I cannot, in my heart, blame Marty. Even though he may have resorted to trickery."

Rutledge was about to make some response to that, but the arrival of two carriages, with Elias and James Warren passengers in one of them, prevented it. Elias made his way slowly to where Virginia sat with her head bowed. She was still weeping. James Warren joined Anton Boyle and they talked softly to each other.

Elias said, "I'm sorry, darling. Marty died before we reached the city. The military hospital doctors did their best."

Virginia looked up, her eyes filled with misery. New tears were making their slow progress down her cheeks. Elias handed her his handkerchief, which she took gratefully.

She wiped her eyes, blew her nose, then looked up at him. "Mr. Boyle told me an unbelievable story about the duel. I'd have to be mad to accept it. And look at Nan. Her arm around that horrible Rutledge. Letting him rest his head on her shoulder. Marty's dead and she's comforting his murderer. It doesn't make sense."

Elias drew her closer and kept his arm around her. "This was not murder. It was a duel Marty agreed to and fully expected to survive."

"But he didn't survive," Virginia protested. "He was killed."

"The way I understand it, Rutledge used a flimsy excuse for the duel, going against the advice of his friends. But it wasn't a duel he wanted. His motive was to have Marty kill him. He was actually commiting suicide. Dying in an honorable way, as they say."

"That's idiotic," she said angrily, forgetting her sorrow for the moment. "And it's the identical, unbelievable story Mr. Boyle told me."

"It's the truth, Virgie. There were two witnesses to this, remember."

"Oh, yes. Witnesses who are friends of the murderer. Who can believe their stories?"

"I can, and you will too, given time to think about it. Marty had been on an extended drunk, as you likely know. Last night he hung one on. When the duel took place, Marty was suffering from a long hangover. It's evident that he came here before the time of the duel and practiced target shooting and was not doing a very good job of it."

"Marty knew how to use a gun. Don't try to convince me otherwise."

"I'll grant you that, but he wasn't in the best condition so far as his reflexes were concerned. Marty fired first. Rutledge deliberately wanted it that way. But Marty missed."

"Then Rutledge killed him," Virginia said adamantly.

"Rutledge deflected his aim so his bullet would miss, but again, Marty, not in full possession of his nerves, did the wrong thing. He tried to avoid being hit by moving aside as Rutledge fired. But Marty moved directly into the path of the bullet."

"If you believe that, Elias, you're a fool."

"I learned the circumstances from the best possible source, Virgie."

"Two witnesses who are certainly biased . . . ?" Her eyes mocked him.

"No, Virgie. I learned it from Marty. He was able to tell the circumstances and his story backs up what Warren has told me and Boyle told you. Marty's death was actually accidental. Rutledge did his best to miss."

"I will never believe that," she said sternly. "Never! And if you do, you're a stupid man. Rutledge insisted on the duel. He thought the whole thing up and carried it through. Marty didn't believe in dueling. Some of his friends did and he used to call them fools. Marty was tricked into this awful business.''

"All right, Virgie," Elias said. "If that's what you want to believe, I won't argue the point. One day you'll know the truth. Is Rutledge hurt in any way?"

"I don't know. I hope he's dying. Look at my sister! She's holding him close to her. She acts as if Rutledge was Marty, not Marty's murderer.''

Elias said, "I'll go over and find out what Rutledge wants to do.''

"I don't give a damn what he wants. We have to consider Marty. What of him?''

"I arranged to have his body returned to Valcour. I'm sure you want him buried there.''

"Of course I do. Go see Rutledge if you must.''

"Thank you. I feel I must.''

"And try to find out if he's going to welsh on the arrangements he made with Marty.''

"My wife, the practical woman," Elias said with a touch of sarcasm that was lost on Virginia. Elias walked over to kneel beside Rutledge and Nanine.

"Mr. Rutledge, I'm Elias Birch. Were you injured in any way?''
"No, Mr. Birch," Rutledge said.

"He's a very sick man," Nanine explained. "But he isn't hurt. I want to get him to his hotel. He is in need of constant attention.''

Elias couldn't help but smile at Nanine's concern. "Are you going to give him that attention, Nan?''

"Who else is there? He needs a woman's touch and sympathy. Elias, Mr. Rutledge is not a murderer even if Virgie insists he is. I know the story.''

Elias nodded. "I believe it. It's Virgie we must convince. She doesn't like the attention you're giving Mr. Rutledge.''

"I don't care what she likes. I'm an adult woman and I can do as I wish. When someone needs help, I want to give it. Mr. Rutledge needs someone to minister to him. I believe I'm the one.''

Elias nodded approval. "He'll be in good hands. Mr. Rutledge, for your peace of mind, I will tell you that Marty testified that you were entirely innocent of his death. I hope that will ease your mind and your conscience.''

"Thank you," Rutledge said. "It does help."

"Doesn't Virgie believe what Marty said?" Nanine asked.

"I'm sure she does not. But, remember, she's under considerable stress. I doubt she's accountable for what she says or does right now. Without even realizing it, she may feel partly responsible for Marty's death."

"If it will help, tell her Mr. Rutledge is not going to back out of the financial arrangements he made with Marty."

"I'll tell her." Elias breathed a sigh of relief that he didn't have to ask that embarrassing question of Rutledge. "It will go far in making her listen to reason. What do you plan, Nan?"

"I'm going to see Mr. Rutledge to his hotel and arrange for a doctor to examine him. After that I don't know. I'm as confused as Virgie must be."

"Let me know when you make up your mind. They'll bring Marty back to the island for burial. I expect that will be tomorrow."

"I'll be there if Virginia allows me to come."

"Allows you? It's your island too, Nan. Bear with Virgie. You know how strong-willed and stubborn she is."

"That's the trouble, Elias, I do know. May we use one of those carriages?"

"That's why Warren and I brought back two of them. May I help you get Mr. Rutledge to the carriage?"

"You'd better not," Nanine said apprehensively, looking beyond him. "Virginia looks furious."

Elias slipped some bills in her hand. "You may need this. You're a most unusual lady, Nan."

He rose and walked briskly back to where Virginia waited. He drew his arm around her waist. For a moment he thought she was going to reject his approach, but instead she leaned her head against his shoulder.

"I know I'll never have Nanine's goodness," she said. "Or her sense of fair play. But I hate her being with that man."

"You asked me to find out what that man's intentions were about the money. I didn't have to ask. He told me he would see the arrangement through. The money will not be stopped."

"Thank heaven." Virginia's sigh was one of relief. "Is Nan coming with us?"

"No. She's taking Mr. Rutledge to his hotel. She wants to see that he gets the services of a good doctor. He's really a very sick man. There's no denying that."

"And Marty's dead," she countered. "We don't deny that either."

eleven

Anton Boyle and James Warren helped Miles to his suite. Nanine accompanied them, but remained in the sitting room while they undressed Miles and helped him into bed. He was still weak from the ordeal and once his head touched the pillows he gave a low sigh of weariness. His eyes were closed, but he opened them when he addressed his friends.

"Thanks," he said gratefully. "I don't know how I'm going to live with the fact that I just killed a man."

"You didn't mean to," Anton Boyle said.

"It was an accident," James Warren added. "We know that. The commandant accepted our story. The fact that Elias Birch was present helped."

"That lady," Miles said. "Miss Hammond. Will you convey my thanks to her?"

Warren smiled. "We'll let you do that. She's in the sitting room, awaiting permission to come in here. She is going to care for you."

"After I killed her brother?" Miles asked. He closed his eyes as if to shut out the painful memory.

"She accepted the story. She's a warm, compassionate woman," Boyle said. "We know she'll give you the best of care."

"I can't let her do it," Miles replied.

Warren chuckled. "I doubt you'll be able to stop her. We're going downstairs to get something to eat. We'll be back tomorrow. Now we'll send Miss Hammond in.''

Nanine was already standing in the doorway of the bedroom, her concerned glance on the figure lying so still in the bed.

She spoke as the two men approached her. ''Does he know I'm here?''

''Yes,'' Warren replied. ''He finds it difficult to believe you'd want to be.''

''Don't worry about him.'' Nanine spoke with quiet assurance. ''I shan't leave him. I've already sent for a doctor, though I think I can do as well for him as the doctor.''

''That's good news.'' Boyle smiled appreciatively. ''None of them have been able to help.''

Nanine excused herself and went into the bedroom. Warren and Boyle left the suite.

In the corridor, Boyle said, ''Quite a difference between those two sisters.''

''Quite,'' Warren agreed. ''Both beautiful. One with a serene disposition and the other quite spirited.''

Boyle smiled despite himself. ''A hellcat, that voluptuous blond. And, as you say, spirited. Elias Birch is quite a man, but he doesn't seem to have tamed her.''

''I doubt any man could,'' Warren mused. ''She has a maddening appeal.''

''I know,'' Boyle agreed. ''I was damn mad at her at Miller's Field and at the same time physically attracted to her. A helluva thing to say, considering the circumstances.''

''Not at all,'' Warren replied. ''I felt the same way—and damned ashamed of myself. Amazing how you could hate her and at the same time want to possess her.'' Warren quickened his step. ''Let's get the hell downstairs, have a drink and get that woman out of our system.''

''Get all that happened out of our system. Poor, gentle Miles. He wanted so much to die. Instead, he has to live with the fact that he killed a man.''

Nanine stood beside the bed and looked down at Miles. His face was dirt-smeared and his hands, which rested atop the coverlet, also showed traces of the sandy ground on which he'd fallen when he fainted.

She went into the bathroom and returned with a bowl of water, a wash cloth and towel. She bathed his face gently, then his hands. While she was doing so, she noticed his brow was very hot. Apparently he was feverish. She knew what that was like. There'd been a time when the slightest exertion weakened her to the point where she trembled from head to foot and had to take to her bed. She noticed the tremor of his hands as they lay on the coverlet. At least, now they were clean. She returned the bowl and towels to the bathroom, then sat beside his bed.

"I'm so filled with shame for what I did today," he said, "I don't know how to express my gratitude for your kindness. I don't deserve it, since I killed your brother. But I'll say thank you anyway, Miss Hammond."

"Please call me Nanine, because I'm going to call you Miles," she said. "Tell me about your illness. Has any doctor told you what it is or what causes it?"

He related a long story of childhood illness that no doctor could either diagnose or prescribe for with any success. He'd lived on an assortment of nostrums and diversified advice from several doctors. More and more, as he spoke, Nanine came to realize that Rutledge was actually relating every stage of her own illness. The blood deficiency she had conquered with the advice and help of a doctor who knew what the disease was.

Rutledge had just ended his sad tale of continued weakness and sickness when a doctor arrived. An aging, fussy little man who made an elaborate examination of Rutledge. Nanine retreated to the sitting room but was within hearing distance.

"You're in no immediate danger," the doctor said to Rutledge. "But you're quite ill. I would advise you to go home, where you can be provided with constant attention. You require it, sir. I'll leave a bottle of elixir. Take it four times a day, a teaspoonful at a time. If you wish, I'll be back tomorrow."

"I'll send for you if it becomes necessary," Rutledge said. "Thank you, Doctor."

Nanine resumed her chair beside the bed. "How often I had

doctors tell me the same thing. And leave the same elixir. I guarantee it will taste awful."

Rutledge managed a smile. "The worse it tastes, the more good the doctors think it does. Please be kind enough to deposit the bottle of medicine in the wastebasket."

"He was right about one thing, Miles. You do need constant attention. Do you have family? Or are you married?"

He said, "No to both questions. My father was killed in the war. My mother died years before it. I have no kin, but you're not to worry about that. I'm wealthy. Very rich, in fact. I lost little from the war. My investments were in the North and in England and are intact. So I can buy all the attention I require."

"The kind you buy," she said, "is not enough. Professional help, of course. But no medicine can take the place of someone truly concerned."

He tried to sit up. Nanine put her arm around him, eased him forward and arranged the pillows to better support him. The effort left her flushed and just a trifle breathless. Nanine didn't deceive herself about it. The breathlessness didn't come from exertion but from contact with this man. She quickly regained her self-control.

"I'm going to provide the attention you need," she said. "I'm going to take you back to Valcour. It's an island. There's no better place in all the world for someone recovering from an illness."

"There's no recovery," he said, again morose. "I'm never going to get better, Nanine."

"Oh, yes, you are," she told him confidently, pleased he spoke her name. "Because I went through the same thing you're going through now, but I was lucky. Elias got a Yankee doctor to examine me. He knew what caused this condition. It's due to a weakness in the blood. He brought me back by prescribing . . . Miles, do you like liver?"

"Abhor it."

Nanine laughed softly. "You're going to learn to love it. This doctor told me to eat all the liver I could and red meat as well. Frankly, it's far more appetizing than the taste of the elixirs, the dozens of bottles I was given. What's more important, it worked and it's going to work for you. And I've more news for you. The treatment begins immediately. Close your eyes and rest. I'll be back soon."

She moved quickly through the sitting room, but caught a glimpse of herself in a wall mirror close to the exit door. She paused and almost exclaimed aloud. She scarcely recognized herself. There was a glow to her eyes that had never been there before. Her cheeks were flushed and when she placed a hand against her neck, she could feel her rapid pulse. She could even feel her heart pounding in her chest. She told herself she must be mad, as she left the suite, heading for the kitchen. She couldn't be falling in love. The fact that she'd been stirred when she propped him up against his pillows could well be because she'd never been that close to a man before. She'd known the man scarcely more than an hour. A man who was more dead than alive and who had no zest for living.

She forced the troublesome thought from her mind and made her way downstairs to the kitchen quarters. There, she cornered the chef, whose first reaction was to regard her with annoyance for having invaded those sacred premises. However, her quiet, serene manner, along with the soft glow in her eyes, captivated him and he found himself giving her assurance he would carry out her orders.

Half an hour later, a generous serving of liver was placed before Miles, along with a small portion of a thick porterhouse steak, very rare. Nanine insisted on feeding him, starting with the liver. He ate it all without even making a face. She was touched by his effort to please her.

He rested against the pillows while she cut the steak, and eyed the steaming red meat from which blood oozed. "I think it's still alive."

When Nanine laughed, his mouth widened in a smile.

"You should smile more often," she said teasingly. "You look quite handsome, especially with that lock of hair falling across your brow."

"It never will stay put," he exclaimed in annoyance, attempting to fingercomb it back in place.

"Never mind it. Besides, I like it," she said. She had a forkful of beef and placed it in his mouth.

He dutifully ate as much as he could, though the portion was not too large. However, Nanine was satisfied.

She brought the tray of dishes to the sitting room, then returned and resumed her place beside his bed, her hand resting on it. "Now—will you come with me to Valcour?"

He looked pleased and his smile warmed her. "You're very kind, Nanine. Quite a dear lady, really. But your sister would never tolerate me. I heard her at Miller's Field, you know. Besides, it wouldn't be fair to her or you. Is there anyone else there?"

"Elias," Nanine said with a smile.

"He'll tolerate me. I heard him speak to you."

"Mama."

"It would be a brutal shock were I to confront her. Most unfair."

"Mama wouldn't be that upset. Then again, maybe she would. She enjoys something to be upset about."

"Your sister—Mrs. Birch. She troubles me."

"I have as much right to Valcour as she. Should she object, I'll remind her. Besides, like you, I have no one to care for. Like you, I'm lonely also." She paused, then added daringly, "You are lonely, aren't you?"

"Terribly," he admitted. "Until now, I never met any woman who gave me a second glance. Not that you have—except out of compassion."

Nanine's hand moved up to his and clasped it lightly. His tightened around it. She felt her heartbeat increase.

"Say you'll come—please. Let me care for you."

"I'll come." His voice was barely audible.

"It's settled, then. I'll go back. You need lots of rest. I shall see that you're well taken care of while I'm gone, and your friends will stop by. I'll return tomorrow or the next day."

Though it seemed unbelievable, his eyes held the same glow hers had when she glanced in the mirror. She leaned forward and kissed him lightly on the lips.

"I'll not desert you, Miles Rutledge. I swear it."

He brought her hand to his lips and kissed the back of it. There was an unevenness to his voice when he said, "I have finally discovered a reason to live."

She turned away quickly, so he wouldn't see the tears. She knew there'd be more—for Marty—but they'd be a different kind. She talked to the manager of the hotel, giving him specific orders about feeding Miles and looking in on him regularly. She reminded the manager that Rutledge was very wealthy and if all this attention was provided, the manager would find it worthwhile.

She then took a carriage to the dock and arranged with a boatman to be ferried to Valcour. She sat in the stern of the boat, her head bent, her mind busier than it had ever been in her life.

She was doing this despite Virginia's certain wrath because she herself had been given back her life by a good doctor. Now it was her duty to pass on this treatment to a man who needed it desperately. She tried to convince herself that was the only reason for her sympathy for Miles. Yet she knew she was lying. Her kiss had not been an impulsive act; but a deliberate one. A kiss from a woman in love. For the first time in her life and she was in love with a comparative stranger. A man who had killed her brother hours before.

There was no one at the dock to greet her though she knew the approach of her boat must have been noticed. This was Virginia's way of registering her disapproval. An indication that the sailing would be rough for Nanine. Still, she walked in a determined manner up the path to the mansion.

Elias opened the door for her and cast his eyes heavenward in a signal that all was far from well. In the drawing room she found her mother and sister seated side by side on a sofa, apparently waiting for her.

Lenore raised her head. "How could you?" she asked.

"Good afternoon, Mama," Nanine said quietly. "If you are referring to Mr. Rutledge and my regard for him, I am well satisfied that I am doing the proper thing."

"Comforting the man who killed your brother?" Virginia asked sarcastically.

"What happened was unfortunate. A tragic accident. I believe that to be the truth."

"The only thing that could have made it worse," Lenore said, "would be for him to have been a Yankee."

Nanine sat down. "Mama, you heard Virginia's story of how all this happened. Will you listen to mine?"

"I disown you," Lenore said sharply. "I don't want anything to do with you or your story. All I know is that my son is dead and that terrible man killed him."

"Very well, Mother."

"Why did you come back?" Virginia asked.

"Why? To attend the funeral of my brother, of course. Besides, this is my home as well as yours."

"You've disgraced it," Lenore said. "I never would have thought this of you, Nanine. You, my ever-dutiful daughter."

Elias, who had been standing in the doorway to the drawing room, quietly withdrew. He might make matters worse. Virginia would believe only what she wanted to believe. Also, he was certain neither she nor Mother Hammond would deter Nanine in what she wanted to do.

"What made you so attracted to this man?" Virginia demanded.

"He suffers from the same ailment that almost killed me. I recovered, thanks to a Northern doctor, and I felt that I could do no less than to pass on what I know about this treatment to a less fortunate person."

"What are you talking about?" Lenore exclaimed.

"Do you mean you're going to help him?" Virginia asked in a shocked voice.

"If I don't, he will die."

"Let him. I insist you stay away from him. I'll not have my sister—"

Nanine interrupted her quietly. "After the funeral I intend to bring Mr. Miles Rutledge to Valcour. He'll find rest and comfort here. Besides, he needs me."

"You're mad. Totally insane," Virginia said.

Lenore rose abruptly, burst into tears and left the room. Nanine knew her mother would go to her bedroom now and cry herself to sleep.

"We're going to have this out right here and now," Virginia said. "I absolutely forbid you bringing that murderer to Valcour. If you insist, you'll have to leave and never come back. I hope I've made myself clear on that point."

"You have," Nanine said complacently. "However, it would be to your benefit and to Valcour's existence if you permit Mr. Rutledge to recuperate here."

"If he dares to set foot on this island, he'll die one minute later. I'll shoot him."

Nanine nodded. "I believe you're capable of it, but you'd be terribly sorry afterward."

"There's no one who would blame me if I killed him," Virginia said.

"You're wrong. I would, and that's where your problem lies, Virgie. You see, if you refuse to give Mr. Rutledge sanctuary on Valcour, he will withdraw his agreement made with Marty."

"He can't!" Virginia shouted in sudden consternation.

"Oh, yes, he can. The sale was made under false pretenses. Marty schemed the whole thing to bring the price so high. That was illegal and if you take this to any court, you'll be turned down."

"This man said he would not welsh—"

"I agree. But I'll tell him to cancel the sale and he will. You can't rescue Valcour without the money he will provide. You have often said you would do anything to restore Valcour as it used to be. Well . . . if you were truthful in that statement, you will permit me to bring Miles here."

The torrent of abuse that almost burst forth from Virginia was held back with an effort. Everything had changed with Nanine's demand.

Virginia said, "Nan, please listen to reason. We're sisters. All our lives we've been close. I respect what you're trying to do even if I think it's madness. But how can you expect me to accept this man in our home? And Mama."

"You will have to," Nanine said quietly.

"Why are you doing this? What does this man mean to you?"

"I don't know. Yet."

"Oh, my God!" Virginia exclaimed. "It can't be that you are doing this for him because of any other reason than to help him because he suffers from the same sickness that troubled you."

"I said, I don't know."

"Nan, don't be a fool. In no way can you feel that you are in love with your brother's murderer."

"I didn't say I was. I said I didn't know."

Virginia rose and quickly went to Nanine's side. She took Nanine's hand in hers. "Poor Nan. You're fooling yourself. You've never had a man in your life. All of a sudden some strange compassion for Rutledge has caused you to think you're in love with him. I know your life has been barren, but you cannot care for a man guilty of murdering our brother. You don't understand this emotion of love. You've been a spinster too—"

Virginia brought a hand to her lips in dismay. Nanine smiled gently.

"It's true. I've been a spinster, and I never enjoyed one moment of it. I'm not certain I'm in love with Miles, or if it's compassion or infatuation. It doesn't matter because in time I'll know which it is. But I am bringing him here if I have to blackmail you into it."

"Mama would never tolerate it. You know that."

"Mama will tolerate anything that will bring back the old days."

"She would never allow you to bring him into this house. Nan, your brother is not yet buried and you—you—talk of aiding the man who killed him. I will not allow it. Mother never would. You can't go through with this."

Nanine rose and began walking out of the room.

"Where are you going?" Virginia demanded.

Nanine paused and looked back. "To my room. I intend to pack a few things and then I'm going to the mainland. To Miles—and I won't come back. I'm sorry, but I can be firm too, even if I rarely showed it before. Right now, I think I may go as far as marrying Miles, if he will have me. Good-bye, Virgie."

"Now wait!" Virginia came to her feet and hurried to Nanine's side. "This will kill Mama."

"Mama is strong enough to bear this and anything else. Tell her you'll not be able to bring Valcour back unless Miles can come here. See what she says and then talk to me about how strong she is."

"I wonder what Phoebe would think of this," Virginia said, desperately seeking a way out of this preposterous situation.

"I'd wager anything she'd be on my side, and you know that.

Now I have your answer to my request. Miles will not be allowed on Valcour. I want that to be a definite answer, because I shall then take steps to see that no money will be forthcoming.''

Virginia walked back to the nearest chair and sat down heavily. ''You know you're taking advantage of me, Nan.''

''Call it what you will. It's quite simple. No Miles, no money.''

''Will you be entirely responsible for him? No one else will go near the man.''

''I don't want anyone else to go near him. Are you changing your mind, Virgie?''

''I cannot afford to lose that money. I must have it and you know that. Let me talk to Elias about this.''

''There's no need. I know what Elias will say. He believes Miles even if you do not. Which is it, Virgie? I must have the answer now.''

Virginia fiddled with the handkerchief she'd been twisting all through the conversation. ''You may bring him here, but not in this house. At least have that much consideration for Mama.''

''Very well. Miles and I will live in the old hospital. I shall ask Moses to get it ready. You will not have to see him. You need not acknowledge his presence here. All I wish is that he be let alone so he can have a chance to recover.''

''Be damned to you,'' Virginia said angrily. ''Have it your way.'' She rose and stalked out of the room, passing Nanine without a glance. She ran up the stairs to her bedroom. Nanine made her way to the kitchen. Belle was sound asleep in her big chair. Nanine touched her shoulder to waken her.

''Yes'm,'' Belle said, blinking her eyes in an effort to focus them. She'd never seen such a determined look on Nanine's face.

''I'm bringing a gentleman here to stay,'' she said. ''He suffers from the same illness that almost killed me. You recall that I was compelled to eat great quantities of liver and as much red meat as I could. He must have that same diet. Everything the same as it was for me.''

''Yes'm,'' Belle said uncertainly. ''Yo' sistah say Ah kin do this?''

"My sister has nothing to do with it. I'm giving you orders and you must obey them. Do you understand?"

"If Missy Virginia against this, Ah'll do it. Yes'm. It riles her Ah does it. From the way yo' look, it sho' goin' to. When yo' bringin' him heah? So Ah kin see to slaughterin' some o' the animals. Ain't much livah from one hawg."

"Do whatever is necessary, but see that it's done."

"Yes'm. Sho' likes to do whut Miss Uppity don' wants me to do. Likes yo', Missy Nanine. Yes'm, likes yo', an' does whut yo' say." Her smile became broader. " 'Co'se yo' cain't git a man to do that much killin' fo' livah. Mayhap yo' pays a dollah sometimes?"

"If you don't fail him by one meal, I'll see that you're rewarded."

"Ah thanks yo', Missy. She goin' to be mighty mad fo' sho'. Yes'm. Mad as hell, Ah 'spects."

"If Miss Virginia makes any complaint to you, come to me."

Belle said indignantly, "Ah sho' will, chile. Sho' will. Do mah heart good settin' her down a peg."

"And please bring a supper tray to my room," Nanine added.

"Yes'm. Sorry 'bout Mistah Marty. Real sad."

"Yes," Nanine agreed. "It was."

She went directly to her room, sat in a chair beside the window looking out over the front of the estate. It was her favorite spot and had been since she was a child. Here she could think clearly most of the time. At this moment she was confused. Admitting that she might be in love with Miles had been as much a shock to her as it had been to Virginia. Now, upon serious consideration, she did wonder if compassion was carrying her away. She wondered if it was possible to be in love with a man who had killed her brother. Not weeks or months ago, but this very day.

In the waning light, she considered what this day had brought. Sorrow, of course. But there was Miles, and he represented something else. She wondered why she didn't feel any hatred for the man.

Marty would be brought back in the morning and laid to rest in the island cemetery. Soon after the funeral she would bring Miles here in the face of opposition that almost crushed her. Yet she knew it had to be done. She was helping another human being. If she fell in love with Miles in the course of caring for him, so be it. Love him or not, she would nurse him back to health. She smiled wistfully at the idea of being in love with him. The only gesture he'd given of his regard had been to kiss the back of her hand. Yet what he'd said more than made up for it.

Belle brought up the tray with a substantial supper on it. Nanine ate and went to bed early. She half hoped Elias might have paused briefly to see her, but she understood his position. In her present state of mind, Virginia was not one to be further defied. Nanine slept well, much to her surprise, and awakened only in time to see the barge dock and the coffin carried to the mansion.

She dressed quickly, hurried down to the kitchen for a stand-up breakfast and then went into the drawing room, already filling up with those who had once lived on Valcour and who had attended a rousing ball only two days before.

Nanine took a chair at the rear of the room and quietly acknowledged the words of sympathy from her old friends and neighbors. Nanine's mother was escorted into the room on Elias's arm and she promptly burst into bitter tears.

Virginia busied herself greeting the mourners, but she never acknowledged Nanine's presence or went near her. Elias came over and sat down beside her.

"I approve of what you're doing," he said. "I think Miles warrants your help. I'll also say this, I believe he never intended to kill Marty."

"I wish you could convince Virgie he didn't."

"For now it's like talking into the wind. I'll do what I can to help you and Miles. Just remember, if you need me, let me know."

"Thank you, Elias. I appreciate your offer."

"I understand you're going to install Miles in the old slave hospital."

"Yes. And I intend to live there with him. I won't enter this house again until Virginia relents and accepts Miles."

Elias took her hand and squeezed it gently. "I'll see that the place is cleaned up and furnished with whatever I can get."

"Thank you. I was going to ask Moses to take care of it."

Elias rose. "I'd better go to Virgie now. The minister just arrived."

The mansion was completely filled with an overflow outside. The minister spoke of Marty's service to the South, of his promotion to general, then offered a brief prayer. The mourners formed a line to pass before the open casket. Virginia was the last to pay her respects, leaving Elias to guide and comfort Lenore, who wore a flowered dress because she had nothing in black, but she had managed to find an old bit of black veiling and that covered her face.

Virginia gently placed Marty's sword at his side and bowed her head in prayer. Marty's body was clad in his uniform, as befitted a general, and some wartime companions of his were attending, also in their gray uniforms. They were to carry the coffin to the cemetery.

Everyone left the room now except for the undertaker's assistants. Nanine went out the French doors leading to the rear of the estate. She could hear the coffin being hammered shut and she shuddered and again wondered if she was doing right.

At the cemetery she stood well back, alone. But Elias left Virginia's side and came to stand silently beside Nanine. The ceremony was short and everyone turned away to return to the mansion.

"Thank you, Elias," she said. "It was lonely here. I hope Virginia does not cause you any trouble because of this."

"She asked me to stand beside you," he said. "She's not completely vindictive. Bear with her. She's going through an ordeal, too."

"I understand. I'm glad she sent you. Tell her that, will you please?"

"Yes. Will you go back to the mainland now?"

"With the others, yes. I saw some of the Yankees who live on the island here. I think that was nice of them. And the old slaves who lined the path and wept as poor Marty was carried past them. There's a great deal of love and compassion here, Elias."

"There is. Bringing Miles here will bring out more of it. If not now, in due time. Call on me if there is need."

He turned back, reaching into his coat pocket. "Oh, yes, I almost forgot. Virgie asked me to give you this letter. We picked it up yesterday at the post office. It's from Phoebe and it came yesterday. She thought you'd like to read it."

"I hope things are going well with her and Tom."

"Read the letter and be assured of it. She's having a great time."

twelve

Before she stepped out of the carriage, Phoebe wrinkled her nose delicately in distaste at what she saw. Tom Sprague removed their suitcases from the carriage. He set them on the sidewalk, paid the driver and moved to stand beside Phoebe.

"I know it's nothing much," he said. "But it only costs fifteen dollars a month."

"Look at the sidewalk. It's filthy," she said disgustedly. "And the building . . ."

"There are far worse. Besides, we're only on the second floor, so you don't have to climb five and six flights. The lower flats are the most expensive."

"Forgive me, darling." Her sunny smile returned. "It's just that the hotel we stayed in was so nice."

"At two-fifty a day." His smile was apologetic. "We can't afford that. Not yet."

"What disturbs me most," she said, and stopped speaking for a moment while two huge drays passed with a deafening clatter. "It's just that I'm used to the quiet and cleanliness of Valcour and this is a far cry from it."

"I know," Tom said remindfully. "I was there."

Phoebe gave him a loving smile. "It's where we met."

"Right." He picked up the suitcases and they went inside to climb the stairs. The flat consisted of one room and had a small double gas burner for cooking. This intrigued Phoebe, lessening her disappointment in the shabby furniture and worn carpet.

"It's for cooking," Tom explained. "It runs by gas. You'd better let me attend to it for a while—until you get used to it. It's really a very good way to cook. You have to be careful with it. Don't ever turn it on without lighting it and don't forget to turn it off. The gas can kill you."

"I never even saw gaslight before we came to New York," she said. "It's wonderful. No doubt of that. How do we pay for it?"

"See that red box under the sink? You put a dime in it whenever the gas runs low. Once a month a man comes around to collect it. Very simple. Of course, everything is going to be different. Not at all like Valcour." His arms enclosed her. "I'm sorry, darling."

"My darling Tom." She kissed him on the lips. "You don't have to make excuses. It's a palace. It's our *home!* When the man comes for the dimes, he'll call me 'Your Majesty.'"

Their laughter mingled, and she went on, "I'm so happy I don't mind anything. In fact, I could cry, but I've been doing that too much lately. It's funny but when I'm happy, I like to cry."

"You're a little crazy," Tom said lovingly.

"What gives me the biggest thrill of all is the way I'm treated. Especially at the hotel where we stayed. Having the bellboys bow to me, the desk clerks going out of their way to answer my questions. The doorman opening the door. All for me—a nigger fresh out of slavery."

He took a step closer and looked down at her. "Don't ever say that again. You're not black. You're as white as I am and don't ever, for one moment, forget it. Do you hear me, Phoebe?"

"Of course I do, the way you're shouting. What's so awful about the truth?" She was shocked by his sudden anger.

"You don't understand," he said. "You just . . . you're fresh from the country, I guess, and you don't know city ways."

"Then I'll have to learn," she said brightly. "I promise I won't say I'm a nigger or I used to be a slave."

"Good." He sat down beside her, suddenly contrite. "Oh, Phoebe, I love you so much. I'm . . . just . . . overwhelmed by the way I feel about you. You say you're happy. I'm glad you are, but I'll bet your happiness is no greater than mine."

She let her head rest on his shoulder. "I'm glad, Tom. I was afraid, after our first few days of marriage, that you'd regret it."

"Never!" he said vehemently. "I fell in love with you on sight. Just as Elias fell in love with Virginia. Everyone told me that would never happen. It only existed in books, but it happened to me."

"I'm going to cry some more if you keep telling me that," she said.

"Well, we surely have to discuss more serious things too, I suppose. You know that I was a school teacher before the war. I taught mathematics. I had other jobs in my day, but teaching became the one I was best at. Perhaps because I enjoy the challenge it presents. I had a fine record before I enlisted and I was sure there'd be a job for me when I came back. But they haven't shown any favoritism toward ex-soldiers. When I went to the school where I used to teach, they said I was one of the best they ever had, but there were no openings yet. There will be soon. Some of the teachers are old, some hate their job. Openings happen all the time. Meanwhile, we have enough to live on if we're careful."

"How careful?" she asked.

"Reasonably. Don't use a carriage when you can walk. Don't buy anything we don't need."

"I have some money. I told you that. Virginia was quite generous. Tom, there are things I need. Clothes, a reticule—shoes."

"Buy whatever you need. Just don't splurge. I wish you could, but not just now."

She nodded. "I promise I won't. Now, let's get our things unpacked and I'll clean up this place. Oh, my, is it always as noisy as this?"

"It's not Valcour," he reminded her.

"I'll live through it. When do you try for a job next?"

"In a few days. I'll keep in touch. I'm going to the Board of Education tomorrow and see if there are openings in any of the other schools. We'll make out. Don't you fret about that."

For the next few days Phoebe was too excited to worry about anything. She spent one full day by herself, going from one store to another and making purchases of inexpensive items merely to glory in the politeness with which she was met. Every time a saleslady called her Miss and thanked her for the purchase, no matter how insignificant, Phoebe felt a glow of something she might have described only as triumph. As if dreams were coming true. She was free. She was white. Her whole world had changed. If not always for the better, nevertheless there were its benefits too. Once, aboard a horsecar, a man had politely tipped his hat and given up his seat for her. She came very close to kissing that stranger on the cheek. A foolish, crazy impulse she'd not given in to.

In the building where she lived, other tenants were gracious and polite too. The owner of the building addressed her as Mrs. Sprague. That took some getting used to also.

That evening, she dumped her purchases on the table while Tom regarded them with some consternation.

"All told," Phoebe said, "they cost a dollar and twenty cents. I bought them just to prove to myself I could buy things and be treated nicely."

"Of course." He hugged her and laughed aloud. "It's hard for me to remember that you never were allowed to have money or buy things in a store. Valcour, the South and the damned war seem so far away."

"Did you talk to them at the Board of Education?"

"Oh, yes. They were very nice. It seems with all the returning soldiers there are five men for every job. Any kind of a job, but there will be openings. Things have to settle down a bit."

"I was thinking it might be a good time to visit your parents. I want to meet them, Tom. I want to know they approve of me."

He gave a negative shake of his head. "Not yet. We can't afford it and I have to be so close by in case I'm sent for. These jobs occur very suddenly and if I'm not on the spot to move in on a vacant one, I'll never find work."

Phoebe nodded in understanding. "I forgot about that. You have to forgive me. There's so much to learn. Please take me to a restaurant tonight, darling. I like to dine out. It's exciting to study the menu, ask the waiter a question and hear his polite answer."

Tom grinned at her eagerness. "Sure, but we can't eat out often.

Not until I'm at work again. Honestly, I'm sorry I had to bring you to this. When we married and left Valcour, I was so confident I'd have a job waiting, but . . ."

He sighed and got up to pace the floor. Phoebe brought him back to her side by holding out both arms.

"It's all right, my darling. Everything is wonderful. I'm not afraid. If we have to face some degree of deprivation, we can do it."

"Yes, we can do it," he said, but without much enthusiasm. "You have to remember, though, that all this is new to you and the bad side of it hasn't hit home yet."

"Could it be any worse than being a slave?" she asked. "Oh, I know I was treated tenderly. Marse Hammond was my secret father and he was very kind. But I was still a slave. I said 'Yes, Missy; Yes, Marse; Yes, ma'am.' I was never allowed to express my opinion. A slave never asked questions. He never got to read a newspaper, or hear what was going on in the world. The less we knew, the less trouble we'd make. If I faced that, I can now face anything and be cheerful no matter how bad things get."

"I hope they won't get that bad. Well, I'm not going to spoil your happiness. We can get along for a few weeks and I'll be back at work before long. It has to be that way. A man returning from the war must be taken care of. Must be given privileges after the sacrifice he made. Everything is going to be fine."

But it wasn't, and before long the newness of freedom, the thrill of a big city, strange but interesting faces and even stranger ways—so different from anything she'd known—began to wear off. Phoebe sensed it more each day. She was now accustomed to being treated like a white and she began to forget she had Negro blood in her veins, though she wondered what made Negro blood different from white. The color was the same, regardless of whether it came from the vein of a white or a Negro. Yet she knew she would always have to remember she had Negro blood in her veins. Secretly, despite Tom's impatience with her when she referred to herself as a nigger, she knew she didn't want to forget. Not out of bitterness, but because she was proud of her people. They'd put up with a lot, done with little, yet few had ever become bitter. They knew better. Lashings with the whip would tame the rebellious ones. If that didn't work, a rope strung from a tree would do it. She'd remember all that, but she was glad she was living in the North. Now that slavery had been abolished, there'd be no stigma attached to Negroes or those who were, but didn't show it. Like herself. People here would be fair-minded. They'd understand.

Still, money was running dangerously low and Tom hadn't found a job. His shoes were worn thin from walking the streets looking for work that wasn't there. Once he'd mildly wondered if they could obtain some assistance from Valcour, but Phoebe had promptly squelched that idea and continued writing happy letters to Virginia and Nanine. She would never let them know that she and Tom were rapidly approaching serious straits.

Often they existed on bread and a dime's worth of bologna, and coffee so weak Tom wondered why it didn't collapse in the cup. Phoebe tried to keep up her spirits and Tom's. He was becoming actually morose some days, after trudging about vainly looking for some way to earn a dollar. He did find one job, on the waterfront, but the work was much too hard for him and he was promptly fired. The two dollars from that work seemed a windfall, but it was gone.

Phoebe said, "Tom, I wonder if I could find work. There are so many rich people uptown, and I certainly know how to be a good maid."

"Don't you dare say that again." He came to his feet as he spoke and waved a finger before her face. "I don't know about the South, but in the North a man earns the money. It's a disgrace to have his wife working."

Phoebe shrugged. "That's a lot of nonsense. There's no difference between the North and South as to women working. It's your pride that's being hurt."

"My pride has nothing to do with it."

"We're in serious circumstances," Phoebe argued. "I know you'll find a teaching job soon, but in the meantime . . ."

"No!" he reiterated harshly.

She gave in, though reluctantly. "Very well, if you're that unsettled about it, but I still can't see your point. I've worked all my life and without being paid for it. I know I'd enjoy working if for no reason other than to see a pay envelope."

"You've no faith in me," he said.

"Darling, I've every faith in you and this would only be a temporary thing. We have to eat, we have to pay rent, and so far as I know—though you don't talk about money very often—we're on the verge of being without funds. What do we do then?"

"Go to Niblo's Garden for dinner," he said with a broad grin.

"Niblo's . . . ?"

"It's on Broadway at Prince Street. You must have passed it. It's a music hall and restaurant."

"Yes," she exclaimed happily, I recall seeing it now. Of course you're joking."

"I'm not. My father sent me a check as a wedding present. I intended to save it until we were settled in our own place and then I wanted to surprise you with it. I wanted to buy you a silver set. Like the one you and Virginia tried to steal off the island when we occupied it."

"Tom, there are so many reasons why I love you . . ." She moved quickly to him, her arms going around his neck. "Dinner out sounds wonderful, but shouldn't we keep it for getting a silver set or as something to fall back on?"

"We can always earn it later on. It will be like a loan to ourselves. It's a hundred dollars."

"That much? But still . . ."

"No arguments. Tonight we're going to Niblo's. They have a fine show there and very good food. You've never been to a theater before, have you?"

She moved back, still holding on to him and shook her head. "Never! There are a million things I never did."

"Put on your best dress. This is a classy place. The headwaiters bow lower than at any other restaurant. And there's enough to keep us for a week or so and by that time surely I'll be called back to work."

"Then we'll forget our troubles and have a wonderful time for ourselves. Your father must be a very generous man."

"He's not rich by any means. 'Comfortable' is the way he'd put it."

"I hope I can meet him soon—and your mother. What's she like?"

"Well, sometimes she reminds me of your mother...that is, Virginia and Nanine's mother. She likes to dress up and serve tea to her cronies and attend every soiree and supper she can. I would say she is very socially inclined."

"I see nothing wrong in that. Tom, can't we spare a few dollars and go to your home, just for a day or two?"

"That would be the day or two when I'd be called and I wouldn't be here. We're not going anywhere until I get my job back."

She released her hold on him and turned away. "You're right, of course. But sometimes...the way you act...I think you might be embarrassed if anyone learned I'm not all white."

He looked incredulous. "How could I be? You're a beautiful girl."

"I'm part Negro," she said.

"It doesn't show in any way. Besides, it's nobody's business."

"Will we have children?" she asked in her blunt fashion.

He regarded her with surprise. "Children! Why do you ask?"

"Because I want them."

"My God, Phoebe, how can we when I can't support the two of us?"

"You've never even spoken of our having babies."

"I never thought of it."

"I believe you have. You take every precaution. Don't you think I recognize that?"

"If I do, it's only because we're in such bad financial condition."

"Will you want a family when things get better for us?"

"Let's wait till they do. What's the sense of talking about it now?"

She rose. "I must iron my dress for tonight."

"You're angry," he said, eyeing her somber features.

"No," she said quietly. "Though I really expected more enthusiasm on your part when we talked about a family. It doesn't matter now. As you say, the whole thing is impossible anyway."

"Good. Let's devote ourselves to having a good time tonight. And stop worrying."

She kissed him on the cheek, then went to the clothes closet with the built-in ironing board alongside. A small, recessed area held an icebox and a cast-iron sink. Above it were three shelves for dishes. They would have to be purchased along with pots and pans for cooking.

They were quiet after that, not finding much to talk about, but when they entered Niblo's and the headwaiter bowed as low as Tom said he would, Phoebe forgot the gnawing hurt that was growing inside her. She looked about in almost disbelief of what she saw. The tables covered with fine linen, silver and china. The ornamented chairs, the potted palms and shrubs making part of the large room look like a garden. There was a stage at the far end of the room. The headwaiter led them, quite grandly, to a table very close to the stage. Phoebe saw Tom hand the headwaiter a coin. Even this gesture was new to her.

She went into ecstasies over the menu. They ordered oysters, turtle soup, beef and crisp vegetables. There was a large cake for dessert. It was a thing of beauty but she didn't think it tasted quite as good as the cakes Belle made on Valcour.

Before they finished their meal, the stage curtains parted and there was a series of singing and dancing acts presented. A tableau of females representing the Four Graces, clad in diaphanous gowns, made Phoebe gasp in astonishment at their elegance and grace. Tom eyed her proudly. She was the most beautiful lady in the room and he was fully aware of the admiring glances of men.

Two performers appeared in blackface to dance, further arousing Phoebe's interest. She frowned as she watched intently, then shook her head in dismay.

"I think they're trying to do a cakewalk, but they don't know what it's all about. Their first dance was supposed to be a Jim Crow, but they were just shuffling and doing it without paying much attention to the rhythm of the music."

Tom nodded agreement. "I remember when you did the Shout on Valcour, along with all the nig . . . the blacks. You were sensational, Phoebe. You knew how to arouse a man, the way you used your body."

"It's a shame to watch those two actors spoiling what could be fine dancing. I don't doubt they can dance well, but they don't know what they're doing. I feel like getting up there and showing them how."

"Don't you dare," Tom laughed. "You'd make a spectacle of yourself."

"Why?" she asked, truly perplexed by his statement. "You do that no matter where you dance—if you dance to African rhythm. They don't even know what that is up here."

"You enjoy this, don't you? Dining out and seeing a show."

"More than anything else since I came to New York."

"As soon as I get work and we can afford it, I'll take you to the Bowery Theater. It's only a couple of blocks away. They're going to put on a new minstrel show that's supposed to be better than ever. They say it's a lot of fun. I wish I could take you there tomorrow."

"We'll get there," she said confidently. "And thank you for this lovely evening."

Each day Tom went hunting work, mainly at the school Board, but nothing came of it. His discouragement became more evident in his somber features and frequent though brief flashes of irritation. Phoebe felt sorry for him, but she could see no way out of their predicament. She was tempted to ask Virginia to send enough to tide them over, but she discovered she couldn't. Instead, she wrote glowing letters about how she enjoyed New York, going into detail about the things she saw and the courtesy and kindness that was extended to her wherever she went.

Staying alone in that one-room flat became more and more difficult. By midmorning she was bored and edgy. With Tom gone, she usually took to walking about. She had soon adjusted to the noise, the dirt and the traffic on both street and sidewalk. One day she found herself on the Bowery. She quickly recalled Tom's story about the Bowery Theater and its new kind of show.

If the dancers were as poor as those at Niblo's, it would be a sorry show, she thought. Those people should take the time to learn what Negro dancing was like. She knew how much she enjoyed it and gave full credit to the Negro blood in her veins. Somehow the term Negro blood amused her, but that's how someone like her was referred to so she accepted it, though she didn't like it.

She paused to study the bright posters outside the theater and even ventured into the lobby. The rows of blackface performers depicted in these posters intrigued her. Purely by instinct and perhaps inspiration, she went around to the stage door and walked into the theater. She heard the piano music and the shuffle of dancing feet as she slowly approached the wings from backstage.

A white man was dancing, and quite well, to the music from a piano. There were two other men seated onstage watching. Theater employees moved about, paying no attention to her, and she finally stood in the wings to watch.

Someone said, "You're next, girlie."

She spun around. A middle-aged, paunchy man signaled she was to go on to the stage. She hesitated a moment.

"I'm sorry," she said. "I don't know what you mean."

"I mean go on and show me what you can do," he said impatiently. "That's what you're here for, isn't it?"

"I . . . just . . . walked in," she said lamely.

"You didn't come from the agency?"

"I don't even know what an agency is, sir."

"How'd you get by the door? We don't allow people to just walk in, as you call it. So get the hell outa here, and if you wanna see the show, buy a ticket."

"Not if what I've seen so far is the best you can offer," she said boldly.

"Now hold on," he said with some heat, "that dancer is one of the best in the business."

"I don't think he's very good. And I saw some dancers at Niblo's Garden some time ago. They were awful."

"What dancers?"

"I don't recall what the card said their names were. They were in blackface trying to do a Negro dance and they didn't even come close."

"Is that so?" His attitude was one of mock respect. "I know the couple you refer to and I'd be proud to have them in my show, but I can't pay their price."

"Then you must conduct a cheap show, sir, because they were not worth much. I'll go now."

"I suppose you could do better?" he asked with open sarcasm.

"Oh, yes." Phoebe spoke with quiet confidence. "Especially with Negro dances."

"Now, how does it happen you know so much about those kind of dances?"

"I . . . grew up on a large plantation in the Carolinas. There were—we had six hundred slaves and we allowed them to dance whenever they wished."

He eyed her speculatively. "That's interesting. Want to go out there and show me what you consider authentic Negro dancing?"

"Oh, no," she said. "I didn't come here looking for . . . work." She hesitated with the last word.

"If you show that performer how to do a real Negro dance, I'll give you two tickets to the show, any night you want to come."

She laughed softly. That would be a surprise for Tom. She nodded eagerly. "Very well, sir. I will."

"Good. Come along. What kind of music do you want?"

"Oh—any Stephen Foster song."

"I'll talk to the piano player. Go ahead, show me." He led her to the male dancer. "What's your name?" he asked Phoebe.

"Phoebe Sprague," she said. "Mrs. Thomas Sprague."

"Fine. I'm Rudolph Duncan and this is Bert Lawlor. He's featured in the show. Bert, she says we don't know anything about Negro dancing."

Lawlor exploded into laughter. "You know, Rudy, she's right. All I do is improvise and I don't even know what I'm improvising."

Phoebe removed her coat. "If you will provide some music, I'll show you how to do Rockin' de Heel."

"Well now, that I'd like to see," Lawlor said.

The piano player went into the spritely music of "Camptown Races." Phoebe quickly picked up the beat. She was slow and awkward at first, more because of nervousness than stage fright, but in minutes she fell under the spell of the music and suddenly she was dancing with Lawlor and showing him some of the steps. They danced for ten minutes until she was breathless and begged to be allowed to stop.

Rudy Duncan applauded and so did the piano player. Rudy took her by both hands and looked her up and down, studying her face, her curves, and making no pretense of it.

"How'd you like to be in my minstrel show?" he asked.

"Oh, no," Phoebe said quickly, but she blushed prettily as she rejected the idea. "I didn't come here for that. I was just . . . intrigued by the posters outside. Also, I'd never been backstage before."

"Twelve dollars a week," Duncan said.

"I'm flattered, Mr. Duncan, but of course I couldn't."

"Your husband wouldn't approve, of course," Lawlor said. "They never do, but damn it, there's nothing wrong with being an actor."

"I agree it must be an exciting profession, but I'm not interested."

"Fifteen," Duncan said. "And that's the best offer I ever made to an amateur."

"Do you really mean that, Mr. Duncan?" she asked, this time looking mildly interested.

"That's what I'll pay. Maybe you'll be terrible. I don't know, but from what I just saw . . . say, what other dances can you show us?"

"The Shout," she said. "That's a very sensual dance. Primitive, you know. And the Jim Crow and the Cakewalk . . . they're more or less strutting dances, but they're fun to watch."

"Can you be here tomorrow at ten?" Duncan asked.

"You really mean it, don't you?" Phoebe wondered how she could contain her excitement.

"Of course I do."

"Suppose you prove that," she took a long breath and wondered where she got the courage, "by paying me two weeks in advance."

"'Advance'?" he asked, like a man utterly bewildered.

"She didn't lie when she said she didn't know anything about the theater," Lawlor laughed. He eyed her with grudging admiration.

"How do I know you'll even show up?"

"How do I know I'll get paid if I do?" she countered.

He removed a billfold from his coat pocket and counted out three ten-dollar goldbacks. She folded the bills, thanked him graciously and tucked them into her handbag.

"I'll be here at ten tomorrow. Thank you very much, Mr. Duncan." She turned to Mr. Lawlor, "I liked dancing with you. You're very nimble on your feet and you have perfect rhythm."

She walked along the stage and disappeared into the wings. Duncan looked at Lawlor and chuckled. "You know, if she looks as good in tights as she dances, she's going to do well."

"If she dances as well as she'll likely look in tights, she'll be a sensation," Lawlor said. "And she's got the nerve to make it all go. You may have picked a winner here, Rudy. Be sure to let me dance with her."

"If she's that good, I'll let her lead the company. Our routines have been awful and they have to get better or I'll lose my shirt. Maybe she could even teach the others."

"If she can, we got us a winner."

"Yeah, provided I can hold on to her." Duncan was eyeing the darkened wing Phoebe had just passed through. A winner, Lawlor had said. Duncan nodded. She had it. They were easy to spot. Now if she only showed up.

─────────────── *thirteen* ───────────────

Phoebe placed the gift-wrapped plush box on the dinner plate and covered it with a handkerchief. She returned to the two-burner gas range and stirred the stew she'd made out of expensive beef. She would have liked to give him a thick steak, but it was impossible to cook on this stove.

When Tom returned, weary and disgusted with the fruitless day, she greeted him with a warm kiss and a hug and tried to keep from showing her enthusiasm for the news she had for him.

"No luck?" she asked.

"I don't think they give a damn whether they ever hire me," he said. "Frankly, Phoebe, I don't know what to do."

"Well, sit down and eat your supper and then we'll talk about it."

He washed and came out of the bathroom drying his hands. He caught a glimpse of the purple plush box, only partly concealed. He picked it up, looked at Phoebe's smiling face. He opened it and took out the gold pocket watch. He snapped open the case and read the time aloud. Then he looked at Phoebe again, sorely puzzled.

"Do you like it?" she asked. "I know your old watch wasn't keeping good time. This is an Elgin. It's fourteen-karat gold. They said it is a fine watch. It cost twelve dollars."

"Have you been keeping money . . . ? No! You asked Virginia."

"Neither, Tom," she said, and felt quite dizzy with excitement. "It's from my first two weeks' pay."

"Your 'pay'." His eyes shifted away from her. Embarrassed color flooded his face. "You got a job as a clerk in a store. Phoebe, you don't know enough about handling money or writing up sales slips."

"It's not work in a store. It's—"

"If you got work sewing in a millinery store or a dress shop, you'll take this watch back and get your money refunded. That kind of work will make you old before your time. It's not fit for anyone. The places are poorly lit, they're unventilated and they work you till all hours."

She looked at the watch in the open case as she took it from Tom's hand. "I thought it was so beautiful and you do need a watch that keeps time."

"Don't you understand? We can't afford it. What in the world possessed you to do such a thing? Or more important—what kind of work did you get?"

"I'm to—be an actress. I'm going to dance—on the stage."

He stared at her silently for a moment, then turned and spoke with his back to her. "You're out of your mind. You've no idea of what being an actress means. I forbid it, Phoebe." He turned back, his face now alight with anger. "Do you hear me? I forbid you to have anything to do with the theater. The people connected with it have no morals."

"Tell me this, Tom," she said. "We're two weeks behind in the rent. Where will we get it? What will we do if they turn us out?"

"There's Virginia." He said it hesitantly, as if the very thought made him uncomfortable.

"Absolutely not," she said. "You wouldn't have considered that before."

"Things are different now." His eyes avoided hers.

"I will write and ask for our fare back to the plantation. We'll be welcome and we can be a part of it. Have an equal share. Virginia told me that."

"I prefer living in the North."

"What about your parents? Won't they loan us enough to tide us over?"

"How can I tell them I've not found work?"

"They're your parents. Surely they'd understand."

"It's out of the question."

"Well, then . . ." Her hands raised and fell to her sides.

He sat down and buried his head in his hands. "You'll regret the day you did this, Phoebe. How do you, in heaven's name, hope to get along in the theater, when you know nothing about it?"

"I know what I need to know," she said logically. "I can dance and both Mr. Duncan and Mr. Lawlor said I did very well."

He got up and started pacing the floor distractedly. "They're going to put you out there on the stage in tights . . . displaying your body."

"What's wrong with my body? You certainly approved of it. You liked my dancing too. You told me so."

"No," he said abruptly, as if to end the discussion. "No, Phoebe. You can't do this. I'll not allow it."

"As I said, show me where our rent money is coming from and I'll back out of the whole thing. But I don't want to back out of that and then be compelled to back out of this . . . this so-called flat. And we do like to eat, both of us."

"I've still a little left out of the hundred . . ."

"And when that's gone—as it will be in a short time—then what? We'll be in the same predicament. But with what you have left of that hundred dollars and the money I have, we can get along until I'm paid again. We can go on from there. You can take your time looking for work and maybe you could even change your profession for something better. All we need is time, darling. A little time to get our bearings. Besides, I love dancing, and to be paid for it . . . I can't imagine getting money for what I love doing."

"You'll not become an actress," he said flatly. "Not as long as you're my wife."

"Be reasonable," she pleaded. "We had no money and you can't find work. Now we have enough to pay this month's rent and next month's as well and even have a little left over."

"No," he said. "We've exhausted the subject. You know my feelings on the matter. Please respect them."

Phoebe eased herself onto the bed. "I'm trying to reason with you. What's wrong with my going on the stage?"

"Everything in the world is wrong with it. You don't know what those people are like. The actresses are whores. The men only want to sleep with the actresses or any other woman they can find. And the people who run the shows are the worst of all.''

"Mr. Duncan is a perfect gentleman,'' she said with some heat. "Besides, I should think you'd trust me.''

"I trust you. I don't trust Mr. Duncan. Who is he?''

"I think he owns the show. Tom, it's the minstrel show you told me about. At the Bowery Theater. You wanted to take me there, remember? You wouldn't take me to a show that was . . . was . . . distasteful. Or would you?''

"Of course not,'' he said impatiently. "How'd you get mixed up in this anyway?''

"I was out for a walk. I passed the theater and I recalled what you told me about the show so I stopped to look at the posters in the lobby. The more I looked at them, the more interested I became so I just . . . went around . . . to the stage door. It was open. I walked in and there was a man named Lawlor dancing on the stage. It was a rehearsal, I think.''

He eyed her disdainfully. "And they talked you into joining. You, an amateur. That proves you know nothing about show business. Don't you know what they're going to want from you?''

"Tom, I resent that. I think you're wrong. All wrong.''

He sat down heavily. "Of all the goddamn fool things for you to do . . .''

"Well,'' she said, almost defiantly, "I've done it.''

"If you do this, it'll be against my wishes,'' he said.

She noted his tone was less adamant. She could commiserate with him. His pride had been struck a severe blow. Nonetheless, she had to bear in mind their situation was desperate.

"I swear that if anything happens which I think is not right, I'll walk out of that theater immediately. But I don't think it will. I don't think the actors Mr. Duncan would hire are that way. Most of them are like me. New at this and trying to make good. They have no time for nonsense or pestering.''

"Don't use that word. It smacks of slavery.''

She couldn't dispute that. "Then we won't talk about it again until after I try out. Maybe I'll fall on my face, but I do want to try, Tom. Please understand. Sometimes I think I was, well . . . made to dance. I love it so. At Niblo's Garden I almost went onstage and showed those two people how it should be done. It made me heartsick to see the way they tried to dance, and they're supposed to be good. Mr. Duncan said so."

"In fairness, I realize it isn't right for me to try to stop you. Nor can I take you to the whipping shed and cure you of this crazy idea. You'll have to cure yourself and all I hope is you're not hurt in the process. And you're right. We'll not talk about it again."

"Thank you," she said gratefully. "If you're right, I'll be the first to admit it. Now tell me how you like the watch. I wanted it to be a surprise."

"It certainly was a surprise," he said soberly. "And I appreciate it. Mine is worthless. Thank you, my dear. But from here on, I'll buy my own watches and anything else I need."

She got up and began to serve the food, which had been slowly growing cold on the unlit stove. They ate, mostly in silence. That night Phoebe lay silently beside Tom, who turned and tossed half the night. She longed for the comfort of his arm around her. She'd wanted him to be proud that her resourcefulness had given them a new lease on life. Instead, it had only embittered him.

She was at the theater early. So early the stage door wasn't even unlocked so she sat down on the steps to wait. A doorkeeper finally appeared. Her quiet, sincere manner plus her beauty convinced him she was going to be part of the show. Then the work began. She had no idea how much was involved in setting up a new show, especially one that wasn't familiar to the theater-going public. A great deal of money was spent on it. Phoebe was accepted readily by the others in the large cast with a greeting and a friendly smile, but she knew she had to prove her worth. She did that when she took center stage and showed how to do the Jim Crow. Everything stopped. Before the morning was over, she was instructing the cast on how to take part in the Shout and the Cakewalk. They didn't stop for dinner and even went right on through until after the supper hour. She didn't even realize it was so late.

She returned to the one-room flat with some anxiety, but Tom was napping and she moved quietly to prepare supper. At the table, she hesitated a moment before waking him. She regarded his sleeping form, then went over and kissed him lightly on the brow, awakening him.

"Do you want to hear how it went?" she asked, speaking close to his ear.

"No," he said curtly. "I don't give a damn how it went."

"Thank you," she said quietly. "I always enjoy encouragement. But I can't help but be proud of how it turned out. I'm to do a featured solo and I think I'm going to get more money if the show goes over."

"That's great." He spoke without enthusiasm.

"Come and eat." He followed her to the table and by the time she sat down opposite him, he was already wolfing his food. She laid down her fork, the hurt inside her now so great she could no longer ignore it. "For the first time since we married, I wish we had a flat with two rooms so I could go into the other one and have a good cry."

He paused and looked across the table at her somber features. His expression softened as he set down his coffee cup. "I'm sorry I was such a prig. You're right about the predicament we're in and you're right in saying we have to find money somewhere. Tell you what. I'll buy an orchestra ticket for the opening show."

She literally flew around the table and almost upset him by depositing herself on his lap. She hugged and kissed him until his arms went around her and he returned her caresses and kisses.

Finally he asked huskily, "Shall we make love or eat?"

She slipped free of his arms. "We'll eat first. Then we'll make love."

"Whatever you say." He escorted her back to her place at the table, seated her, then resumed his chair. "Tell me about the show."

She beamed. Through the rest of the meal he listened to her talk about the theater, the dancing, the rehearsals, the type of music they used and the amount she was going to get, though she didn't dwell on that. He even asked a few questions. Afterward they made love. He hoped she didn't realize how appalled he was, and how helpless he felt. Gnawing at the back of his mind was the thought that she was going to be an outstanding success. He wondered how he could cope with that.

Passing the mailboxes built in the lobby the next morning, Phoebe saw the white envelope through the slits in the lid of their box, but she didn't have a key. There was only one—Tom's. The mail must have been delivered after he'd left. She was looking forward to a letter from Valcour and she could barely wait until she was able to write her family that she was going on the stage as a dancer. The thought that she really had a family warmed her.

It was a final dress rehearsal with all the props and costumes except for blackface. The large company was fun to work with, from the initial walk-around when the curtain went up, to the final parade at the end of the show. She laughed at the jokes between the end men and the interlocutor, for they were new and good. The singing was excellent and the numbers traditional, but always well liked by any audience, and had been a part of minstrel shows during the forty or more years of their existence.

During the middle of the show she danced with Bert Lawlor but, wisely, he graciously and expertly moved away from her and then returned to his chair, leaving her to finish the number as a solo. With the full orchestra and half a dozen banjos onstage supplying music, she knew she was better than ever. Her dancing could have been more polished but the primitiveness of the steps made that unnecessary. With practice she would improve so she could perform other dances and not devote herself exclusively to the Negro rhythms.

Rudy Duncan applauded her efforts and kissed her a bit too warmly after the rehearsal, though she'd observed stage folk kissed without it having any meaning. "You're going to be very good," he predicted. "Perhaps too good to help me."

"I don't know what you mean by that, Mr. Duncan," she said.

"You're that good, somebody is going to see you dance and take you away from me. I won't be able to afford the money they'll offer you."

"Whom do you mean by 'they'?" she asked, still strictly an amateur concerning the business aspects of the stage.

"The big fellows who run big shows. For instance, they're rehearsing right now for a new kind of show at Wallack's Theater over on Broadway. It's a mixture of a play with music. Dancing and singing all through the drama. It's going to be called *The Black*

Crook and if I know anything about the theater, it's going to be the biggest success in years."

"You mean they might want me?" she asked. "Oh, no! How could they? I've not even performed once before an audience."

"You will tomorrow night, Phoebe. I don't say they'll pick you, because I don't know if they could use you in that kind of show, but if they can, I'll wager they'll approach you."

"I'll not take another job until you say I may leave your show, Mr. Duncan. In good conscience, I couldn't. You had enough faith in me to give me a chance."

"Well, I'm grateful to hear that. Beginning tomorrow you'll be paid twenty-five dollars a week and it may go much higher if you become the hit I think you'll be. Maybe I can't meet the kind of money those others pay, but I'll go as high as I can, so you can look forward to a very bright future, my dear."

He patted her hand and touched her cheek in something more than a friendly way. "Oh, your costume came. The seamstress will give you a fitting."

By the end of the day she was as tired as anyone in the troupe but it was a kind of exhaustion that was also exhilarating. She knew she wouldn't sleep that night, though she realized how much she needed rest.

Tom was reading a newspaper when she returned. He looked up, grunted a greeting and buried his face in the newspaper again. He'd already forgotten their joy of last night. Phoebe was determined that his negative attitude would not interfere with her new career, so she paid as little attention to his moods as possible.

"Was there a letter from Valcour, Tom?" she asked as she removed the hatpin from her hat.

" 'Letter'?" he asked. "There wasn't any mail."

"I was sure I saw an envelope in the box on my way out this morning."

"You must have been mistaken. How'd it go today?"

"We're ready for the opening," she said. "It's going to be a very good show. And I'm to be featured. Imagine that? Oh, yes, I've been given a raise to twenty-five dollars a week, even before the show opens. It was a lucky day when I stopped by that theater. It's like a whole new life is opening up for me.''

He laid aside the newspaper. "I'll say one thing, even if I don't approve of it. You are a marvelous dancer—especially those slave dances. If you dance like you did that night on Valcour, you'll bring the house down.''

"Do you really think so?'' she asked, startled by his unexpected support.

"I don't know if I'm going to be able to stand it, sitting in the audience while you're teasing all the men in the theater. That's what the dance is—a tease.''

"All dances are sensual,'' she said. "Every movement is made to stimulate the senses. When the music starts, I want to move with it. Sometimes I feel I'm going to burst—but when I dance, I release my pent-up emotions. Darling, please try to accept this because I have to go through with it.''

"You surely do,'' he said good-naturedly. "I can't find any work. There seem to be ten teachers to every classroom. I don't know what's happened. Before the war I had no trouble, but now . . .'' he shrugged, but gave her a smile of acceptance of his situation.

"Now you can take your time until you find a position you really like,'' she said. She opened the icebox and uttered a sigh of exasperation. "We're out of milk. Tom, will you run down to the store?''

"Of course,'' he said. He moved to her side and kissed her on the lips. "Especially since I drank it all when I got home. I'll be right back.''

"It's chilly,'' she warned. "Better take your coat.''

"It's just across the street. I don't need a coat.''

As he left the room, she picked up his coat, returned it to the closet on a hanger, but as she hung it up she saw a letter inside the inner pocket. For a moment she hesitated. He was entitled to the privacy of his own mail, but she wondered why he had denied the existence of a letter she had seen in the mailbox. She removed it. The return address was that of his parents in New England. She removed the double sheet of paper, and started to read the letter. A stab of pain shot through her after the first sentence. She read only a few lines before tears blinded her and she could read no more. She quickly slipped the letter back in its envelope and replaced it in his pocket.

She hurried to the sink, doused her eyes with cold water and patted them dry with a towel. She was determined to keep her composure. The letter was from his parents, asking why he hadn't brought his bride home. They were anxiously awaiting the opportunity to meet her. Also, since he'd had no luck in securing a position in New York City, there were openings in his hometown. His father had made inquiries and learned that there'd be a class available for him. In fact, there were several openings. Also, with his father's political connections, in time he could easily move up to the top, supervising all education in the state. Or, if he preferred, he could teach at a university.

She finally knew why he didn't want to bring her to his home. He was afraid to have his parents meet her, even though there wasn't the slightest physical evidence she wasn't all white.

Apparently her heritage embarrassed him; made him fearful that, in some way, the knowledge that he'd married a black might become known. She'd told him the truth about herself. That she was the daughter of a union between a slave and a plantation owner. A lusting plantation owner, she thought, though without bitterness. She knew now that Tom regretted he'd married her, but he was too much the gentleman to admit it or to leave her.

She hadn't thought that race mattered so much in the North. She still wasn't certain and knew no one to ask. She'd not dare bring up the subject to Tom.

She thought back to the double wedding. It had been performed by a chaplain in the Northern army. She didn't even know if he was aware of her heritage. It hadn't bothered her at the time because Tom had been insistent that it was of no importance. She'd glowed in the knowledge that he'd loved her in spite of the fact she wasn't all white. Yet she remembered the large article in the Charleston paper concerning Virginia's marriage to Elias. Despite the scarcity of paper, a full column had been devoted to it, relating the history of the Hammond family, their social background, the fact that Virginia had a sister and brother.

No mention had been made of Phoebe. She wondered if the war had protected the Hammonds from the scandal of having anyone learn there was another member of the family who wasn't recognized. Virginia herself had learned it only just before the war. The Hammonds, along with the other families, had had to leave the island to escape the Yankees. The few who had remained lost their homes, which were sold to the carpetbaggers for back taxes. Since they were on the island at the time of the wedding, it was possible they carried the story back to the mainland when they had to depart.

But Virginia had been fair-minded. She'd offered to share what little they had with Phoebe and Tom. Phoebe was grateful, but relieved when Tom refused. She wanted to go North. She knew that, despite the end of slavery, she'd never be accepted in the South. She had no illusions about that. But in the North she'd be treated as an equal. Marse Hammond had seen to it she was as well educated as Virginia. Her skin was almost as fair.

She still loved Tom. She was never more certain of anything in her life. But with him it may have been an infatuation. The beauty and enchantment of the island had cast a spell over him. She'd seen what war could do to people. Some weathered it; some came out of it stronger, while others it destroyed. She knew she was seeking excuses for him. Yet nothing could excuse the fact that if he went home, he had a classroom waiting for him along with promotions and he took no advantage of this. She could think of no reason for it except that he was afraid to expose himself to the possibility that someone would discover she was not white.

He'd also lied to her about his parents not knowing he couldn't find work. The letter proved he'd written to them, using her as an excuse. She made up her mind at that moment to never let him discover she knew the truth. Perhaps, if she was successful, he'd forget his fears. With success, she'd be accepted everywhere. In that case, his parents couldn't object to her.

She heard him coming down the hall and she returned to her cooking, hoping he'd not notice her eyes, still tear-rimmed. He handed her the bottle of milk and kissed her fondly. She didn't turn away. She knew she must go on as if nothing had changed. It had to be that way. She managed to smile and at the table she talked about her dancing. She kept up a constant flow of words to hide the rage and grief she was still filled with. She wished profoundly that she had never read that letter. Because no matter how devoted he was, it would never again be the same.

She claimed sheer exhaustion that night and went to bed early. It was an awful night. She couldn't toss and turn as she wanted to. That might relieve some of the tension in her, but Tom would want to know the reason for her nervousness. So she lay quietly and made herself think about the dancing. It helped. Halfway through the night she must have fallen asleep.

As she stepped through the stage door the next morning, her troubles dissipated. The thought flashed through her mind that this was her life. It didn't matter what Tom thought or did about it. She was determined to show him that she could be what she wanted to be. An important actress, a dancer who would someday be famous. The anger and hurt vanished, to be replaced by a happy glow she hadn't felt in some time.

In the big dressing room she sat before a mirror while the excitement swirled about her. She did her part in talking about the show, but she was mainly concerned with putting on blackface. For the entire cast in a minstrel show wore blackface.

Suddenly she burst into laughter, lifting her spirits even higher, lessening the opening night nervousness. She was part Negro and here she was daubing burned cork all over her face and neck. She was a little uncertain as to how the Shout would go over in the red pants and jacket costume. She'd always done it in bare feet. Then she realized she must capture the audience's attention so completely that they could forget the inappropriate costume and see her in the open, barefoot, wearing some kind of dress that outlined her slender curves as she moved her body. Slowly at first, then sensually, gradually increasing the tempo, making every movement count until it mounted to a passionate pitch. At the end, she fell on her knees and let her head rest on them.

A smile touched her lips when she thought back to what really happened at the end of the Shout. Couples grabbed each other's hands and ran into the forest. They were never interfered with by the plantation owners. They knew that to give them a barrel of whiskey along with food, then let them dance their traditional dances, would arouse them and in the end, produce babies. What their masters called suckers. What Phoebe didn't realize was that she had taught herself the first lesson in show business. She must capture the audience; make them believe the illusion is real. Make them want more and more.

She drew on white gloves and was ready before the others had completed their makeup. Phoebe said, "When we go into the Shout, I must have a lot of hand clapping and there must be stomping of feet. It's a Negro dance and it has to be accompanied by a lot of noise. There'll be banjos playing, so you can pick up the rhythm. Just try to imagine that you're somewhere in Africa and this is a ritual dance. It's done in the open and dedicated to whatever gods they worshiped there. It's a dance to arouse the emotions. But it's a joyous dance, like the Cakewalk. In that, you do a lot of strutting. Don't be afraid to exaggerate the strutting. Throw your shoulders back, lift up your chin and keep your feet moving."

Some asked questions, which she answered knowledgeably. Half an hour before curtain Rudy Duncan came in to wish them all well and to exhort them to do their best. Their future as well as his depended on it. He informed them the theater was sold out and there were critics and reporters in the audience.

"They'll tear this show apart if it's not good," Duncan warned. "Minstrel shows have been around too long and they've slipped in favor, but that's because up to now none of them have been very good. I believe we're going to surprise them. Go out there and back me up."

As she walked toward the wings, Bert fell in step with her and reached for her hand as if to lend assurance, which she didn't need. Not now. There was too much determination inside her to make her even slightly nervous. She believed that if she was sure she'd be good, she would be.

The entrance parade began as the curtain was raised. Phoebe, just another player in blackface, white gloves and a gaudy red uniform, tried to peer beyond the footlights to look for Tom. She was still not certain he would come. She couldn't see him, for the gas footlights were strong enough to blot out the audience.

The first part of the show was lively, the comedy came off well. The audience seemed to be in a mood to accept the show.

Phoebe did her bit in the ensemble, slapping the tambourine, singing with the chorus of voices and all the while her feet kept tapping to the music. By the time her turn came, she was more than ready.

First she danced with Bert, a slow, soft shoe that he had taught her. It held the audience well, for their timing was perfect and they moved in unison with each other. It was almost as if one person was dancing or they were joined together in some way. After the applause, Bert resumed his chair, leaving the stage to her. Phoebe stood center stage, motionless, facing the audience while the others in the dance left their seats and to the soft strain of a brisk tune trotted in line until they had formed a circle around her.

Then all music stopped and there were a few moments of silence. Slowly, Phoebe's arms raised along with her head and she held the pose for three seconds. Then her mouth opened and she uttered a loud, lonely cry—almost a dirge. The banjos started strumming softly, the feet of the dancers started stomping slowly. Then, as the banjos became louder, the stomping increased and the circle began a slow, shuffling movement around Phoebe, who still stood motionless. As the circle around her quickened their steps, she began her slow, sensual movements. First with her arms, then moving her legs, her hips, her torso. When she started to clap her hands, the circle around her stopped and opened in the front of the stage so the audience could view her completely. When her body began to jerk and twitch in a motion that made her quiver from head to feet, the dancers started to clap, slowly at first, then faster. Her legs were spread slightly and her knees bent. She was in constant motion, so much so her body was a blur as it shivered and shook. Her torso undulated in violent spasms. All the while she emitted cries that seemed to emanate from deep in the jungle. She had forgotten she was on a stage. Now she was a slave and part of a ceremony and celebration. She knew it and so did the audience. The applause had started even before she gave a final spasm, fell to her knees and let her head rest on them.

The noise in the theater was deafening. For a moment she didn't know what it was or where she was. But then she came to her senses and got to her feet gracefully. She acknowledged the thunderous applause with a gracious bow. Even the circle of dancers around her joined in the applause, after which they resumed their seats.

The audience wouldn't stop applauding, shouting demands of "more." She was still dizzy from the Shout, but she'd arranged for an encore at Rudy Duncan's demand, though she hadn't expected to get one. She went into the intricate steps of Rockin' de Heel. It was a well-known number, but she surpassed anything seen on the stage and, once again, the applause was deafening. Her heart pounded madly, not so much from her exertions, but because the applause from her solo had equaled that which followed her rendition of the Shout.

Phoebe had been prepared for a limited success, though not in the intensity with which it came. The cast gathered around her after the curtain fell and their enthusiasm rivaled hers. Bert hugged and kissed her.

"You've got it," he assured her. "Nobody ever danced like that before. You were born to dance. You've got rhythm in your blood."

She laughed. Nothing could upset her now. Rudy Duncan added his praises and talked about a contract. She'd even been assigned a new dressing room during her performance. One reserved for a featured player. Rudy escorted her to the door that had her name on it, written in crayon. He patted her cheek, thanked her and walked away.

Phoebe opened the door, still filled with the thrill of the applause. To her astonishment, Tom was there, awkwardly holding a bouquet of roses. His presence and the expression of pride on his face made her happiness complete. She literally flew into his arms. Her joy was so boundless, she never even gave a thought to the letter. Some of her blackface smeared his cheek and they both laughed as she removed it with cold cream. So far everyone had been kept away from the dressing room while she changed and substituted regular makeup for the blackface.

"You," Tom said, and proudly too, "are going to be one of the most famous dancers in the business. I never saw such dancing, and neither has anyone else. I heard some reporters, maybe they were critics, saying you were great."

"Thanks, my love," she said gratefully. "I hoped they'd like my dancing. But your approval means more to me than anything else."

Tom held her to him. "What's going to be difficult is that from now on I'll have to walk in your shadow, but I swear I won't mind or resent it in any way. Talent like yours comes along once in a lifetime. It's unfair for you not to share it with the public. They're entitled to enjoy it as much as you enjoy performing for them. And you do, don't you."

"I love it, Tom," she said honestly. "But you'll always come first. Believe that. Hold it in your heart as I hold it in mine."

They kissed and Phoebe made him sit down until she changed.

There was a party after the show. It hadn't been intended to be lavish, but it turned out that Duncan had sent out for food and drink. The theater rang with laughter and the conversations bounced off the ceiling and walls until it became one long, insistent roar of sound.

People whom Phoebe knew to be important without actually knowing who they were added their congratulations. Her mind was in a whirl before the party ended. There was a carriage to take them home and when they entered the shabby one room, they laughed, hugged each other and swore this would be their last night in this room.

The days that followed were equally exciting. For the first time in her life, Phoebe saw her photograph in the newspapers. She was acclaimed as a coming great performer. There wasn't a single line of adverse comment.

They immediately moved to a five-room flat well uptown, near Thirty-fourth Street. They even hired a maid to come in by the day. At her insistence, Tom gave up hunting a job and settled down to manage her affairs. He was excellent at it and money was coming in beyond their wildest expectations. There were offers, too, of better shows now in the making, but Phoebe turned them down. She would remain with Rudy Duncan until the minstrel show closed. She owed him that, and more.

Still lurking deeply in her heart was the memory of that letter from Tom's parents. For now, she was much too busy. She wondered, with this new found and growing fame, if it would change his mind and he would take her home to meet his parents. Perhaps her fame would now overshadow the strain of a black heritage in her blood. She still didn't know, but hoped it would.

She was content to let everything stand as it was. She knew only that she loved Tom.

On the waterfront of New York City, a husky-looking black man stood at the bar of a saloon that catered only to Negroes who were the stevedores working the docks.

This black man was staring at a newspaper with such intentness he signaled for another drink without raising his head.

"Pay for the last one and the others you owe for," the bartender said.

The black man's lips parted in a huge, glistening smile. "Ain't no reason fo' yo' to git excited now. Ah'm goin' to git mahse'f 'nuff money to buy the place."

"What do you mean by that, Tobal?"

"Means whut Ah says. Jes' now Ah foun' me a nice bankroll. Ain't sayin' nothin' mo', but Ah craves 'nothuh drink. Mah shoulduh aches bad, it do. Nevah did get the bullet out after Ah was shot."

fourteen

It was a cold, bleak January day on Valcour. Lenore Hammond, dressed in black, even to a black veil that concealed her face, walked slowly along the path between the old slave cabins. Cradled in one bent arm was a bouquet of sorry-looking flowers, but she held them as if they were precious, or breakable. She walked with her head held high and each step she took was slow and funereal, almost like someone walking behind a casket.

Inside the low frame building that had once been used as a hospital and birthing house, Nanine stood beside one of the windows and watched her mother pass by. Lenore never glanced in Nanine's direction.

"There she goes," Nanine said, her tone one of resignation. "Every day she marches by on her way to Marty's grave. And makes very certain we see her."

Miles Rutledge occupied the bed, the head of which was raised on blocks so he could sit up in comfort. He said, "I'd call it devotion, wouldn't you?"

"Not exactly," Nanine said. "I'm not saying Mama didn't love Marty. She worshiped him. He was her favorite. But she isn't passing by dressed in black every day at the same time to honor Marty in death. She's doing it partly to remind you that Marty met his death at your hands, and to let me know she considers me in the same category as you because I insisted you be brought to Valcour for rest and treatment."

"I still think you did the wrong thing in bringing me here so soon after I shot Marty. I can understand their resentment."

"They're intolerant and unkind. Especially Virginia. I'm sorry Marty's dead. But she knows he was drinking himself into the gutter. She also knows how she nagged him to sell the plantation. She's never thought she might be responsible for all that happened."

"Do you think she is?" Miles asked softly.

Nanine regarded the gentle figure propped up on pillows and smiled reluctantly. "Of course not. But you weren't either."

"I shot the pistol, my dear," Miles said softly. "That's something I'll never forget."

"I wish Phoebe were here," Nanine said, a smile touching her mouth. "She'd understand."

Miles stared with pleasure at the soft curve of her lips. "How lovely your smile is," he observed. "You are beautiful."

"Oh, Miles," Nanine replied with a touch of reproach, "I'm not."

"Yes, you are, my darling," he said. "And please forgive the endearment. Your mere presence enchants me."

Nanine colored prettily. "No one ever said anything like that to me before."

"Then it's way overdue," he said, chuckling softly.

She went over to the bed and rested her hand over his. "Your spirits are much brighter than when I met you. I think my nursing is doing you good."

"You know it is," he replied. "I think I'm going to owe you my life. But I feel bad that I've come between you and your sister."

"She's very spirited and very stubborn. Just as Marty was. She'll come to her senses." Nanine paused, then added, "I also think she's not got over the fact that I stood up to her. I don't believe I ever did before. Not in anything of importance. Perhaps because nothing of importance ever happened to me before. I mean you, Miles. And I don't feel the least bit embarrassed by it."

"Do you think she'll forgive you?" he asked seriously.

Nanine's smile was thoughtful. "She hated Phoebe once. Now, no one would dare say a belittling thing about her in front of Virginia."

"Why should she hate her sister?" he asked.

"Because her mama was a slave. Papa sired Phoebe. She's almost as white as we are. She's as beautiful as Virginia. They have the same violet eyes and resemble one another closely, though Phoebe's hair is dark, of course. With a soft, loose curl. You'll meet her one day."

"I'm looking forward to it."

"She's Virginia's age. In fact, Papa saw to it that they were educated together."

"Sorry I couldn't have met your father. In spite of his transgressions, I know I'd have liked him."

"You would have," Nanine affirmed. "He had to have a woman. I'm old enough to know now that Mama didn't wish to bed with him, though she loved him. She also loved the material goods he bestowed on her. He indulged her as he did Virginia. And me."

"I'm eager to get out of this bed so I can indulge you."

Nanine sat in the chair alongside the bed. "What Virginia ought to realize is that you could have stopped payment on the draft you gave Marty for the sale of our mainland plantation. Without that money she'd never be able to put her plan into motion. According to Elias, it's already working."

"Tell me about it," Miles said. "I love listening to you talk."

She leaned forward and kissed his cheek. She felt very warm toward this too thin man who, she well realized, might be slowly dying despite what she was doing for him.

"I mean it, Nan," he said. "I can't believe I have you with me each day."

"What was your father like?"

Miles laughed. "He was very wealthy and one of the few not wiped out because of the war. Papa had an uncanny way of looking into the future."

"Now don't tell me he was a soothsayer," Nanine said jokingly.

"I didn't mean it that way. Yet he did foresee a great deal. Before the war broke out, he used to tell me while he favored and loved the Confederacy, he believed those who chose rebellion were wrong. Not because he didn't think they should fight for their rights, but any nation that rebels and courts war is foolish unless it has a good chance of winning, which Papa doubted the Confederacy had. The

245

North had too many people, too many factories, too much money. He thought the war was unnecessary; that the South could have gotten what it wanted by negotiation."

"There were too many hotheads," Nanine agreed. "Maybe on both sides. Here on Valcour the attitude was all for war and glory. The young men from the islands around Valcour came here to march and drill. They looked handsome in their uniforms. They were confident that they could win. The cemetery that Mama is visiting now bears mighty good proof of how wrong they were."

"Well, anyway, my father put a great deal of money in Northern banks, where it was safe and drawing interest. It's now available to me, for he died during the war. My mother died long before the shooting began."

Nanine returned to the window. "Mama's coming back. Oh, Miles, she's behaving so childishly. That bouquet she carries is made of dried flowers and she carries it back from the grave each day, hiding it under her coat."

"If it relieves her sorrow, let her do it," Miles said tolerantly. "So long as I have you close by, I could put up with anything."

"Thanks, you dear man," Nanine said softly. "As for Mama, I couldn't stop her. Stubbornness is a very strong trait in our family."

He eyed her curiously. "I doubt you ever rebelled before."

"Perhaps because I never had anything to rebel about." She returned to the bedside. "Enough talk about me. I notice a little color in your cheeks. Are you feeling better?"

"Yes. At least, that's what I tell myself. Certainly you've done everything possible to improve my physical condition. My mental condition is now perfect, thanks to you."

"Another thing—you get up for a while each day." Nanine's smile was one of encouragement. "You're going to get better. You're going to be able to go to the plantation you paid so dearly for, and get it going this spring."

"What do I know about raising cotton?" he said with a derisive laugh. "I bought the place because with it I thought I might get well with an abundance of fresh air and the food I'd grow there. I know now it was a fallacy. After what happened from that cursed duel, I don't believe I could set foot on it."

"You're going to run it one day," she said. "That plantation is far too valuable to lie fallow as it has been since the war began. It's going to be a challenge for you to face."

"I don't want it," he said.

"Miles, that property is worth a fortune. Getting it into operation will help the South recover. You must do something about it. You must forget what happened. That plantation is your future."

"You run it," he said.

"Me? I can't do that. Besides, I've you to take care of and that's more important to me."

"Then let Virginia handle it. That is, if she'll accept this from the man who she says murdered her brother. And," he added, "stole her sister away."

"She will insist on shares . . ."

"She can have the damn place, Nan. Try to understand. I bought it on a whim and it turned out to be a disaster. I want nothing to do with it."

"If she'll let me talk to her, I'll find out what she thinks. There's a lot to be worked out because I'm not going to let you be cheated."

"Do whatever you wish. You're right about it helping the South. Would you mind now if I take a nap? That's one thing I do well, nap whenever I get the chance."

She drew the blanket up around him, raised his head and fluffed the pillows. Before she was done, his eyes closed and he was asleep. Nanine sat beside the bed for half an hour, mulling over the strange proposition he had made. Virginia and Elias could run the old plantation very well and it would be even more profitable than it had been in the days when Nanine's father ran it. She decided to put it up to Virginia at once, before the idea had a chance to cool. Making certain Miles was comfortable, she put on her heavy coat and covered her head with a woolen shawl.

She reached the mansion and walked up the porch steps. It had been a long time since she'd entered the house. She didn't even want to go in. If it hadn't been that Miles had suggested it, she'd not have come near the place.

She found Elias seated in the drawing room, alone. He rose quickly, startled at her appearance, but he greeted her with a light embrace and a kiss on the cheek.

quickly, startled at her appearance, but he greeted her with a light embrace and a kiss on the cheek.

"You look great," he said. "How is Miles?"

"I'm not sure. He seems cheerful sometimes, morose at other times. His health seems to be improving, but slowly. Much more slowly than it did with me, but then I think he was far sicker when he came to the island than I had ever been."

"I believe you're right," Elias agreed thoughtfully. "Virgie is going to raise the roof when she finds you here. Whatever possessed you to come?"

"I've some important news. Tell me, have you heard from Phoebe?"

"You'll never believe it, but she went on the stage and has become famous for her dancing. Imagine, getting fame and a lot of money for doing something she loves to do. And does so well."

Nanine beamed. "Oh, Elias, that's wonderful news."

They heard Virginia's firm steps coming down the stairs from the second floor. Nanine turned to face the door. Virginia glanced at her casually as she entered the drawing room.

"What do you want?" she asked coldly.

"Virgie, mind your manners. This is your sister," Elias said sternly.

"She's helping a man who murdered our brother and that act severs any relationship between us as far as I'm concerned."

"Will you sit down and let me explain something that is of importance to us," Nanine said. "It's not only important, it's a business arrangement that rivals any you could come up with."

"Say what you have to say," Virginia told her.

"With that attitude, I'll say nothing more." Nanine headed for the door.

"Nan," Elias begged, "please. Virgie, use your head. Nanine wouldn't come here if it wasn't important." Elias raised his voice, "Nanine, please come back."

"Not unless Virginia asks me," Nanine called from the door.

"Do come back, Nanine," Virginia called, with a tinge of sarcasm.

Nanine hesitated a moment and then remembered that Miles's

offer could benefit everyone. She walked back into the room and sat down.

"Miles doesn't want to operate the big plantation," she began.

"I suppose he wants us to take it back and return his money," Virginia said coldly. "Well, we won't."

"How you've changed," Nanine said. "There's not an ounce of compassion left in you, not even an iota of common sense. Miles wishes to turn the plantation over to us to operate."

Even Virginia was startled at that news. "What's he to gain by that?" She was suspicious, trusting neither her sister nor Miles.

"Not a thing. In my opinion, he doesn't even want any of the profits. It's the chance of a lifetime. You know what that plantation can earn."

"There's a trick to this," Virginia said. "I have to think about it."

"Don't take too long, Mrs. Birch," Nanine said serenely.

"If I accept, it changes nothing between us."

"I expected that. I also like the idea of it."

Elias, observing the verbal byplay between the sisters, had difficulty in repressing a smile.

"Find out exactly what he has in mind and have him put it in writing," Virginia said. "Then I'll consider it."

Nanine rose. "You considered it two seconds after I mentioned it and you know very well you cannot turn down an offer like this even if it's been made by the man you accuse of murdering Marty. I'll be going now."

"I'll expect to hear from you soon," Virginia said. "I have to know, one way or the other, so I can arrange for men to be hired and overseers retained to get the ground ready."

"Good day, Elias," Nanine said. Then she turned to her sister in the first signs of anger she'd shown. "One thing more, you have no right to keep Phoebe's letters from me. Elias just told me that she has become an actress. I love Phoebe too. I always did, and that's more than you can say. See that I get her letters, Virginia. Otherwise, I'll write and tell her to stop all correspondence with the family until I've moved away from here."

" 'Moved away'!" Virginia exclaimed.

Nanine smiled. "You never thought of that, did you?"

Virginia's mouth compressed angrily and she turned her back, fearful she might say something that would cause the proposition to fall through. She well knew Nanine's influence over Miles. After all, they were together constantly.

Just as Nanine turned to leave the room, Lenore entered.

"Hello, Mama," Nanine said. "I hope you're well."

"I'm not, thanks to you," Lenore retorted. "My daughter consorting with a murderer. Have you no shame? Living in the birthing house with him."

"Well, Mama, you refused to let me bring him to the house. You and Virginia. Here, you could keep an eye on me. In the birthing house, Miles and I can do as we please. And we do," she added, giving her mother a wicked smile.

"Please, Nanine," Lenore pleaded. "I beg of you not to bring scandal on the good name of Hammond. Your papa caused me enough heartache with Phoebe."

They knew Lenore had no knowledge of Phoebe until the war years. Or, if she did, had never let it be known to anyone—even her husband.

"Well, Mama, if I think the Hammond name is endangered, I'll move away from these parts." Nanine turned and left the room. No one spoke until they heard the door close.

"Do you think she was serious?" Virginia asked fearfully.

"I'm going back upstairs," Lenore said tearfully. "To think my older daughter would say such things to me."

Elias chuckled. "I had no idea Nanine had such spirit."

"She never did until she met that horrible person," Virginia said testily.

"I think," Elias mused, "if she'd had her health, you'd have had a worthy adversary."

Virginia turned on Elias. "Why must you be so contrary?"

"Why must you?" he asked. Before she could answer, he said, "Seriously, Miles is too sick for that. Nanine was needling you. The man can get out of bed for only short periods of time. He can carry on only brief conversations. You may as well resign yourself to the fact that Nanine has come into her own. I believe she cares for Miles. And if you're smart you'll keep that in mind. That is, if you're interested in the proposition she brought. And being a businesswoman, I have a feeling you're very excited about it. The only fly in the ointment is that the property belongs to Miles. You ought to stop hating him and start cultivating him. Besides, Nanine's your sister. What she's doing commands respect. She could also do with a little understanding. Grow up, Virginia. Stop being so selfish and wanting your own way all the time."

"I'm not fool enough to refuse it, if the man is mad enough to make such an offer. Just don't lecture me. I've got to go down to the Haywood plantation and hand a check to the Yankees who bought it. We're rid of our first Yankee, thank heaven. And the rest are shaky. No need for you to come along," she said when Elias rose to accompany her.

"As you wish," he said. "It's going to be dark before you get back."

"I'm not afraid on Valcour," she said.

She went upstairs for her coat. She put a scarf on her head to keep out the cold. When she left the house, she didn't even glance into the drawing room. Nor did Elias look up from his newspaper.

It was twilight as Virginia made her way along the path toward the other homes and plantations on the island. Ordinarily she would have left earlier, saddled a horse and ridden down, but this particular home and plantation was the closest to Willowbrook. She felt no fear here on her island. Which was the way she'd come to think of it. The Yankees showed no hostility, the old Negroes working on the island were trustworthy. There'd been no repetition of her facing up to a Tobal and putting a bullet into his shoulder before banishing him.

She neared some of the old buildings. The sheds, toolhouses. Her attention was drawn to the whipping shed, which was a rather large building. It should have been torn down as the last memory of the old days when it had been put to use so often. As she walked toward it, she had a strange feeling that she was not alone. That someone either followed her at a distance, or was even closer by. There was no sound, no lurking shadows to frighten her. Only this eerie feeling of apprehension. She tried to shake it off as she passed the whipping shed. Only then did she hear the sound of quick movement behind her. A hand was passed over her shoulder to clamp down on her mouth. At the same time she was caught in a grip that she couldn't break.

But she did try to squirm free, to kick, use her elbows, but all this brought only a soft laugh from the man who held her.

"Now, Miss Virginia," he said, "no call to get sassy or scared. Sure don't mean to harm you."

She went limp in the grasp of this man. She didn't try to fight any more. She actually felt a wave of anticipation go through her. Perhaps there was also fear, perhaps even relief. She wasn't sure which, but she didn't resist.

She was turned about; demanding lips pressed down on her mouth and held the kiss. She struggled briefly, mostly out of sheer surprise. Then she ceased to resist. She didn't grant him any encouragement though she was oddly inclined to do so. He let go of her and she stepped back.

"Bradley Culver," she said breathlessly, "I ought to slap your face."

"Go ahead," he invited happily. "Though you're the only woman I'd let do it. I'm sorry I scared you."

"You frightened me out of my wits. What are you doing here anyway? Have you come to loot the island again?"

"I came to see you."

"I'm not flattered, Mr. Culver."

"Didn't expect you would be. Last time I came, I got you into a mess of trouble, didn't I?"

"You nearly got me and Elias locked up."

"I'll bet Ben Bowman won't bother you again."

"Did you set fire to his house?"

"Wasn't even in the neighborhood, ma'am."

"Why did you come here, then?" she asked, knowing full well the answer.

"To see you. That's what I said, didn't I?"

"You're risking your life, Mr. Culver. If you're caught, you'll be a doomed man."

"Will you weep if they string me up?" he asked.

"I'd weep for any man who died that way."

252

"But would you shed more tears for me?"

"I . . . might, seeing I do know you now."

"Good. That pleases me. I'm sure you know that I'm in love with you."

"Mr. Culver," she protested, "that's an awful thing to say. I'm a married woman. I—"

His fingers silenced her by touching her lips. "You're married to a Yankee and that don't count nohow with me. It's like you're not married at all."

"Mr. Culver, I know you risked a great deal coming here, but please let me go and please don't come back."

"Of course I'm coming back, and when I do, I'll send word so you can meet me here. What is that shed I was hiding in?"

"The old whipping shed," she said.

"I should have known. Pity we can't use them again. The niggers in town are getting unruly, you know."

"I didn't know that. Please, I have to go . . ."

"All right, but I demand another kiss to pay me for doing all that rowing. Then I'll go peacefully, but I'll be back. You do want me to come back, don't you?"

"I never said I did. In fact, I don't want you to come back . . ."

"You're a double liar. Lying to me and to yourself. Virginia, do you think I don't know a healthy, passionate woman when I see one? That cold-blooded Yankee soldier can't show you the kind of love I can deliver. You're a woman unfulfilled and mad for the kind of love I will provide."

"If you talk that way, I swear I'll scream . . ."

"No, you won't. You'll let me hold you again and kiss you again and you'll want me back sometime when it's better for both of us. I'll stay awhile next time. You can meet me in the whipping shed when I send word."

"If you do, I swear I will not come . . ."

"Yes, you will, because you're just like me. You know what you want. In my case, maybe not quite yet, but you'll come around. Now . . ."

He put his arms around her so suddenly that she had no opportunity to try to move away. He drew her against him as hard as he could, pressing her against him. His demanding lips closed down on hers and held there. One hand moved slowly up and down her spine, making her quiver with excitement. She raised a hand and almost brought it tight around his neck, but she dropped it in time and hated herself for almost letting him know how she felt and how much she wanted him.

He let go of her. "Good night, my love. I'll give you notice when I'll be back. Think about me. You'll be on my mind until I see you again."

He stepped back, moved away and disappeared into the now fairly intense gloom. Virginia slowly exhaled a long, long sigh. She was weak and breathless and thoroughly aroused by a scoundrel. For one exciting, alluring moment, she felt that she wanted to run after him, to call him back and take refuge in those strong arms. To let herself become part of him. She never realized how much she craved this kind of excitement.

She finally got control of herself and continued on her way to the Yankee household. She made certain she was completely calm before she knocked on the door. She knew she was flushed and hoped no one would notice.

Frank Upton opened the door and stepped back to allow her entrance. He didn't invite her into the parlor and no other member of the family appeared. The lamplight was weak and it was impossible to see if there had been any damage done.

"You don't have to worry that we busted up the place," Upton said bitterly. "We'll be out of here day after tomorrow. We didn't hurt the house any."

"I'm glad of that, sir." She removed the check from her handbag and gave it to him. He studied it a moment.

"Seven hundred! You're buying this beautiful place for seven hundred dollars."

"How much did you pay for it, Mr. Upton? Not one cent more than seven hundred and you've had the advantage of living here for months, occupying the mansion and having full use of the plantation. You lost nothing in this deal."

"That's what you say. I know better. You sure can make a person feel unwanted on this island, Mrs. Birch'. I know you were behind everything that forced us to give up the property."

"I have done you a favor, sir. You couldn't grow cotton. You were unable to handle the blacks, you know nothing of our ways down here, and you'd never learn. It's to your benefit to go back to where you came from and, at least, get your money back rather than go bankrupt. In two days painters and carpenters will come in to repair whatever damage has been done. The place needs renovating anyway. Good-bye, sir."

She let herself out, walked briskly away, but as she approached the whipping shed again, she reduced her pace to a slow walk. Remembering those arms about her, the demanding lips, the utter boldness of the man. And he made no false pretenses about what he wanted and why he was coming back. She told herself the situation was impossible. What she should do, if he gave her advance notice, was to have the military here waiting to arrest him. He was a ruthless murderer, perhaps a rapist as well. He deserved no sympathy, no mercy. But, oh, she thought blissfully, he did know how to arouse a woman. She knew very well that her ideas of having him arrested were foolishness.

But she made up her mind she would not give in to him. If he came again, she would have a clear understanding with him that he was not only an outlaw doomed to hang, if he was caught, but she was a married woman who was not only faithful to the man she married, but deeply in love with him.

She picked up her pace and entered the house. Elias laid down the newspaper.

"How'd it go?" he asked.

"What? Oh—Mr. Upton. He was a bit surly about it, but he'll be gone day after tomorrow. And that, my dear husband, is number one. It's a start and it came about sooner than I expected. I'm sure he appreciated the seven hundred dollars I paid him. I'll put the deed on the desk if you wish to examine it."

"I've no sympathy for the man, even if I am a Yankee," Elias said. "He was lucky to get back what he paid for the place. How much is it really worth?"

"I'd say close to thirty thousand dollars. Meg is going to be so happy to get it back."

"You look a bit flushed," he said. "Do you feel all right? Let me see..." he touched her forehead. "Well, there's no fever. I think you ought to dress more warmly when you go out in the evening. It does get cold."

"I'm quite all right. I am a bit excited at seeing the first phase of my plans come true. Darling, I swear I won't stop until every scalawag is off this island and every family back where they belong. In their own homes."

"I hope you make it. Have you considered Nan's offer any further?"

" 'Nan'? Oh, no, I haven't. I guess I was too busy thinking about getting that family off the island." She wished desperately to change the subject to something that would bring her back to earth after her meeting with Culver. For one scant moment she considered telling Elias about his visit, but she quickly abandoned that idea. At least for now, she told herself. Eventually, though, she would.

"I haven't seen the paper. Is there anything new?" She changed the trend of their conversation abruptly.

"Two Confederate states have rejoined the Union and are going to vote for members of Congress and go to Washington."

"Being defeated is a terrible business, Elias."

"Not in this instance. I believe the South is being very wise to return to the fold. The North needs the South and certainly we need them. This will spur the raising of cotton and tobacco again. People can now go to work patching up the ruin that damn war created everywhere it touched. I'm happy at the way things are going and I hope the Carolinas develop sense enough to come back into the Union too."

"There's nothing else for us to do. Nowhere else to go," she said. "I'm not bitter, but I'm not happy, either. We did have a way of life here that was enchanting. They say it will never come back. I say it will. At least on Valcour."

Elias smiled tolerantly and took her in his arms. He drew her close as he kissed her. To his surprise, she responded immediately, her passion even surpassing his.

"Shall we go upstairs?" he asked, wondering if he was imagining it. She hadn't been so responsive since Marty's death.

"Yes." Her reply was almost a demand.

Elias swooped her up in his arms and carried her out of the room. She rained kisses on his face and neck as they went up the stairs. By the time they reached the landing, he was as impatient as she to get to their room.

What he didn't know was that it was Bradley Culver who had made her feel this way. And in their bed, it was Culver to whom she made love. Afterward, she turned away from Elias and closed her eyes tightly. She felt like a whore and knew she'd behaved like one. She'd never made love with such wild abandon. She hoped Elias would never suspect.

fifteen

Virginia's features registered satisfaction as she stood atop a small rise of land overlooking the fields. From that vantage point she could see the men at work. The fields had been furrowed, the seed planted. In a few weeks the plants would turn the now brown fields into green and, finally, into white. Valcour, particularly Willowbrook, was back to its old glory so far as earning its way was concerned.

Exhilarated by the certainty of success, she acted on impulse in entering Henry Tannet's store. It had once been occupied by the Union army sutler who supplied the occupation forces and the Negroes with bare necessities. Tannet, as he had told Virginia, had taken over the store as insurance against the failure of his cotton crop.

It was a small store, supplying mostly cotton goods, flour, lard, kerosene, candles, lamps, and a few of the fairly recently developed canned foods. The shelves were well stocked and the store was neat, looking as if it were an unqualified success. Virginia knew it was not, knew the desperate straits Tannet was now finding himself in.

"Good morning," she said brightly.

Tannet was a dour individual at best. The sight of Virginia's cheerful greeting and bright smile aroused his antagonism.

"Nothin' good about it. What do you want?" he asked.

Virginia pretended surprise. "That's a strange attitude for a shopkeeper to assume. I don't wonder you haven't done well."

"Well enough," he said with a scowl.

"Oh! The Negroes are paying up, then?"

"I got enough on the books to be solvent. If you came to gloat over my misfortune, think again, you snooty woman."

Virginia still maintained her smile. She could afford to. This man was at her mercy.

"Mr. Tannet, when you took over this store, you knew very well that almost all your business would be with the blacks. You Yankees buy most of your supplies on the mainland. The blacks have little access to the stores in Charleston, and if they did, no cash to buy anything with. So you gave the blacks credit and they bought lavishly, charging everything. You supplied them with goods you bought with money borrowed from a Charleston bank. Am I correct?"

"You ought to know. You engineered the whole damned thing."

"Mr. Tannet, I warned you about this type of business."

"If the goddamn niggers paid up when they got their sharecrop money, I'd be in good shape."

"The Negroes, Mr. Tannet, are quite lax in paying up, as you say. It's not entirely their fault. Before the war, they never had need for money, beyond a silver dollar now and then as a gift or reward for good work. Everything was supplied to them by the plantation owners. Our Negroes have not yet learned the value of money and they have little knowledge of how a retail business is run. They'll pay up eventually, when you refuse them further credit. But you'll get your money in driblets while you have to permit them to buy more of your goods."

"If you're trying to give me lessons in how to run a business, you don't have to go any further. I got one hell of a fine education in it during the last six months."

"Won't the bank carry you?"

"They ain't bein' what you might call polite about it. They hate us Yankees."

"Well, nothing is normal right after a war like the one we endured. Hatreds don't die easily or fast. There's some on your side too."

"You sure ain't been of much help. You grew some good cotton and we didn't. Why?"

"Because you never learned how to grow it, Mr. Tannet," Virginia said patiently. On the Sea Islands we grow a particularly fine type of cotton, which brings the highest prices ever paid for a bale. Our cotton is different due to the type of soil and the methods we use in raising it. The cotton grown here and on the other islands is more silky, it's heavier, it gins better and is processed into fine cloth. Special cotton takes special methods and you folks never learned them.''

"How could we? There was nobody to teach us. You sure refused to help.''

"If our positions were reversed, would you help? You and the other Northerners on the island came down here to enrich yourselves at our expense. We lost everything and you bought what we lost for a pittance and boasted of it. Why should we help you?''

"You got an answer for everything, don't you?'' he asked angrily. "But I know what you're after. We all know. You want to get rid of us and bring your own folks back. Well, it ain't goin' to work.''

"Mr. Tannet, if you have any business affairs to discuss, take them up with my husband.''

"Got nothin' to discuss with him. Besides, your husband's a traitor. We don't do business with traitors. I had my way, he'd be shot.''

"You're not easy to talk with, but I will anyway. I'm going to tell you what's going to happen. You'll not be granted any further credit. The blacks won't pay their bills unless you let them buy more of your goods. But you won't have any goods, Mr. Tannet so they won't pay up. In six months you'll be on the verge of bankruptcy.''

"Even so, I ain't leavin'.''

"Let me point out a few facts,'' she said. "How will you pay your taxes? How will you provide for your family? Your plantation will be taken from you and there'll be nothing left. You have only one chance of leaving here with something in your pocket. I'll buy your plantation for exactly what you paid for it.''

"Now ain't that nice of you,'' he said sarcastically.

"I don't have to do it that way. I can wait until your plantation is put up at auction and I might well buy it for less than I'd be willing to pay you. Good day, Mr. Tannet.''

"Know what you are? A loose woman.''

Virginia was so startled, she was speechless, but she quickly recovered her composure. "What are you talking about, Mr. Tannet?"

"You know dang well what I'm talkin' about."

"I haven't the faintest idea."

"Then I'll tell you. Bradley Culver. D'you s'pose we believe he brought back everything he took from us out of the goodness of his heart? He ain't got one."

"I'll tell you why. I asked him not to prey on anyone who lived on this island. I appealed to him as a Southern gentleman. That's something you will never understand and you ought to be grateful you got back what he and his men looted from you. Tell me how that makes a loose woman of me."

"You oughta know." He smiled maliciously. "A man like Culver don't do no favors for anybody without gettin' certain favors back."

She tensed and held her breath, not in anger but in sudden fear. "You prove that or retract it," she said. "Otherwise I shall take steps to see that you do."

He sniffed contemptuously. "What steps? Anybody'd know why he came back. And anybody'd know why he burned out Ben Bowman. Things add up."

"Can you prove that Mr. Culver came back again because of me? Can you prove that I approve in any way of what a scoundrel and bandit does? Suppose you tell me when he did come back."

"When he brought the stuff back, that's when."

If Tannet had been more observant, he might have noticed the swift release of tension that freed the tight muscles of her body. Tannet knew nothing. He was only making a wild guess.

"Mr. Tannet," she said with considerably more confidence than she'd had half a minute ago, "if I ever had any compassion for you, it vanished after that statement. I predict you'll fail with this store and you'll either sell me your plantation or it will be taken from you. Don't call upon me to intercede at your bank, nor for any type of credit. The sooner you leave this island, the better it will become. Good day, sir."

She marched out of the store. If she'd looked back, she might have derived some sense of satisfaction, for Tannet bent his torso over the counter until his face was against it and sobbed like a man utterly at his wit's end.

Virginia, still filled with anger, walked rapidly back to the mansion. But she'd endured a scare that had left her weak with fear, though she'd managed to keep it hidden. For a moment, she'd thought Tannet knew Bradley Culver had returned to the island a third time, and only to see her. With that information he would have had her completely at his mercy.

Culver, she decided, must never return. It was too dangerous, for him and for her. And yet, even the thought of not seeing him again sent a chill of despair through her. For weeks now she'd lived with the fear of his return and the anxiety brought on by the chance he would never come back.

There were nights when she recalled the deliberate harshness of his kiss and the bold way he'd approached her. He was an outlaw. He would certainly hang some day soon. To be mixed up with him could be courting disaster. Nothing must interfere with her plans. But if he had stepped onto the path at this moment, she knew she would have gone straight into his arms and damn the consequences.

The more she thought about him, remembered about him, the more intense the desire to see him filled her. It was madness. She had a splendid husband, her once glitter-filled world was now in the process of returning. Everything she did had worked out far better than she ever expected. Even the fiasco concerned with Nanine and that murderer Miles Rutledge had turned to her benefit. She'd taken him at his word and had already begun the process of restoring the mainland plantation. She would hire Negroes to work it, hire the best overseers, take an active part in running the place just as her father had done before the war. And she would have all the help Elias could provide, plus Rutledge's money. Everything was in her favor. She'd be courting a catastrophe if she submitted to the charms and the physical magnetism of the man. She would be finished, the island would never come back, those she loved would turn against her in disgust. She had everything to gain by not seeing him again, and at this moment she felt she was fortunate that he did not materialize before her. If he had, she knew what she would have done and her reputation, her life, her plans and friends would vanish like a puff of smoke.

By the time she reached the mansion she was still under the spell of that dilemma, but Elias eased her tenseness when she told him, in detail, of her experience with Tannet. And his reference to Culver.

"The man's orneriness," Elias said, "has grown along with his frustrations regarding the store. I'll stop there tomorrow and tell him off. If it wasn't so serious, I'd tell you to laugh at it. It's preposterous, the ravings of a man who knows he's licked and can't think of any other way to get back at you. From here on, I'm on your side. I no longer feel sorry for them. Now I want every last one of those thieves who stole this island off it and without a dollar of profit. Just as you do."

"Thank you, Elias."

"I know I've criticized you in the past and urged you not to go at this too vehemently. You know why. After all, these people came from the North. I fought for it. But they're selfish and greedy and if they could, they'd kick you off the island. That'll never happen. What's the name of that lazy houseboy who hangs around the kitchen?"

Virginia relaxed, extending both arms to rest against the back of the sofa she occupied. "I do feel better," she said. "And the houseboy named himself a few days ago. He is now known as Brandy."

"If we had any, I'd say he was drinking it." Elias went to a rear window that looked out on the walkway between the mansion and the detached kitchen. He shouted for Brandy and the boy came running.

Elias said, "You want to earn your keep around here and the wages we pay, you better put a little more energy into what you do."

"Don' knows whut yo' talkin' 'bout, Marse, suh."

Elias eyed him, feigning anger. "You know damn well what I'm talking about. Run down to the fields and find Moses. Can you do that?"

"Sho' kin, Ah sees him, suh."

"You'd better see him. Tell him to come here to the house as quickly as he can."

"Yah, suh. Ah runs, suh." He left, but showed no inclination to run.

"What are you about to do?" Virginia asked.

"Put Tannet and every other carpetbagger out of business. I had a little compassion for them before, but that's gone. You'll see what I mean in a little while."

Moses rode up on a mule and Elias and Virginia went out to the veranda to meet him. Elias said, "Ride back to the fields, Moses, and round up every Negro who works for us. I want them assembled in front of the porch within the next half an hour. There's something of importance I want to tell them and you might add that they won't be disappointed in what I have to say."

"Yes, suh," Moses said, mystified, but unwilling to ask for any more details. The memory and habit of the slavery days still had a strong hold on him, for slaves could never ask a question without permission. He rode off as fast as the mule wished to go.

"Sit down and relax," Elias told Virginia. "I want to talk about a few things before they get here. First of all, I'm mighty proud of Phoebe's success. I understand she's practically the toast of New York."

"I'm proud of her too. And Tom must be."

Elias cocked his feet on top of the railing. "I've never told you this before. Never thought it was necessary. Tom served under me as a lieutenant in the occupation forces and he did well at it. Now, you surely recall that Tom was a healthy, strong young man."

"Yes," she said, puzzled by the turn the conversation had taken.

"Why then was a strong, healthy young man assigned to serve as an assistant administrator of an occupied island? He was fit for combat and he should have been in the thick of things where bullets were flying. That's where I was when I got this bullet through my thigh."

"I never once wondered about Tom," she said. "I thought a soldier took orders, obeyed them and that's why he was not where the bullets were flying, as you said."

"Tom was a noncombatant. Not a shirker or a draft dodger. He was drafted, you know. He stated that he was glad to serve in any capacity, even to digging latrines. But he wouldn't be a good soldier in action because he would never be able to kill anyone, nor order any men under him to kill. He was frank about it. I admired him for it. There are a lot of men like that and if they refuse to admit it and go into battle, they often are the cause of loss of life among those around them.''

"What brought that up, darling?"

"Phoebe's success. I wonder if Tom can cope with it."

"Cope with it?" She looked at him, still puzzled.

"She's making a great deal of money. She's busy all the time. Her letter stated he still hadn't found work. I even wonder if he's looking for it. Besides that, he's very jealous and as bigoted as all hell.''

"How do you know?"

"He told me he's jealous of Phoebe."

"Tom is bigoted? I had no idea."

"I didn't either until he said he'd be glad to get her North where her lineage wouldn't be suspected."

"Oh, Elias," Virginia exclaimed in horror. "If Phoebe ever finds out . . .''

"I've an idea she suspects. In her last letter she mentioned the fact that Tom had not yet introduced her to his parents. To me, that's an indication of something. His father is an important man in New England politics."

Virginia had no opportunity to ask any more questions, though she was filled with them. Moses, leading more than a hundred men, was approaching the veranda.

Elias stood up. "You'll have to go along with this, Virgie. It won't be cheap, but it'll work as nothing else will. Trust me, please."

"Infinitely, darling. I always will. But I am very curious."

"Then listen to this." Elias moved to stand atop the veranda steps. The men were closing in, as mystified as Virginia, and despite what Moses had said in the way of encouragement, they expected trouble. It always came in the slavery days when they were assembled like this on short notice.

Elias said, "First of all I want you to know that you have been doing very well here on Valcour and both Mrs. Birch and myself appreciate it very much. We are now about to open the big plantation just outside of Charleston. No doubt most of you are familiar with it, for it's been in the family for many years, just as you men and your women and children have been. So we'll need a large force of men. Perhaps over six hundred as the plantation opens up. Now I don't want any of you to go there, for the work will be harder and men less experienced than you can do it. So, beginning the first of this month, every last one of you is getting a raise to seventy-five cents a day."

Virginia half raised a hand to stop him, but let it drop. The men seemed unable to comprehend the meaning of what he said.

"And we will pay the same wage to any worker who is hired for the mainland farm. There are a great number of men working for the Yankees at twenty-five cents a day. Fifty at the most. I want you to talk to them and tell them of this offer. If you are able to recruit enough men to work on the mainland, we shall repay you with a bonus of ten dollars for each and every one of you."

That was when they began to smile and murmur among themselves. Finally, they could no longer contain themselves and showed approval by howling and stomping their feet in a shuffle induced by happiness.

Virginia hugged and kissed him and exclaimed happily over his plan. "What a splendid idea. I never thought of such a thing."

"Those Yankees brought it on themselves. Every last black will take us up at seventy-five cents a day. I told you it was going to be expensive."

"It's cheap. You've shortened the days of my plans a great deal. Without help, the Yankees are finished. They won't be able to sow a seed without blacks. This is the one thing that will do it. Rid us of these people. Oh, Elias, how can I ever thank you?"

"I know exactly how," he replied, eyeing her speculatively.

"Tell me." Her eyes were filled with admiration for the step he'd just taken.

"Bring Nanine back and make Miles Rutledge feel welcome."

Her face shadowed. "That's asking a lot."

Elias attempted to reason with her. "Nanine was sickly most of her life. You've told me on several occasions of some of the fun and even the beaus you had when you entered womanhood. Nanine had none of that. Now that she's well and truly happy, you can increase her happiness by accepting the man I believe she loves. Is that asking too much?''

Virginia walked over to a chair and sat down. "Yes. She's a traitor.''

Elias refuted that. "No more so than you.''

"What do you mean?''

He smiled. "You married a Yankee. Don't you suppose that rankled a lot of your friends?''

"To hell with them," she replied matter-of-factly.

"Nanine could have said, 'To hell with you.' ''

"She did," Virginia retorted bitterly, "in so many words.''

"Yes," Elias agreed reflectively, "she certainly did.''

"How can Nanine love a man who murdered Marty?'' Virginia demanded.

"Miles didn't murder Marty. I'm not a fool, nor is Nanine. We're both far more fair-minded than you. Marty himself told me in the carriage on the way to the hospital Miles was not to blame. Marty knew he was dying. He also told me something else. I didn't tell you before, but I'm going to now because this has gone too far. Marty wanted to reform.''

Virginia stood up and approached Elias slowly. "Why didn't you tell me?''

Elias frowned. "Because there was more to it.''

"I'd like to hear it.''

"Are you certain?''

"Very.''

"Well, then, Marty told me that he tried to duck the bullet and jumped to one side just as Miles fired the pistol. Instead of avoiding the charge, he walked into it.''

"He wouldn't be such a fool," Virginia said bluntly.

"He wanted to live," Elias said slowly, a hint of irritation in his voice. "He wanted to help bring Valcour back. He said that if he hadn't had such a hangover, he'd have killed Miles. But his hand shook. He arrived there early for target practice. He missed so many times, he was frightened.''

Virginia turned away. "I can't believe he was a coward.''

"I didn't say that."

"You might as well have."

"I'm trying to enlighten you. Miles's seconds also told me Marty jumped to one side. You've got to accept the truth sooner or later. Why not now?"

"Because I can't believe that's the truth."

"I'll tell you how I feel about the whole thing," Elias said, "then I'll drop the subject because I can see we're wasting words."

Virginia turned and looked directly into his eyes. Hers revealed how deeply his words about Marty had cut into her. Nonetheless, Elias felt no regrets at having spoken.

"Just what are your feelings on the matter?" she asked.

"I wish I'd never gone to seek him out that morning. To spur him on to make the sale of the damn plantation. I'm also becoming sick of your obsession with Valcour. That's all you can think of."

"You think of it also," she replied.

"Because I love you so damn much." There was anguish in his voice. "I just hope I'm not making a fool of myself."

"Is that how you think of me?"

"You're stubborn, Virgie," he said quietly. "And it seems that whenever we quarrel, it's about this damn island."

"It started with Nanine and that murderer she's in love with," Virginia said pointedly.

"No," Elias replied with a sigh of resignation. "It started when you asked if you could do me a favor. I don't care to discuss it further."

"Nor do I," she replied. "I don't like our quarreling either."

"We won't. We'll discuss the subject dearest to your heart. And I'm not being sarcastic. But before we do, I'll make one more statement regarding Nanine. Nothing you or your mother do can turn her from Miles. She knows in her heart he didn't kill Marty. I believe him also. And now you know all of what Marty told me before he died. I'll also say Miles would be dead if it weren't for Nanine's care. She's also given him hope."

"Very well," Virginia said quietly. "I'll do this. I'll think about what you told me—Marty's last words. His confession, so to speak."

"That's what it was. He was making peace. Doing the right thing. I always knew he had it in him. It's sad his life had to end just when he realized he had much to live for. Wherever he is, I'm sure he has one hell of a lot of respect for Nanine. And, I might add, so do I. Now let's talk about the plantation on the mainland. At least, you agreed to take on that. Do you have any plans on how you want it handled?"

"We must plow and seed at once," she said. "We'll still be in time for a crop this year. Very few plantations are being planted so far. Nobody has the money to hire help and buy seed or mules. We have plenty and a crop this year will bring a very good price."

"Remember this," Elias said. "We have the money, thanks to Miles Rutledge's generosity. He gave us the plantation and took back none of the money he paid Marty to get it."

"I know. I admit it may influence me, but getting into production is all I can think of now. Elias, would it be possible for you to go to the mainland and take over? You know everything there is to know about raising cotton and you have a knack for handling the blacks. I can take care of everything on the island."

"I don't think there's any other way," he said. "It would be foolish to put some overseer we didn't know in charge. I'll hate every day I'm there because I'll be away from you, but I'll do it."

"I'll miss you just as much," she told him. "Perhaps even more, because it's going to be lonely here with only Mama for company."

"There's Nanine."

"Darling, please. Let me think about it."

"Perhaps without me here, you'll get lonely enough to ask her back. I hope so. We have to make full plans now. Our blacks will get the word to those working for the Northerners. They'll be waiting to get to the mainland by morning. Ashore, in Charleston, the word will spread. There are thousands of ex-slaves willing to work. I can pick the best of them and be in production in a week. First, the fields must be plowed, the seed planted. Then I'll see to rebuilding the house, the sheds and quarters."

"It's a big undertaking," she admitted.

"You're not going to have an easy time of it here. As soon as the blacks begin leaving the Yankees, there's going to be hell to pay.

Then you'll have to arrange to buy the carpetbaggers out, refurbish the houses and bring their rightful owners back.''

"When it's done," she said, "we can begin to enjoy life. Do the many things the war deprived us of. Make up for the years that were bleak and dangerous.''

"I'll do everything in my power to help you forget them.''

His arms extended and she went to him, resting her head on his shoulder. As he stroked her hair, the pins slipped from it and it cascaded almost to her waist. He murmured endearments in her ear and she closed her eyes. Instantly, the picture of a devil-may-care face came into her mind. Bradley Culver. The thought occurred to her that if Elias went to live on the mainland, there'd be far less danger if, and when, Bradley came back—as he swore he would. A shiver of delight passed through her. One Elias misinterpreted, but Virginia didn't mind. As he drew her closer, her face lifted to meet his lips.

She knew Elias loved and respected her. And thus far, she'd been a loyal, loving and obedient wife. But she had to press her lips harder against those of Elias to shut out the memory of Bradley Culver. The very thought of the man drove her mad.

sixteen

Virginia felt the loneliness mostly at night. Elias had been gone a week, though it seemed more like a month. She had really never known what it was like—being without someone to talk to, or even to sit near. Her mother, still grieving for Marty, was no company. If she did come downstairs, it was only to complain that her former friends and neighbors were not returning quickly enough and she'd be unable to plan any kind of social season for the summer months. Virginia tried to reason with her, but to no avail. Lenore's heavy-hearted reply was always the same. She'd gone through so much, it was time for the island to be back in Southern hands again.

More than once, Virginia almost gave way and decided to visit Nanine and the murderer she was nursing back to health. If Elias was right, she wasn't having much luck. Nonetheless, he had certainly caused a rift in their lives. So much so, twice Virginia had thrown a shawl around her shoulders and headed for the door to make amends, but caught herself in time. Now and then, she saw Nanine heading for the kitchen. In the hope of having a chance meeting, Virginia had even gone there a few times and started up a conversation with Belle. Or attempted to. It seemed Belle was forever cooking puddings or some kind of nourishing sweets for the man. She was as devoted to him as Nanine. To add insult to injury, when Virginia attempted to converse with Belle, she was ordered out of the kitchen on some flimsy excuse. Obviously Belle resented Virginia because she'd barred Nanine from the house.

Virginia started taking long walks about the island, telling herself it was to keep the mansions under regular outward inspection, though she had to concede that the Yankees had taken good care of them.

. She got so she dreaded nights and wondered how she could go through another. Lenore retired promptly at sundown, leaving Virginia to herself. She read until her eyes burned. She tried to think of ways to accelerate the speed with which she could be rid of the Northerners. She did take satisfaction in noticing how the cotton fields, except on Willowbrook, were not even planted. Once the island had teemed with slaves. Hundreds of them. Now the young able ones worked only for Virginia and the Yankees could rely only on the older blacks who had nowhere to go and would be unable to work the fields. It was not going to be a profitable year for the Yankees.

Virginia's yearnings were not for the restoration of the island half as much as for Elias. And, she conceded reluctantly, for Bradley Culver. He was coming back and she knew precisely for what purpose. Some male instinct must have assured him she'd not have him intercepted and arrested. His vanity, no doubt. He was fully aware that if she permitted him to land and came secretly to meet him, her purpose would be the same as his. He knew her as well as she knew herself. But, she reminded herself, it was Elias she loved and wanted.

She'd never been as restless before. Nothing seemed to satisfy her. She could not yet bear to submit to Nanine's terms and Lenore had turned into a terrible bore, mouthing the same complaints over and over again.

When Virginia could stand it no longer, she went upstairs and hastily packed a small bag. She wrote a brief note for her mother and was going to leave it on the hall table when she heard sounds in the kitchen. Thinking it might be Nanine, she hastened there. She'd pretend she thought it was Belle.

To her disappointment, it was. Virginia was holding the note in her hand. "What are you doing?" she asked.

"Whut yo' thinks Ah'm doin'?" Belle asked boldly, not pausing in beating the liquid in the glass pitcher.

"I don't know or I'd not ask," Virginia said coldly.

"Ah'm makin' a eggnog," Belle said. "That's whut Ah'm doin'. Fo' Mistah Miles. Also, Ah'm puttin' a li'l brandy in it. Make him sleep bettah."

"Brandy!" Virginia exclaimed impatiently. "We have no brandy."

"Yes, Miss Uppity, we has. Two gen'mun fren's o' Mistah Miles brings it. Say it good fo' him. Ah agrees. Ah don' keeps it in the house, so that good-fo'-nuthin', slothin' niggah named Brandy"— she motioned to the bottle standing on the table close to where she was working—"cain't steals it. Brings it back to the birthin' house, Ah does. Moses say fo' me to."

"I give the orders in this house, not Moses," Virginia retorted.

"Knows that." Belle picked up the bottle, removed the cork and poured a moderate amount in the liquid. "Ah takes orduhs from Moses too. He knows that good-fo'-nuthin' Brandy, same as me."

"I'm going to the mainland," Virginia said, placing the note on the table. "Give this to Mama in the morning."

"Whar'bouts on the mainland is yo' goin'?" Belle spoke as she placed the pitcher on a tray and a glass alongside it. She put the note in her apron pocket.

"To the plantation, of course," Virginia said. "Not that I have to answer to you. You get more impudent by the day."

"Mebbe so. Yo' gits mo' uppity. Won' even let yo' sistah brings that nice Mistah Miles into the house. That gen'mun's real sick. Yo' oughta be ashame' o' yo'se'f."

"You know why I won't. Since you're going outside, tell one of the Negroes to row me to the mainland."

"Glad to," Belle said calmly. She'd picked up the tray and was already at the door. "Gives mah 'gards to Massa 'Lias. That is, if yo' goin' to sees him."

Virginia turned abruptly and left the kitchen. It would have been useless to make a retort. Belle was already walking along the path to the hospital. Virginia wished she'd never gone to the kitchen. Belle always made her angry. Even more so this time, now that Virginia knew Belle had taken Nanine's side. For the first time Virginia realized that perhaps Moses had also, plus the Negroes who lived on the plantation. They'd known Nanine all their lives, were fully aware of her goodness and admired what she was doing.

Virginia snatched up her small satchel and headed for the landing. The Negro was already there. He took the bag from her and held the boat steady until she got in. Her mind churned all the way to the mainland. She resented Belle's audacity. She also resented the fact that she had only one ally—her mother. She felt dubious satisfaction in that. On the mainland, she took a carriage for the long ride to the plantation and slept through most of it, not waking until daylight. It would help, being there, seeing how Elias was progressing with the work, listening to his plans for the rebuilding of the house, which Yankee troops had burned down.

Her breath quickened at the thought of being with him. He was what she needed. What she wanted. She loved him, not only for himself, but for the way he worked and planned with her.

Elias, alerted by one of the workers, came in from the fields to meet Virginia as the carriage stopped at the old barn, now used as Elias's quarters. He was sweaty and his boots were covered with the red dirt of the fields. Virginia ran into his arms with a sob.

"I'm astonished," he said. "I never expected you to show up here. Is something wrong?"

"I couldn't stand being lonely," she explained. "I love you so much, darling. I wanted to see you, so . . . I just came. Aren't you pleased?"

He smiled. "I'm so pleased I can't express myself. I've been lonely too. Working hard, though. Got up before dawn to get the men moving early. We have to get seed in the ground as quickly as possible. It's already late for planting."

"I know, darling. And I'm grateful."

"No need to be. It's a challenge. Have you had breakfast?"

"It must be time for dinner," she said. "How do you feed yourself here?"

"I've hired a cook and some kitchen helpers so I can feed all the help. The cookhouse is in a tent near the fields. Can't see it from here, but the food is good. Come on. Let's walk down there."

She felt a thrill as his arm went around her waist. Her arm slipped around his and she snuggled close to him as they walked along a newly made path, passing by the stark chimneys of the mansion that had stood on this spot. They stopped there for a moment.

Elias said, "I've already got an architect at work drawing up plans for a replica of the house that once stood here. I didn't have time to ask your opinion, but I do now. Is it all right to duplicate the old house? We did find some rough plans and that made it easy to get going quickly."

"Oh, my darling, yes," she said. "I approve with all my heart. How I'd love to see the house standing once again. We could live here part of the year. It always was a joy to spend time here. Papa would arrange some memorable dances and dinners in the winter. You know, Elias, the Charleston society is beginning to emerge again."

"Good. The future looks great to me. Now we've got about everything. This plantation will be going soon. You'll have the island in your hands in no time. It's going to be like the old days."

She hugged him and he paused long enough to kiss her. Her lips trembled with desire. His eyes held a hint of promise as they continued on to the large tent under which tables were set up. The cook was a replica of Belle except in disposition. This one was amiable and eager to please.

"Her name is Eliza," he said. "She used to work here as a slave and remembers you well."

"But not with much relish, I suppose," Virginia said. "I'm afraid I was a hellion. Haughty and headstrong."

"You still are," he said. "The type to drive a man mad." He paused, then added, "What about Nanine?"

She shook her head. "I've thought about it, but I cannot give in. Marty's death is too fresh in my mind and, anyway, Mama would never allow her back into the mansion unless she got rid of Miles."

"That's cruel," Elias said.

"I don't see it that way. And, please, Elias, no quarreling."

A very good pork pie was served for dinner and Virginia enjoyed it, and the apple pie for dessert. Elias respected her wishes about Miles, but it was obvious he'd had hopes she'd relented.

"Is this the kind of food you're serving to the help?" she asked.

"Yes. I'm trying something new. We tried something new on the island when the army controlled it and that didn't work. You can declare the Negroes free, you can pay them a little for a day's work, but it won't be a hard day's work. We found that out. So we're paying them well and feeding them well. It's expensive, but it pays off."

"I hope you're right," Virginia looked dubious.

"We've been plowing and putting in seed. That's hard work, but I'm getting two or three times the amount of work done here compared to what we got on the island. These people are happy. They have a little money, their bellies are full and they show their gratitude by the diligence with which they work."

"We're not used to coddling them this way, but you may be right."

"I know I am. There's little slothing here and a man who tries it is brought up real fast by the others. They know they have a good thing and they don't want it spoiled. I'm happy you came. I knew I missed you, but it didn't really hit me until you arrived."

"I couldn't stand the separation any longer," Virginia confessed. "I could never again do without you. Now, where do we sleep?"

"You're going to stay?" he asked, in mild surprise.

"You don't think I came all this way to spend a mere hour with you. Darling, my body aches for you. You and your love. And I want to love you."

"There's the slave hospital the Union soldiers forgot to burn down. I've outfitted it, but it's rough. Not like Willowbrook. If I'd known you were coming, I'd have—"

She placed her hand over his mouth, cutting off his words. "Darling, it'll be like a palace as long as you're there. I won't mind if I get my hands dirty or perspire a little. I want to help."

He brightened. "There's some bookkeeping. The payroll, food bills and supplies. Things like that. You'd be a big help because I have to spend so much time in the fields."

"Then you tell me what to do, turn the books over to me and we'll get to work."

She did shudder slightly at the accommodations in the old hospital. It never had been much of a place and there were few fond memories connected with it. During the war, when life was at its lowest ebb, when she and her family were both destitute and hungry, they'd taken refuge in this building. She'd hated it then and she had no special fondness for it now.

There was a rough table she would use as a desk. An old four-poster brass bed was lined up against one wall, a relic probably discovered amidst the ruins of some other burned-out place. There was fresh linen on the bed, a new blanket and new pillows. There were lanterns for light and the place smelled slightly of kerosene.

"It will do fine," she said. "You run along now. I'll work on the books. I've done it before. Come home early, darling."

He grinned and kissed her. "If you can call this place 'home,' you'll learn humility yet. I'll be as quick as I can, but we don't quit until it gets so dark we can't see the furrows. If you want anything, Eliza will get it for you. You'll find her at the tent."

He was gone seconds later and Virginia sat down at the desk, opened the ledgers, studied the pile of bills and the carefully laid-out plans for both the house and the plantation itself. She had to concede that Elias was doing a splendid job. Perhaps, she reasoned, he was more ambitious and smarter than her father or Marty ever were.

She went to work and was still at it when the light began to fade and she had to light the lanterns. Still, there was light enough outside that Elias might not return for another hour. She walked back to the tent and made arrangements for supper. She looked forward to a long supper hour, another long hour to talk and then to bed. She ached for the thrill of his body close to hers. Somehow, Bradley Culver came to mind. She realized she'd not once thought of him. Coming here was the right medicine for her.

She unpacked the bag she'd brought along and put on a thin cotton nightgown with a heavier robe over it. She brushed her hair and lavished some precious *eau de toilette* on her skin. She knew she was trembling with desire.

Elias came back, dirtier than ever, sweat-soaked and eager for the hot bath she'd arranged, taken in a large washtub, for there were no other facilities here yet. She had a fresh nightshirt laid out for him. Over it he put on a plaid wrapper.

Eliza and two kitchen aides brought trays laden with good food. While they ate, they could hear the blacks, lodged in tents half a mile away, singing and dancing to music supplied by gourds and what sounded like a banjo.

"Elias, it's like old times," she said contentedly. "I almost feel as if there'd never been a war. Papa used to go down and listen to the slaves. He believed they had the best talent for music and dancing in the whole world. He . . . Elias . . . Elias . . ."

He stirred, shook his head vigorously and smiled sheepishly. "I dozed off. Sitting here at the supper table. I just . . . fell asleep while you were talking. I apologize, darling. What were you saying?"

Virginia's smile was one of understanding. "No need to apologize. Not after the long day you put in. Finish your supper and get in bed. You're exhausted."

He fell asleep moments after his head rested on the pillow. Virginia sat beside the table, her spirits low, trying to read a newspaper in the weak light of a lantern she had turned low. His exhaustion was so complete, she doubted even a cannon shot off beside the bed would waken him. She stood this as long as she could, but each time she glanced at his prone figure, she wanted to join him.

Finally, she slipped out of the robe and got into bed beside him. He was facing her and she kissed him gently. He didn't stir. She lay motionless for what seemed to be hours. Then her hand raised slowly and she let her fingertips move lightly along his brow, down his cheek, along the outline of his ear to his neck. Her hand slipped beneath his gown, moving in an exploratory manner to his shoulder, then down to his chest. He still didn't move nor did he show any response when she caressed his face again and, with parted lips, pressed gentle kisses along his upper and lower lips. Still she elicited no response.

She turned on her back, sighed dismally and got out of bed. It was cold at this time of morning and she put on her robe, tying it securely around her waist. Even then, she could feel the chill through the thin fabric. She paced the floor, her fists clenched in frustration. Finally, she walked out of the building and trudged up and down the path, increasing her speed until she was running. Only when exhaustion overcame her did she return to the hospital. She slipped out of her robe and got between the covers, pressing her body close to Elias's to absorb the heat. He didn't stir, but by now she didn't care, for she was tired from her exertions.

She slept, but it was fitful and she knew it would be useless for her to remain here, for each night would be the same. Elias was pouring every ounce of energy he possessed into supervising the regeneration of the plantation. She was grateful, knowing it was necessary, but for her it was agonizing. If she'd not thought of it before, she knew now that she was the type of woman who needed a man's love. If not love, then lovemaking. She couldn't do without it. She couldn't spend another night here.

Over morning coffee in the gray light of early dawn, she told him so. "I'm afraid I'm doing more harm than good staying here, Elias. Besides, I must confess it's most uncomfortable. Do you mind if I return to Valcour?"

"I wish you would, Virgie. That's an awful thing to say after your coming here, but conditions are not good. And I have to be in the fields every working moment. This is no time for mistakes and the workers can make them by the dozen. I swear this won't last more than a month longer, but we have to endure it."

She nodded agreement. "Better days are coming. Besides, I've a great deal of work to do on Valcour. We've got the scalawags on the run now and we mustn't let up. I suppose the houses will need refurbishing. Also, I can't leave Mama alone. She fusses."

Elias said, "Neither of you has to be alone. There's Nanine."

"I miss her, but I can't abide the thought of that man in the house."

"Miles feels guilty because he's caused ill feeling."

"He should," Virginia asserted.

"The ill feeling's yours, not Nanine's. Show some compassion." Virginia sighed. "Am I such an ogre?"

"You're a beautiful, desirable, passionate woman. I'm the envy of every man who looks at you. I love you madly. You know that."

She smiled and patted his arm, thinking of her attempts to arouse him last night.

"Try to remember that Nanine never knew love before," he went on. "She never had a man to care for before or one who valued the beautiful qualities she possesses. Show her you're pleased that she's happy. Remember, you've had love. This is her first and it's a love that may never be fulfilled."

"What do you mean?"

"Simply that. Miles is too ill. Put yourself in their place."

Virginia said gravely, "You've given me something to think about. I know I miss you terribly."

She hugged and kissed him a dozen times before she finally let him go back to the fields. It was just after dawn and even then she knew he was late. She tidied up the books she'd worked on, but it was an effort. She wanted to get away from here more than she'd wanted to come. She arranged for a young black to drive a farm wagon back to the city and the journey seemed to take hours. She fidgeted nervously and once or twice talked aloud to herself, to the bewilderment of the boy handling the reins.

She checked into a hotel and had her bag brought up. She ate dinner alone and didn't enjoy it. She luxuriated in a hot bath and fresh clothes. Still she was restless, goaded on by some inner feeling she tried not to heed or even comprehend.

In an attempt to ease her restiveness, she went on a shopping tour. It was a relief not to have to worry about money. She could thank Miles Rutledge for that. When he refused to take back the money he'd paid for the plantation, and even deeded it back, her problems had been solved.

She was standing at the shoe counter of one of the big stores still sparsely stocked, but at least there were a few things even if they were ridiculously high in price. She suddenly realized that Miles had deeded the plantation back and she'd been so happy about that, she'd never given much thought to the deed. It had occurred to her that the deed was in Nanine's name alone. Certainly Elias had noted that. She supposed he hadn't wished to worry her about it. She didn't grow angry over what Miles had done. She readily saw why he did it, but she must accept Nanine and, worst of all, accept Miles too, for without him, Nanine would never agree to any reconciliation. If that was the case, she could do it.

A small roughly dressed man brushed against her. It might have been by accident, but it could easily have been deliberate. She shrugged it off, left the store with her purchases and headed for a dress shop where she hoped to find something for Lenore. Her mother whined so often about not having anything new to wear that it often irritated Virginia. She did have her mourning dress that she'd insisted on once she learned they had money.

Out on the busy street again, which still showed so many of the marks of war and destruction, she saw that small man. It was not by coincidence. She felt certain of that, and she began to develop the first stir of fear. She wondered if he could be some sort of spy set on her trail by Ben Bowman, who, she believed, was still in charge of the Freedmen's Bureau. But even Bowman would hardly have hired a scurvy-looking creature like this man.

There was a great deal of petty crime in Charleston these days, much of it inspired by desperate and hungry men. She thought about going directly to the headquarters of the occupying Union army, where Elias's friend Captain Delaney was in charge. If this man followed her there, she might be able to have him seized and questioned.

Then she forgot about him, for she spent the next hour in the dress shop. This time when she emerged she was so laden with packages that she had to summon a carriage for the trip to the dock. Seated in the carriage, she felt at ease once again and believed her imagination was running away with her. That small man she'd thought was eyeing her was probably just a beggar trying to get up the courage to ask her for help.

The carriage stopped at a street crossing to allow two heavy vans to go by. Suddenly she saw the little man. He was running straight toward the carriage. She opened her mouth to scream, but all the man did was hand her a very soiled envelope. Then he was gone, to vanish somewhere down the street.

She didn't open the envelope then. She knew who it was from and she felt that restlessness returning with an ever increasing intensity. She hired a boat to take her back to the island and during that rather long journey by water, she kept tapping the edge of the unopened envelope against her thigh. Once she raised it to throw it overboard, but she stopped short of doing that. Finally she succumbed to curiosity.

The note was so brief it could be read at a glance.

*　　*　　*

My dear One, I'm coming tonight and I'll wait in the whipping shed where, together, we'll change the name of that shed, you willing. Don't disappoint me. Nine o'clock.

B.C.

She tore the note into small pieces, raised her fist, opened it and let the small pieces be caught up on the breeze and borne out to sea. She closed her eyes tightly and cursed Elias for not responding to her last night. If anything happened . . . but, no! No! She would not go to the whipping shed at nine o'clock. Nothing in the world would cause her to go. She even considered writing a note to the Union army commandant telling him that the outlaw Bradley Culver might be caught tonight on the island.

She gave up that idea promptly. How could she explain she knew he'd be there?

By the time the boat docked she was uneasy, worried, hungry again for the warmth of a man's arms, for his kisses and caresses. Elias should have realized that. He admitted she was a passionate and loving woman. Since he knew it, he should have given her the love she needed. That was why she'd gone to him.

Lenore was downstairs to greet her. Virginia, without much enthusiasm or interest, handed her mother the packages. Lenore kissed Virginia and promptly hurried upstairs to change into one of the two new dresses Virginia had bought. They were, of course, ready-made, something new since the war, and ordinarily Lenore would have felt humiliated at the thought of wearing one, but she was pleasantly surprised. They were the latest fashion and most becoming. She wore one downstairs.

"You're lucky, Mama," Virginia said. "There were only five in the whole store and these two were in your size. The fit is perfect."

"Were they expensive?" Lenore asked.

"I won't tell you. Confine your criticism of costs to food. You do grow worrisome when it comes to talking about money, Mama. Especially when you know we have enough and more."

"I don't know. Nobody ever tells me."

"Thanks to Miles Rutledge, we have."

"Do not utter his name in this house," Lenore said angrily. "You know how I feel about the man who murdered my son."

"I know, Mama, but come along. I want to show you something."

She took her mother's elbow and led her to the library. There, Virginia removed the deed to the mainland plantation from the desk and opened it to hold the document before her mother's eyes.

"It occurred to me a short time ago," Virginia said, "that this deed to the mainland plantation is made out in Nanine's name alone. Rutledge did that because I suspect he didn't trust us. I can't blame him, but you must realize that Nanine is the sole owner of the plantation where Elias is working so hard to get back into production. We cannot operate that plantation without her consent."

" 'Consent'? How could she deny us? It's our plantation."

"Not legally. And we've punished Nanine sufficiently, I think. Besides, if we go too far, she might turn against us, and then what? There'd not be as many new dresses or shoes or chocolate cakes. I managed to scrape up some chocolate in the city today so Belle can make you a cake. There'd be less of that too."

"I will not allow that man in this house. That is final, Virginia."

"Mama, I'm beginning to think we'll have to."

"There is no reason great enough to make me change my mind."

"Mama, there's a chance Nanine may have fallen in love with him."

"Nanine in love? Nonsense! That's absolutely ridiculous . . .."

"It's far from that, Mama. As we shun him he may, in turn, shun us. He may take Nan off to live in New Orleans, where he comes from. Then what happens to the big plantation? You know Nan defied us. Regardless of what we think, she's a warm, merciful woman. We've both learned she's also a very determined one. We'd be wise to show we can forgive."

"Forgive what?" Lenore demanded angrily.

Virginia smiled. "Nothing, really. Let's hope Nanine will forgive us. Elias has convinced me how unfair we are."

"Elias is a Yankee. Never forget that. I've accepted him, but he's a Yankee and I despise them. They killed my husband. They took everything away from us . . ."

"Think about it, Mama, and quickly. There are times when

everyone has to admit an error. We have to take Nanine back and Miles with her. I just hope we're not too late."

"He will enter this house against my direct wishes. Nanine . . . well, she is my daughter and I do love her, but that man . . . no. No, Virgie! I will not consider it."

"As I said, think about it. And don't waste too much time."

"You've ruined my happiness at having new clothes," Lenore said petulantly. "I don't understand you, Virgie. I swear I never did."

She went off in a huff, but she forgot the whole incident a few moments later when she discovered a pair of new shoes among the purchases Virginia had made.

Virginia went upstairs and lay across the bed, angry at herself, at Lenore, at Elias and especially at Bradley Culver. She couldn't lie there. She was too nervous, too upset. She went out for a walk. That didn't work so she had a horse saddled and she rode for most of the afternoon. That didn't help either. Lenore refused to come down to supper, so Virginia ate alone and that only aggravated her restlessness. She took a bath, slipped into her nightdress and wrapper.

By the time it grew dark she was almost beside herself with indecision. She blamed her mother, she blamed Elias and transferred some of the blame for her uneasiness to Nanine, then to Miles Rutledge, who she didn't even know well. At eight, alone again because Lenore refused to leave her room, Virginia went upstairs. She let her hair fall free and brushed it with so much energy she tore some of it from its roots. She slammed the brush onto the metal tray, removed her robe and got into bed.

She tried to read, but the light didn't seem to be right and she adjusted the bedlamp two or three times. Finally, she tossed the book onto the bed, extinguished the lamp and slid down beneath the covers. She tossed restlessly, but was unable to sleep despite the fatigue from her journey. She pressed her hands against her brow in an effort to quiet her nerves, but there was no relief.

Finally, she jumped free of the bed as if it were afire, unbuttoned her nightdress and let it drop to the floor. In the dark, she put on soft-soled slippers, went to the closet and took a satin peignoir she'd purchased that day, from its hanger. Still in darkness, she went to her dressing table and got a bottle of *eau de toilette* she'd also purchased and splashed it generously over her body. Its floral fragrance excited her. She slipped into the peignoir and tied its wide flowing ribbon into a bow at the neck.

She made her way down the dark stairway. At the door she hesitated a moment. She cautioned herself to consider what she was doing and then thrust the thought from her mind. She closed the door softly and ran down the path toward the whipping shed. Twice she looked over her shoulder to see if, by some chance, she was being observed. There was no light in her mother's bedroom window. Nanine's place was out of sight by now.

She moved more swiftly as she neared the shed. There was no light there either. She grasped the leather thong by which the door could be opened and stepped inside. Instantly she knew he was there. She came to an abrupt stop in a shaft of moonlight that slipped through a hole in the roof. Neither said a word. She unbuttoned the peignoir and held it away from her, exposing her nakedness and her intense desire. She heard his hissing breath and then she was in his arms to discover that he too was naked.

There was a pile of blankets from the stable on the floor. He lowered her slowly, not taking his lips away from hers. They stretched out on their makeshift bed and she was quickly and somewhat roughly relieved of all that tension and emotion that had built up in her from dawn, when she'd said good-bye to Elias.

She had no idea how long they lay there and she didn't care. She would not have arisen if Elias walked in with a lantern held high.

"I knew you'd come," he said, showering kisses on her shoulders. "Shall I light a lamp?"

"Please don't. The moonlight is enchantment enough. What made you so certain I'd come?"

"I knew from the way you kissed me, held on to me. Your desire matched mine. I almost went mad waiting, but I knew you'd meet me."

"How did you find out I was in Charleston?" she asked.

"I've people all over who work with me and for me. They're a brutal bunch, indolent and lazy, until it comes to raiding and looting. And raping," he added with a lopsided grin. "I asked them to be on the watch for you. They keep the island under observation too, at my request. They saw you leave it yesterday, saw you return today. I take it your husband is not the most attentive of men or responds to your desires."

"Elias works too hard. He . . . fell asleep last night as I lay beside him," she said, laughing softly. "I'm glad he did now. Brad, do you love me or am I just another conquest?"

"Mistress mine, I'm a man doomed to die with a rope around his neck if a posse's bullet doesn't cut him down first. I can't afford to fall in love. I have to take it where I can find it. But this I'll say. It will never be the same. Not after you."

She felt no offense. "I'm not in love with you either. Isn't that strange?"

"Not strange at all. We were attracted to one another the moment our eyes met and our bodies touched that day in the forest. Admit you wanted me as much as I wanted you."

"I admit it, harlot that I am. I wanted you. Though I didn't realize it until I got your note."

"Yes, you did. You just fought it."

"True," she admitted. "I lost the battle, quite willingly, I might add."

"Will you come again?"

"Whenever you wish. That is, provided it is safe for both of us. I don't want you caught."

"Why should you care, when you don't love me? A woman like you would have no difficulty finding another mate whose passion matches hers."

"Damn it, I told you I needed you. I always will and I know very well what it all means and how it will end. Especially if we are caught."

"No need to be. I'll know when it's safe to come. How are you getting along with Miles Rutledge?"

"I despise him. Do you know the man?"

"I've thought about taking him. Perhaps kidnapping him, I don't know. Do you want me to dispose of him?"

"No!" she exclaimed vehemently. "If you harm him, I'll never see you again. What do you know about him?"

"Just a few things. The most important of which is that he's very wealthy. I think he must be as close to a millionaire as the defeated Confederacy can produce. He's never married. He's always been sickly. He has no one. All his people are dead. I don't know what keeps him alive. He always looked like a walking corpse."

"Don't harm him. Do you know anything detrimental about him?"

"No. He enjoys an enviable reputation. Brilliant too, I'm told. If he lives, he'll probably make another million before long."

"That's all I wanted to know. Now tell me about you."

"Little to tell. My father is dead, my mother lives in a small Maryland town. She gets along well enough and probably has no idea of what I'm doing. I've neither brother nor sister, nor other kin. I went to West Point, stayed there until I realized the war was coming and I went home. I rose to the rank of colonel in the Confederate army. If the war had continued, I'd have gone up another one or two ranks. I was a good soldier. About the only thing I can be proud of."

"Why do you go about stealing and looting?"

"For one thing, I got too much war, and I loved every moment of it. There's something to have a gun in your hand while you're stalking a man you want to kill. And there's a great feeling of . . . I don't know what. When you break down a door and loot and burn and kill. It gets you. It's very much like what we've just done, I get a feeling of relief, a great wave of joy. I can't exactly describe it, but . . . I know I want that as much as I want you."

"I'll worry about you."

"Don't. My finish is foreordained. When it comes, I'll take it like a man."

"Then I'll say that I'll miss you."

"That's better. A hell of a lot better. Come closer to me. It's a night I want to remember always. You're wanton. You're beautiful. You're full of life and daring—like me. I'll never love you, but I'll adore you and want you like nothing else in this world."

She moved closer to him and she gave way to him, to his lusty, almost violent lovemaking and she loved every moment of it. She lost track of the number of times they made love. She only knew she'd never given of herself with such wild abandon. Never known the ecstasy of such complete fulfillment.

seventeen

Virginia hesitated a moment, her hand half raised to knock on the door of the old slave hospital. She let her hand drop, began to turn away and then, turning back with a resolution characteristic of her, she knocked, perhaps too hard.

Nanine opened the door. Her face betrayed open surprise.

"What do you want?" she asked quietly, yet her manner was firm and unyielding.

Virginia, for once, was without words. She'd not planned a speech. Even if she had, the sight of Nanine standing there, so close, touched her heart.

Slowly Virginia raised her arms. Nanine watched with wonder and then, with a cry of happiness, the sisters embraced.

"Virgie, Virgie, I've missed you so," Nanine said.

"I don't think you missed me any more than I've missed you. I came here to apologize and admit I was wrong. It's taken me a long time to realize it and perhaps even longer to accept it. Please forgive me, Nan."

"Now that you're back, there's nothing to forgive." She released Virginia and brushed away tears. "Please come in."

Virginia dabbed at her eyes with a handkerchief and arm in arm they entered the room where Miles Rutledge sat in a large chair beside a window. He was almost encased in blankets, a stocking cap covered his head and he seemed, to Virginia, to be thinner than ever.

She managed a smile, though it wasn't easy. Miles looked like a very sick man.

"Thank you, Virginia," he said. "I've been praying for this day."

Virginia moved to his side, bent and kissed his cheek. "I must ask your forgiveness also, Miles. Thanks for accepting me when I wouldn't even acknowledge your existence."

"You two have been tearing your hearts out all because of me," he said. "Seeing you embrace in the doorway warmed my heart. Tell me the reconciliation is permanent."

"For the rest of our lives," Nanine said firmly.

"I agree." Virginia's tone matched Nanine's. "Are you happy here, Miles?"

"With this dear lady at my side, looking after my slightest need, never doubt it." His hand reached for Nanine's; she held it between both of hers.

"He's coming along. It's slow, but there is an improvement." Nanine regarded Miles as she spoke and the softness in her eyes bespoke her regard for him.

"Please forgive me for not standing, Virginia," he said.

"Don't even try," she replied. "I'm going to sit down, though I won't stay long."

She sat in a straight-backed chair facing him. Nanine released his hand and her arm went around his shoulders.

Virginia said, "I'm glad I came. Elias said you two loved one another. Of course," she gave them a wry smile, "that infuriated me. It doesn't now. I'm as happy for both of you as he is."

"Thanks, Virgie," Nanine said.

"I also want to say something else," Virginia went on. "Elias told me what Marty admitted on his way to the hospital. That he tried to escape the bullet. I know also that you tried to avoid hitting him, Miles."

"Yes," Miles sighed. "It isn't easy to live with the knowledge you've killed another human being. I had really hoped to be the one to die. At the time, because of my health, I had nothing to live for. With Nanine, I have everything. Yes, Virginia, I love your sister."

"And I love Miles," Nanine said quietly. "I've never been so happy."

"I can see that," Virginia said. "I'm happy for you both. I also know Belle is quite taken with you, Miles. And she doesn't take to very many people."

He chuckled. "She makes great eggnogs. My friends—Anton Boyle and James Warren— the gentlemen who were my seconds, brought me a case of brandy from the mainland. I'd like you to take some back."

"If there should be need for any," Virginia said gratefully, "I'll come after it. Belle says the houseboy, Brandy, isn't to be trusted around a bottle."

"She should know," Nanine said with a laugh. "Nothing escapes her sharp eyes."

"I've never managed to escape her sharp tongue," Virginia replied. "I hope, once she knows I came here, she'll be a little more civil."

"She likes scolding you," Nanine said. "Just to make you angry. You're even more beautiful then, Virgie. And I swear that's why she does it. I've seen her chuckle when you've stomped out of a room after she's given you a verbal barb."

"I just wish for once I could best her," Virginia said good-naturedly.

Nanine said, "She told us you went to the plantation. How is it coming along?"

"Very well. I think there are about four hundred blacks working there now. Many of them came from this island. You know how Elias got them, of course."

"It was a shrewd idea," Miles said. "I don't see how you could get the island back otherwise."

"Two families have left," Virginia informed them. "I'm sure two or three more won't last out the month. I suppose I'm being cruel, but how else could we help our friends get their property back?"

"They deserve anything you might do to get rid of them," Miles said. "They're mostly a ragtag bunch anyway. Besides, they bought the property for practically nothing. It wasn't right."

"I'm glad you agree with us," Virginia said gratefully.

"If you're in need of financing, temporarily or otherwise, don't hesitate to call on me. I've already told Elias that."

"That's nice to know, but you've already been too generous. However, if we should need to borrow, things are going so well on the mainland, we'd be able to pay it back."

"I wouldn't hear of it. After the care Nanine has given me, you'd have to put it down as a medical fee."

Virginia said, "Nanine, will you come back to the house?"

"No." Nanine promptly rejected the offer. "I will not leave Miles and I know Mama well enough that she'd never stand for his being under the same roof with her."

"You're right about that," Virginia agreed. "I meant that I want you to feel free to come there whenever you wish. You belong with Miles until we can get Mama to change her mind."

"I don't blame your mother," Miles said. "She'd be the hardest to convince that I did not kill her son by intent. Nan, I'll be all right if you wish to move back. Just so I see you each day. I'm feeling better."

"No, Miles," Nanine said firmly. "I'm staying here. My place is with you."

"Thanks, my dearest," he said with a smile. "Sooner or later though, it's going to cause gossip."

Virginia almost laughed aloud at the idea. "There are only the Yankee carpetbaggers here and nobody cares what they think," she said. "Miles, I'll do all I can to change Mama's mind. In the meantime, Nan, come to the house whenever you wish."

"I'd like to go back with you now," Nanine said. "Just for a little while. I do go to the kitchen."

"I know. I've seen you. I may as well confess I visited the kitchen recently in the hope you'd be there, but I always picked the wrong time."

Nanine slipped a shawl around her shoulders. "I won't be long, darling."

"Take your time," he said cheerfully. "I'll be fine."

Nanine turned to Virginia. "How is Phoebe? I know she's an actress. Elias brought me her letters to read. Thanks for sharing them with me."

"I haven't heard from her for a week, but I'm sure she's doing very well. I want to show you the books. Our island plantation is going to make money this year. Lots of it. Cotton is easy to sell in this very short market. Especially our crop. It's better than ever."

"That's good news," Nanine said.

She kissed Miles, adjusted the blankets and brought him a tall glass of milk. She and Virginia left the hospital and walked slowly back to the mansion, arm in arm.

"He's really very ill," Nanine confided. "I am worried about him. He isn't doing as I'd hoped."

"He's too thin and his color, well, it's not like yours was when you began to recover."

"He isn't responding as I did. I know I'm treating him in the only way possible. But he was in such terrible condition when I got him here. Then the duel . . ." She broke off. "No sense in bringing that up. How's Mama?"

"As full of complaints as ever and very set on not allowing Miles into the house. I'm not even sure she'll agree to let you come back, if only to visit. I'll fight her on that, but you know Mama."

Nanine smiled. "The three Hammond women are stubborn. I suppose I surprised you when I insisted on bringing Miles here."

"Very much. Now I'm glad. You've given him happiness."

"It's he who's given it to me," Nanine replied. "I feel alive for the first time in my life."

"You're really in love with him, aren't you."

"Of course I am. It seems to me I've waited for him all my life. I knew that as soon as the shock of that insane duel left me."

"Strange," Virginia mused. "If it hadn't been for the duel, you'd never have met him."

They reached the veranda stairs and then crossed to the front door. Lenore was halfway down the stairs when they entered the house. There was no welcoming smile on her face.

Virginia said, "I've brought Nan back, Mama. This is where she belongs and you know it."

"Did you send the murderer packing?" Lenore regarded Nanine coldly.

"Miles will remain at the old hospital," Nanine said. "Haven't you even a smile for me, Mama?"

"How can you look me in the face? Your brother lies in his grave on this island because of that man."

"Mama," Virginia said sternly, "let's stop talking about it. I now admit that I was wrong in judging him as I did. I went to him and apologized. I hope one day you will."

"That's heresy," Lenore said angrily.

"Please, Mama," Nanine pleaded. "He's very ill. Worse than I ever was."

"I hope he dies," Lenore said coldly.

Nanine turned away, bringing a hand to her face as the tears began.

"You ought to be ashamed of yourself," Virginia told her mother. "I've asked Nan to come here as often as she wishes. There are many things Nan and I have to discuss and if you can't be courteous, stay upstairs while she's here. Miles will remain where he is. You don't have to worry about him being in the house. He understands your feelings."

"I would stand in the doorway to prevent him from entering," Lenore said defiantly. "That's how I feel and I'll not change. Nanine is my daughter. I do not condone what she is doing, but I certainly cannot object to her being in her own home. Now—please excuse me."

She walked back up the stairs. Virginia emitted a long sigh, shook her head in dismay and led Nanine into the drawing room. They sat side by side on one of the settees. Virginia drew an arm around her sister's shoulder.

"At least we've broken the ice," she said. "It will go easier from here on. I wish Elias was with me. Mama listens to him even if he is, in her words, a horrible Yankee."

"I'll try to forgive her," Nanine said. She wiped away the remnants of her tears. "I know how she is, how she thinks. I'm sure it will work out eventually."

"What of Miles? Has he asked you to marry him?"

Nanine tried to smile. "No. He's too despondent. He's sure he isn't going to live very long and he's said, so often, that all he can bring to those who love him is sorrow."

"He needs a good talking to," Virginia said.

"He can be stubborn too. I guess each of us has a degree of it. Anyway, I'm happy we're together again, Virgie. I'm sure Elias will be glad too."

"I can assure you he will be. He told me how wrong I was almost every day."

"He's a good man, Virgie. Have you heard anything more about that bandit who came here to plunder the island?"

"No," Virginia lied skillfully. "He has no further business here, I hope. He's supposed to be an evil man. But that day in the forest, the first time I confronted him, he was a perfect gentleman."

"All men are gallant to you, Virgie. You're so beautiful. I think you've even grown more beautiful since the war."

"It's nice to hear that, of course, even if it's not true. What we went through should have turned me into a wrinkled old maid. Oh, Nan, I didn't mean anything by that," she added contritely.

Nanine smiled tolerantly. "Those are just words. They were true in my case once, but no longer. I'll admit that if Miles had the energy and strength, I'd get into bed with him today, tonight, anytime. Do I sound like a harlot for saying that?"

"You're talking like a girl in love. Make Miles well again. Let me help in any way possible. If you think he should go North for treatment, go with him."

"He's better off here. They'll treat him exactly as I'm doing now. It has to work. Remember how I looked? Like someone already measured for her coffin. There were times when I wished I was in it. I know what poor Miles is going through. I'll make him well. I must."

"You will, Nan. I'm sure of it. And don't let Mama worry you. She'll come around. It'll take time, but she's not completely stupid. Or hateful. Marty was her only son. Her pride and joy. Also, she's dramatizing the situation and calling attention to herself. Once the social life begins here, she'll get over it. Now, come into the library and let's go over the books. You're the one who always attended to them and I've had to do it since . . . since Miles. I've likely made a hundred mistakes.''

They spent an hour going over the books, which turned out to have been meticulously managed. Then Nanine became concerned about having been away from Miles so long. Virginia accompanied Nanine out of the house. They stood on the veranda and shaded their eyes as they caught sight of a small craft being rowed toward shore.

"It seems to me there are two men . . . in Yankee uniforms . . . ,'' Nanine said.

Virginia cried out in fear. "I hope nothing's happened to Elias . . .''

They ran down to the dock and waited there anxiously, until the rowboat docked. Captain Delaney, in charge of the Union Occupation Forces in Charleston, stepped ashore and saluted Nanine and Virginia.

"Captain, is there trouble?" Virginia asked worriedly. "Is it Elias?''

"No, Mrs. Birch,'' Delaney said. "Last I talked to Elias, he was working from dawn to dusk at the plantation.''

Virginia breathed a sigh of relief.

"I saw him this morning, in fact. He was in the city to do some banking and buying. I asked him the same question I'm about to ask you. And you, Miss Hammond. We learned that last evening Bradley Culver was seen as a passenger in a boat rowed by one of his men and heading out to sea in the direction of Valcour.''

Virginia's fears over Elias's welfare were minor to the terror that now invaded her.

"Did he show up here, ladies?''

"Not that I know of,'' Nanine said.

"Nor I,'' Virginia added hastily. "Why would he come here, Captain?''

"Why would a man like Culver do anything? Last evening a group of his men attacked a small settlement three miles out of Charleston. They killed two men. I'm sure they didn't treat the womenfolk gently. They stole whatever they could carry and burned down three homes. All because the menfolk living there had appeared at a town meeting and suggested the best thing to do was recognize the Union and hold an election.''

"Is Culver that intolerant of anyone joining the Union?" Nanine asked.

"Culver doesn't recognize the fact that the war is over, ladies. He's an evil man bound to end up with a rope around his neck. The sooner, the better."

"But you said that last evening Culver was seen in a rowboat," Virginia said. "How could he be in both places?"

"The raid took place well after midnight," Delaney explained. "He was seen in the boat before that. We're doing all we can to arrest that man and we follow every lead we get. That's why I'm here. We know he'd been on Valcour twice before, the last time to return the loot he'd previously stolen from the Yankees on the island."

"That's true," Virginia said. "We didn't understand it either."

"As I see the situation, Culver did not steal anything from your family, Mrs. Birch, but everyone else was robbed."

"Mr. Culver," Virginia said, striving desperately for calmness, "first came to the island and looted the Yankee homes. At that time he confronted me as I was riding back from the other end of the island. Naturally, I was terrified. When I learned what his mission was, I begged him not to burn or destroy anything. I explained who I was and he seemed to change from a man to be feared into a polite Southern gentleman."

"But he did steal from the Yankee homes."

"Yes, Captain. However, he harmed no one and then, to our surprise, as to yours, he returned with the stolen articles and left them on our veranda. We returned them."

"It was a strange thing to do. For a man of his evil reputation," Nanine said.

"We don't understand it," the captain said. "But then, some of the niceties and methods of your cavalier Southerners are beyond the comprehension of a Yankee anyway. Meaning no offense, ladies. I admire chivalry as much as the next man, but Culver, that murderous rascal, being chivalrous?"

"Well, you may be assured Mr. Culver did not come here last night," Nanine said. "Or if he did, he certainly kept it a secret."

"I saw no stranger last evening," Virginia added. "You must be mistaken, Captain."

"I realize that just because he was seen in a rowboat doesn't necessarily mean he came here," the captain admitted. "I told Elias I'd make certain you were safe."

"Thank you, Captain," Virginia said graciously.

"I'm relieved to know you're safe. Sorry to have disturbed you." Captain Delaney looked beyond them to the mansion and the part of the island in his line of vision. "You're doing wonders here. I'm glad. A place like this should be preserved forever, just as it is. I envy Elias. Thank you and good day, ladies."

He saluted again, stepped aboard his boat and was promptly rowed back to the mainland while Nanine and Virginia walked toward the mansion.

"I wonder if Culver did come here last night," Nanine mused.

"Why do you say that?" Virginia's tone held a hint of irritation. A fact not lost on Nanine.

"Why Virgie, you seem annoyed I should say such a thing."

"I am. For heaven's sake, why would he come here?"

"I don't know, of course. But then, according to the account you gave of your first meeting with him, he did treat you like a lady. And he did return the loot. Just as you asked. No one was hurt, nothing destroyed, and destruction is what he and his men seem to dote on."

"Meaning just what?" Virginia asked.

"Why, nothing, except that it was possible the man may have become infatuated with you and decided to pay another visit. You are an extremely beautiful woman. A very sensual one."

Virginia eyed Nanine indignantly then she began to laugh. For perhaps two or three minutes, neither spoke. Then Nanine looked sideways at her sister.

"I do declare, Virgie, when Captain Delaney brought up the subject of Culver, you actually blushed."

"I did not. I had nothing to blush about. Mr. Culver means nothing to me."

"I'm sure he doesn't, but I thought perhaps you had a slight regard for the man after the courteous manner in which he treated you. And respected your wishes not to harm anyone on the island."

"Mr. Culver is a renegade, a murderer and worse. He is doomed to be executed."

"He deserves it," Nanine said quietly.

Virginia said, "I was upset, though. I was so afraid Captain Delaney was bringing bad news about Elias."

"Of course that was the reason." Nanine spoke with new awareness. "Well, one thing's for certain. Mr. Culver has brought a little excitement into our lives."

"Indeed, yes. I'll walk you back to the hospital and look in on Miles again. Nan, I'm glad we're together once more. I missed you terribly."

Nanine nodded. "It was the same with me."

Miles was dozing when they returned and Virginia didn't stay. She walked slowly back to the mansion. From here on she knew she would have to be very careful in the way she responded should Culver's name be brought into any conversation.

And, she told herself, she must never see him again. Not ever, for it was much too dangerous. To her reputation, and to Culver's very life. The authorities were hot on his trail now and would never relent until he was captured and disposed of.

She tried to figure out some way to reach him, but it was impossible. He moved about all the time and if he had any emissaries or spies abroad in Charleston, they were not likely to make themselves known, even to her.

If he came again, surreptitiously in the dead of night, she must turn him away. She told herself that, yet with every step she took the resolution to do so grew weaker. If he had suddenly appeared in the path before her, she would have gone with him. Yet it was difficult for her to understand why, for she would go with him only to the whipping shed and never beyond. She would never leave the island for him. She could never adapt her ways of life to his. She didn't even love the man, she assured herself. And yet . . . she yearned for him. For the passionate way he made love. Ways that brought out a wantonness in her that she'd never been aware of.

She began to believe she was much as her father had been.

Lusting for life and love and daring anything to fulfill her desires. Yet her behavior puzzled her, for she firmly believed she was deeply in love with Elias.

Culver was a cutthroat, a desperado. He was evil personified. He should be killed out of hand by anyone who faced him. There was no mercy in him and he expected none. He was feared and hated and should be, especially by someone like Virginia. Yet, even aware of that, her mind was striving to find a way to reach him. To warn him, certainly, but mostly to be with him once more. She knew she was completely under his spell.

eighteen

"The Bijou Theater," Tom ordered as he settled down in the carriage beside Phoebe. The vehicle made a turn on to Third Avenue to ride beside a noisy horsecar.

"At least," Phoebe observed, "we don't have to ride in one of those anymore."

"You'd be very uncomfortable on a horsecar these days," Tom said. "Everybody in New York recognizes you. They'd be asking questions and wanting you to write your name on some bit of paper."

"I love it," Phoebe said. She looked radiant and felt that way, for she was dressed in the latest fashion. Everything had gone well with them. She was the star of the minstrel show, she was written up in the newspapers and *Leslie's Weekly* had written a story about her, mostly concocted out of thin air, for little of it was true, but it served to enhance her reputation.

"When will the minstrel show close?" Tom asked. "I know that date has been postponed twice, due entirely to you."

"In a month, darling. That's why I'm going to see Mr. Lowell Stuart this morning. He's almost ready to begin rehearsals for a musical play. It's bound to be a success. Look what happened to *The Black Crook*. It sells out every performance. People from as far away as Rochester and Boston come to see it."

"Hold out for plenty," Tom advised. "Those shows make enough to pay you a thousand a week."

"It will be more like six or seven hundred to begin with. But if the show really goes over, then I'll demand more. I really don't care about the money end of it, Tom. I so love working on the stage, I'd do it for nothing if I had to."

"After what we went through," he said remindfully, his smile wry.

"I know. I remember it very well indeed. Do you ever try to find a teaching job anymore? Not that you have to," she added hastily. "It's wonderful to have you free to accompany me when I need you."

"I drop by once a week. I'm treated with a great deal more respect because of your reputation, but . . . no job. They keep promising, but there are so many teachers ahead of me, all looking for any opening."

"What do you do with yourself all day and in the evenings?" she asked.

"Walk about. I drop into the theater every night to watch the show for a while. Thank you for getting me that pass. I'd never be able to afford two and a half dollars every night."

"Doesn't it get boring?" she asked.

"Boring as all hell," he said. "It's not normal for a man to loaf all day while his wife works. It does get under my skin."

"Maybe I could find something in the theater—"

"No! I'm a teacher. I'd never be satisfied with anything else. There'll be an opening one of these days and, as you say, we can wait."

"Why don't you try for a teaching job elsewhere?" she asked, her memory of that letter from his mother still fresh in her mind. "Perhaps in the town where your parents live."

"Phoebe, I couldn't stand it, being away from you."

She patted his cheek with a gloved hand. "Thank you, darling. I hope one of these days I'll be free long enough to pay your parents a visit."

"I write them and send them clippings. They know all about your success. As you say, one of these days . . ."

"Yes," she said, "one of these days."

The tone she used caused him to glance her way with some

apprehension, but she seemed perfectly calm. The carriage brought them to the Bijou, a new theater not far from the Bowery. It was already a proven success and was of a caliber equal to Niblo's Gardens, the Bowery Theater and Wallack's. Its owner and producer was noted for his fine shows and his lavish method of living. Lowell Stuart also had a reputation as a rather high-class roué.

They entered the outer office where a mannish-looking secretary looked up from her desk with her usual haughty glance. It changed instantly when she recognized Phoebe.

"Mrs. Sprague!" She came to her feet. "Mr. Stuart is waiting. Please . . . this way."

Tom followed the two women. Before she opened the door, the secretary turned to Tom. "You will have to wait, Mr. Sprague. Please make yourself comfortable."

Tom shrugged, returned to the row of chairs and sat down. he felt ill at ease. This happened every time he was in the company of these theatrical folks. They seemed to be a breed apart and showed little enthusiasm for anyone who was not integrated into their world.

In the large and lavishly furnished office, Mr. Lowell Stuart rose from behind his desk, the largest Phoebe had ever seen. He came forward to greet her, holding out both hands. He was a middle-aged man, somewhat portly, with muttonchop whiskers, but no beard or mustache. He was dressed in gray trousers, a morning coat with a high, stiff collar and a string tie. His face was somewhat florid, attesting to some very fine living, Phoebe thought. Since her hands were gloved, he kissed her cheek.

"I've wanted to meet you so much, my dear," he said. "You've made quite a name for yourself in the minstrel. When you get up to dance, the audience becomes mesmerized. A tribute to your talent."

"Thank you, Mr. Stuart," she said quietly. "I do the best I can."

"Where in the world did you learn to dance that way?"

"From watching Negro dances on my father's plantation. I used to join in. They taught me everything I know about this form of dancing."

"They taught you well. It's new and it's different. Now we have a part for you in this new show that's going to ensure that you will be the most talked-about actress on any stage. The script isn't ready yet and the songs are now being written by the best songwriters we could find. In about a week we'll be ready for casting and rehearsals. I want you to sign a contract for the duration of the run. I can offer you four hundred a week."

Phoebe smiled and sat down before the desk. "Mr. Stuart, let's not play the usual games. Six hundred to begin and after one month, if the show is a success, you will pay me a thousand dollars a week. I make six hundred with the minstrels. I cannot lower my wage scale even for you, sir."

"That's a tough bargain," he said cheerfully, "but I'll meet it and we don't have to haggle. Now let me tell you about the show, the plot and the place in it for you."

She listened to him describe what she instantly knew would be a highly successful show that could run for months, even years. While she gloried in the chance to play her part in it, she didn't let Stuart realize how very anxious she was.

"Mr. Stuart," she said finally, "I agree it will be a very fine show. I'm happy to be in it and I ask that you now prepare the contract to go into effect the day we begin rehearsals."

"You don't dicker, do you, Phoebe? I like that. Yes, I like everything about you. We're going to get along fine. Besides talent and beauty you have intelligence—which explains your good business sense."

"Thank you." She rose. He came around the desk to step close to her.

"You're a charming girl," Stuart said. "I predict one of the brightest futures in our world for you. With the proper management, of course. I should like to take over that task."

As he spoke, he rested a hand on her shoulder in a fatherly sort of way that changed somewhat as his hand slid down her arm, then moved over to pass gently across her breast.

Phoebe smiled coolly and stepped back. "If you do that again, Mr. Stuart, I'll not only walk out of your show, but I'll tell the whole world why. Or do you wish to cancel the negotiations now?"

"Why, Phoebe," he said, taken aback. "I certainly meant nothing. In the world of show business, we often grow very affectionate with one another. There is no other meaning to—"

"And as for taking over the management of my affairs, Mr. Stuart," she interrupted him, "my husband is quite capable of doing that. Now, if you'll excuse me..." At the door she looked back. "Please let me know when rehearsals start and have the contract ready before then. Good day, sir."

She walked out serenely, proud of the way she'd handled herself. Tom came to his feet and took her elbow to escort her out of the office. In the corridor, she slipped her forearm around his. It didn't matter now that he was afraid to take her to meet his parents, or that he did suffer some degree of embarrassment over the fact she was an ex-slave. He was Tom, and she loved him and the rest of it was of no consequence.

Tom rode with her in the carriage to the theater for the matinee. He dismissed the carriage and accompanied her to the stage door. There she embraced him and kissed him warmly.

"There's no sense in just hanging around," she said. "I'll see you at suppertime. Pick a nice place to eat and meet me here after the show."

"I'll find something to do," he said. "I go to the library quite often so I can keep up with my profession. They have a lot of books about teaching and one day I'll go back to it. Don't worry about me."

She left him and he turned away, reached the street and wondered which way to turn. Uptown or downtown. It didn't matter. Wherever he went, he was bored. He often stopped at a saloon on Fifth Avenue and he'd become fairly well known there. He wondered if he was drinking too much. Phoebe never suspected where he spent some of his time and he never drank so much as to make it visible.

He had his early afternoon brandy, then meandered in the direction of the library. He'd told the truth about that. He enjoyed the quiet of the big reading room.

As he walked, he was accustomed to stopping before the windows of large stores to examine their displays. He was admiring a tailor's array of fine tweeds when he noticed the reflection of a lanky, neatly dressed man in the window. He'd caught a glimpse of him before, several times. Dressed in a green plaid suit, unusual for a wardrobe these days, he was easy to notice.

A block away, Tom came to an abrupt stop, raised a foot to a projection in the wall of a building, and pretended to tie his shoelace. Sure enough, the man in the green plaid suit was half a block away and he had also come to a stop. As he had no window to peer into so innocently, he stood awkwardly in the middle of the sidewalk. Apparently, he sensed he'd been observed and was embarrassed at being caught in the open like this.

Tom went on, sorely puzzled. He was tempted to round the next corner, step out as the man came by and seize him to demand an explanation. But that would raise a fuss. If the man resisted, Tom would have to do battle. He detested even the thought of any kind of altercation. Also, the police might come into it, along with Phoebe's name. That would give the story major significance and result in it being written up in the newspapers.

So Tom kept walking and entered the library. He proceeded directly to the stack room, where he found two volumes he wished to examine. He carried these to the huge open reading room, where he sat down at a long table.

At first he thought he'd either eluded the man in the green plaid suit, or he'd only imagined the man had been following him. But after a few minutes, the man appeared. He entered the reading room, looked about, saw Tom and came directly toward him.

There was no one close by. The man settled himself into a chair beside Tom. He even raised himself slightly so he might move his chair closer to Tom.

"All right," Tom said with some heat, "who are you and why are you following me about?"

"Keep your voice down, Mr. Sprague," the man said. "They get sore if you talk too loud in here."

"Never mind that. What's this all about?"

"Keep your voice down," he whispered harshly. "What I got to say is important, but it ain't something you'd want anybody else to know about."

"I'm sure I don't know what you're talking about," Tom said. "Speak up, if you do have anything to say to me."

"Oh, I got plenty, Mr. Sprague. Yes, indeedy, I got plenty. You ever hear of a man named Tobal?"

"Tobal?" Tom searched his memory vainly. "I'd remember that name all right and I never heard it before."

"He's a big, dumb nigger."

Tom felt the first twinges of apprehension. "Begin at the beginning, will you? Who are you?"

"I'm a lawyer. Well, that is, I never passed the bar exams. Don't make no difference to me. I get along, see? You can call me Darby. Bill Darby it is."

"Very well, Mr. Darby, will you fill me in, please? You've been following me for some time. You must have a reason for it."

"You sure do a lot o' walkin', Mr. Sprague. I kept after you until I got you in a place where you wouldn't be apt to raise a fuss or curse me out loud. This is the best place I ever saw."

"I can still make a big fuss and curse you out," Tom warned.

"Yep, reckon you can at that. Now don't get sore. This big buck works on the waterfront. He comes to me one day . . . I got some clients down there and somebody told him I could help him."

"Help him in what way?" Tom asked, growing more and more fearful that this man did have something important to divulge.

"Well, you see, this here buck, he used to work on an island down around the Carolinas. I think he said the name of the place was Valcour. I'm not sure about the name. The nigger talks kinda funny, a lingo that don't make much sense sometimes."

Now Tom knew what was to come and he grew icy cold inside.

"Well, what's this buck got to do with me?"

"You know where Valcour is, don't you?"

"Yes, I know where it is."

"Well, this here nigger he says your wife is a nigger too."

Now it was out. Now Tom knew and it scared him half to death. He didn't know how to handle this situation and he knew he must use tact. Above all, he must protect Phoebe.

"You tell your Negro friend that he's crazy. You've seen my

wife's picture. Maybe you even went to see her in the show. If she's a Negro, you got big spots before your eyes."

"He didn't say she was all nigger. He says the Southern gent who used to own the island and the plantation on it is her papa by a nigger woman. A slave. He says her ma wasn't coal black either, but she sure was a nigger and your wife's got plenty nigger blood. And she was born a slave."

"Suppose you're right about this. What do you intend to do with this information?"

"Do? Why nothin', Mr. Sprague. Nothin' at all. This nigger says he's mad as hell at everybody on that island. He got into some trouble there. They made him leave and he says the only work he can get in New York is heavy stuff on the docks and he ain't up to it. So all he wants is for you to give him a little money every week. Like payday. You know . . . enough to live on. Then he'll keep his mouth shut real tight."

"In plain English, this is blackmail," Tom said angrily.

"You can call it that, you want to. This here buck's got to be paid or he's sure goin' to the newspapers an' tell what he knows. They'll be glad to pay him."

"Mr. Darby, I don't know where you got this crazy information, but it won't work. If you attempt to extort money from us, I'll have you thrown into jail and the buck as well. You tell him that."

"Now Mr. Sprague, that ain't usin' your head none. Your wife now, she dances . . . nigger dancing. They say she's better'n any nigger ever was on any stage. But what if the newspapers gets to know she's a nigger? It'd make a mighty fine story and they sure wouldn't miss it. A white woman who dances like a nigger and really is a nigger. They'd make somethin' of that now, wouldn't they?"

"This buck you talk about. Where can I meet him to verify what you've just told me."

"I can tell you where right now. You go down to the docks. Just a little above the Battery you'll see a saloon that's called Mike's Place. You go in there late this afternoon. You want to handle this right away, and I'll have the nigger there."

"What do you get out of this? How are you involved?"

"Well, you could say I'm his lawyer, but I ain't a real lawyer so just say I'm his agent."

"And if I don't go to the police, how much do you think this information is worth to be kept secret?"

"We figured maybe a hundred dollars..."

"That's absurd. A hundred a month—"

"A week," Darby corrected him smoothly. "Just remember, Mr. Sprague, your wife is going to be in a big show and make lots of money. But if this comes out, they'll fire her sure. Niggers ain't welcome on the New York stage. Not lessen it's to be a butler or somethin' like that. A hundred a week ain't much and it lets her make lots more'n that."

"I'll be at this saloon around half-past four. You have that man there."

"Sure. Be glad to. Ain't no reason you should get sore about this. What the hell, all your wife's got to do is ask for more dough. She'll get it. And you know what? She is a mighty good dancer. Yes, sir, she dances just like a nigger and that's goin' some."

Tom rose abruptly, closed the book he was reading, returned it to the stack room and left the library. Darby was still sitting at the table when Tom departed. He walked the streets for an hour, not even knowing where he went. Right at this moment, when Phoebe was riding so high, this had to happen. If it became known that she was part Negro, she would surely lose her job. Tom's parents would know he'd married a girl with nigger blood. Everybody would know. It would be very embarrassing and it might go so far as to literally kill Phoebe. That this man Darby was in contact with some buck who used to work on Valcour was very evident. He couldn't possibly know all he did without that. A hundred a week. It was a lot of money, but Phoebe was going to receive a thousand a week. Perhaps a hundred was cheap.

But he couldn't tell her. If he did, he knew very well that she'd defy Darby and the buck, even go to the police and damn the results. She was not one to deny what was true, even if it cost her the glittering future that was certain to be in store.

He would have to submit to this blackmail. There was no other way. He did have a fleeting idea of killing Darby and the buck, but

311

he shrugged that off at once as being not only impractical, but impossible. No, he'd pay and somehow he'd keep Phoebe from knowing. He owed her that much. It might also relieve him of this burden he carried, in that he was living off his wife. Now, in protecting her, he was giving something in return, even if she wasn't aware of it.

At four-thirty he walked along the waterfront, having dismissed the carriage some distance away. Mike's Place was easy to find, for it sported a large, somewhat dirty-looking sign over the door. The windows were dirty, the door window had a lace curtain that looked as if it had been last washed about the time of Bull Run. Tom felt uneasy entering the place, for its patrons were dockworkers, tough and looking for a fight at the least provocation. The patrons were a mixture of black and white, also an unusual condition in New York City.

Darby was seated at a little round table along the far wall. With him was a bulky Negro, dressed in shabby workman's clothes. Darby stood up, waving to attract Tom's attention. Tom crossed the room, aware that he was being observed as a rare curiosity by the other patrons, but no one tried to intercept him. He sat down at Darby's invitation. Tobal presented Tom with a big, toothy grin.

"Yas, suh," he said. "Yo' sho' lookin' fine, Mistah Lieutenant."

"What's the 'lieutenant' business?" Darby asked.

"Mistah Sprague, heah, was a Yankee soldier all durin' the wah. He was runnin' things on Valcour."

"Were you a slave there?" Tom asked.

"Yas, suh, sho' was, suh. Right till yo' comes an' say we is free. Mighty happy to welcome yo', suh. Bein' free is mighty nice."

"Why did you leave Valcour?" Tom asked.

"Tells yo' why, suh. Tells yo' why Ah been aimin' to tell whut Missy Phoebe is. 'Cause she a sistah to that sonabitch Missy Virginia who owns the islan' now. Yo' know whut she done to me? She puts a bullet in me, that's whut she done. An' it keeps hurtin' like hell. Sho' do, all the time. So Ah ain't one to like Missy Virginia, an' Phoebe bein' her sistah, Ah hates her too. Gots to get money 'cause bein' shot that way make me a real sick man, suh. Real sick. Cain't wuk much no mo'."

"You know if I go to the police, you'll spend much of your life behind bars," Tom warned.

"Sho' knows it, suh. Cain't be none diff'runt from bein' a slave, suh. Ah gets used to it, but Missy Phoebe she goin' to be laughed at. Yas, suh, this heah whole town goin' to laugh they haids off they evah knows she a niggah."

"How do I know you won't be asking for more than a hundred a week?"

The buck gaped at Tom. Then he looked at Darby with slow, raging anger written on his face. "A hundrud dollahs a week? Yo' says mayhap ten dollahs we gits."

"That's what I told you," Darby said hurriedly and with some alarm. "But I got thinkin' this woman makes a lot o' money an' she ought to pay us more. So I asked a hundred."

"Now ain't that somethin'," Tobal rolled his big eyes. "This heah bastahd goin' to cheat me. Goddamm iffen the folks heah in the No'th ain't wuss than the folks in the South. One hundrud dollahs. Yas, suh, Ah likes that."

"We won't ask for more than that," Darby said. "It's enough for Tobal to live on and I can use my ten percent."

"Whut's 'ten percent'?" Tobal asked suspiciously.

"Ten dollars. You get ninety."

"Thinks that's fair 'nuff, but yo' cheats me an' Ah tells yo' now, Ah busts yo' skinny neck. Yo' heah?"

"I heard you." Darby turned to Tom. "Is it a business arrangement?"

"It's blackmail, but I'll pay," Tom said. "How do we arrange it?"

"Let's say every Tuesday you go the library and take out two books. In one of them put a hundred dollars and when I come in, you kinda shove the book my way so nobody notices. I'll take out the money and go away. Until next Tuesday."

"All right. I'll be there Tuesday. If I can't raise the money, I'll be there anyway and let you know."

"Yo' sho' bettah raise it, Mistah Lieutenant," Tobal said.

"You keep your nigger mouth shut tight," Tom warned him. "If you ever tell this to anyone, I swear I'll put a bullet where it will kill you. Understand me, Tobal?"

"Yas, suh, ain't settin' to make no mo' trouble, suh. Yo' pays an' keeps me happy an' nuthin' goin' to happen."

Tom rose and walked out. He hailed a carriage and was driven home to find Phoebe already there, helping the maid in the kitchen. She came out to greet him with a kiss.

"You're out late this afternoon," she said.

"I got lost in a book at the library. And I've been doing a lot of thinking. We'll talk about it after supper."

She brushed a stray lock of hair back over his forehead. "You sound so serious, darling."

"Well, it's serious business, but not all that important. I'm starved."

They ate while Phoebe chattered about the performance. "I swear I keep getting more and more applause," she said. "And it makes me want to do better. Aren't we lucky people, darling? Just think...not many weeks ago we had that one ugly little room..."

"I wish I'd had even half your success," he said. "And that's what I want to talk to you about."

"Talk now," she said. "I'm curious."

"All right. It's just a straight business proposition. It's bothered me for some time that you're carrying the whole load of this family, Phoebe. I can't get a job and you're making ten times as much as I would be getting if I had a job. So, to make up for the part I haven't played in our finances, I'm going to suggest that I act as your manager."

"Why, Tom, I had that very idea in mind. I hesitated suggesting it to you for fear you might resent it. I'm relieved."

"Thanks. I'll handle the money. Take your checks to the bank. I suggest we have a joint account. You can draw on it whenever you wish. But I'll pay the bills and keep track of your contracts and any other business deals that might come up."

"I never heard anything I'd like better." She looked pleased.

Tom breathed a quiet sigh of relief. "It will make things easier all around. I'll see that you are paid what you deserve. Also, I'll invest your money wisely."

"Our money," she corrected him.

"Thank you, my sweet," he said with a smile. "Someday I'll add to it on my own. However, in the meantime, I'll be doing something to earn my keep.''

"If there are papers to sign, legal arrangements to be made, you make them, darling. You know,'' she said, her eyes teasing him, "it's going to be fun going to bed with my manager.''

nineteen

During the following week, Valcour had settled down to a quiet interlude. There were two letters from Elias reporting that the big plantation was doing fine, and though the greening of the plants had already taken place, he was working harder than ever.

There was also a letter from Phoebe, enclosing several reviews and articles in newspapers praising her talent for exotic dancing. She was well, working hard and Tom had not only taken over the managing of her career, but the financial affairs, and had invested a part of their income, apparently with great success.

At Valcour, the only unpleasantness was from the Yankee carpetbaggers who were slowly reaching the stage of near bankruptcy. None of them came with much money—but with a total lack of understanding of the South, its people and, most important of all, the growing of cotton. One family gave up during that week and moved away, leaving the interior of the house in a shambles. They'd taken their anger and frustration out in the destruction of walls, doors, stairs and anything else that could be rendered useless.

"From here on," Virginia told Nanine, "I shall insist on inspecting the premises before I buy the house, and then only a few hours before they are ready to leave. If the house is in the condition the last one was in, I'll refuse to buy until it is restored to its original condition."

"Be careful," Nanine warned. "I think some of those men might actually become dangerous."

"The women aren't exactly friendly either. I can't blame them for that, but they seem proud of what their men did."

"I just hope they don't turn on us. I'm more fearful for Miles, than for any of us."

Virginia nodded sympathetically. "How is he?"

Nanine's brow furrowed. "I don't know. At least I don't think he's any worse. I remember how I felt when I was so ill. There were times when I could barely stand up. That's how he is now. I try to get him outside for a little exercise, but he says he's too weak. I walk him around the hospital. It's large enough so that he gets some good out of it, but he has to lean on me most of the time."

"I've tried to change Mama's mind, but to no avail. Do you want to defy her and bring him here? I'll back you up. I'm tired of her childish behavior."

"Thanks, Virgie," Nanine said with a sad smile. "Miles is content where he is. His coming here—even if he would—might do him harm. Certainly Mama would get highly emotional. She might even become ill. We don't need that problem."

"You're right," Virginia agreed. "Too bad Elias isn't here to visit Miles."

"That would be pleasant," Nanine said. "His friends Anton Boyle and James Warren come regularly and always bring fruit or vegetables and, of course, brandy and bourbon. They even brought four cases of wine two days ago."

"You'll have a wine cellar there," Virginia laughed. "Does Brandy know about it?"

"Oh, yes," Nanine said laughingly. "He totes it from the boat and Belle walks back and forth with him every step of the way. She doesn't trust him out of her sight, though I don't believe he'd steal anything."

"You mean Belle's suspicious of him are groundless?"

"I mean he's terrified of her," Nanine said. "I saw him try to slip some fruit in his pocket and she raised her foot and booted him so hard he fell on his face and skidded several feet across the grass."

Virginia laughed heartily. "I wish I could have seen it. Elias would have enjoyed it too."

Nanine said, "Thank goodness things are going well for him on the mainland. Now, I'd better get to work on the bookkeeping. Elias sends enough of it from the mainland and the business dealings are getting complicated."

"I'll visit Miles," Virginia offered. "I can keep him company for a while."

"That would please him. I'll be back by sundown."

Virginia walked slowly along the path to the hospital. From a low rise in the ground overlooking the cotton fields, she surveyed the rapidly growing whiteness of the plants. This was a thrill that never lessened with the viewing. It was almost as it used to be before the war. She guessed that the Yankees would not be able to hold out longer than autumn. Some were in dire straits already.

Miles showed little improvement. He was just as thin and perhaps paler than ever. But he was cheerful and Virginia's entrance brought a smile to his lips.

"I've learned to live with it," he told Virginia when she commented on his cheerful attitude. "Since I've come here and been with Nanine, I'm enjoying life to the fullest extent I'm capable of."

"Do you really love her?" Virginia asked.

"I'm so in love with her it's driving me mad," he confessed.

"Then why don't you ask her to marry you?"

"How can I? For one reason, I stand accused of killing her brother. No matter that I'm not entirely to blame for what happened, I must accept responsibility for a duel I insisted Marty fight. My sole reason for it, and a selfish one I now admit, was that I actually intended to let him kill me. I wanted to die."

"Long ago," Virginia said, "I learned to disregard what anyone thinks. If I'm in the right, it doesn't disturb me. I want you to marry Nan, for her sake as well as yours."

"I'd only make her miserable," he said with a shake of his head. "She's doing all she can for me and I grant that without her care I'd probably be dead by now. But I'm not getting better. I know that and I have no desire to marry her just to add to her burden."

"She loves you," Virginia said earnestly. "She's never been so happy. To bear your name would complete her rapture."

He lowered his eyes.

"Now what?" Virginia asked, sensing his sudden change in mood.

Without looking up he said, "I could never consummate the marriage."

Virginia leaned forward and rested her hand over both of his, still clapsed in his lap. "For Nanine, that marriage will be consummated when you slip the ring on her finger."

He raised his head and studied her carefully. "Do you really believe that?"

Virginia nodded. "Miles, perhaps one of your troubles is your expectation that you won't get well. Convince yourself that you will. Certainly Nan will be at your side to give you all the encouragement you need. It's not fair to say you won't marry her because you feel you're not going to live long. After all, who knows what will happen tomorrow to any of us? Live, Miles. Live and enjoy it."

"I'll sure give it thought," he promised.

"Do more than that. Don't make Nan ask you to marry her. She's about to do just that, Miles."

"Are you serious?" His astonishment wasn't feigned.

"Completely. Don't let her humble herself."

"Your mother! She'll be horrified."

"Consider yourself and Nan, never mind Mama. Perhaps once you're married, Mama will relent and accept you. Don't count on it, but don't let her stop you."

Miles seemed more animated than Virginia had seen him before. He clasped his hands, looked up and drew back his head.

"Damned if I don't think you're right. My illness must have made me stupid."

Virginia smiled encouragement. "I'll send Nan back as soon as I return to the house. I'd like her to tell me the good news this very evening."

"Yes, Virginia. Yes, I'll ask her. I've been a fool not to do so before now. I'll make her as happy as I can, but if it should happen that I don't get better, I'll leave her everything I own. And that's a considerable amount. My only desire is to make her happy. Count on me."

320

That evening Nanine appeared at the mansion while Virginia and her mother were still eating supper.

"I'm going to shock and offend you, Mama," Nanine said, "but I will not do something secretly that you do not approve of. Miles and I are going to be married next week."

Lenore's eyes revealed shocked disapproval. "I will not consent to you marrying the man who murdered my son, your brother."

"I'm over thirty, Mama. I don't need your consent. I have a feeling Marty would approve."

"So do I," Virginia stated firmly. "I'm all for it."

"I intend to bring a preacher here. Miles is too ill to go to the mainland. It will be a quiet wedding. I intend to invite no one except Virginia and Elias—and you, Mama."

"I will not attend," Lenore said, an angry gleam in her eyes. "Please do not refer to this again. I cannot order you off Valcour, but I will not acknowledge the fact that you are married to this . . . this . . . maniac. If you bring him to this house, I swear I shall clear out as quickly as possible and never return. That is all I have to say."

"Where will you go, Mama?" Virginia asked.

"It doesn't matter," Lenore said testily.

"I'm sorry, Mama," Nanine said. "I would do almost anything not to hurt you, but in this matter I must have my way. Miles and I are in love. Once, you were in love, too. Try to remember that. But do not try to stop me. I'll tolerate no interference."

She turned abruptly, her hands at her side clenched into fists, and left the room. Virginia followed, accompanying Nanine to the front door.

"You handled it properly," she told Nanine. "Don't weaken now. In time she'll realize she's been wrong, but even if she never does, go through with it."

"I have no intention of changing my mind," she said. "I've got to run. I don't want to be away from him any longer than necessary."

"I'll go to the mainland and arrange for a preacher," Virginia said. "The least I can do is to help prepare my sister's wedding. I only wish Phoebe was here."

"You could ask her," Nanine said hopefully. "There's time."

"She opens in that new show next week. It would be impossible. I don't think I'll even let her know until after you're married. So she won't be tempted to come down and perhaps ruin her chances. It's going to be a very quiet wedding anyway, but I promise you that when we have the island back to its former glory, I'll arrange a dinner and ball in honor of this wedding and it will be an affair no one will ever forget."

Nanine embraced her sister. "Thank you, dear Virgie."

When Virginia returned to the dining room, her mother, already in tears, started to sob aloud. Virginia almost went to her in an effort to comfort her, but she sat down at the other end of the table instead.

"You can stop your tears now," she said. "No matter how many you shed, it isn't going to change a thing. Nan is in love. Miles is a fine man and they're well suited to one another."

"The murderer of her brother," Lenore moaned. "The killer of my son—and your brother too. What do you expect me to do? Cheer?"

"It would help," Virginia said. "It might even help you. The fact remains, they're to be married and you'll have to get used to it, even if you refuse to accept it. I had Belle bake one of your chocolate cakes. I'll tell her to fetch it."

"I couldn't eat a thing," Lenore said tearfully. "I cannot bear to sit at this table another minute."

"As you wish, Mama," Virginia said, offering neither solace nor encouragement.

As she reached the doorway, she turned. "A large serving, if you please. Belle does get so stingy at times. I'll have it upstairs."

Virginia exhaled in a great sigh of relief. She'd expected the news to be received with more tears and anger than Mama had shown. Mention of the chocolate cake dissipated the tears instantly. Virginia issued the order to Belle, who grumbled because Lenore would not be served at the table. Virginia went to her rooms after she finished her coffee. In the parlor she sat down near the window, bent her head and covered her face with her hands. The day had been an emotional strain on her also.

The mention of marriage had brought upon her that savage and overwhelming desire to see Bradley Culver again. She was ashamed

322

of herself, devastated by the realization he had become so great a part of her life. An obsession to be relieved only by his physical presence.

If Elias had been an angry man, a suspicious man, she might have felt less guilty, but he was so trusting, so loving and so occupied with the plantation. He hadn't given a single thought to her loneliness and the fact that she might be desiring him. Elias had never been demanding. Always kind and gentle. Bradley Culver, on the other hand, was possessive and demanding in his lovemaking. Yet she wanted him again. If there'd been any way to reach him, she would have sent him word.

With a sigh of frustration, she prepared for bed early. She hoped she might fall asleep quickly so she'd not be haunted by dreams of Bradley Culver. That sort of dreaming had been occurring too often of late. She'd wakened herself one night calling his name. She was relieved that no one was there to hear.

The mansion had grown silent. She heard Belle leave for the cabin she shared with Moses, after the maids and even the houseboy had gone to their respective lodgings.

She blew out the bedlamp and felt her restlessness slowly leave her. She had no idea how long she did sleep, but as she slowly wakened, she had the eerie feeling that she was not alone. She sat up suddenly. The room was so dark she could see nothing, but she was sure someone was in the room with her.

Sudden terror brought one short-lived scream to her lips. A hand promptly covered her mouth, cutting off the cry. Someone sat on the edge of the bed. The hand over her mouth was slowly released and in its place, demanding lips fastened against hers. Two arms enveloped her and drew her close. Her hands touched a bare chest. The man was naked!

"Brad!" she cried out. "Oh, Brad!"

"Shhh," he warned. His hands were already exploring her body in a way to arouse her. "Your mother is just down the hall. I almost got into her bed. Now wouldn't that have been something?"

"How did you get in? What time is it?" She held him close, covering his face with kisses.

"I picked the lock. I can open most any door. And it's early. We can have the entire evening. Right up to midnight. Then I've got to get back to the mainland before someone sees me."

"Stay the night," she begged. "All night. Dear Brad, my body ached for you. I've needed you so!"

"Can't. Too dangerous. I'll come to you only when I believe it's safe. It's easier when your husband isn't on the island. Now let's make love; arouse me, woman. Then give yourself to me. I can't wait any longer."

She was aware that he was already aroused, for he was holding her so tight she could hardly breathe, and his hands kneaded her buttocks. Virginia was as eager as he. Their lovemaking was violent, short-lived and intense. Afterward, she lay in his arms, staring at the ceiling and feeling as if she floated through space. A sense of peace flowed through her. All tension and nerves were gone.

"How did you know I wanted you to come tonight?" she whispered.

"Because of the way I felt. We're alike, Virginia. We must somehow convey our desire and need to one another."

"I wonder if you'd be as attentive and loving if we were married," she said lightly.

"Never! I'd be seeing another woman."

"Brad, you wouldn't," she admonished him, but not seriously.

"Indeed I would. I'm not a man to settle down ever. With us, it doesn't make any difference. We don't need love. We need only one another and for one purpose we're very good at."

"You're not a romantic," she said lightly.

"My romance comes in looking for danger. My thrill is a good fight."

"But I'm not fighting you, Brad. And you did enjoy my body."

"That's what it's for—my pleasure. Don't ever deny me. I'd have you anyway. Don't you believe me?"

"Completely. And I want it just the way it is."

"Good! Things are getting a bit tight on the mainland. They seem to be closing in. They've spies out trying to infiltrate my band of men. They've not made it so far, but there's a growing determination to get me strung up. I may come again soon. It had better be soon. There may not be much left for me."

"Brad, stop it now. Stop all this violence and go somewhere. Hide! Wait until it dies down. Please, for my sake."

"I didn't think you cared. You so much as said you didn't."

"But I do. I think I'd die if I no longer had you. For my sake, go away. Quickly."

"But not so far that I can't slip back to see you. Is that it?"

"Yes," she admitted boldly. "I want you alive. I want your wild, passionate body. I'd go mad without it now."

It was well past midnight when Virginia lit the bedlamp, turned it low and hastily dressed while Bradley put on his clothes.

"Where do you think you're going?" he asked in a whisper.

"With you, to the dock. Is that where your boat is tied up?"

"Got a man waiting there. No need to go with me."

"I'm going," she said. "Don't stop me."

"We've got to be careful. Did you hear a dog barking just before I got into the house?"

"I was asleep. I heard nothing."

"Some Yank might be prowling about. If I'm right, and he comes our way, I'll slit his throat."

Virginia carried the bedlamp to illuminate their way downstairs to the front door. There she blew out the lamp and turned to Brad, thinking how tall he was . . . a big and dangerous man. He drew her to him and held her for a moment while her passion began to rise again. She struggled out of his arms.

"You've got to go," she whispered. "Please—don't take any chances. Please be careful."

"I'd rather stay a while longer," he said. "You can easily drive a man to madness, but not quite to the degree that would make me stay longer. But I'll be back."

"When?" she asked, without the slightest feeling of shame.

"When I can. Come along now, if you insist on going to the dock with me."

They moved quickly along the path. Twice they heard a dog bark, and not too far away. It sent chills of apprehension through Virginia and she noticed that Bradley had drawn a hunting knife from a belt scabbard.

They reached the dock with no trouble. He kissed her with his

325

customary violence and she loved it. She stood on the dock while the man waiting in the rowboat pushed off and began to apply the oars. The boat quickly faded out of sight into the darkness. Virginia turned back, walking slowly, in a dreamlike state, toward the mansion. The dog barked again, this time close enough to alarm her. Moments later a large black dog stood in the middle of the path, baring his teeth and growling.

"Hush up, you," someone said. "Git! Go back where you belong."

The dog backed up a few steps and then ran off into the darkness. A man's form came out of the night and Virginia opened her mouth to scream for help.

"What you doin' out this hour of the night, Mrs. Birch?" the man asked.

Virginia peered at the speaker. "Mr. Tannet?" she asked, not being able to identify him except by voice.

"Kinda funny you bein' out like this," he said. "Yep, I'm Tannet."

"What's funny about a person taking a walk, even at this hour? I couldn't sleep."

"Ain't sleepin' much myself these days. Got too many money troubles."

"I'm sorry about that."

"Did you hear a boat out there, off the dock?"

"I heard nothing. Did you?"

"Sure did. You hear things a long way off in the middle of the night like this. Somebody was snoopin' around."

"No one has ever, as you call it, snooped around Valcour, Mr. Tannet."

"Maybe not in the old days afore the war. Anythin' can happen these days. You got a minute? I want to talk to you."

"Very well, but be brief. I'm getting tired and that's what I came out for."

"My store is sellin' everythin' I can lay my hands on."

"How fortunate, Mr. Tannet."

"Only the damn niggers ain't payin' for anythin'."

"You have to wait until the harvest, Mr. Tannet. When the crop is sold, they are paid."

"Don't do me no good now. The people I buy from don't wait that long."

"I'm sure they don't. But I can't help you. Good night, sir."

"Now wait a minute. I been thinkin' maybe you can help me some."

"Help you, Mr. Tannet?"

"You could advance me some of the money you're goin' to pay the niggers."

"Mr. Tannet, I only pay when the crop is sold. You're aware of that."

"Won't hurt none you pay me some of what they owe me."

"I cannot do that. It would be against the law, sir."

"There are a lot of things against the law, Mrs. Birch. Askin' for money owed me is one of the smaller things, wouldn't you say?"

"I don't know what you're referring to, Mr. Tannet, and I don't particularly care. I'm very tired. Please excuse me."

"I could say Culver was here tonight."

Virginia steeled herself to show no emotion, no trace of worry. "Was he here, Mr. Tannet?"

"Like I said, I could say so."

"Then go ahead and say so to anyone you choose. It would be a lie. Now, please excuse me."

He blocked her path. "I heard a boat out there and you were on your way back from the dock."

"For all I know, and for all you know, it may have been General Grant or General Lee out there. Please get out of my way."

"Like I said, it wouldn't look so good . . ."

"Mr. Tannet, you're annoying me with that absurd talk. You're about to lose your store and with it your house. I was prepared to buy both, but I have, at this moment, changed my mind. I will now buy your house and store only for the taxes you owe. You will profit nothing."

"We was talkin' 'bout Culver bein' here. They'll believe me on the mainland."

She looked at him in studied contempt. "Believe the word of a scalawag carpetbagger against that of a Southern lady? You're very naive, Mr. Tannet, and very annoying. Please let me by.''

He stepped aside, furious, but unable to think of a suitable retort. She passed by him and walked casually up the path, not indicating how much she wanted to run, to get inside the house and bolt the door.

He was moving, but not in her direction, and she reached the veranda. A moment later, she was inside with the key turned. She set her back against the door and tried to relax. She told herself that he had seen nothing, although he may have heard the faint slap of oars. If he'd actually seen Brad, he'd have been far more aggressive.

It had been fortunate, though, that Brad had left when he did, for later on Tannet might have been closer, or his dog in a mood to attack. It would have been too bad for Tannet if he had encountered Brad. The result would have been disastrous. Virginia shuddered at the mere idea of it.

They would have to be more careful. She realized that she was already planning and hoping for his return. But she experienced no shame, no remorse. She quietly went upstairs to her room and to bed.

twenty

Late Thursday morning Virginia was at the dock to welcome Elias who had come to attend Nanine's wedding. Elias kissed her and held her close for a long moment. Then, arm in arm, they walked up the path to the house. If Elias was pleased to be back, Virginia was overjoyed.

"I've missed you," she exclaimed. "You've no idea how lonely it can be here, even with Nanine and Miles close by."

"And your mother?" Elias asked with a grin.

Virginia looked discouraged. "She spends the days in her room, forgoes meals, and indulges in crying spells that can be heard through the house. I've given up on her. She won't listen to reason."

"Don't fret about it. In time she'll come around. How's Miles?"

"I worry about him. So does Nanine, though she no longer speaks of it. I fear she's resigned herself to the fact that he will never be well."

"We have other troubles," Elias said. "This year's crop is going to be excellent—if we can get it in. Finding enough help is hard. I can get overseers with no trouble. They stand in line for the job, but the blacks still can't realize that they have to work for a living."

"That will change," Virginia predicted.

"Of course, but when? The cotton plants won't just sit there and wait. Hoeing is badly needed and when the crop is ready to harvest, we're really going to be in trouble unless we can find help. What we have is good. They're fed well and are content to stay."

"Here on Valcour we're lucky. Our crop is a bumper one too and we have the blacks who never had any desire to leave. Also, we got more from the Yankees, thanks to you. They work well. I won't say as hard as before, but enough that the crop won't spoil."

"We'll be rich in just a few short years," Elias ventured. "Thanks to Miles's generosity. Let's hope the marriage will serve as a tonic. For his sake and Nan's."

"Yes, indeed. How long will you stay, darling?"

" 'Stay'?" He laughed aloud. "I have to go back right after supper and I'm staying for that only because I presume it will be Nan's wedding celebration."

"Oh, Elias, I hoped . . ." Virginia's high spirits vanished.

"I'm sorry," he broke in. "You know the place needs constant supervision. The house and some of the new outbuildings are coming along too and I have to be there. The carpenters are always coming to me with questions. I'm sorry. There's nothing I'd rather do than be with you."

She sighed. "When will we be together again? I've too much time on my hands here. There's little to do just now. Nan stays with Miles, as she should. Mama spends her time sulking and crying."

"I know, my love." Elias's arm enclosed her waist. "I'm lonely too. Do you want to come back with me?"

"I must oversee here."

"I know. What about the Yankees?"

"One moved out since I saw you last, and left the house in a shambles. Malicious destruction of property. I've put a stop to that. But as the Yanks grow more and more worried about losing the houses, they also grow more angry. Oh—another thing. Tannet stopped me when I was taking a stroll in the night. He hinted he could blackmail us into loaning him money."

" 'Blackmail'? What kind of crazy talk is that?"

"I think he's bluffing. He said he heard someone leave the island in a boat and he surmised—that's what he said—it was Bradley Culver."

"Good God! What's the matter with the man?"

"He, and others, I'm afraid, seem to think that Bradley Culver returned the loot he'd stolen from them because Culver is our friend.''

"If I ever lay hands on that outlaw, they'll find out how much of a friend I am to that rascal. I understand he's been getting bolder and bolder.''

"Did you know that Captain Delaney also came to see me? It seems someone had seen Culver in a rowboat heading toward the island and Delaney wondered if he had come to Valcour. Why do people think that bravo is a friend?''

"Doug Delaney doesn't. Yes, I knew he was coming here. He reassured me of your safety and that of the family when he returned.''

"That was kind of him. But why should he assume Culver came here?''

"Culver's second visit is responsible. Nobody can understand why he came back and returned the booty he'd stolen. It's out of character for him.''

"I agree," Virginia replied.

"I must confess I'm puzzled also. If I were here, I'd like to set up a lure of some kind to entrap him. Then hand him over to the authorities.''

Virginia shuddered inwardly. "That might be extremely dangerous, seeing that he controls so many outlaws.''

"I suppose so. It's a dismal subject. Let's get to the house.''

They found Nanine alone in the drawing room. She looked enchanting in her wedding gown. Miles had given Virginia the address of Anton Boyle and told her he'd know where to take her to get the best wedding gown available. When Virginia protested that nowhere in the South could one purchase a wedding gown, Miles laughed.

"My dear," he said, still chuckling. "Money has a loud voice. Anton looks after my investments, He's completely trustworthy, as is James Warren. Don't return until you have a gown for Nanine.''

Miles was right. Virginia returned with the gown, veil, slippers, silk stockings and blue garters. All purchased in a lovely house in a residential section of Charleston. She was aghast at what was in there. One could furnish a house or purchase a wardrobe.

Anton had laughed at her astonishment. "Don't ask questions, my dear. I don't own this place, but I do have connections. Rather, I should say, Miles has."

Both Virginia and Elias stood still and watched Nanine slowly move about the room, her train cascading out gracefully behind her.

Elias went over and kissed her. "What a beautiful bride you'll make."

"Thanks for taking the time to come for the ceremony. I only hope the preacher arrives on time."

"Reverend Thompson told me he'd arrive at two o'clock," Virginia said. "I'm sure Anton will see to it, since both he and James Warren will be here."

"If you ladies will excuse me, I'd like to pay Miles a visit," Elias said.

"He's looking forward to seeing you," Nanine said. "I hope you'll be able to say you see an improvement. I think he's as eager for the wedding as I."

"I can vouch for that," Virginia said. "Run along, Elias."

Virginia led Nanine to one of the sofas and they sat down side by side. Impulsively, Virginia hugged and kissed her sister.

"You look beautiful," she said.

"I wish we could have had a big wedding," Nanine said, "but even if it were possible to invite our friends, I don't think Miles could stand up under all the noise and confusion."

"I agree. Besides, our old friends would then be under an obligation to bring gifts and you know they couldn't. One day it will all change."

"I pray it happens as we hope for. I talked to Moses a short while back and he told me the Yankees are growing angrier by the day and making threats to do all sorts of things if we don't help them."

"Just talk, Nan. What can they do? Tannet and I had a run-in a few days ago. He wanted me to pay the bills owed his store by the blacks. He knew beforehand that they pay only when the money from the crop is shared, but it seems he can't wait that long."

"I don't like that man," Nanine admitted. "But I do feel sorry for all of them. They came here with high hopes."

"They came because they were looking for the spoils of war," Virginia said harshly. "I'm not sorry for their troubles. All I want is to get them out of here so our friends can return and Valcour will be as it once was."

"I used to think that would never happen," Nanine said. "But now I'm much more encouraged. Oh, Virgie, I can scarcely believe it's my wedding day. I won't be an old maid after all. I feel so lucky. I've a fine man. A gentle, kind man and . . ." She paused, then added soberly, " . . . a very sick man. I'm going to try harder than ever to make him well. I love him dearly."

"One of these days," Virginia vowed, "we'll celebrate your wedding as it should be. Did Mama come down?"

"No," Nanine said, and there was sadness in her voice. "She hasn't and she certainly won't come to the wedding. We've decided to hold it at the old hospital and not in the house. I don't want Miles to be humiliated. Anton and James will be here, but they won't stay. I don't want Miles to tire."

They waited on the veranda in the warm, bright sunlight watching Elias escorting the clergyman up the path. Anton Boyle and James Warren followed. Elias left the three men, who headed for the hospital. He approached Nanine and Virginia.

"The wedding ring," Nanine exclaimed in dismay. "We forgot the ring."

Elias laughed. "Anton has it. He'll give it to Miles when they get to the hospital. I'll now escort the bride."

He held out his arm. Nanine placed her hand on it.

Virginia said, "I'll follow and hold your train up."

When they reached the cottage, Belle, Moses and the other ex-slaves were lined up. Virginia wasn't even surprised to see tears in Belle's eyes. Belle, to Virginia's surprise, even shifted her eyes enough to give a bare nod of approval to her.

Virginia addressed Belle. "You may bring everyone in to watch the wedding." She happened to catch a glance of Ivy, standing in the background and a little apart from the others. "You too, Ivy."

Virginia leaned forward and spoke softly in Nanine's ear. "I looked back once and caught a glimpse of Mama upstairs in the window. I'll bet she's sorry not to be a part of this."

"I'm sorry she isn't, Nanine said rapturously. "But I'm too happy to let it bother me."

When they entered the hospital, Miles, dressed in white, was on his feet. Reverend Thompson stood beside him. Virginia went to his side, but he didn't appear to be in need of support. He was smiling widely. Anton Boyle and James Warren stood alongside Virginia.

Moses, Belle and Ivy entered, followed by the others. They remained at the far end of the room. Elias escorted Nanine to her place beside Miles. Reverend Thompson was ready. The ceremony was short, but it brought tears to Virginia's eyes. Belle had been dabbing at hers all through the ceremony. Once it ended, she moved over to the table covered with a linen cloth. On it were crystal, china and sterling. There were sandwiches, sliced meats and a large cake.

Anton opened the champagne and filled the glasses, which were passed around for all to toast the bride and groom. Miles walked over to the table with Nanine and his hand rested over hers as she cut the cake. She looked radiant and though she never left Miles's side, he seemed quite capable of standing and engaging in light conversation.

However, Nanine didn't allow the festivities to go on. She knew he had been making a supreme effort and she signaled Virginia it was time for everyone to go. Since they were aware of Miles's state of health, the room quickly emptied. Nanine told Belle to give the remainder of the food to the ex-slaves, even a small serving of the wedding cake for luck.

Virginia accompanied Elias to the dock. "How much longer, Elias?" she asked. "I want you terribly."

"No more than I want you," he said. "Just remember, when the loneliness gets too unbearable, it was what you wanted. That's the only thing that carries me through each day. Don't forget, I'm a man. As I said, come back to the mainland with me."

"You know I can't."

"Then we'll have to wait."

She tried to appear happy, but it was a considerable effort. A situation like this couldn't go on endlessly. With Elias once again gone, the boredom, the loneliness and that maddening fire of desire would be quickly rekindled. Soon she'd begin looking forward to Bradley's next visit.

Their embrace at the dock was brief, for Reverend Thompson hailed them. He asked to return with Elias, since Miles's friends were remaining a little longer.

Virginia remained on the dock until she could no longer see the craft. Then she walked slowly back to the mansion. She couldn't even go down to the hospital. Nan and Miles would wish to be alone, once his friends left. So she went directly to the library and tried to bury her frustrations in work. She tried to console herself with the rapid success she'd had with the island and with Elias repeating the success on the mainland. He'd not be away forever, even though it would seem that way before dawn.

The library had been fully restored, the furniture was new and the old table had given way to a spacious desk. The rest of the house had been refurnished and Virginia gloried in walking from room to room, admiring the charm and beauty of the house once again. She tried her best to duplicate as much of the original furnishings as possible and, failing that, ordered a close facsimile of it. She wished that she'd delayed this difficult and time-consuming project so it might take up her time now and release some of the tension and burning desire that brought Culver to mind so intensely.

Lenore didn't come down for supper. Virginia dined alone, picking at her food listlessly. The only consoling thought she had was the memory of Nanine's bliss as Miles slipped the gold wedding band on the third finger of her left hand, then sealed their troth with a gentle kiss.

She considered stopping at her mother's rooms, but decided against it. She was too disappointed in her mother's unforgiving attitude toward Miles. She could at least have come down to see Nanine in her wedding gown and, perhaps, given her the slightest bit of encouragement, if not an expression of a mother's love. There were times when Virginia felt she could easily hate her mother, but reason always prevailed and she realized that would be childish.

She went to bed early, for there was absolutely nothing else to do. By day she could keep reasonably busy with the plantation help, with visits to Miles and Nanine, but by night everything seemed to stop and she felt more alone than ever.

It was such a drastic change from the old days when the mansion would almost always be filled with guests, relatives and gregarious friends, some of whom stayed a long time. There were servants about in profusion. Now she had only Belle, who was more apt to be sullen as not, and Ivy, who worked quietly and never intruded. Then there was Brandy, the houseboy, inept, but somehow likable.

She dreamed of the days to come, when the house would again be filled with laughing, friendly people. When she'd have gowns and jewelry and maintain an important social life, both on Valcour and in Charleston.

She was awakened by someone screaming. She sat up in bed, trying to clear her wits and wondering if she'd been dreaming. But it came again and close by, from her mother's rooms.

Virginia rushed down the hall, entered her mother's rooms and found her at the window peering into the night. There was no need to ask her why she had screamed. The darkness was broken by red and yellow flames rising above the treetops. Virginia hastily ran back to her rooms to dress. In minutes she was ready to leave. Her mother had grown frantic with fear.

"They're burning everything on the island," she cried out in horror. "They'll burn us out too. Those damnable Yankees!"

"Only one place is on fire," Virginia said. "I think it's the Laurel Porter house. Nobody is burning the island, Mama. Go back to bed. I'll do what I can about this."

When she ran down the path, she met Nanine, also dressed and alerted to the possibilities of what this fire meant.

"I've been afraid of it," Nanine said. "For days I've been afraid."

"Of fire? Why should you be?"

"The Yankees are very angry. I thought they might take their hate out on us by burning all the houses. I think it's the Porter place."

"So do I. We'll get down there and see what we can learn. If this is the first of an attempt to wreck the island, I'm going to bring in the Yankee soldiers. If we have to depend on them, then we must, and Captain Delaney is an understanding man. He'll provide the help we'll need."

A group of Yankees stood well away from the burning house. It was completely engulfed in flames. No one had made any attempt to start a bucket brigade. They merely stood in silence to watch the house being consumed.

Tannet was there. He left the group and came over to speak to Nanine and Virginia. "Reckon you can take this for a lesson, ladies. Mel Hutton said he wasn't going to leave anythin' for you to just take over."

"Do you mean he deliberately burned down the house?" Nanine asked in dismay.

"Ain't sayin' he did, an' ain't sayin' he didn't. Sometimes nobody can tell how a fire starts. Not even if it starts in every goddamn house on the island. Reckon you know what I mean."

"I shall see that Mr. Hutton is properly punished if he committed arson, Mr. Tannet. There are laws here. Even if they are being administered by Northern soldiers."

"What can you prove?" Tannet asked. "Ain't nobody here goin' to say they saw Mel Hutton set fire to the house. Mel can say it just happened. It does sometimes. But even so, if you did prove he set the fire, you can't do nothin' to him. A man can burn down his own house he got a mind to."

"Please inform Mr. Hutton that he and his family will leave this island at once, or I will have the law on them. And anyone else who has plans to destroy property better be very certain it isn't to avoid taxes or mortgage payments. For then it becomes a crime."

"You been lookin' for somethin' like this, the way you been treatin' good folks on the island. You don't own the place, Mrs. Birch. Not by a long shot you don't. An' you ain't no queen either. You can't tell us what we got to do."

"Are you ready to go back, Nan?" Virginia asked.

Nanine nodded. They walked away in spite of the fact that Tannet was still issuing ominous warnings of more trouble to come. Neither spoke on the way back to the hospital where Miles was waiting somewhat impatiently.

"It's the old Porter place," Nanine told him. "They set it on fire so we wouldn't be able to buy it back. They're threatening to burn everything. Maybe even our own house."

"Virginia," Miles said, "I'd be obliged if you would provide me with a gun. I know how to use one despite the awful spectacle I made of myself in that duel. If those people have plans to burn everything, a few of them won't get to lighting the match."

"Elias provided guns. I'll send a rifle," Virginia promised. "I'm sorry this had to happen on your wedding day, Miles."

"Maybe that's what they were celebrating," he said lightly.

"I'm afraid that's unlikely," Virginia said. "Honestly, I don't know what to do about this. How I miss Elias."

"I just thought of something," Nanine said. "This fire will easily be seen on the mainland and someone is bound to come out to see what happened."

"It's going to be a long night," Virginia said, agreeing with her."

Miles was wearing a heavy robe. He drew it closer around him against the chill of the night air invading the hospital.

"You two better get down to the dock," he said. "They'll surely send someone. I'll be all right. Don't worry about me."

"I hate to leave you," Nanine declared, "but Virgie shouldn't be alone now. I'll get back as soon as I can."

Virginia went outside while Nanine helped him remove the robe so that he could climb into bed. She kissed him and tucked the covers around him. She managed a reassuring smile as she bade him good night. His eyes were already closed in weariness.

"If those terrible people get it into their heads to burn everything"—Virginia spoke as they made their way to the dock—"it's going to make restoring the island almost impossible. It would cost a fortune to rebuild. Elias must come back. It's beyond me."

"I'm worried too, Virgie," Nanine admitted. "You heard what Miles told us. They might get it into their heads to burn everything . . . the hospital, the mansion . . . everything. How could we stop them?"

"I'm going to try," Virginia declared. "Perhaps the military can help."

They were at the dock some time before they heard the approach of what turned out to be a large launch, rowed by six soldiers with Captain Delaney directing them. He came ashore as the boat was tied up.

"What burned? How bad is it?" he asked.

"One house," Virginia said.

"Anyone hurt?"

"Not so far as I know."

"I'm glad of that. From the mainland it looked as if the whole island was on fire."

"It may be, sometime in the near future," Nanine spoke up. "One of the . . . the Northerners warned us these people would rather burn their houses than let us buy them back."

"It's been done in other places," Delaney said. He turned to order his men to go down to the scene of the fire and find out what they could about its origin and its extent.

"There'll be nothing left but the chimneys," Virginia said. "You'd think General Sherman had marched over the island. That fire was purposely set, for a house built like that wouldn't be completely engulfed in such a short space of time."

"I'll send word to Elias if you wish, Mrs. Birch."

"Please do, Captain. We're so alone and unprotected here. If they fire all the houses, this island will be a disaster. It's one of the loveliest places on earth. It must be preserved somehow."

"I'll go down there and give them a lecture," he promised. "That's about all I can do. I can't order them off the island. I can only promise severe penalties if they burn any more places. And I'm not even certain I can do that. I know of no law that says they can't burn down their own houses, unless they wish to profit from the loss and they certainly can't be suspected of that."

"Please inform us of what you learn, Captain. My sister and I will be glad to receive you in the mansion."

"I'll get back to you. Remember, there's not much I can do. Maybe I can scare them into abandoning any idea of burning everything, but some of those Yankees can be awful stubborn."

"And some can be very kind and understanding, as you are," Nanine said. "We're grateful, Captain."

Lenore was downstairs when they entered the house. "What is it,

Virgie? What happened?'' She directed her questions to Virginia, never once looking at Nanine or greeting her in any way.

"Mr. Hutton set fire to the Porter house they were going to lose in a few more days, Mama. The soldiers from Charleston are here."

"Yankee soldiers, I suppose."

"Yes, Mama, Yankee soldiers. And we're damn lucky they came."

"And what do you think they'll do?" Lenore demanded. "Nothing! Absolutely nothing! They'll likely be very pleased at what's happened."

"I doubt that, Mama. Have you noticed that Nanine is with me?"

"I have tried hard not to," she answered.

Nanine said, "Mama, I'm now Mrs. Miles Rutledge. And I am also your daughter."

"Are you?" Lenore asked angrily. "You've betrayed me and betrayed your dead brother. Maybe the Lord will forgive you, but I never shall. I would be pleased if you left my home."

"Mama," Virginia broke in quickly, "Nan is not going to leave here and she may come anytime she wishes. You are not only unreasonable, you're a bad mother."

"That's heresy," she exclaimed indignantly, then turned to walk to the door. They heard her climbing the stairs.

"Poor Mama," Nanine sighed.

"I'm not going to let her get away with this, Nan. As soon as all this awful incident dies down, I shall insist that you bring Miles here for supper. Or dinner. But he is to come here and Mama will have to like it. There's no other way to handle her and I'll not have your happiness ruined by her stubbornness. Besides, you and Miles belong in this house, not that hospital."

"Don't be too hard on her, Virgie. Mama just doesn't understand. I'm happy with Miles. We're never lonely so long as we have each other. Give her time."

"That's what Elias said. I'd like to give her the back of my hand," Virginia was still furious. "This is your wedding day. She did her best to spoil it."

"If that was her intention, she failed," Nanine said. "I'm still radiating joy. Not even a deliberately set fire can dampen that. Let's

340

make some coffee for the captain and the men he brought. Belle may have some cookies or cake left in the kitchen. We haven't raided it in years. Come on."

They soon forgot their troubles in the excitement of raiding the kitchen. They giggled like school girls over the explosion that would emanate from Belle when she arrived in the morning to find all the leftovers from the wedding gone. They did manage to have two large pots of coffee ready, and an assortment of cakes, cookies and biscuits.

Captain Delaney gave them a gloomy report as he sat down to eat. His men were also at the table and they ate as if they hadn't encountered home cooking in months.

"As you said, the fire was deliberately set, Mrs. Birch. They admitted it without the slightest measure of shame or guilt. I believe it's not past them to burn down the other houses. One by one, as they get ready to abandon them. I don't know what I can do about it. I would never be permitted to establish a camp here to guard the island. You'll have to consult with Elias about it. Perhaps he can offer some kind of solution. Unfortunately, I cannot."

"Then we stand the chance of losing everything on the island," Virginia said wearily.

"I'm afraid so. They also made certain to burn the cotton in the fields that Mel Hutton had planted. They're not going to leave anything."

"This is something I never considered," Virginia admitted. "And I can see that there's no way to stop them. At least, none that I can think of now."

"I'll send word to Elias in the morning."

"Please, Captain, don't. Not tomorrow. He'll rush here and abandon the work on the big plantation. He came back today to attend my sister's wedding and he remained not an hour after the ceremony."

"But, Virgie," Nanine broke in, "you said he had to come back. That it's got beyond you."

"I know what I said," Virginia replied. "But it's out of the question."

Captain Delaney rose and bowed to Nanine. "Congratulations, Mrs. . . ."

"Mrs. Miles Rutledge," Nanine said proudly.

"Ah—yes." Delaney sat down heavily. "I wondered what had happened to him."

"He's been on the island ever since . . . that unfortunate accident," Nanine explained.

Delaney nodded. "I know the story of that duel, Mrs. Rutledge. The two men who acted as your husband's seconds came to me and explained the whole matter. When you say it was an accident, I am positive that is exactly the right word. And in Miles Rutledge you have a man of excellent character and"—he smiled—"a great deal of money. Not that I think money played any part in your marriage, I assure you."

"Thank you, Captain."

"When shall I notify Elias, Mrs. Birch? For I feel I must."

"Give me time to try and reason with these people. Elias had enough on his mind. Give me until day after tomorrow. If things really are beyond my control, I'll send for him."

"Certainly. I wish there was more we could do, ladies. My men and I thank you for your Southern hospitality. We experience very little of it. After what happened here tonight, it's understandable."

They saw the men to the door and then returned to the table to finish what was left of the coffee. Neither felt any desire to sleep.

"Virgie, what are you going to do? Are you sure you don't want Elias to know immediately?"

"I need time to consider this. Elias may get angry and they'll burn everything at one time in defiance. Perhaps I can talk to some of them, offer them more money. They're in such desperate straits they might accept. I'd rather spend a few extra thousand and have the houses intact."

"I don't think they'll listen, Virgie. Not from the way they acted tonight."

"At least I will have tried. If it doesn't work, then Elias will have to handle it. But I must have the chance."

"All right," Nanine agreed. "I'd better get back to Miles."

"I'll go with you. No telling what those carpetbaggers will be up to. I put nothing past them, especially that man Tannet. I don't like the way he looks at me.''

"Be careful, then. If anything happened to you, I think I'd die."

"No, you wouldn't, Nan. You'd just step in the space I occupied and carry out what we've planned. I know you. Besides, you now have Miles to help. Give me a moment to fetch a rifle and bullets. I'll feel better if Miles is armed.''

twenty-one

Nanine saw them first, a group consisting of all the Yankee owners on the island, as they marched determinedly toward the Willowbrook mansion. She was able to leave the hospital in a hurry and reach the mansion before the crowd. Virginia, who had been working on the bookkeeping, had no indication the march was on the way until Nanine burst into the house with the news.

"I don't know what they want," she reported, "but I don't like the look on their faces."

"We'll confront them," Virginia said. "I've even been considering calling them together. After last night we surely need to let them know what the consequences of arson can be."

They were standing atop the veranda steps when the group arrived. Tannet seemed to have taken charge of them and acted as spokesman.

"We got somethin' to tell you an' I'm warnin' you we ain't foolin' about this. You saw what happened last night. Well, it's goin' to happen again an' again. We decided we'd burn down every last one of these houses rather than let you get your greedy hands on them."

Nanine uttered a soft cry of anguish, but Virginia stepped forward and tried to control her anger as she replied to this open threat.

"May I ask what the alternative is?"

"You can buy our houses for what we say they're worth, not what we paid for them. We won't take a penny less."

"Let me point out to you that every last one of you is indebted for taxes. If you burn your houses, you can be accused of doing so to avoid payment. That would be arson."

"Who's goin' to prosecute us? What you two women forget is we Yankees licked you good an' proper an' we ain't goin' to take no sass from any of you. So you'll pay up, or we'll burn."

"My thought right now is to let you go ahead and burn your homes. But don't come near this plantation, because if you do, you'll be met with guns and bullets."

"Ain't aimin' to burn you out. We know better. Just askin' you pay what our houses are worth. An' I speak for ever'body. Ain't that right, folks?"

The group shouted assent and they seemed more sure of themselves than when they first arrived. Tannet's threats had given them courage.

A slim, narrow-faced man moved forward, elbowing Tannet aside. "An' you got to pay me too, even if I burned my place."

"You must be Mel Hutton," Virginia ventured.

"I know how to fire these houses," he boasted. "Did a mighty good job on mine, didn't I? But you got to pay for it or there ain't no deal."

"I'll have to consult my husband on this matter," Virginia said. "I will take it up with him as soon as possible."

"You got a week," Tannet shouted. "One week from today. We don't aim to stay on this island any longer, but we sure ain't givin' up what we own. Not for what you'll pay. One week is all."

They marched away, talking among themselves and apparently feeling certain of success. Virginia walked back into the house and to the library with Nanine. They sat down and neither spoke for a few moments.

Then Nanine bent her head in despair and began to weep. Virginia busied herself with some arithmetic and when she finished, she sat back.

"Stop it, Nan," she said. "They haven't fired the places yet."

"They mean to," Nanine said. "I know they do."

"Well, I know that too, Nan. I also know that there is no way we can pay them what they demand. If we do, we'll have to mortgage Willowbrook, if we can find a bank with enough money to handle it. Suppose we talk it over with Miles. He may be better at handling a thing like this. I admit I'm at my wit's end. And, of course, we have to send word to Elias, much as I hate to bother him. Damn!"

Miles provided little comfort. "If they burn the places down, I doubt anything will be done to them. It's a criminal act, but with postwar conditions as they are, I doubt we'd be able to convict them. If there is a crime involved, which I'm not certain of."

"We'll have to put it up to Elias," Virginia decided. "I'll send one of the blacks right away to ask Elias to come home."

"There is one way and I know it will work," Miles said.

"Miles," Nanine exclaimed in surprise, "please tell us what it is."

"I've more money than I'll ever be able to use. Enough to pay them off."

"No, Miles," Virginia said promptly. "We can't accept an offer like that."

"Why not? I'm a member of this family now. You want the island restored and I don't blame you. Eventually, as your old neighbors come back and progress, they'll be able to pay some of it back."

"I'll not let you do this," Virginia said again. "Elias wouldn't hear of it."

"We'll see what Elias has to say about it," Miles countered. "If he agrees, the problem's solved."

"Perhaps there may be another way," Virginia said. "At least it's worth trying. I'm going to talk to a lawyer, our banker and Captain Delaney. They may be able to give me some advice."

"It's too late for a trip to the mainland," Nanine said. "I don't want you to try it in the dark. We have a week's time. Tomorrow will do."

"You're right," Virginia agreed. "But first thing in the morning I'm going to Charleston and I'm going to send word to Elias to meet me somewhere in the city. We'll be back by nightfall tomorrow. Let's hope they do give us the week. Frankly, I don't trust them."

Virginia and her mother had little to say at the supper table.

Virginia had explained the situation and Lenore responded with her usual tears.

"There's just one thing I want you to realize, Mama," Virginia said. "Miles has offered to buy up every house on the island at the price those carpetbaggers will dictate. I think you might regard him in a better light after such generosity."

"He killed my son. He murdered your brother. I will not permit you to accept such an offer. He made it only to force or buy his way into the family. I'd rather lose Valcour."

"Mama, he's part of the family. That's why he made the offer."

"Under no circumstances—"

"Mama, I'm going to Charleston in the morning and I'll bring Elias back. Whatever decision he makes on this matter is how we'll handle this situation. And I swear if you shed another tear at this table, I'll smash every dish on it."

"Every day," Lenore complained, "there's another crisis. I don't know how I can stand any more. I wish your father was here. He'd know what to do with these contemptible people."

"Perhaps. But he isn't here, Mama. And Elias is not going to take this without a fight. That's all I have to say. I'd much rather conduct a pleasant conversation at supper. One more thing. Don't mention Miles's crime against Marty again. That's an order."

"What pleasant topic can you find these days?" Lenore asked.

"For one thing, Molly Peters is moving back to the island next month. To her old house that was vacated last week. She's one of your oldest friends and having her here will help."

"She'll never return. They'll burn down her house too. They'll even burn this one if they can."

Virginia pushed her chair back, touched a napkin to her lips and rose. "Good night, Mama. I have work to do in the library. Go upstairs and have another good cry."

She walked out of the dining room, knowing very well she should not have allowed her anger to take control. Yet she'd been through so much these past twenty-four hours that her nerves were on edge and she was beset with the danger of her plans and hopes vanishing in the flames from a score of homes. It seemed to her that the Yankees had just won another war.

No matter how many times she went over the finances of Willowbrook, she couldn't hope to raise enough money to meet their demands. She could accept Miles's offer, but Elias would have to agree to that. Perhaps he might find some way. He had influence with the Occupation Authorities. Captain Delaney might be prevailed upon to warn the carpetbaggers that there would be dire consequences if they fired the island homes.

She closed the heavy ledger and tore up the scraps of paper she'd done her arithmetic on. As she rose from the desk, she thought she heard a sound just outside the room.

"Nan?" she called out. "Is that you?"

There was no reply. She turned back to the desk and blew out the lamp. In the darkened room, there was a rush of feet behind her and she was roughly seized with a hand clamped hard against her mouth. She struggled, but the man's grip was too strong. Someone thrust a piece of cloth between her lips and tied it behind her head. She was forced against the desk, her wrists thrust behind her and quickly tied.

Someone grasped her arm and straightened her up. She tried to struggle again. For one hopeful moment she thought this might be Bradley Culver, but the two men she could barely distinguish now were certainly not Brad.

"You behave an' you ain't gettin' hurt," a rough voice warned. "You don't an' you sure goin' to be might sorry."

Each man took an arm and between them propelled her out of the room. In the better light of the reception hall, she saw that they were rough, bearded men wearing soiled clothes, with matted and uncut hair. They were obviously ruffians of some kind who'd not bathed in some time.

The gag was uncomfortable and made her mouth sore. Her tied wrists began to ache from the pressure of the tight bonds. One on each side of her, they propelled her along, sometimes actually lifting her feet off the ground. They seemed to be in a hurry.

The trip ended in front of Tannet's little store, where the Yankees were gathered, guarded by a dozen armed men, as rough-looking as her captors. She was thrust into the midst of the terrified Yankees.

A tall figure emerged from the gloom. It was Bradley Culver. He held a bowie knife and he calmly bent down and wiped blood from it on the grass. He replaced the knife in a scabbard beneath his coat and then he walked slowly toward the group.

"You all know who I am," he said. "I warned you before not to make any further trouble here. Last night you burned down a house. I don't cotton to such damn foolishness. You burned the property of what was once the dwelling of fine Southern folks. I have people on this island who keep me informed as to what's going on here. I heard about your promise to burn every house. You wouldn't take my warning. You don't believe that my whole purpose in life anymore is to keep Yankees from ruining the South even more than they have."

Tannet stepped forward. He was shaken and pale, but he did seem to have more courage than any of the other men.

"We can burn our own property—" he began.

Bradley Culver walked slowly toward him and, without warning, he struck Tannet in the face so hard that he was lifted off his feet, and he fell to the ground, bleeding from cut lips and loosened teeth.

Culver sought out Virginia next. He grasped her around the waist cruelly, until she groaned in pain despite the gag. He turned her about to face the Yankees.

"I'm going to ask this lady, this real Southern lady, what she wants us to do with you. I know what I want to do, but it's up to her."

He moved behind Virginia and fumbled with the gag. "Play up to me," he whispered.

The gag removed, he next untied her wrists. She didn't look at him. She gently massaged her swollen wrists and moistened her lips. Bradley left her, went to where Tannet lay, grasped him by the neck and lifted him to his feet.

"You better hear this too," he said. "Seeing you appear to be the main skunk around here." He looked at Virginia. "Speak up, ma'am. Say so and we'll get rid of this scum before morning."

"Please," Virginia begged. "Don't hurt anyone. These people have not harmed you."

"They've harmed the entire South by the way they behave.

Talking about burning every house on the island. Just say the word, ma'am . . ."

"Please go away," she begged, and she meant it with a sincerity Bradley must have noticed. "You have no right to tell anyone what to do. You're an outlaw. You don't represent the South. I want you to leave."

Bradley bent his head acknowledging her little speech. "As you wish, ma'am. But let me warn these yellow-bellies that we'll be back if they make any more trouble for you or anyone else. And just to prove I mean what I say, you can look for the man who burned his house down last night. All of you, stay right where you are. Make one move and we'll kill the lot of you. If you know what's good for you, you'll get out."

"Please go," Virginia pleaded.

"Yes, ma'am, but I figured you might be a little more appreciative of what we're doing. This is not the first time we've come to the help of some women beset by Yankees, and those others were mighty glad for our help."

He waved his arms and he and his men quickly faded out of sight in the dark and the brush. The Yankee men stood as if transfixed, afraid to move.

"What did he mean about Mel Hutton?" someone asked.

Virginia gasped. "Hurry and fetch lanterns. Did anyone see him?"

Nobody had. They only knew that he had not been among them when Bradley Culver's men rousted them from their homes. Several hurried to obey Virginia, and soon they were back with lanterns. They spread out, somewhat warily in the fear that Bradley and his men had not left the island.

There was a shout from one of the searching parties. Virginia hurried to the small cleared spot in the brush. Mel Hutton lay on his back in a pool of blood. His throat had been slashed. Virginia turned away, her stomach rebelling at the sight and her mind filled with horror. She was suddenly possessed of a loathing for the man to whom she'd given herself and whom she dreamed about.

She stumbled along the path toward Willowbrook. The hospital was lighted. Nanine and Miles must have heard enough to be awake.

Nanine came out and with one look at Virginia's face, she quickly led her into the building.

Virginia sat down, defied the urge to weep. She spoke firmly and with a burning anger.

"Bradley Culver and his men were here. Two of them tied me up and forced me down to Tannet's store, where every Yankee on the island had been rounded up by Culver's bandits. Bradley must have had twenty or more men with him, all ruffians. All . . . horrible men."

"Did he hurt you?" Nanine asked in horror.

"No. His men gagged me and tied my hands behind my back, but he was not punishing me. He made me stand up before all those Yankees and beg mercy for them. He had heard about the fire and somehow he'd learned about their threats to us. He said he had spies here on the island. Blacks, I suppose, whom he must have terrorized into working for him."

"But what was he up to?" Miles asked.

"He threatened to harm, perhaps kill, the Yankees if they carried out their threats."

"Kill them?" Nanine exclaimed in fresh horror.

"He was trying to scare them," Miles offered.

"It was more than a scare, Miles," Virginia said. "We found Mel Hutton, the man who burned down his house last night. Someone had cut his throat."

Nanine couldn't speak. Miles sank back against the pillows. Virginia now could hold back no longer. She began to weep and as she did so she wondered if she wept for Bradley Culver, or for the evil he'd committed on Valcour.

Miles recovered first from the shock of what had happened. "There's been a murder," he reminded them. "Word has to reach the mainland. Damn it, if I could only be of some help."

"Your ideas and presence are enough," Nanine told him. "You're right. Elias must also be told."

"I'll go to Charleston in the morning," Virginia said. "What is going to happen now? They're going to say that we called in Culver. At least Tannet will think so, for he's been suspicious of that all along."

"We know we did not," Nanine said. "Tannet can talk all he likes. It was impossible that we could have called in Culver if we'd wanted to."

"Tannet is sure to say we did, though," Virginia said.

"How could we contact such a man? The police can't even find him. He roams about, never staying in one place long. Besides, nobody from the island went to Charleston since the fire."

"Somebody told Culver," Miles reminded them. "He knew what was going on."

"Virgie, stay here tonight," Nanine suggested. "There are a lot of cots left from the hospital days."

"I can't, Nan. By now Mama must be awake and fretting. There certainly was enough noise to awaken her and when she finds me gone . . ."

Nanine nodded. "You're right. Will we see you before you leave for the mainland tomorrow?"

"Of course. In case something has come up. You never can tell in a situation like this."

On the way back, through the darkness, Virginia was more than apprehensive. She was scared and had to steel herself from breaking into a frenzied run for the house. As she had surmised, Lenore was awake and moving about the first floor, from one window to the next.

"Where in the world have you been at this time of night?" she demanded as Virginia entered. "You're quite unconcerned about me, Virginia. You have no respect or love for me."

"Mama, stop whining. That outlaw Culver was here with a number of his men. They bound and gagged me, forced me from this house and took me down to where his men had herded all the Yankees on the island. He warned them against setting another fire and . . . he murdered one of them."

"Murdered? A Yankee?" Lenore seemed reassured when Virginia nodded. "At least it wasn't one of us. Why does that man tantalize us so?"

"Because he's still fighting the war, against all Yankees and Southerners who have given in to the Yanks. The man must be mad.

He can't win. They're going to find him someday and they'll surely hang him along with every member of his gang."

"Well, I can't say I blame him. Someone should remind the Yankees that we aren't completely subdued. Culver must be a romantic sort of person."

"He's a cold-blooded murderer, Mama. Don't you dare take his side. Not when you treat Miles as you do."

"What are you going to do?"

"Leave for Charleston in the morning. If I'm not here when you wake up, you don't have to worry. I shall probably bring back the Yankee soldiers and I hope Elias can return too."

"Must you go?" Lenore asked petulantly.

"Mama, a man has been murdered. The island was invaded by an outlaw. This has to be reported."

"Well, I hope there's no more excitement tonight, Virginia. I'm exhausted and there seems to be one crisis after another these days."

"Good night, Mama," Virginia said, knowing for once her mother made sense.

She waited until her mother was in her own rooms. Then she entered the library. It was like a place of refuge to her after the violence, threats and uncertainty. She sat down, the lamplight low, and she thought about Bradley Culver. She didn't yearn for him and his lovemaking. Tonight there was no carnal desire in her. Culver had proven to be as ruthless and cruel as he had professed to be during some of their intimate moments. She wondered how she ever submitted to such a man. Twice he'd come to her, and twice she'd given herself to him willingly, even joyfully. She thought now that she must have been mad. If anyone had discovered their liaison, if Elias ever found out, her world was going to crash down and engulf her. The whole thing had been madness.

She didn't sleep until dawn and then only briefly, for she soon awakened to the memory of what had occurred and the realization that she had to go to Charleston. She ate a hasty breakfast in the kitchen, at the same time trying to explain to Belle what had happened.

"Sho' made plenty o' noise," Belle said. "But we sho' wasn't lookin' fo' no trouble, so we minded ouah own business, Moses an' me. Whut's goin' on heah, anyways?''

"A great deal, Belle. I'll tell you about it later. Mr. Birch will return with me this afternoon and I hope he'll stay the night. Please have a good supper waiting for us."

"Yes, Miss Virgie. Sho' glad to have Massa back."

Belle had no idea of how much Virginia wanted him back. Yet, during her sleepless hours, Virginia had returned to the question of Bradley Culver and she realized that what he had done was for her benefit. He was helping her. His method may have been crude, direct and cruel, but he had risked his life to come to her aid in the only way he knew. How much good he'd accomplished she had no idea, but the sharpness of her attitude toward him had mellowed somewhat. Perhaps he had kept the Yankees from burning all the homes on the island. A certain amount of warmth for him returned, but no part of the yearning she once had. She believed he had destroyed that and she was grateful to be free of the burning desire to be in his arms.

She was dressed and ready for the journey to the mainland when two men arrived to see her. Both were middle-aged Yankees living on the island, whom she recognized, but without knowing their names.

"We came to talk," one said. "My name is Otto Mason, my neighbor here is George Hall."

"If you came about what happened last evening," Virginia informed them, "I am just leaving for Charleston to inform the authorities, so they'll return and take charge of this terrible situation."

"Yes'm, we appreciate it," Mason said. "We got poor Mel Hutton's body at my place, but we got no coffin."

"I'll see that you get one," she promised. "Please extend my sympathies to his widow."

"Thank you kindly, ma'am. But we really came to talk about something else. We talked most of the night and we're aiming to leave this island. It's never been lucky for us, anyway."

"And we hope you can buy the homes," George Hall added.

"All of you?" Virginia asked in disbelief.

"All but Tannet and one other. Harry Rhodes says he's goin' to ask all he can get 'fore he goes."

"I see. There isn't time to talk fully about this now, but I assure you we'll take it up as soon as this trouble is finished with. My husband will return and handle the whole matter. I appreciate what you have decided."

"That man comes back, he'll kill us all. My wife an' kids are scared to death."

"I don't mind saying, so am I, and my folks," Otto Mason added. "Guess we know when we're licked."

"I hope no one believes I had anything to do with Culver's coming last evening."

"No, ma'am. Most of us figure he'd have treated you more like a lady if you sent for him."

"I take it Mr. Tannet and the other gentleman believe I did send for him. Is that right?"

"Reckon," Otto Mason admitted. "Tannet's kind of crazy, anyway. He's ready to go broke in that store and that makes him mad."

"I'm sorry about that, and will you tell Mr. Hutton's widow that there is a small cemetery on the island and if she wishes her husband buried there, we have no objection."

"Reckon she'll like that. I guess we ain't that sore at you Rebs. Leastwise, I ain't. Anything we can do to help, let us know."

"Thank you," Virginia said. "I'm sure we can come to some amicable agreement about the houses. And I'll send the undertaker immediately I get to the city."

One of the blacks assigned to row her to and from the mainland was waiting. She stepped aboard, sat down and when the boat was well out to sea, she looked back at the lush greenness of the island and she felt that now it would be hers once more. Hers and the homes of those who had been forced to abandon them.

She thought also that it had been Bradley Culver's doing that was making it possible, even if it had been crude. Until he came to murder and threats, she had seen no way to stop the Yankees from burning their own property and reducing the island to ruins. Perhaps it was the only way a man like Culver could help, though she did not approve of the deadliness of his methods. She realized also that in killing that Yank, Culver had likely committed a murder that would make the hunt for him relentless. He was bound to be caught. Every Yankee patrol and sympathizer would be looking for him. It was highly unlikely that he could escape.

Now she had to report to Captain Delaney and have someone sent to notify Elias. She ached to see him again. Perhaps now he'd stay.

─────── twenty-two ───────

Virginia returned from the mainland in a launch rowed by Northern soldiers. She was seated beside a casket and accompanied by Captain Delaney and Elias, who sat beside her, holding her hand. His anger was revealed in his stern features.

"Culver has pulled his last raid," Elias swore. "The murder on Valcour is his ninth since the end of the war."

"He deserves no mercy," Virginia said.

"There are a number of outlaw bands like this. They claim to be Southern patriots for whom the war has not ended and they feel entitled to prey on any Yankee or Yankee sympathizer they come across. Am I correct, Captain?"

Delaney nodded. "Indeed. You've been very fortunate, Mrs. Birch."

"For a time last night, I didn't think so."

"Are you certain Culver killed that man?" Delaney asked.

"No. But Culver held a large, blood-smeared knife that he wiped off on the grass. Later, he said we'd find Mel Hutton and he was an example of what would happen to the rest of the Yankees if they defied him."

Elias's brow creased thoughtfully. "What I don't understand is why he spared you. Another question comes to mind. Why would he want to help us get rid of the Yankees? It doesn't make sense."

"It's the way he works," Delaney replied. Culver seems to quiet any guilt he may feel by proclaiming that what he does is to help some true-blue Rebel. Excuse the expression. The war is over. But we've never had direct evidence against Culver. Now we have and any chance he had of convincing a Southern jury and judge that what he did was for the benefit of the South won't work. Culver went too far on this one. He'll hang now, when we get him.''

Virginia closed her eyes.

''Have you any idea where he hides out?'' Elias asked the captain.

''Not the slightest. After something like this, his band dissolves and the members go home. Since nobody knows who they are, they're safe and live normal lives, until Culver sends for them again. I doubt their own families know what they're doing.''

''Culver will surely hide for a long time after this,'' Elias said. ''Nonetheless, I intend to find that man and turn him over unless I have to kill him when we meet. We must put an end to this.''

''I agree. If you develop any suspicions as to where he is, let me know. We'll smoke him out if we can locate his hiding place.''

''You can be sure it's close by the island. Apparently he is keeping an eye on it. It puzzles me why.''

''I have but one answer to that,'' Virginia said. ''The first time I ever saw him, he pulled me off my horse and held me and kissed me. He apologized and said he thought I was a Yankee. If I had been, I shudder to think what would have happened.''

''Why would that make him favor you and even go so far as to invade the island and kill a man so we could have our way? Which is what he did.''

''He apologized when he learned who I was. He knew Marty fought for the South. He swore he was sorry. Perhaps he felt so badly about that, he did what I asked him to do.''

''What did you ask him to do?'' Captain Delaney said.

''He and his men claimed to be Southern soldiers still fighting the war. They were about to pillage the whole island and perhaps burn everything, as they usually did. I begged him not to harm anyone living there or damage any property because I wanted to restore the island for Southern families who once lived there. As you know, he didn't burn anything or harm anyone.''

''He even came back with the stuff he'd stolen from the Yanks,''

Elias said. "I agree with you, Virgie. He was either smitten with you or so apologetic for grabbing a Southern lady that he decided to help you as payment. There can be no other reason."

Virginia disputed the first part of Elias's statement. "I doubt the man could be smitten by anyone. He's cruel and vindictive."

"All of that," Captain Delaney agreed.

Virginia cast a quick look at Elias. His impassive features gave no hint of what he was thinking.

"I'm going to try and figure out a way to trap him," Elias declared. "If I do, we'll get an answer to some of these questions. We've another reason to rid the island of Culver. Our brother-in-law, Miles Rutledge. He's very ill and extremely wealthy."

Captain Delaney nodded. "Which makes him a likely subject for kidnapping. An act which he'd probably not survive."

Virginia shuddered inwardly, recalling Culver had brought up that very subject. She'd begged him not to, but she had no faith he'd respect her wishes in the matter.

"How is Miles?" Captain Delaney asked.

"His marriage has seemed to act as a tonic," Virginia replied. "I only hope he continues to improve."

She related, for Captain Delaney's benefit, Miles's offer of sufficient money to purchase the remaining homes on the island. She had already informed Elias and Captain Delaney of the visit of the two owners and their offer to sell.

"Do you really believe they were serious?" Elias asked.

"They're terrified," Virginia said. "I don't believe anything other than Mel Hutton's murder would have forced them to go, but this time I feel they can't get off the island fast enough. Except for Mr. Tannet and one other."

"Tannet's been a troublemaker all along," Elias said.

"Mrs. Birch, why do you think Tannet won't leave?" Delaney asked.

"He still believes we're in league with Culver and we've asked Culver to frighten the Yankees so they'll get off the island."

"Why should Tannet think Culver would do this for you?" Delaney asked.

"I already told Elias that Tannet confronted me and stated Culver came to the island to see me."

Elias said, "I should have punched Tannet in the nose long ago. His arrogance is unbearable."

"When did this happen?" Delaney resumed the questioning. "The more facts I can get, the better."

"A few nights ago I couldn't sleep and I walked down to the dock. On my way back, I heard a dog growl, then Tannet appeared, blocking my path. He asked me if I'd heard the sound of someone rowing a boat away from the island. I hadn't, nor had I seen anyone at the dock. He insinuated that it might have been Culver. That he'd come to see me."

"If Tannet made any direct threats against you, Mrs. Birch, I'll haul him off the island today."

"There were no threats."

"There'd better not be," Elias said grimly.

Nanine was at the dock to meet them. She embraced Elias and greeted Captain Delaney in her usual friendly fashion, then asked, "Will you have your men deliver the coffin to the home of Otto Mason? They took Hutton's body there."

"Of course. I have to go there anyway to question the others who saw and heard Culver."

Lenore was actually pleased to see Elias and even kissed him on the cheek. "I hope you'll stay, Elias," she said nervously. "When you're away, everything seems to go wrong."

"I'll stay as long as I can. But the plantation on the mainland is far from ready to run itself. Perhaps I can arrange not to be away for so long a time."

"I hope so. What with those insufferable Yankees and that brigand Culver who murdered one of them, this place isn't safe."

"Calm down, Mother Hammond," Elias said, comforting her. "Just now we must bury that murdered man."

"Not here I hope," she exclaimed in dismay. "Not on Valcour. Elias, you cannot do this. I forbid it. A Yankee in our graveyard? Never!"

Virginia exhaled slowly. She'd not even thought of this problem. "Mama, the Yankees will be leaving soon. We cannot refuse to bury this man on Valcour. I gave them permission. He's not going to harm any of the others buried here. Or us."

"Why wasn't I consulted?" Lenore demanded.

"There wasn't time," Virginia said impatiently. "Besides, you'd have refused."

Elias spoke quickly. "Perhaps one day in the near future, his people may wish to send for his body for reburial in the North. In fact, I shall suggest it. So this will be only a temporary thing."

"In that case, I will agree. But it is totally against my wishes. Excuse me, please. I have a severe headache. But once again, Elias, welcome home."

"She's beginning to soften," Elias said after Lenore had left. "Or she's forgotten I'm a Yankee."

"Mama's never going to change," Virginia said.

"She has nothing now to occupy her mind or her time," Nanine spoke with her usual tolerance. "Once things are as they were on the island and her friends have returned, she'll change."

"Pray the day comes soon," Virginia said earnestly. "Will we go to the funeral, Elias?"

"Unless you're as set as your mother," he responded with a grin.

"I think we should," Nanine said. "Regardless of what they've done or how they regard us, that murder was horrible."

"I arranged for a clergyman," Elias said, "and he'll be here shortly after noon. Now, Virgie, let's have a look at the bookkeeping. Nan, I'll be down to see Miles shortly."

In the library, Elias made a quick study of the ledgers. "It's going well," he told Virginia. "I'm proud of you."

"Elias, are you staying? Please do! I've missed you so."

"Of course I am. For a couple of days if things go well. I've missed you too, but right now I haven't time to prove it."

"Tonight," Virginia said, giving him a knowing glance, "will do very well indeed."

He rose and went around the desk to lift her out of the chair. He held her close and kissed her with a fervor that set their blood flaming.

"Thank God you're back," she said, her voice unsteady. "My body aches for you."

"And mine for you." His voice was as unsteady as hers. He rained kisses on her face and her neck. His hands moved gently up and down her back in a caressing fashion, sending Virginia's passion soaring to new heights. Her mouth sought his and she deliberately aroused him further, making him cry out.

He thrust her from him. "My God, Virgie, not now. Not here."

"We can go upstairs. There's time." She spoke with her mouth against his.

"There isn't. I must pay Miles a visit."

"It's always something," she cried out, her voice as frenzied as her desire.

"Quiet, Virgie, your mother will hear you," Elias cautioned.

"I don't give a damn if the whole island hears me. I'm your wife. You have a duty to me."

"I don't consider it a duty," Elias said soberly. "I love you. I always will. But just now there are other considerations."

"To hell with them," she retorted, turning on her heel and running upstairs.

Elias eyed her sadly, started to follow, then turned and left the house. If only she could understand he was going mad without her by his side at night. His passion slowly turned to anger when he thought once again that he was working himself until he felt sometimes that he would drop, and doing it because of his love for her.

Damn! He'd been going to dress before he went down to see Miles. He hoped Virginia would dress now and he'd have upstairs to himself when he returned. He wanted no more quarrels. There'd been too many and all because of restoring Valcour and the plantation on the mainland. Sometimes he hated the very name of the island, feeling it was a slowly growing buttress, separating them.

Upstairs, Virginia bathed her face with cold water. She paced the floor until she'd reached a degree of calmness, then she changed to a pale green dress, one she'd never worn. She wondered if Elias would notice. She was already ashamed of her behavior. If only she didn't have such a passionate drive. She hated herself for it.

She dressed slowly and redid her hair, making herself as attractive as possible, then went downstairs so their suite would be available to him when he returned. She'd heard the door close and from her window had caught a glimpse of him heading for the hospital. He would have to change his apparel when he returned. She put on a straw bonnet, trimmed with violet pansies and a green silk ribbon with streamers long enough to bow beneath her chin.

She was at the foot of the stairs when Elias returned. He paused, breathless at sight of her.

"You're beautiful, my darling," he said.

"Thank you, Elias," she replied quietly. "I'm sorry I lost my temper. Please forgive me."

"I'm the one to ask that. I must dress. I'll be fast."

She smiled. "I'll be waiting."

"Oh," he paused. "What were the names of those men who paid you a visit?"

"Otto Mason and George Hall. They were very gentlemanly."

"Good. I'll talk to them after the funeral."

Nanine, Elias and Virginia went together to the home of Otto Mason, where Elias offered his services as a pallbearer. There was no hesitation in accepting him. He was, after all, a Northerner.

At the grave, Elias stood with Nanine and Virginia. The services were short, but what amazed Elias was that the grave was alongside that of Marty. He could imagine the scene when Lenore discovered her son, a brigadier general in the Confederate army, buried next to a Yankee.

Nanine said softly, "Marty wouldn't have minded."

Virginia was more practical. "Mama will."

Following the services, Elias suggested Virginia and Nanine return to Willowbrook, adding he'd join them shortly. Virginia knew he wished to discuss the subject Mr. Mason and Mr. Hall had broached to her following the murder of Mel Hutton.

Elias sought out the pair he'd met at Mason's house. "Gentlemen, you know whom I am. I'd appreciate it if you'd take a brief walk with me. I've something of importance to discuss."

They were mystified, but agreeable. At a spot well away from the mourners who were walking back to their homes, Elias told them what was on his mind.

"I'm sure you, as much as I, would like to see this man Culver delivered his just dues. Am I right?"

"After what he did to poor Mel, we sure do, Mr. Birch," George Hall said.

"I feel the same way," Otto Mason added.

"Good. Now it appears that Culver knows what's going on here on Valcour. Probably he's enticed one of the blacks to keep track of things."

"Sure ain't one of us," Mason said.

"Of course not," Elias agreed. "Now I want this spy to receive enough information to believe that not all of you Yanks have entirely given in to my wife. That you plan to move in a few days' time, but before you do, you intend to burn every house on the island, in defiance of Culver's threat. Can you start gossip to that effect so it will reach the right places?"

"That sure ain't hard to do," Mason said.

"But it'll bring Culver back and this time he may kill all of us," George Hall protested.

"It will bring him back," Elias said, "but to be killed, not to kill. I'm going to do my best to place him under arrest. Don't worry about it. A large number of Northern troops will be waiting for him too."

"We'll be glad to cooperate," Mason said.

"I'm grateful. While I ask that you not mention this to the others—when we buy your homes, we'll add a considerable sum to the price for your cooperation. And I thank you both. It's to our mutual advantage to put an end to Bradley Culver."

──────── *twenty-three* ────────

Two weeks had passed during which time Virginia negotiated the purchase of all but seven of the homes. Elias had returned to the mainland after the funeral but all was going well. The Yankees were packing up, even those who had rejected Virginia's offer, for they knew very well that eventually they would have to accept.

Nanine was kept busy writing letters to the former owners that they should begin making plans to return to Valcour. The terms were generous. Virginia would deed the homes to them at once and they were under no obligation to pay unless they felt it a moral responsibility and then only in the future, for all were practically destitute. She also arranged for carpenters, painters and plasterers to begin coming in the following week to restore the homes. When all was ready the move back would begin and then a soiree would be held to celebrate.

The ex-slaves who worked the cotton fields were retained and paid according to Virginia's wage scale, which made them happy. Both Virginia and Nanine knew that once the former owners were back, the fields would be properly managed and the cotton crop brought in as it always had been until the arrival of the Yankees.

Valcour began to regain its former glory. The success of Virginia's planning had never been brighter.

Much to her surprise, Elias returned unexpectedly on a Sunday morning. She greeted him with a cry of delight as she ran into his arms. They embraced warmly and murmured endearments between ⟍

kisses. That evening they talked far into the night, discussing decisions and future plans.

"We'll have the Yankees off the island in a month or less," Elias predicted. "Then, as soon as repairs are made, the old families can begin moving back. I understand about half the Yankees will be leaving in four or five days."

"Some may go tomorrow," Virginia said with quiet satisfaction. "They'd have been gone sooner, but they had to arrange for their possessions to be brought to the mainland. I cannot find much compassion in my heart for them."

"Well, for that matter, neither can I. When I arrived on the island to take command, we turned over the plantations to the ex-slaves to run. That was the idea of the whole thing. To see if the slaves, turned free, could fend for themselves. We soon discovered they could not."

"It was an impossible idea in the first place," Virginia said.

"Just remember, my love, we of the North were quite ignorant of how things worked in the South. Just as you were ignorant of the potentials of the North to put down the rebellion. If both sides had known one another better, perhaps the war would never have been fought. So now we're back at the point where it began and I'm sure Valcour will be the gainer for it."

Virginia gave him a warm smile. "I love you. I'm so happy you're back. How long can you stay?"

"I don't know. It all depends on how much time it takes to trap Bradley Culver."

"Trap him?" she asked in sudden alarm.

"That's what I came back for," Elias said quietly.

"You . . . have a plan in mind, then?"

"Oh, yes. I just hope it works out."

"Can you tell me what it is?"

"I don't see why not. Before he left, following the murder of Mel Hutton, Culver warned the Yankees that if they burned another house, he'd come back and kill every one. You know that."

"I'm the one who told you. But do you think he'd be so reckless?"

"We'll find out. I still wonder why he's so intent on helping us.

I've tried to figure it out. My only conclusion is that the island is a focal point. He wants to show that his methods do work. He saved the island by driving out the Yankees. All part of his plan for carrying on the war, which ended months ago. I believe he thinks of himself as a modern-day Robin Hood.''

"But why Valcour?" she asked, and hoped Elias wouldn't detect the note of fear and anxiety in her voice.

"That's an easy one to answer. One helpless Southern family against an island of carpetbaggers. Since the war ended, he's been fighting carpetbaggers.''

"If he's captured, do you think they'll hang him?"

"No doubt about it. He'll be turned over to the Yankee garrison in Charleston. You see, there's been some talk about Culver doing what he's been doing only to help the South, or to avenge its loss of the war. That makes him well liked by some. In fact, there are other bands, perhaps not quite as violent, who were rounded up, tried by Southern courts and found not guilty by Southern juries. Culver won't get that opportunity. A Yankee trial will be held without a jury. It will be a military matter and they don't show mercy when it's not called for. Culver is known to have killed, with his band of outlaws, several others besides Mel Hutton. He won't have a chance before a military tribunal.''

"But, Elias, wasn't he acting for what he believes to be a rightful cause?"

"Rightful?" Elias chided. "He displayed far more greed than patriotism. He and his men looted all they could lay their hands on. He's a doomed man and I've come back to put an idea into motion.''

"You intend to trap him here, on Valcour?"

"It's all set up. The idea is quite simple. He threatened to come back if any more homes were burned. I have arranged that he gets word the Yankees intend to burn every house before they leave. One great big bonfire. And it's to be done this evening. What Culver will see, if he takes the bait, is a big fire here. He'll come and we'll be waiting for him. With luck, we'll have ended his career and captured his entire outlaw band.''

"Won't it be dangerous?" she asked in genuine fear.

"Not the way we have it planned. Two of the Yankees, Otto

Mason and George Hall, have cooperated in this and I promised them they'd be rewarded generously for their houses."

"It's frightening, Elias. You might be killed."

"I'll take damn good care to see I'm not."

"There's also Mama, Nan, Miles and the Yankees," Virginia said worriedly.

"And you, my darling," Elias said softly. "The most precious person on this island so far as I'm concerned. I'm not taking a wild and reckless risk. Captain Delaney is in on it. This is one fight Culver won't win. That is, if he comes here."

Virginia was trying to control her nerves. "I'll be glad when it's over."

"He has the island terrified," Elias said, as if thinking out loud. "Miles has a gun, true, and I'm certain he'd use every last ounce of strength he had should he need to aim and fire it. But his strength is limited and that band of brigands would have no trouble with him. Or with your sister."

"My God, Elias," Virginia cried out in genuine fear. "Can't you stop it?"

"I'm trying to. I know you're tired of trouble and violence. I know you went through hell during the war. I want to end it. I hope to be back here permanently soon. I have a new manager for the big plantation. A young fellow who shows a great deal of promise, Christopher Savard. A West Point graduate, a real Rebel patriot, fought in half a dozen big battles. But a sensible sort too. He accepts the idea that the Rebel cause no longer exists and wants to not only bring back the South to what it once was, but to better it."

Virginia looked her relief. "At least you've some good news. I can't wait to have you on Valcour again."

"You don't think I enjoyed being away from you, Virgie. I've been looking for someone like Chris ever since the first furrow was plowed. Experienced and trustworthy people aren't easy to find."

Relief flowed through her, and she hugged and kissed him. She would be a constant wife with him now by her side. Yet, deep within her was a worry that Bradley Culver would be caught and punished. There were memories that refused to go away.

What she had done was wrong and 'immoral. She'd debauched

herself in an adulterous relationship with Bradley Culver. There'd never been any actual love between them, not even a pretense of it. She'd gone to him eagerly and debased herself. yet she was far too practical a woman to feel shame over what had been done. She had been unfaithful to Elias, even though she loved him. With Culver, it had been only a wild infatuation. Yet, she hoped he'd escape the trap.

At the supper table, Lenore favored Elias with a series of hostile glares and she had no word of welcome for him. Elias was accustomed to her moods and made nothing of it, but Virginia's nerves were on edge with the knowledge there might well be violence once again on Valcour before dawn.

"Mama, what ails you? Elias has come home for the first time in two weeks and you greet him like a stranger."

"I greet him the way I do because I thought he had become a gentleman, worthy of running Valcour."

"What on earth makes you think I'm not?" Elias asked, more amused than angry.

"You are supposed to be in control here, even over my daughters. And you allowed that carpetbagger to be buried beside my son. My son. It is not right. I want that Yankee's body removed."

"Mama, stop it," Virginia said sharply.

"Mother Hammond," Elias said, "if it bothers you that much, perhaps sometime in the near future we can have it removed. I make no promises, but it is possible."

"Then my regard for you is slightly improved," Lenore declared. "Just so someone has respect for the sanctity of my son's place in the cemetery. Virginia would do nothing, not even give me hope. I have faith in you, Elias." She hesitated a moment. "Even if you are a Yankee."

"Thank you, Mother Hammond." He got up, went to the head of the table and kissed her cheek.

After supper Lenore promptly went upstairs to read the Charleston and Atlanta newspapers Elias had brought from the mainland. Elias and Virginia remained at the table to enjoy more coffee. It seemed to be in more plentiful supply these days and Elias had brought a whole sack of it.

"Tonight," he said earnestly, "I beg of you, stay inside the house. Don't leave it for any reason. I'm going to ask Nan and Miles to do the same thing. Someone could get hurt."

"Elias, please stay here," she implored. "Let the soldiers do it. They're paid for that. It's their duty to capture the man, not yours."

"It's everybody's duty to rid the South of men like Culver. All he does is to slow down the process of the final peace and reconciliation. That's more important than anything else."

"Very well. I'll stay in my rooms and I'll see to it that Mama does too. I wish Nan and Miles were here with us."

"I'll see you later, then. I think everything is about ready. Wish me success, darling. Once it's over, we can concentrate on Valcour. And each other."

He next sought out Otto Mason and George Hall.

"It's all set," George Hall reported. "We've got piles of hay and a lot of things the families were leaving behind when they moved. The hay is spotted around so it'll look like the whole damn place is on fire."

"Good. What about any chance of information getting to Culver since you put up the material for the fires?"

"Nobody has been allowed to leave the island since yesterday. Every boat is accounted for and guarded, and it's too far to swim."

"You two will find this profitable. Now, when the trouble begins, see that everyone stays inside, including you two. If we miss, we don't want Culver to come back at you. However, we're not going to miss."

"You say the time," Otto said. "We're ready."

"It's getting dark now. Say, at eight o'clock when the fires are bound to be seen on the mainland. Light the fires and then go home. Leave the rest of it to us."

"Us?" Mason asked.

"The Yankee garrison in Charleston is sending out a good-size patrol. Very secretly. Culver will find a warm reception when he gets here."

"After what he did to poor Hutton, I hope they break his neck," Mason said.

"Have no doubt about it. They will. I've got to get down to the beach now. Wait until eight, then light up the sky."

Elias walked slowly down to a part of the island shore where the shrubbery and trees seemed to go out to meet the tide. This was where Culver had made his landing before because of the shelter, and this was where he'd surely make it again. Everything was in readiness. He examined the pistol stuck under his belt and a short hickory club bored out near the top and filled with lead. It would crack any skull. Elias sat down to wait. He also had a flare, a rocket to be shot into the sky. A relic of the war, given him by Captain Delaney to be used as a signal.

He sat, quite alone, bringing to mind all the questions he'd been asking himself for some time. Why did Culver make such a grandstand play of it on Valcour? Why did he come the first time? When he'd encountered Virginia, why did he honor her request not to destroy any property?

Then, too, why had he returned a second time, to give back the loot he'd stolen on his original visit? It didn't make sense, except for Virginia's guess that Culver was trying to be a Rebel Robin Hood. That didn't fit Culver either. He'd deliberately slit Hutton's throat and he'd warned the Yankees that should they burn again, he'd be back to destroy every one of them.

Elias had considered Culver's motive from every angle without reaching a conclusion. It must be simply an eccentricity on Culver's part. He'd become fascinated with Valcour and what had been done to the former residents. His activities here could be a showcase, a building-up of a reputation Culver so eagerly sought. A man who dealt out violence to those who deserved it, and bestowed only good fortune to those who merited it.

Elias cautiously lit a match, guarding the flame from being observed from the sea. In its feeble light he consulted his pocket watch. In two minutes now, Mason and Hall would begin starting the fires.

"The only chance of failure would be that Culver had taken off for some other part of the state. A remote possibility in Elias's opinion because, since the murder of Hutton, Culver had been diligently hunted both by Charleston lawmen and, especially, Captain Delaney's garrison.

Under those conditions, Culver wouldn't move about. Elias had a strong feeling that he was going to fall into this trap. Somewhere on the island, even Elias didn't know exactly where, Delaney's soldiers were hidden and waiting. Once Culver and his band of cutthroats came ashore, the signal would be given, either by the flare Elias carried, if he saw the invasion first, or by one of the garrison officers, if Culver came his way.

Elias felt himself growing nervous. It was going to be a dangerous undertaking.

Promptly at eight, the fires were started, and the red light of the flames rose in three or four minutes. Soon the whole sky over the island grew red with fire. The bonfires were arranged to last just about as long as it would take the houses to burn. Old houses that were vulnerable. Given an hour before the fire would die down, another hour for Culver to get into motion, the action should begin about ten o'clock.

Elias fought off a desire to return to the mansion, if only for a little while. He and Virginia had missed so much by their separation. Soon, though, he would be able to spend more time on Valcour. He'd been lucky when Christopher Savard had wandered into the plantation looking for work. He'd been a sergeant in the Confederate army. A tall, well-built man with a no-nonsense way about him. Unmarried, he had no ties and could devote his time to the plantation. Besides, he'd quickly demonstrated that he was quite capable of handling the blacks, some of whom were inclined to sloth, as the slaves used to do when no one was looking.

But this was no time to let his mind wander. Elias settled down to wait and listen and keep his eyes glued on as much of the ocean as he could see in the darkness. The splash of oars might give away the raiding party, but Culver might very well see that all oars were wrapped and carefully dipped to make very little sound. Elias would have to depend as much on night vision as on the acuteness of his hearing.

Now the time began to drag. The fires had been reduced to smoldering spots. Elias checked his revolver, hefted the truncheon a few times and let it strike lightly onto the palm of his left hand. He was no longer beset with any doubts, any puzzling details of the why and wherefore of Culver's actions on Valcour. He now concentrated on what might prove to be a bloody battle before it was done with.

A flare lit the night sky. It came from the hiding place of the soldiers. Elias began running back toward the other houses. Once ashore, it wouldn't take Culver long to realize he'd walked into a trap. All he had to see was the houses still standing and, perhaps, the smoldering bonfires. By then, Elias prayed, the soldiers would be between the raiding party and their boats.

Nearing the sound of the fracas growing louder and accompanied by several gunshots, Elias saw a dark figure go loping off toward the center of the island. Elias began running to intercept the man before he reached the mansion. Suddenly the outlaw turned and fired. The bullet went wide. Elias brought the man down with one shot, ran up to him and discovered the bullet had pierced his chest. The man was already dead.

It was not Culver. Elias ran back toward the shore, taking an angle that would lead him to where the soldiers had been concealed. He came upon a soldier being beaten off by two outlaws. Elias gave vent to a great shout and joined the fight. He used the truncheon on one man, sent him unconscious to the ground. The other one shouted in fear and threw up his hands. The soldier knocked him down with the butt of his rifle and promptly handcuffed him. Then, with only one set of handcuffs, he used the second outlaw's belt to bind his wrists and legs, though Elias doubted that was needed. The weighted truncheon had done a fine job.

There were other scuffles nearby. Some shouting, loud swearing and then it grew quiet again and to Elias that was ominous. He moved about until he found a Union sergeant.

"Culver," Elias asked. "What about him?"

"Don't know, Major Birch, sir. We haven't found him yet. A few of 'em got away in the brush, but we're rounding them up. We'll find Culver. Don't Worry."

But Elias did worry. He hurried down to the beach where half a dozen boats had been dragged ashore. Two Union soldiers stood guard over them.

"Any sign of Culver?" he asked, after he identified himself.

"No, sir. Not yet."

"Do you know if he came ashore?"

"Sure did. We got one of his men and clubbed him till he told us. Culver is on the island for sure."

"Keep an eye out," Elias warned. "He's tricky and dangerous."

Elias hesitated a moment, not quite knowing where to turn, but he realized quickly enough that his duty now lay in protecting Virginia, her mother, Nanine and Miles. If Culver reached the old hospital to look for shelter, he'd have fine hostages in Nanine and Miles, neither of whom could put up much of a defense.

The hospital was on his way back so he knocked, called out his name and a terrified Nanine opened the door.

"Culver's loose," Elias told her. "Keep everything locked and your gun handy. Don't hesitate to use it. Miles, do you hear me?"

"Hear you, Elias. I've got the gun right here and strength enough to pull the trigger."

"Is Virginia safe?" Nanine asked.

"That's where I'm headed now."

Elias ran the distance almost to the mansion. Approaching it, he slowed down and skirted some of the brush close by the house. If there'd been trouble, Virginia would certainly have put up a fuss and her mother's screams would have been heard a quarter of a mile away. Unless he was too late . . . or too early. Culver might still be on his way.

Elias dropped to his hands and knees and began crawling toward the front door. A large row of lilac bushes offered not only ample protection from being seen but provided him with a fine view of the front and rear of the mansion. The only place he could not observe was the offset kitchen, but he guessed that if Culver was coming here to provide himself with a hostage, he wouldn't go to the kitchen. He'd merely break his way into the mansion proper.

Ten or fifteen minutes went by. The sound of action near the waterfront had died away. Apparently Culver's outlaw band had been captured or killed. Now it was up to Culver to use his skill and brains to get away.

Leaving the island was impossible, and he knew it, for by now all the beaches would be under guard. It was impossible to swim to the mainland and every boat was protected. He had to come here. The taking of a hostage was his one and only way out of this predicament.

If he relied on being hidden, that would be useless, for at daybreak soldiers would begin a sweep of the island from one end to the other. Unlike the mainland, there was nowhere to hide that could not be discovered by searchers.

Then Elias heard him. Just the sharp crack of some small dried branch inadvertently trampled upon. Elias waited, hardly daring to breathe. He sought more sounds, looked for a fleeting shadow. Nothing happened. Time began to pass with an irritating slowness and Elias grew restless. He hadn't counted on anything like this. He grew chilly, crouched down close by the earth. Chilly and unaccountably sleepy. The mansion remained dark, no sign of any activity. He knew Virginia would not be asleep and if Culver entered, she would fight and scream. So far there was nothing.

By dawn, Elias was standing up and moving about. The lieutenant in charge of the soldiers approached the mansion and Elias gave up the vigil to move out and intercept him.

"Major, sir," the lieutenant reported, "we've got just about all of Culver's band. I doubt any are still loose. We've combed most of the island and we're heading this way to sweep this part."

"Are you sure Culver came along?" Elias asked.

"At least half a dozen of his men swear he did. They're talking their heads off, looking for a chance to avoid being strung up. We killed four. We got two men hurt but not seriously."

"Good," Elias said. "Culver will show up. He's bound to. I can handle him."

"I'm going to send half the men to the mainland with the prisoners and the dead and wounded. You say the word, sir, and I'll keep enough men here to keep watch for Culver."

"It won't do any good. He's hiding now and in a place that seems to be safe. But have your men sweep this area. If he's not found, take your men away. But before you do, make sure only one boat is left. Take the others in tow and don't cut them loose, for he'll try swimming to them. If there is just one boat left, he'll make a play for it."

"I could spare some men to help, sir."

"No. Likely he has things under observation, or he's prowling about and he'll know you've gone and taken all the boats with you. He'll soon find the one tied up on our dock. That will be his only chance."

"Yes, sir. I see your purpose. So, as soon as we finish the sweep, I'll order all boats towed and we'll go back to the mainland. Good luck, sir."

"Thank you, Lieutenant. Tell Captain Delaney I'll bring the prize in. I'm sure of that."

Elias then walked openly up to the mansion. As he approached, he sensed Virginia was watching. She unbolted the door, let him in, bolted it again and then clung to him as all the terror of the night subsided in the warmth and protection of his embrace.

"Culver is still on the island," he said. "I'm certain of it. Can you fetch me something to eat? I'm starved."

"You look awful, darling. You need sleep."

"Not yet, my dear. As it is set up now, the soldiers and their prisoners are soon to leave the island. First, they're going to make a sweep of this area, but they won't find him. He's too clever for that. But while the soldiers are doing that, Culver must, by necessity, lay very low and there's little chance he can see me making for the dock."

"Are you going to leave the island?" she exclaimed in fright.

"No, of course not. But there's only one boat left and that's where it is, on the dock. What I want you to do, after I have a bite of something, is to go upstairs to our room and draw all the curtains, as if you're darkening the room so I can sleep. Meantime, I'll get down to the area near the dock and wait for him. He may suspect it's a trap, but he has to take the chance."

"If . . . he comes at you, shoot him, Elias. Don't take any chances."

"My, you're bloodthirsty this morning," he observed with a smile.

"Dear Elias, I don't want you hurt." Her voice was a plea.

"I know. While you're getting me something to eat, I'll doze off a bit. The patrol will keep Culver under cover, so I've enough time."

Virginia hurried to the kitchen and raided the icebox of ham and bread to make a sandwich. She also supplied a glass of milk. Belle was nowhere to be seen. Likely she'd not budged from her cabin after the shooting and yelling began.

Elias was sound asleep when she returned and she was tempted to let him sleep. But he stirred and finally opened his eyes. He ate hungrily and then went into the library, where he added bullets to his revolver in place of those spent on the outlaw he'd killed.

Elias peered out of windows at the sides of the house. Soldiers with fixed bayonets were combing every foot of ground. They were heard to enter and and search the kitchen.

"Time to get down there," Elias said. "No telling when he'll make a break for it. But if the soldiers leave and he thinks I'm sleeping, he may try. Don't forget to draw the curtains. Wish me luck, darling, and don't worry. It'll take more than an outlaw to finish me off. Make sure your mother doesn't somehow give the play away."

"She won't budge from her rooms for two more days," Virginia predicted. She was trying to be lighthearted, but the effort wasn't fooling Elias. He held her for a few moments, caressing her face, his hands moving across her head, smoothening her silken hair. Then he kissed her, very hard, opened the door and slipped out.

Soldiers were still moving about. One of them quickly aimed his rifle, but recognized Elias and lowered the weapon. Elias didn't use the path, but made his way down the slope toward the dock well concealed by the lilac and laurel bushes and the elms and magnolia trees. He was certain that, except for a few seconds, his departure from the house could not have been observed.

Reaching the dock, he knew exactly where he would hide. A boathouse, once used as an icehouse, was close by the dock. He wasn't worried that Culver might already be using it as a refuge, for the Union soldiers had searched it thoroughly.

Entering the shed, Elias left the door slightly ajar. Through this crack he had a fine view of the dock and the boat, so temptingly tied up there. Even the oars lay on the dock for quick seizure if Culver could get away with it.

There was going to be no quick solution to this problem. The Union soldiers had to make their departure and surely Culver wouldn't dare make a break until he was certain all the soldiers were on the mainland and unable to intercept him.

Elias fought off the desire to doze. He shouldn't have eaten. It made him drowsy. There were a few times when he forced his eyes to remain open and he concentrated on recalling what he knew about Culver's unsavory reputation. He moved about, stretching his cramped muscles. The morning passed and at the middle of the afternoon he began to wonder if his scheme had failed, and that Culver had somehow made good his escape, even if it seemed impossible that he had done so.

More than once Elias was tempted to risk going out into the sunlight, but he'd sacrificed so much time now that his common sense told him not to take such chances and that Culver would act soon.

Culver came late in the afternoon, when shadows and daylight intermingled. When work in the fields had subsided and there was less chance of his being seen. Whatever route he'd chosen must have taken him through thick woodsy areas, for there were scratches on his now heavily bearded face and rips in his clothing. He didn't look much like a romantic outlaw now. He was moving toward the boat, his eyes darting in every direction, for he certainly suspected a trap. Elias saw that he held a large knife. A bowie, the kind that he'd used on Hutton. Elias cocked his pistol and stepped out of the shed.

"Stand where you are," he warned. "Or I'll kill you."

Culver whirled about and he seemed to relax, like someone glad it was over. There was even a slight smile on his face, though Elias reasoned later it was more likely a sneer.

"Well, now," Culver said. "If it's not the master of Valcour. Major Birch himself. You want me, you'd better shoot because I'm not dropping this knife."

"You're too rotten to kill quickly," Elias said curtly. "I'd rather see you hang. I'm coming, Culver, and this time you're not getting away."

"I'm waiting," Culver said. Elias thrust the gun under his belt, a bit of bravado he knew, but he spoke truthfully when he said he wanted Culver alive. But from that same belt he drew the truncheon, the lethally-loaded weapon that could do as much damage as a bullet at close range.

Elias sprang forward. Culver anticipated that. He moved aside agilely and made a wild swipe at Elias with the knife. Elias whirled about, bent low and went into a tackle. Culver tried again to use the knife, but Elias came in too low and too fast. One arm grabbed at Culver's legs and brought him down.

Culver was like a cat. He jumped to his feet and leaped at Elias, kicking him between the legs so cruelly that Elias came very close to lapsing into unconsciousness.

But Culver was too eager. He raised the knife for the kill as Elias squirmed aside and swung the weighted club. It hit Culver squarely between the eyes and he dropped as if shot through the temple with a heavy slug.

Elias rose, bent over in agony. He kicked away the knife, which had fallen from Culver's hand. He used a foot to turn the outlaw over. Culver was breathing, but unconscious.

Elias leaned heavily against a rail that bordered the little dock. He regained his breath slowly, all the while watching Culver for any signs of a recovery. He doubted there would be. The club had been swung far too hard.

Elias ached, his right thigh seemed to be alive with pain. That was where a bullet he caught during the battle of Bull Run had hit and was still lodged.

Finally he grasped Culver by the legs and began dragging him up the slope, moving slowly because of the pain. He was tempted to throw him aboard the rowboat and take him directly to the mainland, but if Culver came to, in the boat, there might be a battle Elias could lose. He decided on a safer course of action.

He kept dragging the unconscious man until Moses spotted him. The elderly ex-slave came running to help. Elias was happy to see him, for he felt he was at the end of his stamina and the pain was increasing.

"Help me get him into the whipping shed," he said. "I want to spancel him to the whipping post."

"Yes, suh," Moses said. "Yo' sho' put him to sleep, suh. Yo' sho' he ain' daid?"

"He's alive and that's how I want him to stay. Grab his other leg. Don't worry if we bang his head on rocks a few times. He has worse than that coming to him."

They dragged him into the whipping shed. There, Moses propped him up against the thick iron post to which slaves used to be spanceled and whipped.

"Where are the spancels?" Elias asked.

"Ain't none, suh. Ain't been no spancels since aftah the wah stahted. Us slaves throwed 'em all into the ocean."

"You didn't throw away the larger snake though," Elias said as he took down the tin rawhide whip from its place on the wall. He took a knife from his pocket and cut lengths off the long whip to fashion stout ropes of rawhide.

While Moses held the unconscious man against the post, Elias tied his wrists and ankles, fastening him to the post so tightly that if he did regain consciousness he'd not be able to make a move. Next, Elias wound another length of cord around his middle and another around his neck, pulling it tight, just short of strangling the man. Finally, he applied a gag and then a blindfold.

He stepped back, tested the bonds and nodded. "He won't get out of those and he can't yell for help. I'm going to the house and tell Miss Virginia. You get yourself down to the dock. I want you to row me to the mainland so we can bring back the soldiers."

"Sho' be nice we could take him too." Moses eyed the burly, tall prisoner.

"The boat is too small and I can't row. He got me between the legs and I'm not capable of much just now. I'll meet you at the dock."

"Sho' 'nuff, suh. Yo' all right? I mean, yo' wants me to go with yo'?"

"I'll be all right. Wait on the dock. I won't be long."

Limping badly, doubled up in pain, Elias made his way across the grassy approaches to the mansion, and before he reached it, Virginia came running out to meet him.

"You're hurt!" she exclaimed in horror. "Elias, you're badly hurt."

"I'm all right," he insisted. "It's just temporary from a kick. Culver's in the whipping shed. I got him tied to the whipping post and there is no chance he can get free. I'll be back with soldiers in an hour. Stay away from him. Lock the door and arm yourself with the rifle in the library. If he happens to get loose, which I'm sure he won't, kill him if he tries to break in."

"Elias, I should go with you. I'll even go to the mainland . . . but, no. I'd be too slow. Just go. And hurry, darling. Please—hurry and please be safe."

"Back to the house with you," he said. "Everything's fine now. It's over. By the time I get back, I'll be in good shape. This is nothing. Moses is rowing me so don't worry about me. Just be glad this is the finish of it."

She wanted to stand there until he was aboard the boat, but she knew he'd not approve of that so she hurried back to the mansion and sat down in the drawing room, close by a window overlooking the approaches to the house.

And then she bent her head and wept. As Elias had said, it was over. Especially for Bradley Culver.

twenty-four

Virginia dashed cold water on her face, dried it and then went down to the library, where she took down a rifle from the gun rack. She loaded it automatically, placed it across the desk. Her mind was in torment. Too much had happened. Elias was surely hurt more than he had admitted. She could tell by the drawn look on his face, by his limp, and his wincing with pain at every step.

Bradley Culver was beyond any possibility of escape. He'd be taken ashore as soon as soldiers arrived. There'd be a trial; then they'd hang him. She wondered, with painful anxiety, what he would tell. It was within his power to destroy her and Elias. To place an onus on Valcour that could never be wiped away. Would he?

She idly let one hand caress the stock of the rifle. It would be so easy . . .

Her mother made a great deal of noise coming down the stairs and in the reception hall she demanded in a loud voice where Virginia was. At Virginia's reply, Lenore entered the library and sat down heavily in a chair.

"I'm so upset. I wish someone would tell me what's going on around here. There seem to be soldiers everywhere and so much shooting and yelling. I don't like it. We all might be in danger."

"It's finished, Mama," Virginia said.

"What's finished? I was told to stay in my rooms and I did, but I can't spend the rest of my life there. What is going on?"

"Elias set a trap for Bradley Culver. There was some shooting, of course. Culver is, at this moment, tied up in the whipping shed."

"I saw Elias going down to the dock. I'm sure he was in the boat that left for the mainland. Who is guarding this outlaw?"

"No one, Mama. Elias tied him so firmly there is no chance he could get loose."

A calculating gleam shone for a fleeting moment in Lenore's eyes. "What are you doing with that rifle?"

"I'm keeping it handy in case Culver should get free, or they missed one or two of his band of murderers."

"I'd best get back upstairs, then. Virgie, do you know what I was thinking?"

"No, Mama. I haven't any idea."

"I thought, perhaps, you were considering going down to the whipping shed and . . . killing that awful man."

"Mama," Virginia cried out in exasperation, "where do you get such foolish ideas?"

"He deserves it. After all, you told us he held you and kissed you. In my day that called for quick revenge."

"The war ended the old days, Mama. Everything is changing. But I will admit there may be some danger still, and I would advise you to go back to your rooms and keep the door locked."

"Will you be down here, then?"

"I'm going to visit Nanine and Miles. Then I'll come back. You'll be safe enough if you stay inside."

"Very well, then, but don't dally at Nanine's. Let that . . . that man protect her. If he can."

Virginia said wearily, "He can and he will if it becomes necessary."

After she left, Virginia unloaded the rifle and placed it back in the rack. She left the library and walked the floor in the drawing room for a few moments, her mind still whirling under the decisions she had to make.

Yes, Bradley Culver was an evil man. A murderer. But with her he'd been kind. He'd tried to help her. His capture had been caused by his desire to see that the Yankee carpetbaggers were driven from Valcour.

She could, in her fancy, feel his arms around her, feel the strength and the passion of the man.

She moved quickly to the kitchen. Belle was not there. Virginia procured a sharp knife, not too large, but with the keenest possible edge. She then hurried upstairs, placed a shawl over her head and shoulders, beneath which she could conceal the knife.

She left the house, being careful to lock the door. With a rapid pace she went down to the old hospital. Nanine let her in after making certain of her identity.

"I meant to come sooner," Virginia apologized. "Culver is a prisoner down in the whipping shed. Elias captured him and has gone to the mainland to bring back soldiers who will take Culver away."

"Why didn't Elias take him in?" Miles asked.

"There was a fight, Elias was injured. He was in great pain and afraid he wouldn't be able to cope with Culver in the same boat. So he got Moses to row him."

"What of Culver's men?" Nanine asked.

"Elias is sure all of them were captured. Just in case one or two managed to get away and are on the island, I wouldn't relax. Stay inside, lock the doors. In another half an hour or so, it will be over. Finished!"

"How'd Elias accomplish all this?" Miles asked, then added, "There'll be time enough to talk about that later."

"Where will you be?" Nanine asked.

"In the house. Mama's scared to death."

"Go along, then, Virgie. And don't tarry," Nanine said.

"I surely won't," Virginia said. She was holding the knife beneath the shawl and as she turned to open the door, she let the shawl slip open. She masked the knife quickly and prayed that Nanine had not seen it. She started straight back toward the house, but when she knew Nanine could not be observing her, she changed direction and broke into a run.

She paused before entering the whipping shed. She looked about, listened well, but saw or heard nothing. The blacks were in their cabins, the Yankees were locked in their homes. The whipping shed was more or less isolated from the other structures.

Virginia opened the door. It creaked. Loudly enough to be heard on the mainland, she thought. Entering, she moved up behind Culver. She saw that he was blindfolded and gagged. She stepped close to him.

"It's Virginia," she said. "They've gone to fetch soldiers to arrest you."

Culver gurgled behind the gag. Virginia promptly untied it. Culver exhaled in relief. "What are you going to do?" he asked. "And please uncover my eyes."

"I'm sorry," she said. She untied the blindfold, let it drop to the floor.

"I hope you're going to cut me loose," he said. "If you don't, I'll swing within a week."

"Brad, will you promise you'll go far away and never come back?"

"Strange you should ask that," he said with a note of derision. "I've been thinking the same thing."

"Do you promise?" she insisted.

"My word is no damn good and you know it, Virginia. But I'll promise, anyway, and it's quite likely I'll never come back. I have a sensitive neck."

"I'll cut you loose, then . . ."

"No, wait!" he said sharply. "There's no sense in getting yourself involved. Though I wouldn't mind causing trouble for your husband. He hit me with something that felt like a cannon ball."

"I have to cut these straps . . ."

"Bend down, raise up my right trouser leg. Go ahead . . . do as I say. Strapped to my ankle is a small knife. Use that."

She pulled the small blade free of a thin leather holster and, without any further talk, she cut him free. He massaged his swollen wrists and ankles while he smiled crookedly at her.

"You may be letting yourself in for a lot of grief, Virginia."

"I realize that."

"Good Lord," he exclaimed, "are you in love with me?"

"No," she replied promptly. "But I remember . . . things . . ."

"So do I. The few happiest moments of my worthless life. I'll go far away. You'll never hear from me again. I promise, on whatever honor I still possess."

"Please go," she said.

He looked down at her, a resentful smile on his face. "I'll be damned."

"You are," Virginia replied calmly.

To her amazement, his eyes were regarding her tenderly. Always before, they'd mocked her.

"Mrs. Birch," he said, "I think I'm in love with you. And it's hopeless. Give me the knife."

She had a few seconds of doubt, but she gave him the knife and quite unconsciously braced herself. But he raised his right hand and, holding the knife in his left, he drew it across his wrist. Blood spurted from the shallow cut. He quickly pressed his fingers over it until the bleeding stopped. Then he deliberately made two more random cuts on his hand.

"I'll take off the strap on my ankle and throw it in the sea. When they find the bloodstained knife, they'll think that I had the blade hidden somewhere within reach and I got it free. They may wonder how, after the way your husband lashed me to that post. But this way they'll not suspect I was helped. You'll come under no suspicion. Go now—back to the kind of life you deserve. Forget me. Pretend it was all a beautiful dream. Damned if I ever thought I'd talk this way. Pretend I never existed."

Without touching her with his bloodstained hands, he kissed her on the lips. A long kiss of desire, longing and even sadness. It seemed to express each of these emotions.

Virginia gently touched his face, kissed him quickly and then fled back to the house. Culver was free. She could forget him. There were Yankee boats along the shore by now and he'd find one. It was over. Bradley Culver never existed.

Back in the safety of the library, she was devoid of feeling. She sat dry-eyed, telling herself over and over that what she had done was right. Not legally. She could be jailed for setting him free. All she prayed for was that he'd manage to slip through Charleston. Once out of that area, the danger would lessen. She hoped he'd go to the Far West where a man of his type might find his proper place. She wished him well.

He'd have to move fast now. By this time, Elias and the soldiers would be on their way back. She recalled that Elias had warned her to keep a gun handy, so she took down the rifle again. And she picked up the kitchen knife she'd taken with her and, with a sigh of relief that she'd remembered it, went to the kitchen and replaced it in the drawer.

Everything was now accounted for. She'd lie about it, but it would be a necessary lie. No one would suspect her of a thing. Especially Elias, and he was the most important of all.

She was still sitting in the library when she heard someone call out a greeting. She hurried to the front door. Two men were moving briskly along the path. She saw that one of them was Moses. A few moments later she recognized the other as Captain Delaney. Elias was not with them and she was overcome with sudden fear as she ran down to meet them.

"Where is Elias?" she asked. "Please . . . tell me . . ."

"He's fine," Delaney assured her.

"Sho' is, Missy," Moses added. "Kinda wore out some reckon, an' the doctah say he stays in the hospital fo' a while."

"You're sure he's in no danger?"

"Positive," Delaney assured her. "Take our word for it, Mrs. Birch. He is all right. In some pain, but that will pass. They're going to give him a complete examination in the morning."

"Thank you. Do you think I should go to him?"

"Missy, he say yo' to stays heah," Moses said. "Say Ah gots to tell yo' ain' no reason to fret an' you' sho' got business heah on Valcour. That whut he say."

"Very well," she conceded. "I suppose you've come for that terrible outlaw . . ."

Delaney laughed softly. "We've got him already. He got free somehow. I want to go to the shed where he was tied up and try to figure out what happened."

"He . . . got away?" she asked in dismay. She clenched her fists to fight the wave of weakness. She thought she was going to faint.

"Knowing Culver as we did, as soon as Elias came to us with the news Culver was a prisoner on Valcour, I sent out all the patrols I could spare to cover the entire waterfront. Sure enough, they saw him rowing to shore. He gave up without a fight. He says he cut himself free. Elias says that was impossible. Will you please come down to the whipping shed with me?''

"Of course. Moses, will you fetch lanterns, please?''

"Yes'm, sho' will.''

She and Delaney walked slowly toward the whipping shed to give Moses time to bring the lanterns.

Delaney said, ''I'm glad Culver will finally be brought to justice. He was one of the greatest menaces I and my men had to contend with.''

"Will he be tried soon, Captain?''

"In two or three days. We're not going to delay this trial. Culver is far too tricky and shrewd. So long as he breathes, he won't give up hope of escaping again.''

"He's a very strange man,'' Virginia commented.

"Yes, indeed, Mrs. Birch. Odd though, how he gave up so easily when we discovered him. We expected a fight on our hands, but he was no trouble. I suppose he knew he was finished and just gave up.''

"I'm glad he didn't hurt anyone else.''

Moses, supplied with two lanterns, led the way into the whipping shed. The first thing Captain Delaney noticed was the small, blood-smeared knife at the foot of the whipping post. He picked it up gingerly.

"He told us he had a knife hidden on his person and apparently he didn't lie. Elias admitted he hadn't searched him thoroughly. Culver reached the blade somehow and got himself loose. His story seems accurate. He cut himself in manipulating the knife, but got free. We wondered if one of his men had managed to keep hidden, and came here to set him free. Now it's apparent Culver did it all by himself. Not surprising. He's a clever man.''

"Cain't see how he got hisse'f loose,'' Moses said. ''Massa 'Lias he gots him tied up so he cain't move no way.''

"He managed, though, Moses,'' Delaney said.

"Thank you, Moses." Virginia dismissed him. "You'd best see to Belle. She's probably still scared out of her wits."

"Yes'm, Ah thanks yo'," Moses said.

"You were a great help," Delaney told him. "I appreciate it, Moses."

Moses' face spread in a smile. "Does whut Ah gots to do, Cap'n, suh."

"Well," Delaney put the knife into a pocket, "it's finally over."

He took Virginia's elbow and guided her along the path to the mansion. They walked in silence for about half the distance.

"Captain, what sort of man is Culver? Really, I mean, I had contact with him for a few brief moments and even in that short time I sensed he was not just some ignorant ruffian."

"You're right. We did a study on the man and we were surprised to learn he attended West Point. His father was once a senator in Georgia. A wealthy and highly regarded lawyer. His mother was a society woman, known all over the state for her soirees, her charm and wit. Bradley was an only son. Everyone had great hopes for him. He was bright, a handsome young man, kind in everything he did. The war changed him. His father and mother both died; he began to rage against the North. When he went into battle, it was with the sole purpose of killing as many Yankees as he could. And he became expert at it. He risked his life several times. However, all that killing did something to him. The killing and the hate. Too bad! Even his early history and family connections can't help him now."

"Thank you. How . . . very sad."

"Thank heaven it's finished. I'll report to Elias at once when I go ashore. And please don't worry about him. I fully expect he'll be back tomorrow. You know how doctors are. They don't want to take chances."

Delaney escorted her to the door, saluted graciously and set off for the dock. Virginia went directly to her rooms. She was tired, shaken and near the point of exhaustion. Without removing her dress, she lay on the bed to rest.

So Bradley was a prisoner. What she had risked so much to accomplish had been for nothing. And she wasn't really sorry.

Violence such as he'd inflicted on others couldn't be tolerated in a civilized society.

Nonetheless, she remembered with warmth his kisses and embraces. Especially that last kiss after he'd revealed his love for her. Memories she must thrust from her mind. Yet she knew she never could. Neither would she forget that bloody moment after he had murdered Mel Hutton and calmly wiped the blood off his knife. That would remain with her as well.

Bradley was, in her opinion, two completely different people. He could have changed that, but he'd chosen not to, in the full knowledge of what it would finally mean.

·twenty-five

The hospital was still overflowing with wounded from the war. Doctors were harried and short-tempered, nurses perhaps even more so. Elias, however, had been given a small private room. His face lit up with a welcoming smile when Virginia and Nanine walked in.

"You shouldn't have made the trip," he chided them gently, though it was apparent he was overjoyed to see them. He looked wan and tired.

"You couldn't keep Virgie away," Nanine said.

"When will you be able to come home?" Virginia asked. "You'll surely rest better and recover sooner."

"Not right away," he said. "I tried to walk around this morning. I lasted exactly three steps. I was ordered to get back in bed."

"Just what do the doctors say?" Virginia asked.

"It's that wound I suffered at the beginning of the war when I was shot in the thigh. The bullet is still there, of course. It used to give me some distress, but nothing I couldn't stand. Brad Culver changed that. He kicked me exactly where he shouldn't have. I suppose the bullet moved closer to nerves and that's what makes the area so painful."

Virginia's concern heightened, though she kept her voice down. "What are they going to do about it?"

"I suppose there will have to be an operation."

She was flooded with guilt, knowing he had expended himself at the large plantation to the point of exhaustion. "I'm sorry, darling."

395

He gave her a reassuring smile. "It's not the kind of surgery that's especially dangerous. They'll likely remove the bullet and it will hurt like hell, but will eliminate any further trouble."

"Then the sooner it's done, the better," Nanine said in her practical way.

"I gather I'm to be sent to a military hospital in Washington."

"I'll go with you," Virginia said promptly.

He shook his head. "You can't, darling. Not right now. Moses can't handle Valcour alone. Chris Savard is practically a stranger here and may need your advice. We can't take any risk with the first crop. It's going to make us or break us. Tell me, how are the Yankees doing on Valcour?"

"About half have already left," Virginia told him. "And the others are in the process of doing so. We're not having any trouble with them except for Tannet. I don't know why that man hates me so. He swears he's not going to leave and said not even Brad Culver can make him go."

"Brave words when Culver is locked up," Nanine commented.

"Oh, yes, Bradley Culver," Elias said. "Have you heard the latest about him?"

"'The latest'?" Virginia asked. "Don't tell me he's escaped again."

"Oh, no, nothing like that, but it seems he has a few friends after all. People who regard him as a brave man because he still fights the war. They've hired a lawyer who's had the trial postponed for three weeks."

"Well," Virginia said, "I'll grant that he deserves the same rights as anyone else. Especially where his life is concerned. But after what he did to you, I've no sympathy for him."

"He'll be convicted. Military law doesn't provide for civilian juries. He'll be judged by a panel of Union officers and I'd say he hasn't a chance."

"I should hope not," Nanine said.

"Speaking of Tannet," Elias told them, "I understand he's talked to Culver's lawyer and he's going to be called as a witness for the defense. I don't understand that."

"Will you still be here?" Virginia asked. "I mean—won't they need you as a witness?"

"I have no idea." Elias studied her face. "Darling, do you feel well? You look a little peaked to me."

"I feel very well," she responded with surprise. "Nan, do you think I look peaked?"

Nanine studied Virginia's face. "You look tired."

"You've got to stop worrying," Elias chided her gently. "I'm having a good rest and I'll be in much better shape after surgery."

"I'll continue looking after Valcour," Virginia said. "And the large plantation also if you wish."

Elias brightened. "Will you and Nan pay it a visit? Meet Christopher Savard. I'd like to know your opinion of him."

"We'll hire a carriage and ride out tomorrow morning," Virginia promised.

Elias addressed Nanine. "Can you leave Miles alone? How is he?"

Nanine beamed. "He's doing well. He has more strength and has begun to move about. I'm greatly encouraged."

"Who'll look after him while you're on the mainland?" Elias still seemed concerned about Miles's welfare.

Nanine smiled. "Belle. And Moses. And Ivy."

"Ah, yes," Elias said reflectively. "I'd forgotten about Ivy."

Virginia wondered if she only imagined an added warmth in Elias's tone when he mentioned Ivy. She was beautiful. In the way Phoebe was beautiful. Virginia stifled her jealousy of the young girl who had given not the slightest cause for it.

Elias said, "Miles will be able to help you in the business matters of the plantations. And you'll find Chris Savard highly knowledgeable and very eager. Don't hesitate to consult him. Or he may have need to consult you, since I'll not be here."

"Don't worry about business matters," Virginia said warmly. "We'll manage."

"Thanks," Elias said. "You know I think I'm going to enjoy a vacation. I only wish they could perform the surgery here. I'll miss my family."

"We'll miss you too, darling." Virginia squeezed his hand lightly.

"Any word from Phoebe?" he asked.

"We're going to see if there's any mail at the post office as soon as we leave here. And we're going to do some shopping," Virginia said.

"There's so much to be done in the houses that have been vacated," Nanine explained. "We have to arrange for supplies. Also, for the banking. Miles told us what to do."

"Fine. It's a relief to know things will go smoothly." Elias suppressed a yawn.

They both rose, taking the hint gracefully. It was evident he had begun to tire. Nanine bade him a farewell and left the room so they could have a few moments' privacy. Virginia came out shortly.

Walking down the hospital corridor, Virginia paused before a large mirror and studied her face. "I look fine," she declared. "That's how I feel. Now—let's buy Mama a gown and a hat. Since the Yankees have been leaving, she's been planning dinners and dances. A dinner gown will cheer her up immensely." Virginia laughed, then added, "She can always wear it dining with me."

They did their shopping and on the way back to the hotel where they had a room for the night, they picked up their island mail. There was a letter from Phoebe, which they saved until supper to read.

Virginia scanned the brief note and handed it across the table for Nanine to read. Nanine folded it, placed it back in the envelope and put it in her reticule.

"Something is troubling her," Nanine said soberly.

Virginia said, "You mean her saying that she has yet to meet his folks and doubts she ever will?"

Nanine gazed at her somberly. "Yes. And she never mentions the show and we know it got excellent reviews. The brief postscript said she missed us terribly. She can't be happy."

"I suppose we shouldn't read between the lines, but I'm afraid it has to do with Tom—and Phoebe's color."

"I hope you're wrong."

"So do I," Virginia said. "She loves him dearly."

"If what we surmise is true, she must be hurting dreadfully."

Virginia mused, "It could be because she's working and Tom isn't."

"Let's hope that's it. She's too practical a person not to remedy any trouble between them."

"If we're right, it's Tom who must do the remedying," Virginia replied. "Let's eat our supper. We must get an early start tomorrow. I'm anxious to meet Mr. Christopher Savard."

"So am I," Nanine said. "It will give me something to tell Miles about when we return."

"We'll retire early and leave at dawn for the plantation. Then return so we'll have time to go to the bank and hire carpenters, painters and whatever else is needed to get those houses in order."

As the carriage approached the plantation, Virginia stood up to better survey that part of the fields within her vision. At the same time she saw a man hurrying to meet them.

"Nan," she said, "I've never seen a better crop, nor a better tended one. And I suppose that's Mr. Savard coming to meet us."

As Savard neared the carriage, which had now come to a stop before the framework of a large shed, Virginia saw that he was about thirty, older than she'd expected. A tall, slender and solid-looking man. As he swept off the big straw hat he wore, she noted that he had curly brown hair and deep blue eyes. A firm chin and mouth, with rather high cheekbones, but overall he was a handsome man.

Virginia said, "I'm Mrs. Birch. And this is my sister, Mrs. Rutledge."

He bowed again. "Welcome to your plantation, ladies. Elias sent word last evening that you would come."

Virginia extended her hand to be helped off the carriage, then Savard assisted Nanine. He stepped back a pace.

"We had a fairly good look at the fields along the way," Nanine said. "You're doing a fine job of it, Mr. Savard."

"Most of it was already done. I've not been here long enough to take credit for this crop, though it's surely going to be a good one."

"My husband is pleased with your work and feels the plantation will be in good hands during his confinement in the hospital," Virginia said.

"I'm sorry he has to go through that," Savard said. "But he'll feel much better afterward. He drove himself relentlessly here. Some days he limped quite badly."

Nanine said, "One need only glance around at the buildings going up to realize how hard Elias worked."

"I must say it's a pleasure to work for him," Savard replied. "I've learned a great deal in the time I've been here."

"If you have any problems while my husband is away, please come to the island," Virginia said. "He asked us to drive out today to meet you."

"Thank you, Mrs. Birch," Savard said. "May I show you both around a little?"

"Please do," Virginia said with a sigh. "Just standing on this ground gives me a nostalgic feeling. We had such happy times here."

"I'm sure you did," Savard replied. He stepped between them, took their elbows and guided them along a rather rough path.

"The mansion won't be in heavy work until after the sheds and toolhouses are built," he explained. "But it's going to be fine."

"It's going to be enormous, isn't it?" Nanine asked.

"Yes, Mrs. Rutledge. I believe your sister discussed the plans with Elias. Am I correct, Mrs. Birch?"

"You are, Mr. Savard," Virginia replied.

Savard said, "Now—the fields. Let me take you to one experimental patch Elias began. He thinks he can grow the same kind of silken cotton that grows on Valcour."

"Impossible, Virginia said. "Papa tried. Valcour plants will grow only on Valcour."

"I want to show you this part anyway."

They spent two hours going over much of the plantation. It was well staffed with men who seemed to be working hard. Women and children were also busy and the size and color of the plants proved it.

On the way back to the city, Nanine cast a sidelong glance at her sister. "What did you think of him, Virgie?"

"Mr. Savard? Why . . . he seems to handle his job very well."

"He's handsome too."

"Very. I'm more than pleased with the progress Elias has made. I'm afraid, though, he drove himself too hard."

"What better way could he prove his love for you?"

"What do you mean?"

Nanine looked startled at Virginia's sharp tone. "Only that everyone knows you're obsessed. Look darling, Papa would have been proud of you. We all are."

Back on Valcour there were many things to be done besides the growing of the cotton. They had made extensive purchases, and new furniture for the mansion had been delivered by large barges. Willowbrook was assuming its old state of glory. Painting had been done, papering where necessary. New curtains and draperies were installed and more modern furniture filled, the rooms and gave them even more dignity than they'd had before. To Virginia's relief, Lenore was enthusiastic and began discussing plans for a grand ball once the other houses were occupied by their former owners.

Most of the Yankees had already left, sometimes utilizing the same barges that had brought the new furniture to Willowbrook. Five families were still in residence, four of them because they were still trying to find a new location. The fifth, Mr. Tannet, moved about with an enigmatic smirk. Virginia tried to avoid him. Although he had lost his store, he had not yet legally transferred the property, including the house.

Time went by quickly with so much work. Elias was in Washington, not yet operated on and he wrote he doubted he'd be back for at least a month. There were certain complications, though none of them serious. Plans for the trial of Bradley Culver were going on and the consensus was that it was a waste of time and he should be taken out and hanged summarily.

Virginia dreaded the thought of being in that courtroom, but Elias had agreed with her that if Valcour was brought into it, someone should be there to defend it.

Virginia finally admitted to herself that she was feeling unusually tired. She attributed it to the long hours she was putting in. She had to make many trips to the mainland, had to interview each family now preparing to return to Valcour, and overjoyed at the prospects.

Most of them were in serious financial straits and Virginia gladly helped out. Without these people, Valcour wouldn't exist, even if they did come to control all of it. These families were old friends, reliable people, and Virginia believed financing them would tide them over until their crops came in next year. Cotton that brought the highest prices in the world because of its superior quality. With very large increases in the price of cotton, they were on the verge of tapping a gold mine.

"It's strange we haven't had even a brief note from Phoebe," Virginia said one evening when Nanine stopped by.

"It's been on my mind too," Nanine said.

"She's probably forgotten us," Lenore said coolly.

"Nonsense, Mama," Nanine said. "You read her last letter. We thought it sounded as if she was having some sort of trouble."

"Well, I saw nothing like that in the letter, but then I'm not her mother," Lenore said.

Nanine and Virginia knew better than to pursue the subject.

Two days later they dressed for the trip to Charleston and Bradley Culver's trial. Virginia felt nervous about it. She prayed it didn't show, but she did find her hands shaking slightly and she had a difficult time concentrating. Besides that, she'd had several severe headaches. She attributed them to overwork and her concern over Elias.

Much to Virginia's and Nanine's surprise, Lenore walked down to the dock with them.

"If that outlaw is to be hanged," she said, "you should stay for the event."

"I don't know what's come over Mama," Nanine said once they were under way. "She's savage when it comes to Culver."

"Of course she is," Virginia said listlessly. "Culver invaded the sanctity of Valcour."

Nanine said, "Virgie, are you feeling well?"

"Yes; I'm just exhausted. I'd prefer to just sleep for a whole week. The thought of attending this ghastly trial upsets me."

"It won't be a long one, I'm sure," Nanine said, hoping to comfort her. Virginia had looked tired and drawn for days. Nanine was more than a little concerned. Even Miles had noticed.

— twenty-six —

The courtroom was packed, but Virginia and Nanine, as possible witnesses, were given front row seats. The trial proceeded swiftly. One after another, people who had suffered at Culver's hands testified. Culver seemed bored by the whole procedure. The defense attorney, a rather young man named Roberts, was clever enough to bring out the fact that not one witness could claim to have seen Culver actually committing either murder or rape, or even setting fires.

All of which, to the military officers on the bench, was inconsequential. Culver was with those who did murder and rape and commit arson. In fact, he was the admitted leader.

On the second day of the trial, Culver's lawyer put Tannet on the stand. Finally, the reason for Tannet's smirking and defiance on Valcour came to light.

"Yes, sir," he replied in answer to the lawyer's question, "it is my opinion that Bradley Culver not only came to Valcour several times, but he was welcomed there."

"By whom?" he was asked.

"Well," Tannet said, "he sure came to see Mrs. Birch, 'cause the second time he came, he brought back everything he'd stolen from people on the island."

"And the other times?" he was asked.

"Well, now, there was one night, near midnight it was, and I was taking a walk. I ran into Mrs. Birch coming back from the private dock she owns. And at the same time, Culver was rowing away in the darkness."

"Now hold on," the military prosecutor interrupted, "I want this witness instructed that there is a penalty for perjury."

The defense lawyer shrugged and turned the witness over. Roy Martin, the prosecutor, lost no time in destroying that accusation.

"The night you met Mrs. Birch, you saw Mr. Culver rowing away from the island. Please describe to the court what Mr. Culver was wearing that night."

"Well," Tannet acknowledged, "I never got that close."

"In fact, you never even saw him that night, did you? Tell the truth. If you saw him, you know how he was dressed. You have just said that you saw him well enough to have identified him. Is that true?"

"Well, it ain't exactly that way."

"Did you actually see Culver that night? Just answer yes or no."

"I . . . guess I didn't."

"It was more your imagination, wasn't it?"

"Well, he'd come before. He said if we did anythin' to make trouble for Mrs. Birch, he'd come back."

"Isn't it true he came back only because he saw fires on the island and he thought you and some others were destroying all the buildings on the island?"

"I guess so. He said if any more houses were burned, he'd come back and kill all of us."

"When he did return, did you see him? Not the way you thought you saw him one night when you encountered Mrs. Birch."

"I sure did. Yes, I saw him, so did everybody else. He murdered poor Mel Hutton. Just cut his throat."

"Describe the murder, please."

"Well, now, I didn't actually see it happen."

"Strike out the evidence of this man," the ranking court officer ordered. "I doubt he ever saw anything worth testifying to."

The defense attorney put Culver on the stand and this created a substantial ripple of interest. Virginia closed her eyes as he was sworn in. Listening to the evidence so far presented, she knew there'd be but one verdict and she was sorry she'd come to witness the terrible end to this man.

Culver readily answered the questions. "Sure I was on Valcour a few times. The first time I got there I meant to raid the place and maybe burn a house or two because I thought there was nobody on that island except Yankee scum. Cheap, conniving carpetbaggers."

There was a murmur of approval from the audience, composed entirely of Southern men.

"When I got there I saw this lady riding a horse and I thought she was a Yankee and I wanted to show her what I thought of someone like her living on Valcour. Making a joke of what we'd fought for. So I hauled her down off the horse and I guess I got carried away. I kissed her. Only then did I learn she was a Southern lady, a member of the Hammond family that owns so much of Valcour. I felt ashamed I'd done such a thing."

"Did you return after that visit?" he was asked.

"She asked me not to hurt anybody or destroy any property. Well, by that time my boys had already stolen as much as they could carry. So I brought it all back."

"Was that your second visit?"

"Yes, sir."

"When was the third?"

"When one of those scalawags burned down the house he had to move out of. I warned them if any more places were burned, I'd come back and make them mighty sorry for it."

"And did you come back another time?"

"Sure did, sir," Culver said with a broad smile. "I walked right into a trap."

"Did you murder a man named Hutton during the third visit?"

"Never heard of him," Culver replied straight-faced.

"With the court's permission," the defense attorney interrupted. "I would like Mr. Culver to identify the lady he dragged off her horse during his first visit. I ask that he approach the lady and place a hand on her shoulder."

"Granted," the chief justice agreed.

Culver climbed down off the stand and walked slowly toward Virginia. By identifying her he would bear some substance to the testimony of Tannet, even if it had been thrown out. Culver never glanced at Virginia. He placed a hand on Nanine's shoulder, much to her discomfiture and surprise. Then Culver walked back to the stand.

The prosecutor gave a short laugh. "The court should know that Mr. Culver has been accused of going back to the island several times and being in contact with the lady he met on his first visit. That lady, whose name is Mrs. Birch, was not the one he identified. The one he did identify is Mrs. Rutledge, the sister of Mrs. Birch."

When the court adjourned, Virginia and Nanine left immediately. Virginia said, "I'm sorry, Nan. It was unfair to you and Miles."

"Don't worry about it," Nanine replied. "It was unsettling, but I'm glad Mr. Culver perjured himself. Tannet might have planted the seed of doubt in the Military Court."

"I'm still sorry, but I'm glad we were there. If we hadn't been, the defense attorney would have said we didn't dare show our faces."

"True," Nanine agreed.

At the hotel, a messenger awaited them. He'd been sent by Moses with the message for Nanine that Miles was ill and had asked that she return.

"I'm sorry you'll have to be alone tomorrow," Nanine said. "But I must go back at once."

"Of course you must. I can manage. Just get back and see to Miles."

"He seemed to be coming along so well," Nanine replied anxiously. "That's why I felt safe to leave him."

"I'll pack your things and bring them back. Please go at once."

The sisters embraced and Nanine departed.

Virginia ate a solitary supper that night and went to her hotel room. A wave of giddiness swept over her as she prepared for bed. She studied her reflection in the bathroom mirror. There were dark circles beneath her eyes, a drawn look about her mouth. Elias had been right. She didn't look well. Her stomach felt queasy, she had spells of weakness at which times she shook visibly. She'd attributed it to nerves. However, since she was in the city, she decided to see the doctor. With Elias in the hospital and Miles suffering a relapse, she couldn't afford to become ill.

She attended the trial the next morning and resumed the same seat. There wasn't much to be done now. It was almost finished. She fully expected to be called, but Culver's lawyer never glanced her way. In his plea to the court, he begged that Culver be freed and given the opportunity to reform. However, the lawyer's presentation was weak. He had little to base it on.

The military prosecutor in his speech claimed that Culver was a bloody-handed murderer if nothing else. Some of his men had already been tried and sentenced to death. As a leader of this band, Culver deserved the same fate.

The court conferred without leaving the bench. After a ten-minute conference, Culver was declared guilty. He was to be hanged after one week's time.

Virginia held back the tears that threatened to flow. She averted her eyes as Culver was led away in chains. On all sides she heard only satisfaction at the verdict. But even if he was guilty of all the foul deeds testified to, or insinuated, he was, to some degree, a part of her. He had held her and possessed her, made love to her as no other man had. No man had ever stirred her to the depths of her being or inflamed her passions as he had.

To keep from belaboring herself with memories, she decided to visit the doctor who was caring for Elias and had been the Hammond family physician. He was a venerable, kindly man who had spent all the war years in service and was now once again building up his practice. He had officiated at Nanine's birth, at Virginia's and Marty's as well. She had no doubt but that he'd also attended the birth of Phoebe. Their father would have seen to that.

She went through the examination after having been asked routine questions. As she dressed, she supposed she'd be given some kind of tonic. Tension and overwork would be his diagnosis and, no doubt, the proper one.

"Well," he said, "you told me you've not been feeling well the last few weeks. I found nothing wrong with you, Virginia. You're a healthy young lady who will likely live to a very old age."

"I'm relieved," she said.

"Good," he replied, his smile kindly. "And your child will watch you grow old, Virginia. You're going to have one."

She stared at him for a moment and then, without a sound, she slid out of the chair and went into a dead faint.

Someone patted her hand tenderly and she opened her eyes to look into the smiling faces of the doctor and his nurse.

"My," he said. "I've never seen that kind of a reaction in a woman who was told she was to be a mother."

"Virginia sat up slowly. The nurse, who was also in attendance, steadied her with an arm around her shoulder.

"I'm sorry," Virginia apologized. "I guess it was so...so...unexpected. I just don't know what to say, even now."

"Elias is going to be delighted," the doctor said.

"Yes...yes, he's wanted a family," she admitted. But in her mind was the unthinkable thought that this was not Elias's baby.

"You'll be all right now," the doctor told her. "Come to see me in a month's time. And give my regards to your mother and your sister. I can well imagine they'll be pleasantly surprised."

"They will," Virginia agreed.

"There's a small annex where we have a couch," the doctor said. "Nurse Gillem will take you there. Just stretch out and rest for a while."

"I'm quite all right now," Virginia said, managing a smile. All she wanted to do was get out of here before she panicked. It had been, indeed, quite a shock. "Thank you, Doctor. And you, Nurse Gillem."

She returned to the hotel, slipped out of her dress and her corset, unlaced her shoes and lay across the bed. She was so confused and shaken by the news that she'd developed a severe headache. Of course the child was Bradley Culver's. It didn't take much figuring to realize that, but in some way she had to convince Elias that he was the father. There was a time difference, but not too long a one and he shouldn't be suspicious. It would be her secret forever. Not even Nanine must know about this. Somehow she had to keep steady nerves and face up to this with courage and resignation. She would have to share Elias's joy when he heard the news. It wouldn't be difficult. Elias would be so delighted to learn they were starting a family that he'd never doubt the child was his.

Her thoughts turned to Culver, the father of her child, now doomed to hang in a week's time. She buried her face in the pillow. This time she gave way to tears and she cried and sobbed for an hour. For Culver, for Elias, for the child within her and for herself. But she could not resist a desire to see Culver. He deserved to know. She could trust him. He'd deliberately turned any suspicion away from her by identifying Nanine. That had been his grand gesture. He had proven he had a streak of decency. He'd protected her name.

She made up her mind quickly. What had to be done, must be done now. She washed and dried her face, applied face powder and some rouge, mostly upon her lips. She dressed, pinned back a few stray wisps of hair and put on her bonnet. Her eyes were still swollen, but that couldn't be helped.

She made her way straight to military headquarters, where Culver was being held. Captain Delaney saw her at once.

"This may sound very strange and you may reject my request, Captain," she said, "but if it is at all possible, I would like to speak to Mr. Culver for a few moments."

"Well, now," Delaney began. "It's highly unusual and might cause comment—"

Virginia interrupted him. "I know, Captain, but Mr. Culver was kind to me—to my dreams. He did not destroy Valcour as he might have. He even returned the booty he'd taken from those unfortunate Northerners. I wish only to thank him for that. Little enough for a man about to die."

"It could be arranged, I suppose. His lawyer is with him now, in a visitor's private room. If you wish to see the man, it can't do too much harm, I suppose."

Captain Delaney called an orderly who escorted Virginia through the barracks and to the jail. As the door to the visitor's room opened, Culver's lawyer emerged.

"Mrs. Birch," he said in surprise, "what are you doing here?"

"I wish to tell Mr. Culver that I am beholden to him for not destroying Valcour. I believe he deserves that, if nothing else."

"I see." He was suspicious but not overly so. "Culver does feel concerned about you, Mrs. Birch. To be frank, I wanted to put you on the stand to see what I could develop in his defense and he told me that if I put you on the stand, he'd personally kill me."

"I had nothing detrimental to testify to," she said. "I'd have been quite willing to take the stand."

"Well, he wouldn't have it. He's a brave man, Mrs. Birch. I know his reputation is horrible, and I don't know of a soul who feels the least sorrow for him. Except me."

"I do also, sir," she said quietly. "For anyone who faces death at the hangman's rope."

"You're a compassionate woman, Mrs. Birch. Good day."

She walked into the room and Culver came out of his chair instinctively, as if to take her in his arms, but recovered in time. He motioned her to a chair and sat down again.

"What the hell do you want?" he asked loudly, as the orderly closed and locked the door.

"I came to thank you for what you did, Mr. Culver," she said. She lowered her voice. "Can we be heard?"

"Neither heard nor seen. I want to take you in my arms. Just once more."

"Brad," she said, "I am carrying your child."

He gaped at her. "Are you certain?"

"At the time of conception, Elias was at the big plantation and for days before and after. It is your child. I thought, under the circumstances, you might derive a bit of satisfaction from that. Oh, Brad, why did it have to happen this way?"

"What are you going to do?" he asked. "How can you explain...?"

"Elias won't suspect. I'm sure of it. The time element is close and he wants a family so badly he won't even think about that. I'll have no trouble with him."

"I see. Do you believe I'll weep and wail because I'll never see my son? Well, I won't. I will go to that damned scaffold and feel great about it. About leaving behind some part of me. I want you to take care of that boy."

"It may not be a boy."

"It has to be! Don't you dare have anything but a boy. They won't let you stay long. My dearest love, I want to take you in my arms so

410

much that I ache for you, but I can't. I'll not torture myself that way, nor torture you. Please go now. Thank you from the bottom of my heart for coming here to tell me that you and I . . . who thought we were not even in love . . . Damn it, it's the only decent thing I did in my life. Loving you. For I did—and I do. Forgive me and forget me.''

"With your child, how can I ever forget, Brad? How could I ever forget?''

"Try! Try hard, goddamn it! Get out of here, will you? Go—back to your island paradise. Raise my son there, teach him well and never let it be known to him, or anyone else, that his father was a man who killed and robbed—and died at the end of a rope.''

twenty-seven

Virginia braced herself before approaching the door to the old slave hospital where Nanine and Miles were making their home on Valcour. She wondered if she could hold this secret, from Nanine especially. Their association over the years had been so close that Nanine might guess purely by some instinct.

Nanine was not of a suspicious nature this day. Miles was once more confined to his bed and he seemed thinner, paler and weaker than usual. He seemed almost as ill as when he first came to Valcour.

Naturally the sisters did not discuss Miles in front of him and Virginia thought she saw a way to cheer them up with her surprising news. Surprising to them, disastrous to her.

"What happened at the trial?" Nanine asked. "We haven't heard a word."

"There could be only one conclusion. Mr. Culver was sentenced to hang in a week's time."

"He richly deserves it," Miles commented. "Though he did show some mercy here. Even helped some. Still, murder is murder."

"Just the same," Nanine said, "I can't help but feel sorry for him. I told you what he did, Miles. His lawyer was trying to involve Virginia and when Culver was asked to identify the woman that Tannet claimed Culver had been on Valcour to see, Mr. Culver promptly identified me."

"It was a grandstand play," Virginia said. "But it worked. If Culver went to Valcour so many times to see a woman and that woman was alleged to be me, then he spoiled that conclusion by identifying Nanine. No one would believe ill of Nanine.''

"Are you sure he didn't think I was the one he pulled off the horse that first time he came?" Nanine asked.

"He told me he did it purposely to save me any embarrassment.''

"Told you?" Nanine asked, somewhat startled by Virginia's statement.

"I paid him a visit yesterday afternoon.''

Nanine's eyes widened in astonishment. "You actually went to the jail?"

"Yes, Nan. I wanted to thank him for what he had done. It did save both of us a great deal of heartache.''

"She's right, you know," Miles told Nanine. "If Virginia was on the stand and had been asked a straightforward question as to whom Culver had visited, she would either have had to lie or . . .''

"Of course," Nanine agreed. "I don't blame you for wishing to thank the poor man.''

"There's something else too," Virginia said. "Something rather unexpected.''

"I hope it's good news," Nanine said.

Virginia smiled. "Remember Elias saying I looked peaked? And you told me I wasn't looking well. Since I was in the city, I went to see the doctor.''

Nanine eyed Virginia worriedly. "Are you ill?"

"Not exactly," Virginia said, and suddenly she felt happy and serene. The impact of impending motherhood struck her with a force that gave her an inner glow in spite of the circumstances. A feeling of pride swept through her.

"I'm going to have a baby," she said.

"Oh, Virgie, Virgie—how wonderful," Nanine exclaimed. "I'm overjoyed.''

"If you're overjoyed," Miles said, "think of how Elias is going to feel.''

Virginia had dreaded the first time someone would refer to Elias as the father, but she discovered it wasn't even of mild concern. She was going to have a child. Nothing else mattered.

"What a wonderful welcome home for him," Nanine said. "He's wanted a family so much, Virgie."

"He informed me of that several times," Virginia said with a smile. "I haven't told Mama yet. I wonder how she'll take it."

Nanine laughed. "She'll be as pleased as we."

"Of course I'm excited," Virginia admitted, giving Nanine a hug. "But I'm a little scared too."

"Let's go tell Mama right now," Nanine suggested. "I want to see her face when she hears the news."

"Run along," Miles said. "I'll be eager to learn her reaction."

They began their walk up the path to the mansion. Nanine seemed to have lost much of her enthusiasm.

"I didn't suggest this just to see Mama. I wanted to talk about Miles. He's not doing well. In fact, I'm afraid he's slipping."

"Nan, you'd best get Dr. Hawley over here."

"I'm going to, but I doubt he'll be able to help. I recall what that Yankee doctor told me when he prescribed for me. He said that some respond well and some only seem to, and for them it's just temporary. I fear Miles is one of those. My recovery, though slow, was steady and I had no setback. Miles seemed to improve for a while though it was only slight. Now he looks as ill as when I brought him here."

Virginia looked contrite. "And I had to break in and tell you my good news. I'm sorry, Nan."

"Miles was as pleased to hear it as I. We have to face reality. We learned to after what we went through during the war. Perhaps Miles will get better. I keep praying that he will. Tell me, Virgie, didn't you even suspect you were going to have a baby?"

"Not for one second. It never occurred to me. Actually, I didn't want to begin a family this soon. There's so much to do in restoring Valcour. I told Elias so and disappointed him very much, I'm afraid."

"How do you feel about it now?"

"It's . . . just grand. Wonderful! I'm very content. I have such a beautiful feeling inside me."

"I'm glad and happy for you. Tell me—what do you really think about Bradley Culver now that it's all over?"

"It's hard to say. There's no doubt he's done some extremely evil things, but he comes of a fine family. I'm sure he's quite intelligent, and certainly he's courageous. If circumstances had been different, he could have made a success of his life."

"Strange, I thought so too, even when everybody was calling him such a bloodthirsty man. It's too bad he has to die."

"I'm afraid, as Miles said, he deserves it. I think we should try to forget him now, Nan. Dwelling on it won't help him, or us. Let's concentrate on Mama."

Lenore came downstairs reluctantly. Every time someone returned from the mainland with all the available newspapers, she liked to devote herself to searching every column for the names of people she used to know.

"Mama," Nanine said, "Virgie has something to tell you."

Lenore brightened. "You've gotten rid of the last Yankee on Valcour! I've waited for this."

"It's about me, not Yankees," Virginia said. "I'm going to have a baby."

Lenore sat down on the nearest chair. She bent her head as if in deep thought for a moment and then she looked up at her daughters with what seemed to be a puzzled expression.

"You're going to make a grandmother of me! How could you, Virginia? How could you do such a thing at this time of my life?"

The two sisters looked at each other in amazement.

"Mama, is that how you feel?" Nanine asked. "Is that the only way you feel?"

"Of course not. It's wonderful for you, Virginia. Absolutely wonderful for you and Elias, but think of me. I'm not old enough. Or am I? Perhaps I should be very, very happy."

"I can't wait to hear what Elias has to say when he learns the news," Nanine said. "Tell Virgie you're happy about this, Mama."

Lenore hesitated a moment and then, in one of her rare displays of affection, stood and embraced Virginia. Then told her she was delighted.

"I suppose I am old," she said reflectively. "Yes, the war . . . I lost those years. I'd forgotten how many. Imagine me thinking I was too young to become a grandmother. I'm happy about it, really.

Especially since you're my only chance to be a grandmother. Marty is dead. Nanine and that . . . that . . . man cannot have children. At least I don't think they can."

"Mama," Virginia said sharply, "you disgust me."

"It's all right," Nanine said. "Even having a child couldn't make me any happier than I am right now."

"I'm sorry, Nan," Lenore said. "I didn't mean it to sound that way."

"Suppose we drop that angle of the conversation," Virginia said. "Within another two or three days the last Yankee carpetbaggers will be gone. We're already refurbishing some of the houses and our old neighbors are already packing up to return."

"How soon will they be back?" Lenore asked eagerly.

"That's hard to tell. I'd say in about three months."

Lenore did some fast figuring. "Then I can begin planning for our first big social event. It will bring Valcour back to all its wonders and glory and it will be the most fashionable event of the season here or anywhere. I shall begin work on it at once."

To Nanine's and Virginia's relief, Lenore excused herself and went upstairs.

There was much for Nanine and Virginia to do and the next two days were busy. They'd spent a tiring day going over a half-dozen of the recently vacated houses to estimate the cost of replacing paper, replenishing paint and some of the woodwork.

Virginia intended to sleep late the following day, but she was awakened by Nanine, shaking her out of a sound sleep. She sat up quickly.

"What is it, Nan?"

"Miles. He's terribly sick. Virgie, I can't leave him and I don't trust any of the help to get Dr. Hawley. Will you go with them, please? I know you shouldn't, but . . ."

"Please ask Moses to have someone at the dock to row me ashore. I'll be ready in minutes. Go back to Miles."

"Thank you. I don't think he's in any danger, but . . . he's so weak and . . . and . . . oh, Virgie, if only there was something I could do."

"Dr. Hawley will help. He'll be here within two hours, I promise. There's no need to tell Mama. You'll only alarm her."

"I rather think she'd be cheering instead," Nanine said bitterly. "He'd be better off in the house."

"Then you have Moses provide men to carry him here and be damned to Mama. She has to accept him sometime. When Miles is as sick as he is now, his place is here."

"I will. Bring Dr. Hawley here. Mama can rant all she wishes."

Virginia dressed quickly and was ready to leave in twenty minutes. By eight o'clock she was at the doctor's office to beg him to hurry.

"I'll go," Dr. Hawley said. "There are some new medicines I've learned about. I'll stop at the drugstore for something that will help."

"I'll go back with you. Poor Nan is terribly upset."

"Well, now, I think you might prefer to stay in town. Elias is back and checked into the hotel where you always stay, I talked to him last night. The operation was a success so there's nothing to worry about."

"Elias is here? He sent no word . . ."

"He got in late. He intends to go to Valcour this morning and I imagine he'll be delighted to have you for company. Go on—surprise him."

"Thank you, I will. Do what you can for poor Miles. He's very ill."

"Trust me. Whatever I can do, Virgie. Oh, yes, another item to interest you."

"Another? You're full of surprises this morning."

"So it seems. Some time after midnight last night, about fifty outlaws from all kinds of illegal bands of cutthroats surprised the Yankee garrison and set Brad Culver free. He's on the run. Elias can tell you more about it."

Virginia made her way to the hotel, scarcely aware of anything about her. Elias home so unexpectedly—and Brad Culver free once more. Two surprises to worry her. Thank God, she hadn't fainted. If it hadn't been for her concern for Miles, she might have.

She learned at the desk that Elias was in his room and she went there directly. When he opened the door to her knock, he was as startled to see her as she had been to learn he had returned. He took her in his arms and kissed her and then suddenly let go of her and stepped back, pulling her into the room.

"What on earth brings you here?" he asked. "How did you know I was back?"

"I didn't. I came to ask Dr. Hawley to go to Valcour. Miles is very ill."

"Poor Miles. How bad is he, do you know?"

"Only what Nan told me and she was extremely worried. Elias, I've some news . . . rather wonderful. At least I think so. I hope you will."

"Sit down, Virgie. Your news can keep. I have two items of extreme importance. You're not going to like either one."

"Is it about Culver escaping? Dr. Hawley told me."

"No, but that man is certainly lucky."

"How did it happen?"

"Culver's escape? Quite ordinary. Nobody got hurt, thank heaven. It seems Culver and half a dozen other bands of renegades have been plundering ever since the end of the war and they relied upon one another to help in getting out of scrapes. A large number slipped into the city and conducted one of the most efficient attacks on the garrison that I've ever heard executed. There were so many, the garrison was overwhelmed in less than two or three minutes. They gave Captain Delaney a choice of unlocking Culver's cell or getting his head blown off. Captain Delaney is the bravest of men, but he is not suicidal. Culver even thanked him for the kind manner in which he was treated and then took off with the band of outlaws."

"In a way, I'm glad. Culver did us no harm . . ."

"He could have. What irks me is the fact that I managed to trap him and get myself into a hospital as a result."

"Dr. Hawley said the surgery was a success."

"Yes, in a way. That's one of the things I want to talk about. But first there's something of vital importance. While I was in Washington, some British cotton merchants contacted me. Now you know we grow the best cotton in the world on Valcour. The British, all during the war, were mostly dependent on Suret from India and the quality was poor and will never be any better. The British market is starved for good cotton and willing to pay heavily for superior stuff. We've been selling regular cotton for about twenty cents a pound, Valcour cotton for a little more. What would you say if I should get forty cents a pound for our crop?''

" 'Forty'? We'd be millionaires in no time.''

"Exactly. I may not be able to get that much, but I'm aiming for it. As soon as the crop is in, the first picking, send me fifty pounds.''

"Of course—'' Virginia stopped short. "Send you . . . ?''

"This is very sudden, I know, but it can't be helped if we want Valcour cotton sold before it's picked. I came back yesterday, but I was too busy to send you the word. I have to go to England and I'm sailing tonight.''

She fought the wave of weakness that overwhelmed her. "Elias! You can't!''

"I must. The future of Valcour depends on it. You know how the factors are in Charleston. Worse since the war ended. They take too big a bite out of our profits as commissions. I can save that by doing the selling myself at our prices. I bought passage on a ship and I've bought everything I need. I don't have to go back to the island. In fact, I haven't the time.''

"Oh, Elias, I don't know that I approve . . .''

"You'll have to. It's already done. I'm sorry, but that's the way it is.''

"Then there is little sense in my trying to change your mind.''

"You couldn't. Too much depends on this move. Now, there's something else. You won't like this either, any more than I did.''

"Elias, there can't be anything worse than what you have just told me. But perhaps I can take away some of the sting . . .''

"Listen to me before you say anything more. At the hospital in Washington, I was informed that the kick Culver aimed at my thigh did dislodge the bullet. They were able to take that out, but . . . that bullet had long ago done its main damage. Virgie, that bullet I took at Bull Run did irreparable damage. I can never become a father.''

She closed her eyes quickly to keep her swimming senses from

420

putting her on the floor in another faint. She managed to steady herself.

"I . . . don't know what to say, Elias. It's such a shock . . . all this, so sudden . . . such devastating news. . . . And Miles so sick." She sat on the side of the bed, her hand gripping a poster.

"That's how it is. I suggest you go home now. I detest tearful farewells and there isn't time for me to go back to say good-bye to Nanine, Miles and your mother. I ask you, please, don't tarry here. It's going to be bad enough as it is. Just . . . go!"

She rose slowly. "I don't like this, Elias. I don't like it at all, but if this is what you wish, then I can do nothing but obey you."

She stepped up to him, raised her head and kissed him on the lips.

"Good-bye, Elias," she said. "Let us hear from you."

"Often," he assured her. "There'll be a great deal of business between our British friends and Valcour. You'll be rich from this, I can assure you."

"I care little about that without you."

"I know, but it helps, being rich. I'm going to turn my back now. When I turn around, I want you to be gone. I can't stand farewells, as I told you. Please—make it easy for me."

She looked squarely at him, their eyes met for a moment, and in his, she saw deep sadness—and the truth. She stepped back and he turned around. She left the room, closed the door gently behind her. Along the empty corridor the tears came. She had to stop because she could no longer see.

She leaned against the wall for a few moments before she recovered her wits. Then she left the hotel, hailed a carriage and was driven to the waterfront. There she discovered Dr. Hawley. He was just getting into the boat. She joined him.

It occurred to her that a lifetime had passed since she went to the doctor's office and sent him to Valcour. A lifetime in thirty or forty minutes.

"Did you see Elias?" he asked.

"Yes, Doctor, I saw him."

"I'm sorry, Virgie. I could bite my tongue off."

"You told him I was pregnant?"

"I thought I'd congratulate him, steady him for the surprise he was going to get when you and he were reunited."

"I see. And after you told him?"

"He handed me a letter from the doctors in Washington. It explained that the original bullet wound had severed a part of Elias's reproductive system. The only permanent damage was in the fact that he could never father a child."

She nodded. "I suspected that when he told me he was leaving for England tonight."

"So that's how he's going to handle it."

"In his own quiet way, with a plan that will save me embarrassment and shame. It's like him."

Dr. Hawley said, "He asked me—when the child is born—to put his name on the birth certificate."

She rested her head on his shoulder and sighed deeply, but she shed no more tears. They sat side by side and his arm enclosed her shoulders.

"I'm not going to ask any questions, Virgie. I'm not condemning anyone. If Elias is incapable of producing a child, it's better this way, for you may now consider raising a family with someone else as your partner."

"There is no one else, Doctor."

"I can hazard a guess about that. But there may be. There will be. You're young, exceptionally beautiful. You're charming, vibrant, intelligent and on your way 'to becoming' very wealthy."

"Does that matter?" she asked.

"In a way it does. Without money you couldn't do what you and Nan are doing—bringing Valcour back to what it was, with the same families there. I know you financed the whole thing and will continue to do so. It will keep you busy. No time for regrets or dismal thoughts."

They were words of wisdom. She'd abide by them. She was young, she'd have a great deal of money between the cotton grown on Valcour and that grown on the big plantation, which would have to be run by Christopher Savard from now on. She was lucky to have him, as he'd proven to Elias that he was an excellent man at the job and was trustworthy. She also had Valcour. She knew that would always be important in her life.

But there was Elias. He'd never come back.

She accompanied Dr. Hawley to the mansion where Miles was already installed in one of the bedrooms. When she and the doctor entered the room, Nanine came to Virginia and led her out. There were tears in Nanine's eyes.

Virginia put an arm around Nanine's waist and brought her to her suite. "Cry, sister. It will help. I know. I shed copious tears in Charleston. I'll be back shortly."

Nanine did. Tears that had been held back too long. She was drying her eyes when Virginia returned with a tray on which were two cups and a pot covered with a cozy.

"A little tea will do us both good," Virginia said, already pouring. She sweetened it with a lump of sugar and added some milk.

Nanine said, "Miles is gravely ill. I know the symptoms of that dreadful illness only too well."

"Let us hope Dr. Hawley can help him. Sit back for a while. I know you're concerned for Miles, but until Dr. Hawley completes his examination, there's nothing you can do. I have some things to tell you."

Nanine took a sip of her tea. "Thanks, Virgie. This does help. Now what news have you brought?"

"Bradley Culver escaped last night."

"From the military?" Nanine exclaimed in astonishment.

"Yes, with the help of a great many of his friends and, I suppose, what was left of his own men. Anyway, that's the smallest part of what I have to tell you. I beg of you to consider my request that what I say from here on, will be your secret and mine."

"Whatever can it be? Of course I'll keep your secret."

"Elias came back yesterday."

"But . . . why didn't he come to Valcour?"

"That's what I'm getting at. He's going to England. Sailing tonight. He's to act as agent for Valcour. He was approached by British merchants when he was in Washington. What he is doing is for the benefit of Valcour and, of course, for us."

"Why did he leave so suddenly?"

"When he returned, he had a letter to deliver to Dr. Hawley from the Washington hospital. Dr. Hawley took it upon himself to inform Elias that he was soon to be a father. That was before Dr. Hawley read the letter."

"What's the harm in that, except I think he might have let you spring the surprise."

"The letter stated that the bullet which wounded Elias at Bull Run had severed a part of his reproductive system. He could never become a father."

Nanine leaned back in her chair. "Did you tell Brad Culver?"

Virginia managed a small smile. "How did you guess?"

"The night he escaped from the whipping shed, you came by to see Miles. You were wearing a coat and holding a knife beneath it. I caught a glimpse of the knife as you turned to leave."

"I wondered if you had."

"I feared you were going to kill him."

"The thought entered my mind. I had a gun in my hands in the library. Mama came in and saw it."

"So Elias made it easy for you."

"He didn't give me a chance to say anything. But what could I have said? What am I to do, Nan?"

"Have your child and pray he will not inherit the tendencies of his father."

"Now you've given me fresh worries."

"Were you in love with Brad?"

"I . . . didn't think so. I needed him. At the time my body craved him. It was animal passion. He even told me he was not in love with me."

"He's a cad!"

"Not completely. When I saw him in jail, he said I was the only good thing that had ever happened to him and that he did love me. I told him about my condition. Perhaps after he heard of his child, he made plans to get away. To start over again somewhere."

"Let's hope so. Virgie, Elias will get over it in time. Believe that."

"No, Nan. Elias will not be back. Ever!"

twenty-eight

Tom stepped from the carriage and assisted Phoebe to the sidewalk in front of Delmonico's. Several people gathered to watch and someone clapped, an homage taken up by others. Phoebe nodded graciously, slipped her hand around Tom's arm and they entered the restaurant.

Inside, they were received by the *maître d'hôtel* and one of the captains to be escorted to a table in the center of the splendidly decorated room. They could be seen best there and that was what Delmonico's desired. Any celebrity should be shown off. Not many objected, though Phoebe would have preferred a degree of privacy.

"You've developed quite a following," Tom said after they were seated. "And accomplished it in the period since the new show opened."

"I was in the minstrel show for weeks," she said remindfully. "I think that's where I received the most attention. But I rather like it, don't you?"

"I would if it was meant for me," he said.

"Tom, don't be like that. You're just as responsible for my amazing success. You're my business manager. And you're handling our investments. I suppose you're making money for us in the market."

"We're doing rather well," he admitted. "We're not millionaires, but we don't have to worry about the size of the check we're going to get at the end of this meal."

Tom, now acclimated to such restaurants, ordered champagne. Then, for himself, a steak, his customary fare. Phoebe ordered lobster and a salad.

"I have to watch my figure these days," she confessed. "But I am hungry. Not eating before the show is one of the penalties I have to pay if I wish to dance well."

He laughed. "Honey, the way you dance up on that stage, you shake the fat off."

The waiter poured their champagne and Tom raised his glass in a toast. "To the most important lady in the theater."

"Stop it," Phoebe chided, though her embarrassed smile showed she was pleased. "I'm a long way from that. I'm just happy with the success I'm enjoying. And it happened so fast."

"With your talent it could happen no other way." Tom emptied his glass and the waiter, standing to one side, refilled it.

"What I mean is," Phoebe said softly, when the waiter had retired to a discreet distance, "not too long ago I was a slave. I was accepted into the family, educated with Virginia and had no idea of the fact that I was different until one day I was taken aside and the facts were explained to me."

"What facts?" Tom asked.

"I could no longer play with Virginia. And I had to wear the same kind of shapeless dress the other slaves wore. Before, I wore Virginia's castoffs."

Tom regarded Phoebe over the top of his glass. "That must have hurt."

"Not really," she replied, "because I was always treated kindly by the family. James Hammond saw to my education and I'll be forever grateful to him for that. Nanine was my favorite. She's a dear, lovable lady and treated me like an equal."

"You are now," Tom said.

"I was then," Phoebe replied. "However, I didn't realize the blood relationship until one day when Virginia couldn't decide on which gown to wear to a soiree. She had on one gown and insisted I put on the other so she could see how it looked. Our figures were identical. Without thinking, I arranged my hair in the same style as hers and stood before her so she could observe the gown. She stared at me in disbelief, then seized my arm and propelled me to the standing mirror. She made me look into it with her head close to mine. It was then, for the first time, she noticed I had the same violet eyes she had. Our facial structure was identical and my skin was almost as white as hers. She was enraged."

"I can well imagine," Tom said, chuckling.

"I wasn't sure if she was going to kill me or shoot her father dead, especially once she learned he was also my father. She made a great show of how she felt about it. Nobody thought of asking me how I felt. I couldn't have answered them. I wasn't sure if I wanted to be white or black."

"You're white now," Tom said in a low voice. "Never forget that."

"I know, darling. I wouldn't want to go back. Not after this . . ." She indicated the beautiful room and its well-dressed patrons. "Still, if I had to, I'd face it and make the best of it."

"May that day never come," Tom said tensely. "It would be a disaster."

The arrival of their entree caused them to drop that line of conversation and they never returned to it. The evening was pleasant. Phoebe basked in Tom's admiring glances.

"At least," she said in the carriage on the way home, "you can't say that you're not doing your part."

"I don't know what you mean?" he said, in a somewhat startled voice.

"I mean when you were bemoaning the fact that I was making all the money, but now you have those investments to handle and that means you are earning money too. It's worked out very well indeed."

He looked thoughtful. "You understand we take losses too. Even a tycoon has to take a loss now and then."

"I understand that." She paused, her eyes suddenly wistful. "When we get home, I'm going to write Virginia and Nanine a letter. This was such a pleasant evening, my mind is filled with thoughts of the past. Suddenly I realize how much I miss my family."

When Tom didn't answer, she looked over at him. His eyes were closed. She smiled tolerantly. The champagne had made him sleepy. She didn't waken him until they reached their apartment.

She did write when she returned and the next day she carried the letter to the post office. She made some purchases, found that she was carrying little money, walked to the bank where she and Tom had their account.

She wrote a check for two hundred dollars and presented it to one of the cashiers. He hesitated a moment and then excused himself, went to the rear of the bank and she saw him consult a ledger. Next he stopped by a desk and spoke to someone. That man rose quickly and disappeared.

Phoebe placed no importance on the procedure. She had little knowledge of banking practices. Presently the cashier returned and counted out the money.

"Mrs. Sprague," he said, "Mr. Paul Warren would consider it a favor if you would stop by his desk for a moment."

"Mr. Paul Warren?" she asked.

The cashier pointed. "The gray-haired gentleman at the second to the last desk. He's vice-president of the bank."

"Of course I'll stop by," she said. "Thank you."

Mr. Warren rose, moved to the side of his desk and held a chair for Phoebe. "So nice to meet you, Mrs. Sprague. I attended your new show and enjoyed your performance better than any I've seen since the minstrels, where I saw you twice."

"Thank you, Mr. Warren. I'm honored."

He resumed his chair. "I'm most reluctant to tell you, Mrs. Sprague, that the check you have just cashed is quite a sum above your present account. Not that it made any difference. We'd honor any check of yours."

"Do you mean I'm overdrawn?" she asked, her puzzlement genuine.

"I'm sorry to have to admit you are."

"Are you sure? My husband does keep very good accounts."

"This one was fine until you drew out that money. I'm only advising you. Your credit is good here for any reasonable amount, Mrs. Sprague."

"Thank you," she said uncertainly. "I'm sure there's been a mistake. I shall take steps to rectify this at once."

When she returned home, Tom was reading a newspaper. He rose and greeted her with a hug and kiss. Phoebe removed the pin from her hat, took off her short jacket and sat down.

"I cashed a check at the bank a short time ago, Tom. They told me the account was overdrawn."

"Oh, damn," he said, "I meant to see to that. It's no great problem, darling."

"It is to me. Embarrassing too. They honored the check, but they let me know about it. How do we stand financially?"

"Fine. I'm playing the Wall Street game. Our money is carefully invested."

"I turn almost a thousand a week over to you. Does all of it go into the market? Isn't that taking foolish risks?"

"I'm not gambling. The investments are sound. There have been large bills for furniture. Your wardrobe is expensive . . ."

Phoebe said, "I'd like to see the books, Tom. Not that I don't trust you, but I have to learn something about keeping books myself and this is a good time to learn."

"Of course," he said uneasily. "We'll go over them one of these days."

"I mean now," she said with a trace of irritation. "I have a right to know our exact worth."

He eyed her reflectively, as if turning over in his mind what to say.

"You're keeping something from me," Phoebe said. "What is wrong?"

"Trust me," he begged. "Please, darling, trust me."

She recalled the letter from his parents, the existence of which he had denied. He'd never told her there were openings for teaching in his hometown. It hurt when she'd learned he was avoiding taking her to meet his parents. For the first time since that letter, suspicion of Tom once again gnawed at her.

"Now," she said firmly. "This very minute. You can spread the books and the bills on the dining room table so I can go over them with you."

"I can't. They're not up to date."

Phoebe quieted her doubts and rose. She kissed him tenderly. "Darling, you're holding something back. I've a right to know what it is."

He bent his head, ran fingers through his hair. "Let it alone, darling. For your own sake, let it alone."

"No," she retorted quickly. "Now I'm sure something is wrong."

"You really want to know? I can handle it and you'll not have any heartache, but it involves money. Our expenses are lavish. There's not too much left each week. We do live high."

"I thought we could well afford it, Tom. If there's something wrong, I have the right to share in it, good or bad. Now tell me."

"Very well," he said. "We're being blackmailed."

"We are what?" she half shouted in surprise and dismay. "What are you talking about?"

"Lower your voice and calm down. I'll tell you the whole story. As I said, I can handle it although it's expensive. When you lived on Valcour, did you know a slave named Tobal?"

"I don't recall anyone by that name."

"Well, it happened after we left Valcour. Virginia and Elias had some troubles with this buck and Virginia shot him."

"Oh, yes, she wrote about that. Go on."

"He's in New York. He saw your picture and read about your success and . . . he knows you have Negro blood."

She leaned back in the chair. "So that's it! You've been paying him to keep quiet. How much, Tom?"

"It began with a hundred a week, but after your new show got into production he demanded three hundred."

"You should not have paid him a penny," she said severely. "Why didn't you tell me?"

"I didn't want to worry you. You had the new show on your mind."

"Damn the show." She was trying to hold her temper in check. "I suppose you meet him and pay him off."

"He has a go-between. He's shrewd and won't stand being argued with. Last week when I objected to all that money, he threatened to raise it to four hundred a week."

"That's outrageous. Tell me how you meet them, where and when."

"What are you going to do?" he asked in alarm.

"I'm not sure yet, but I want to know everything about this disgusting business."

"Phoebe, if it comes out that you have Negro blood, your career is ended. You're regarded as the white dancer who knows how to perform nig—Negro dances. They'll destroy you once they learn you're a Negro. Your reputation will be forever ruined."

She could scarcely believe it was Tom saying this. "Is that what you really think?"

"I'm stating a fact. The newspapers will consider this a great story. They'll make the most of it and people will laugh. Yellow journalism dotes on this sort of thing."

"They didn't laugh when they believed I was white. If it's my dancing they enjoy, why should they laugh when they discover that I'm part Negro?"

"Darling, you don't understand. You're not used to the ways of a city like New York. The papers thrive on scandals. One tries to outdo the other. It increases circulation. Everybody wants to read that ghastly stuff."

"When," she repeated quietly, "and where do you meet?"

"The public library. In the reading room."

"Thank you," she said briefly.

Tom was genuinely upset. "Phoebe, if you let this come out, it'll ruin you."

"You may be right. When do you meet to pay them?"

"Tuesday. For God's sake, Phoebe, think carefully before you do anything."

"I will. I'll let you know my decision."

She remained in the bedroom the rest of the evening, deep in thought. Tom didn't intrude. He even settled down on the large sofa. He was still there, deep in sleep, the next morning. An empty whiskey bottle lay on its side on the floor. She gave a despairing shake of her head.

She ate sparingly, dismissed the maid for the day and took a carriage to Police Headquarters. There, she stated she had a problem that required the services of a detective. She was brought to the office of a detective captain named Malloy, where she identified herself.

"Why, Mrs. Sprague," he said, "I've attended your shows ever since the first minstrel you were in. I consider it a great honor to meet you in person. Now tell me what's bothering you."

Malloy was middle-aged, somewhat stout, florid of face and a man of integrity. An Irish policeman who respected his profession and whose subsequent behavior proved it.

"A great deal," she said. "It's not an easy story to tell, but it must be told. My husband, for a number of weeks past, has been paying blackmail. I didn't know about it until he admitted the fact to me last evening."

" 'Blackmail.' I see. You'll have to give me specific details."

She nodded. "Since you've seen my show, you know my success is due to the fact that I'm skilled in performing Negro dances."

"I can vouch for that," Captain Malloy said.

"I dance them that well because I was raised on a plantation in North Carolina."

"That's a well-known fact."

"And I'm known as a white woman."

"You are." Captain Malloy's features did not betray the fact that he was already aware of her plight.

"I'm a Negro and I was a slave on that plantation."

"I understand, Mrs. Sprague. I wonder if you do."

"My husband has already acquainted me with what could very well happen when the fact becomes known."

"The gossip columns of the newspapers would have a field day," Captain Malloy stated. "You'd even make the front page of some. Are you certain you wish to go through with this?"

"I will not condone abetting a crime. I want the people involved to be arrested and punished."

"At the risk of all you know will happen? Or you think you know. Your career could be ended. Do you realize that?"

"Yes."

"Very well. Give me what facts you have regarding these individuals. I can just about guarantee they'll spend time in prison. I must also know how much is involved, plus when and where the payoff is."

She told him as much as she knew. It was, he told her, sufficient. He then began to lay out plans. It was evident that blackmailers were no strangers to him. He sketched the probable interior of the library reading room and showed her just how it would be worked.

"I wouldn't let your husband know the real reason why you want both blackmailers to meet you. The less he knows, the better. We don't want that pair scared off."

"When will this take place?"

"You said your husband was to meet for another payoff on Tuesday, just before noon. That will suit me fine. And if he shows surprise at some changes in the reading room, don't comment on them."

"I shan't. I've never been there before. My husband and I will be there on Tuesday."

"I admire your courage, Mrs. Sprague."

"I'm more angry than courageous," Phoebe said seriously. "Also, I believe I'll be treated fairly by the American public."

Captain Malloy sobered. "Don't count on it, Mrs. Sprague."

That evening she put her heart and soul into her dancing, drawing more encores than ever before. She had even instructed the orchestra to stop playing in the middle of the number, and in the quiet theater, she improvised a number that brought the house down. When the applause became deafening, she nodded for the orchestra to resume. She completed the dance and ran to her dressing room, where she changed as quickly as possible and left the theater before anyone could gather to talk to her.

Tom was waiting with half a glass of whiskey in his hand. He didn't rise.

"Need I ask how the performance went?" he asked.

"Well enough, Tom. Tuesday you are scheduled to make the weekly payment. I insist on being there and I want both men present, especially the Negro who says he knows me."

"I refuse to arrange such a meeting," he said flatly. "You don't know what you're doing, Phoebe. If you buck them, it will be the end of your career."

"Tom, unless you arrange this meeting, I shall advise the bank that you will no longer handle any of my money. You won't be able to pay them and you'll have to arrange a meeting then. What's the difference, Tuesday or a month from then?"

He drank most of the whiskey. "I won't do it, Phoebe. For your own good, I absolutely refuse."

"For my good!" She had removed her coat and hat and seated herself directly in front of him. "Do you really think I can be so easily deceived? You're allowing this incredible situation to continue for the good of Tom Sprague, not his wife."

"I gain nothing," he protested.

"A short while ago, when we were on the verge of being removed from that awful room, you lied to me about a letter I saw in the mailbox. You no doubt remember the incident. I read that letter. I thought it might be from Virginia and there was something in it you didn't want me to see. It was from your parents. There was a job waiting for you in your hometown and your parents wished to meet me. You never let me see that letter. Now I know why."

"Phoebe, for your own good—"

"For my good?" Phoebe broke in. "We were on the verge of starving to death, but you didn't dare bring me to meet your people because you were afraid that, somehow, they'd discover I had Negro blood. That's behind everything you do. I married a man I believed to be strong, who swore he didn't care I'd been a slave. I thought you loved me as I have loved you. I know now I was wrong."

"Darling," he protested earnestly, "all I'm doing is protecting you. If it's made public that you are part Negro, your career will be ruined."

"Then let it be. I can't help what I am, but I do have Negro blood and I will not be ashamed of it nor allow those I love to try to protect me from having this truth known. Will you arrange that meeting for Tuesday or not?"

"If you insist. What's going to come of it? The black buck will just show his teeth and tell you he wants more. That's what will happen. They're both greedy and they can make trouble for you."

"I ask only that you have them both at the library at the time you always meet them."

"They'll be there. Do you want me there as well?"

"I think you owe me that much."

He nodded, drained the glass and got up. "I'm going to bed. There's no sense in arguing with you. I thought you'd realize why I became a part of this rotten business, but apparently you don't care if it becomes known you're part nigger. With this blood in your veins you'll not be accepted in the South. Why do you think we of the North are any different? Use your head, Phoebe, and think this over. Don't make a mistake that will cost you everything you've built up."

"It's costing half of what I make now."

She went to the second bedroom. There she took a long bath to relax. It didn't work. In bed, she cried herself to sleep.

On Tuesday, she accompanied Tom to the reading room of the library. He led her to one of the long tables and held a chair for her as he looked about, idly wondering since when did the library decide to exhibit tall, thick, potted shrubs and palms, especially in the reading room. He sat down, paying no further attention to them.

They waited for fifteen or twenty minutes, with Tom growing more nervous every passing moment. Phoebe seemed as calm and cool as an iceberg, but inside she was trembling with a combination of fear of what was to come and heartache caused by her disappointment in Tom Sprague.

The pair finally appeared. Phoebe paid little attention to the scrawny white man. She studied Tobal, the huge Negro, who was flashing his best smile as they approached.

"Well, now," he said before he sat down, "if it ain't Missy Phoebe lookin' 'zac'ly like a white gal. Yo' sho' is lucky, Phoebe. Ain't good to be black like me no mo'. Nevah was, reckon."

"Why did you insist on meeting Tobal?" The man Tom had introduced as Darby was suspicious and uneasy.

"Because I wanted to be certain my husband wasn't paying money to people who were taking advantage of him and didn't really have enough evidence as to my birthright."

"Yo' knows we was both slaves on Valcour," Tobal said. "Sho' ain't foolin' yo', Phoebe. Reckon yo' satisfied now Ah knows whar yo' sprung from.''

"Yes," she said. "I'm satisfied."

"Then pay the money—" Darby began.

"Hol' on now," Tobal broke in. "Ah sho' don' likes the way Ah was made to come heah. Ordered 'roun' like Ah wuz a slave once mo'. From heah on, Phoebe, yo' pays me half o' whut yo' gets fo' actin' like a white gal doin' all them niggah dances. Half, an' Ah knows whut yo' gets.''

"You understand that this is blackmail, of course," she asked.

"Don' knows 'zac'ly whut it is, but knows whut happens, yo' don' pays me whut Ah says.''

Phoebe opened her handbag and withdrew a thick wad of bills. She slowly and carefully counted out six hundred dollars and slid it across the table. Darby reached for it, but Tobal pushed him away so that he almost fell out of his chair. Tobal gathered up the bills, grinning widely at Phoebe.

Before he could put the money in his pocket, four men emerged from behind the shield of potted shrubs. Captain Malloy removed the bills from Tobal's grasp. Darby was seized by one of the men and Tobal was promptly handcuffed.

"We will advise you when you may testify," Captain Malloy said to Phoebe. He ignored Tom completely.

Tom sat down heavily as the blackmailers were hustled out of the library. "Now you did it," he said. "That pair will tell everything. You'll be ruined. You've ruined your career, wrecked everything, Phoebe. I thought you had more sense.''

"Sorry I disappointed you," she said curtly. "You must excuse me now. I have a matinee to do.''

She walked briskly out of the library, leaving him still seated at the table. She summoned a carriage and was driven directly to the theater. She knew no one had heard of the incident yet, but it wouldn't be long before the news reached the theater. Lowell Stuart, the producer, came by to inform her, happily, that the show was on a standing-room-only basis for three entire weeks. She merely expressed her pleasure at the news.

At the end of the second act, where she did most of her dancing, she became aware of a none-too-subtle change in the attitude of her fellow performers. Some seemed to be outwardly snickering at her, a few turned away, others seemed almost sorrowful, but they didn't approach her.

She closed her dressing room door, changed into costume for the last act and she was ready and calm when she was called. She went through the performance, took her customary solo curtain calls and then went directly back to her dressing room, aware that backstage seemed more crowded than usual. The news had leaked out faster than she had anticipated and she avoided the reporters by taking advantage of an escort provided by some of the performers. She entered her dressing room and locked the door.

As calmly as if this was just the end of another matinee, she removed her makeup, dressed in street clothes and wondered if she'd ever return to this dressing room again. It would be a disappointment to those who had bought tickets for the evening show, but she comforted herself with the realization this was something beyond her control. What she did, she had to do. It would have been criminal to avoid the issue.

A series of strong knocks on her door brought her to her feet.

"It's Lowell," the producer called out loudly. "Open up, Phoebe. We've got to talk."

She expected this so she promptly unlocked the door and stepped aside. Lowell Stuart came in quickly and slammed the door in the faces of half a dozen reporters. He turned the key, removed it from the lock and dropped it into his pocket.

"Well," he said, "you really did it, didn't you? Why the hell did you allow it to happen? Why didn't you come to me?"

"Why, Mr. Stuart? To delay the truth coming out? Short of murdering that Negro who recognized me, nothing could have stopped the fact that I too am a Negro, from becoming known. What difference does it make when the story was going to be told anyway?"

"Two main reasons," he said. He walked closer to her. "One, you've probably ruined the show, though I'm not at all sure of that yet. This kind of publicity could sell even more tickets."

"And the second reason, Mr. Stuart?" she asked, knowing very well what the answer was going to be.

"You've stood me off like I was a leper. You've refused to have supper with me, or to see me alone. You're a damned beautiful woman. It doesn't make any difference to me you're touched with a tarbrush. You're very desirable, but you acted as if you were so goddamn above me, I couldn't touch you."

"Don't touch me now," she warned, in a voice gone deadly cold.

He made a derisive sound in his throat. He placed a hand on her shoulder, let it move swiftly down across her breast, where it paused and secured a firmer hold.

Phoebe put both hands against his chest and pushed him back, throwing him off balance. She was surprised at her own strength. He laughed as he regained his balance and moved toward her.

"If you touch me again," she warned, "I'll scream to high heaven until someone breaks down the door. Then I'll tell them all what happened. Those reporters will enjoy that far more than their interest in me as a Negro. Do you understand me, Mr. Stuart?"

"Who the hell are you to be talking to me like that?" His face was flushed with rage. "You're nothing but a nigger. Oh, don't you think we in the North knew how you lived in your great, wonderful South? You slept on the floor at the foot of your master's bed. When he wanted you, he crooked his finger and like a good slave you got up, crawled into bed and when he was through with you he put his foot against the small of your back and kicked you out of bed. And here you are, threatening me, pretending to be a saintly little girl—"

"Are y'all through, Mistuh Stuart, suh?" She assumed a mild Negro lilt to her voice. "Ain't yo' goin' to give me the key? O' does yo' wants me to kicks yo' right in the balls?"

He puffed out his cheeks and exhaled. "You show up for tonight's performance."

"They's a stand-in. She do jes' fine, suh, an' she deserve a chance. Now, suh, the key."

"You're leaving the show?"

"Yas, suh, Ah sho' am, suh."

"There's a contract—"

"Ah declares it void."

"You'll never cross another stage. I warn you . . ."

Phoebe resumed her natural way of speaking. "I don't expect I'll ever wish to go on the stage again. Now if you don't produce the key, I'll do exactly what I threatened to do."

He took the key from his pocket, stepped closer, but instead of handing it to her, he slipped it down her décolletage. She shook her head and looked at him in studied contempt. She had to unbutton her blouse to get the key and she did so quite nonchalantly. She buttoned her blouse, suddenly turned toward Stuart and slapped him across the face so hard it reddened as her hand moved away.

She unlocked the door, stepped out and, using her shoulders as a battering ram, she moved through the crowd, aided by a few members of the cast. She finally reached the stage door and got out. The carriage she always had waiting was on hand and she got aboard. As the driver whipped the horse into action, the crowd erupted from the theater, but too late. Phoebe exhaled in relief. Her hat was askew, but she straightened it and grew as serene as if this was just another ride home from her usual afternoon performance.

She dreaded going into the fashionable apartment building where she lived, but the lobby was deserted. The reporters hadn't gotten this far yet, though she fully expected they'd not be long in coming. She reached her flat and let herself in.

Every gaslight in the apartment was burning. As she closed the door, she sensed that it was too quiet. Too empty.

"Tom," she called out as she removed her hat, gloves and coat. "Tom, are you here?"

There was no reply. She hurried to their bedroom, then to the spare bedroom and even to the kitchen. On inspiration, she returned to the bedroom and opened the walk-in closet. The portion allotted to Tom was empty. She quickly pulled open bureau drawers. They too were empty. A look in a larger storage closet solved that. The suitcases were missing.

She sat down on the edge of the bed. The tension she'd been filled with gave way to tears. She lay down, face against the pillow, and she wept. Presently there was a loud commotion outside the apartment and a series of bangings on the door.

Phoebe rose, entered the living room and, without opening the door, made her first statement.

"If you will be kind enough to give me five minutes, I shall let you in."

There was a roar of assent. She went to the bathroom and washed her face. She patted it dry with a towel, removing all signs of her weeping except for a slight redness of the eyes. She tidied her hair and applied a little rouge and powder to her cheeks.

Then she walked back to the living room, unlocked the door and opened it wide.

"Come in, gentlemen," she said.

twenty-nine

In the morning there were a few glances her way as she passed through the lobby. Following her was a carriage driver lugging three large suitcases. She rode in the open carriage through the teeming streets and no one paid the slightest attention to her. At the railroad station she passed a newsstand and saw two newspapers carrying her picture. Above it were large headlines. She didn't buy one.

At the ticket window she asked for a first-class ticket to New Orleans. She learned there was a train in half an hour already prepared for boarding. A fact she had already determined before she left her flat.

Again she went unrecognized. She decided New York was a fine city to get lost in.

She was tired, sleepy, and she settled into the private compartment on the train with a sigh of relief. She hadn't slept all night, but she'd sleep now during the long journey to New Orleans.

She almost decided on Valcour, but after some contemplation she decided not to. For one of the very few times in her life she was uncertain of her next step.

Tom was gone. If he ever sought to return to her, she would refuse him. The love she'd had for Tom Sprague had evaporated in the reading room of the New York City library. It would have been impossible to live with him after his show of weakness.

However, the way he had fled saddened her into crying for half the night.

She would have found solace and sympathy on Valcour. She'd been sorely tempted, but she decided she couldn't face them. There was far too much indecision on her part and she had to clear that up first.

In the space of a few hours she had lost both husband and career. She'd discovered that life as a white woman was far above that granted an ex-slave, even one with a white skin. She could never escape her heritage as a black. Nor did she want to. What she didn't know was where, in society, did she belong.

She slept well on the train in her virtual isolation. She had her meals brought from the dining car. When she reached New Orleans, she felt rested and ready for whatever was going to develop. The first thing she wished was a long talk with her mother. She wanted her ideas on how to handle this situation. Not that her mother had ever had to experience what Phoebe was going through, for she'd never taken it upon herself to try to be accepted as white. In her case, it might have been difficult, for she did not have the same unflawed white skin.

Phoebe took a carriage to the section of the city where most of the houses of prostitution existed. She recalled the first time she'd come to see Fannie Dawkins, her mother, who ran a high-class house of prostitution. It had been during one of the worst phases of the war—when the Hammond family was destitute, hungry and about to become homeless. Phoebe, on her own, had visited her mother to request money. Fannie had been cold and unresponsive at first, then offered to do so, provided Phoebe would become a prostitute. Having convinced herself of Phoebe's sincerity by sending her lover up to Phoebe, her mother stopped the charade and granted Phoebe money that was the salvation of the Hammond family.

Phoebe wasn't sure of how her mother felt about the distinction between black and white, especially Negroes who could pass for white. But she sensed that her mother was possessed of an unusual ability to consider and judge such things.

The house was an old stately residence with the usual two lamps, their chimneys painted red. A young, pretty Negro girl in a spotless uniform of a maid admitted her. As Phoebe entered the house, she sensed that it was too quiet. Evidently business had been suspended for some reason.

She suspected the reason when a six-foot two-hundred-fifty-pound Negro giant came downstairs to greet her. He was the one her mother had used to test Phoebe to see if she was willing to prostitute herself so the Hammonds might get food and shelter. She'd undressed before him in the full realization of what was going to happen. But he stopped short and called in her mother. That was when Phoebe knew it had been just a game to test her.

"Sam." She extended a hand, then stood on tiptoe and kissed his cheek. "Something's wrong. It's Mama, isn't it?"

"Sho' is, Miss Phoebe. Fannie's fixin' to die. Take some time, but whut she got, there ain't no way out fo' her. Reckon she'll be mighty glad to see yo'."

"The place isn't doing business any more?"

"Not while Fannie's so sick. Closed it up myse'f, Ah did. Sent all the gals away. Yo' wants to see her now?"

"I want to see her more than I ever wanted to see anyone in my life."

"She likely goin' to cuss yo' out some, but she crazy 'bout yo', Phoebe. Nevah stopped talkin' 'bout yo' aftah yo' lef'. Bless the Lawd he sen's yo' heah now when she needs yo'."

"Does she know about what happened in New York, Sam?"

"Sho' does. Ain't sho' she likes whut yo' did o' not. Yo' damn soon finds out. We goes to see her now. She goin' to be mighty s'prised. An' pleased."

"If she shows it," Phoebe said, her smile reminiscent.

Phoebe walked into a room that looked like something out of an Arabian Nights fantasy. It was a large room, papered in dark red flocked wallpaper. The overstuffed furniture was covered with red damask. There were thick rugs on the floor, rich hangings over the bed, which was twice as wide as an ordinary double bed and half again as long. Phoebe approached the bed. Fannie was asleep.

She was thin, almost emaciated, but the lines of her face still bore signs of the beautiful woman she had been. Phoebe bent down and kissed her cheek. Sam closed the door quietly.

"Hello, Mama," she said.

Fannie slowly opened her eyes. She stared at Phoebe. "Well, goddamn, have I gone to heaven already? Phoebe . . . oh, Phoebe!"

Phoebe bent forward, kissed her mother's brow and her cheeks. She straightened, sat on the side of the bed and slipped her hand beneath her mother's, which lay on the silken red coverlet. Phoebe was touched by the frailty of the woman, but managed a smile. "I'm sorry you're sick, Mama."

Fannie managed a weak laugh. "You can bet I wouldn't be lyin' in this bed alone if I wasn't. You come to pay me a visit, child?"

"I'm here for good, Mama," Phoebe said.

"The hell you are. You belong on Valcour. Or don't they want you?"

"They love me and I love them, but I wanted to see you first."

"The New York stage business, eh?"

"It doesn't bother me anymore. I lost my husband and my job, but the hurt didn't stay with me. Not even the fact that I'm now known as a nigger."

Fannie laughed again. "We got a lot to put up with, child. Maybe too much, but when we make the best of it, we get along fine. You have any plans?"

Phoebe shook her head. "Only to be with you."

"Well, that's not going to be for too long, baby. I'm finished and I know it and I've accepted it. I've lived a long time and I've lived. Oh, my God, how I've lived!" Her shrunken eyes glistened in the memory. "You know, child, we have to make our own happiness."

"I'm learning, Mama," Phoebe said.

"What have you heard from Valcour?"

"Not too much. There's been a lot of trouble there getting rid of the Yankees who bought everything on the island except the Hammond place. And there was trouble with a bandit who raided the place. I gather there was more to it than that, but Virgie was holding back."

"Let me tell you about Virgie," Fannie said. "I never saw her until her father—who was also your father—used to come down here for a visit and a bit of dalliance. He said Virginia had grown up to be a beautiful and highly passionate girl. I don't know how he knew this, but he sure seemed to. Not that I hold it against the girl. I was too, and if you don't believe it, go look in a mirror because that's why you're here."

"I know all about it, Mama. James Hammond told me."

"You could go back to the stage, spit in the eye of a few people and dance again. I declare I don't think you'd lose a ticket buyer. I never saw you dance, but you got it from me and I was good at it too. Not a nigger dance I didn't know. Honey, I'm so damned glad you're here. Have you ever forgiven me for what I did to you the first time you came to see me?"

"It was a dirty trick, making me undress in front of Sam."

"Sure was, but he'd never have touched you. I just wondered how far you'd go for the Hammonds. When I found out, I knew they'd taken good care of you."

"Mama," Phoebe said, "you talk just like me. Where did you learn?"

Fannie's chuckle was almost a croak. "One night a white gentleman came into my place. Spoke beautiful. He was from the North. I'd been recommended. I got a mighty good reputation for what I deal in."

"I'm sure you have, Mama," Phoebe said with a smile.

"Anyway, he tells me he teaches English in a Northern university. Well, I offer him a hell of a lot of money if he'll stay here a year and teach me to talk proper. I did that because Mr. James told me he was having you educated. He said you were real intelligent and as beautiful as Virginia. I never really expected to meet you, but now I'm damn glad I had enough sense to think that if you had an education, I could at least speak proper. Not perfect, but good."

"You speak beautifully," Phoebe said. "I take it the professor stayed."

"He sure did. For a whole year. He had his pick of the girls and got paid besides, but so long as he taught me what I wanted to know, they had orders to please him whenever he wished." She paused, then added, "With me though, it was strictly business. All I wanted from him was to learn to talk like an educated woman."

"You succeeded."

"You like a drink?" Fannie asked.

"All of a sudden I crave food," Phoebe said. "I couldn't eat before. But I'll have a drink too. Guess I could use one."

"Go to the door and get Sam. He's so damn concerned about me, he stays close. Probably listening too."

The door opened. "If Ah am," Sam said, sticking his head in, "it's to see if yo' call out an' want anythin'."

"Want a bottle and some glasses and steak and potatoes and coffee for my baby. She hasn't eaten in God knows when."

Phoebe remained by her mother's side all day, and from their talk, Phoebe knew what she was going to do. Not now, for she intended to remain with her mother until there was no longer a need.

That time came five weeks later. She discovered Fannie had gone to her eternal sleep without awakening during the night. Phoebe didn't cry. Fannie had instructed her, somewhat profanely, that she was not to shed a tear. But Phoebe came very close to it at the funeral. She'd never seen anything like it. There were three bands and at least a thousand people, among them faces she recognized as being important nationally. There were uniforms too. The chief of police, the fire chief. They were all there. It became one of the most strenuous days of Phoebe's life.

When it was over, she and Sam returned to the house and collapsed in kitchen chairs with a bottle of fine bourbon on the table before them. Sam poured long drinks.

"Here's to mah gal Fannie," he said. "Finest woman Ah evah knowed, Phoebe."

"I'll drink to that. What now, Sam?"

"Me? No place Ah kin go. No place Ah wants to go, 'cept to stay right heah. She lef' me the place, yo' know. Free an' clear, an' with the bes' gals evah pleasured a man. Goin' to do right well fo' sho'. Whut 'bout yo'se'f?"

"I'll be going back to Valcour. Mama convinced me that's where I belong."

"Funny, ain't it? Yo' comes heah durin' the wah an' asks her fo' money. She sends yo' away with 'nuff to take keer o' yo' fam'ly. Now she sends yo' away again. This time yo' gots 'nuff to take keer o' the whole damn state o' Louisiana."

"I don't understand, Sam."

"Reckon yo' one o' the richest gals in this heah United States. She lef' the whorehouse to me an' some money, but eve'ythin' else she lef' to yo', an' bless mah soul, it ain't mo' than mayhap neah half a million."

"Dollars?" Phoebe asked in awe.

"Gal, yo' thinks runnin' a whorehouse the way Fannie run it ain't profitable? She been pilin' it up fo' yeahs an' she tells me, right aftah yo' comes back, that she finally knew whut she would do with it."

"I don't know what to say," Phoebe exclaimed.

"Whut yo' does with all that money yo' business," Sam said. "But sho' hopes yo' does some good with it. Thass whut she wanted."

"I'll do my best. I'll leave tomorrow if you don't mind."

"Sho' don't. Soon's yo' gits outen heah, Ah calls in the gals. Fannie wouldn' res' easy Ah didn' keep the place goin' like always."

thirty

The deep green lawns of Willowbrook swept down to the dock and the sea. Magnolias were in full bloom and looked down upon by the stately oaks. Maples would soon begin to turn color, for it was early autumn, a season when everything reached its peak. The entire island never looked better. It was a good year for Valcour. The Yankees were gone, even Tannet, who departed in a blast of profanity that made Nanine cringe a bit, but Virginia bore it easily.

The families were returning now. In a matter of a few days, all who survived the war would be back. Those who had not, left the privilege of living on the island to heirs who were more than happy to respond to Virginia's invitation.

The cotton crop on Willowbrook was exceptional and already baled and stored in the warehouse until it could be sent on to England for the best price ever paid for cotton, even of this superb quality. The crop from the other island plantations was poor but might bring in a few dollars, so it had been harvested and would be in the hands of cotton factors for sale. The quality of this crop was further proof that it required a knowledge of how to grow cotton and the proper handling of the men and women who tended it in the fields.

Virginia and Nanine walked, hand in hand, down the path to the dock. In the distance they'd seen the barge approaching the island and they would soon meet Phoebe, who was returning to Valcour.

Virginia and Nanine were dressed for the occasion in new gowns sent from Atlanta and were in the latest style.

"Do you suppose she's changed?" Nanine asked.

"I doubt it. Phoebe was always a steady person—like you."

"I'm thinking of what she's gone through, all that she's lost. I doubt I'd have the courage to face it."

Virginia slipped her arm around Nanine's waist. "No one has more courage than you. To present such a brave exterior each day when you knew your husband was dying. Even now, you're not wearing widow's weeds."

"Miles made me promise not to," Nanine said. "We had enough of Mama walking past the window of the hospital each day in her mournful black with the bouquet of artificial flowers cradled in her arms."

"Mama's been quite a trial since Papa and Marty died."

"When I think of it, I'm glad Miles died in his sleep, free of pain."

"A pity for such a beautiful person to have to die."

"Dr. Hawley said Miles was too far gone to recover, even with the kind of treatment that saved my life."

"A pity Phoebe never met Miles," Virginia said.

"I could say a pity she met Tom," Nanine replied. "But she did have some happiness with him. It wasn't all in vain."

"We'll know better after we talk with her, though I daresay her reasoning will match yours."

They reached the dock early, for the barge was still some distance away. They hadn't talked much lately. Too many things had happened and there was so much to do. Then, all of it culminated in the death of Miles Rutledge.

"What will you tell Phoebe about the baby?" Nanine asked.

"The truth," Virginia responded quickly. "She's our sister."

"You're not showing yet and she'll surely be surprised and pleased. Did you invite Mama to come down and meet her?"

"She informed me that as Phoebe was not her daughter she saw no reason why she should."

"That's typical."

"She did say, however, she was quite willing to receive her as a member of the family. She hasn't forgotten what Phoebe did during the war. I wonder how the other families on Valcour will receive her at the soiree. If she is snubbed by a single person, I'm going to be very angry. Phoebe may not bear the name, but she is a Hammond and she will be respected as one or I swear I'll raise a special kind of hell.''

"After what you've done for them," Nanine commented, "it would be in bad taste for them not to accept Phoebe."

"True," Virginia agreed. "But I'm thinking of that horrible publicity in the newspapers."

Nanine smiled reflectively. "I'm sure you'll think of some way to hold them in line should they become obnoxious."

"I couldn't hold Elias," Virginia said.

"He may relent," Nanine said. "Don't give up hope."

"He'll never return. He handled a delicate situation like the true gentleman he is. However, he's doing wonders for Valcour. The families will have the sale of their crops guaranteed and with that they can get loans from the banks and not the factors, who charge far too much."

"Do you think Valcour will return to its former glory?" Nanine asked.

"I wish I could answer that, but we've been through so much..." She switched her attention to the approaching craft. "Look, Phoebe's waving."

They both waved back energetically and waited impatiently until the ungainly craft bumped the dock. Nanine secured the rope.

Phoebe jumped ashore and the sisters embraced and kissed and brushed away the tears.

Virginia said, "Welcome home, sister. We missed you."

"I missed you both." She addressed Nanine. "I'm sorry about Miles."

"Thank you, Phoebe," Nanine said, her smile grateful. "At least we had a few months of happiness."

"I suppose I can say the same thing," Phoebe said. "It's the only intelligent way to think of my marriage."

"Strange how things have a way of happening," Virginia mused. "I know you suffered greatly in New York, Phoebe, but if things hadn't happened as they did, you wouldn't have been with your mother when she needed you."

"I thought of that," Phoebe said reflectively. "I'm sorry about Elias. You said he left you, though you didn't tell me why in the letter you wrote me when I was with Mama."

"I will," Virginia said. "We've a lot to talk about."

"How is your mother?" Phoebe asked.

Nanine sighed. "No change. I doubt she ever will. I hope you won't pay too much attention to her."

"I shan't," Phoebe promised. "I'm happy to be here."

"No more so than we are to have you," Virginia said. "We may not have our men, but we still have each other. Plus a lot to talk about."

Phoebe looked around, her eyes still moist with tears of happiness. "The island hasn't changed either. Oh, I'm happy to be back."

"Come along," Virginia said, to break up any chance of further tears. "It will take us a week to tell you all that's happened here."

"Are the families back?" Phoebe asked.

"In three days they'll all be here and next weekend we're going to put on a soiree the likes of which no one's seen since we had to hurry away from the island when the war began. We're not going to miss a trick. As Mama says, it will be the most important social event of the whole season, even if it's limited to the island inhabitants."

"I'll look forward to that," Phoebe said. "I'm also pleased that you aren't in mourning, Nanine. The longer you mourn, the more you feel sorry for yourself. That's what Mama told me before she died."

"I agree," Nanine said.

With Phoebe between them, they walked slowly up the path to the mansion. Two young field workers came down to carry Phoebe's baggage.

"Look, there's Belle," Phoebe exclaimed happily.

"The pretty girl with her is Ivy," Nanine explained. "She works in the house."

"She reminds me of you," Virginia said.

Phoebe said, "I can see why. She's as white as I. But I don't recall ever having seen her."

452

"You probably didn't," Virginia said. "Papa sold her mother because she couldn't seem to have suc—" She broke off in embarrassment.

Phoebe laughed. "Suckers. It's all right, sister. I haven't forgotten. Apparently the mother had one after she left the island."

"She did," Virginia replied. "Her grandma still lives here and she asked Elias to get the girl. That was during the war. It seems news came that the household where Ivy lived with her mother was burned to the ground. The mother burned up in it."

"How sad," Phoebe said. "I'm glad the girl is here. We must help her."

Virginia gave Phoebe a sidelong glance. "She is intelligent. And talented. I hadn't thought of helping her."

"I'd be the one to think of it," Phoebe said.

"Yes," Nanine said. "Especially after what you've been through."

"Not just that," Phoebe replied seriously. "I haven't forgotten I was educated here. Treated as a member of the family . . ."

"Until you were grown." Virginia finished the sentence. "That's over now. Let's not bring it up. I'm proud of the way I behaved."

"As you say," Phoebe's arm enclosed Virginia's waist, "it's over. Now I must greet Belle."

Belle, her broad frame drawn up to its full five feet four, her hands on her ample hips, regarded Phoebe sternly. "Ah says it now, Phoebe, yo' gits tellin' me whut Ah gots to do an' sweahs Ah hides yo' good. Ain' askin' yo' wuks in the kitchen like yo' did, so yo' bettah stays out o' it fo' Ah fo'gets."

"Belle, you old darling." Phoebe embraced her. "Hello, Ivy. My sisters have been telling me about you."

The girl curtsied, smiling.

Belle said, "Gits to the house, Ivy, an' unpacks Miss Phoebe's bags."

Ivy headed for the house at a run.

Phoebe walked into the big hall. "You've restored the place," she marveled. "Everything looks as it did before the war. Virgie, what a wonderful job you and Nan did. How good to see this again."

She began to walk toward the drawing room when she looked up and saw Lenore halfway down the grand staircase. Phoebe bowed her head and curtsied daintily.

"I'm happy to see you looking so well, Mrs. Hammond," she said.

Lenore resumed her slow and stately way down the stairs. At the bottom, she studied Phoebe with a critical eye.

"You look beautiful, Phoebe. Welcome home."

Virginia and Nanine exchanged stunned glances of surprise. However, Lenore's statement eliminated the tension the two sisters felt. Phoebe kissed Lenore on the cheek and received a warm smile in return. Phoebe then pirouetted several times to reveal her pleasure.

"You're as slim as ever," Lenore went on. "Your sister Virginia won't be for long."

Phoebe gasped and turned questioning eyes to Virginia.

"Yes," Virginia said, "I'm pregnant and I'll start showing soon. In fact I already have, but I can still hide it."

"How perfect a homecoming," Phoebe said.

"Not too wonderful," Lenore informed her. "Marty is dead; Miles died, and to my everlasting sorrow I never knew what a great man he was. I should have loved him as much as I loved poor Marty, but I shall miss them both equally. Now you girls get your stories told. We soon have to begin decorating. You know about the ball, Phoebe?"

"Yes, I've been told."

Lenore gazed steadily at Phoebe for a moment. "I'm afraid I have to say this because sooner or later it has to be said. Phoebe, you are a member of this family. Everyone who will live on the island knows about you. You grew up here, you were in the public eye recently. All of them know you are not completely white. They will have to accept you as their equal and treat you accordingly, or they'll hear from me. Now let's forget it. I have a headache. Why did you have to come back during all this confusion, Phoebe? Please excuse me now."

She went back upstairs. Nanine laughed. "Well, Mama's still in character."

"I don't know," Virginia mused. "She's beyond me."

Phoebe said, "I want to hear about the baby."

Virginia said, "You will have to, of course. First, I suggest we open a bottle of champagne. I hope my story won't shock you."

Ivy, summoned to bring the glasses and champagne, poured it expertly and withdrew.

The three sisters raised their glasses in a toast to their reunion.

"Please," Phoebe entreated, "the baby."

Virginia sobered. "It concerns Bradley Culver, the outlaw. In fact, he's the father of the child I'm carrying. You undoubtedly read about him."

"Yes. He's an escaped murderer," Phoebe said. "But Elias . . ."

"That's why he left," Virginia said. "I wrote you about his surgery. The doctors told him then he could not become a father."

"I still don't understand," Phoebe said.

Virginia went into detail then, explaining Elias's long absences from the island, her first meeting with Bradley Culver in the forest and the subsequent ones. She related every part of the story in detail, ending it by stating that only she and Nanine and the doctor in Charleston were aware that Elias was not the father. She also told how Elias had requested of the doctor that Elias's name be put on the birth certificate as the father of the child."

"Do you love Bradley Culver?" Phoebe asked.

"I'd like to say I didn't," Virginia replied. "At first, I know the attraction was carnal. At least that's what I thought. I'm a little frightened to be carrying the child of a man who doesn't seem to have a single redeeming quality to anyone."

"To anyone but you," Nanine said. "You love him, Virgie. Elias was hurt, but he understood. We do too."

"Yes," Phoebe said quietly. "And we love you. Nothing else matters now except the baby."

"Let's fill our glasses and drink to that," Virginia said. "Then we must dress for supper. Since the mansion was restored, Mama insists on everything formal. Every day Belle threatens to quit. I'm a bit shaky that she just might, right before the ball."

"Not Belle," Phoebe said. "She just likes to assert herself now and then. I'll have my bath and get ready for supper. I'd hate to disappoint your mother after the warm greeting I received."

Upstairs Phoebe discovered that Ivy had made all preparations for her bath, and while she washed, Ivy laid out her clothes after being told which gown Phoebe would wear.

Phoebe seated herself on a bench before the dressing table. Ivy stood just behind her. Phoebe studied her reflection.

"Ivy, you're almost white."

"Yes'm. Reckon so."

"Does it bother you?"

"Bothers me some. Don't know which way to turn."

"You could pass easily. Your skin isn't quite as white as mine, but you could easily pass."

"I think about it, ma'am, but after all I am black . . . some, I guess,"

"I was born on this island, Ivy. I was raised in this house. I was a slave too. I'm part black, just as you are. My father owned this plantation. I'm accepted as his daughter by the family."

"Miss Phoebe!" Ivy exclaimed in awe. "I can't believe it."

"Sometimes I can't, either. But listen well, Ivy. You're young, susceptible to praise and also to criticism. You'll get plenty of both, but never forget that you are part Negro, and be proud of it. We're unique, you and I, and everything will work out for you as it did for me. Almost," she added.

"Thank you for telling me this, Miss Phoebe. For confiding in me. I feel so much better about myself."

"Before we're done, we're going to find out who you are. In the meantime, we'll be friends."

She stood up and studied Ivy in much the same manner Virginia had regarded her. "Ivy, you do remind me of someone, though I've not the least idea who. It's odd I should think this way." She shrugged. "Nothing to it probably. Please help me dress."

The next days, up to the time of the ball, were as hectic as anything ever known at Valcour. There were the decorations, lavish this time, for more decorations were on the market, along with more kinds of food. They'd decided to spend extravagantly, for never again would there be a party quite like this one.

On the island itself, activity was intense. Furniture movers toiled up the slopes to the various houses. Every one had undergone a complete refurbishing. Some were in sorry condition. The one given up by a still irate and frustrated Tannet was among the worst, for he'd apparently done everything he could to make the restoration difficult. Yet it had been done.

To the head of each family Virginia had given a clear deed. She'd supplied money to buy furniture, arranged with banks to grant loans and had done everything in her power to get the people who belonged on Valcour once again in their homes.

Even before the work was done, the menfolk had returned to begin preparing their plantations for next year's crop. Valcour was teeming with activity.

No outsiders were to be invited. This was an affair for Valcour people only, and they were in sufficient number to fill Willowbrook mansion.

Everything was in high style. The three sisters had visited Charleston to buy gowns and an outfit for Lenore. The table was set with fine linen, china and silver, all direct from New York. Belle fussed about the dining room, cursing under her breath, but never as happy.

This time no barges were needed to bring the guests. They were already on Valcour. At dusk the procession of guests began their journey to Willowbrook in spanking new carriages.

A lavish banquet had been prepared for the several hundred blacks who worked on the island and were an essential part of it. Before long, the singing and shouting from their affair could be heard, making it seem like old times once again.

Nanine, Virginia, Phoebe and Lenore formed the receiving line at five. They looked stunning in their gowns of the latest fashion.

The guests arrived in a state of high excitement, which grew as the evening progressed. There were no speeches, just excellent food and wine, with a limited supply of good brandy for the men. Belle and her kitchen staff outdid themselves albeit to some of the most astonishing vocabulary that had been heard on Valcour.

Moses came to eat in the kitchen with Belle, and Ivy joined them. It was an evening that would be long remembered on Valcour. It didn't end until half through the night, during which time not one soul shied away from Phoebe, or even seemed to know that she was not all white. Or if they did, pretended ignorance. They begged her to perform one of her dances, which she did to the furious handclapping of the guests.

Even Lenore expanded. "Phoebe," she said when they were away from the main throng on the dance floor, "you are not my daughter, but I wish to heaven you were. Take care of my children, Virginia and Nanine. For you, of all people, can do so."

Phoebe recalled James Hammond had made the same request of her.

When the music finally stopped and the musicians wearily packed up to go back to the mainland, Nanine was collapsed in one of the big chairs, Lenore had gone to bed, Virginia rested her head against the high-backed chair.

Phoebe, seated on a stool, said, "It was a beautiful homecoming."

Nanine nodded. "Phoebe, you were readily accepted. You are now an important part of the island."

"I'm flattered and happy," Phoebe said, "but so exhausted I may not make my bedroom. May I say good night, sisters?"

"I'll go with you," Nanine said.

Virginia remained seated. The great house had grown quiet, just as it used to in the old days. The drawing room was still cleared for dancing, with only a few chairs on hand for those wearied by the activity. All lamps and candles were still lit, but soon a houseboy appeared and began extinguishing them.

"Just leave that big lamp near the door," Virginia told him. "Get yourself to bed."

The boy bowed and hurried to obey that order. Virginia sat a long time in the semigloom. The gaiety had passed. It was time to think, to remember and reflect.

Marty should have been here. Miles should have made his debut to the island society. Elias should have been giving orders and been by her side. Tom Sprague should have been here to lend his charm.

And Bradley Culver should have been lurking about somewhere. The party couldn't have been complete without him. She gently massaged her abdomen, which would soon swell with his child. She looked forward to it with nothing but happiness. She wouldn't even allow the absence of Elias to interfere with that.

Two years ago the war was still in all its fury. The months and weeks and days since then had been filled with activity. Some happy, some sad, some good and some bad. Now another year would begin in a few weeks and that was when Valcour would fully recover. The South would be far slower in its recovery, but Valcour would be complete. This was how Virginia had wanted it to be. The dreams she'd had during and just after the war had come true and she was more than satisfied.

She walked into the dining room. Some of the decorations were already beginning to fall down. The party was over. Virginia made her way upstairs, and in her rooms she prepared for bed. It wasn't long until dawn. Not that she minded. She went to bed, but left the night lamp on, turned low, for she wasn't quite ready for sleep. There was still too much thinking to do.

But her eyelids closed despite her efforts to keep them open. She turned on her side and blew out the lamp. But heavy-lidded or not, her eyes would not entirely close. After half an hour of near sleep, she rose and went into the bathroom to prepare a mild sleeping draught. This done, when she got in bed her eyelids seemed to snap closed and she was promptly asleep.

Yet it seemed that her dreaming didn't stop. Once she felt as if someone was in the room. Someone who seemed to float on air. Who stepped to the bedside, bent over it and caressed her face. Who kissed her lips and gently buried his face between her breasts.

It seemed so real that despite the effects of the sleeping draught, she awoke. Now she thought it seemed too real. She lit the lamp beside the bed, prepared to get up quickly to see if there was anyone in the room.

It was empty, the house was quiet. She smiled at the memory of the dream and lay back. As she pulled up the bedcovers, something moved toward her. Startled, she drew back a little and then she reached out and picked up the battered, sweat-stained campaign hat of a Confederate army officer.

She drew it under the covers, held it tight against her and the sleeping drug exerted itself again and she fell into a dreamless sleep.

The morning came slowly to Willowbrook. Even the servants slept late. Lenore sent word she would remain in bed until supper.

Nanine was the first at the breakfast table, soon followed by Phoebe. Virginia came down when they were finishing with their breakfast.

"Well," Nanine said, "what brings those stars to your eyes?"

Virginia smiled vaguely, gestured helplessly with her hands and looked more pleased than ever.

"What time did you go to bed?" Phoebe asked. "What happened after we left?"

"What makes you think anything happened?" Virginia asked.

"You wouldn't look as you do if nothing happened," Nanine said.

"I had a pleasant dream. A wonderful dream. Someone caressed me. Someone kissed me. I thought I dreamed it, yet it seemed real."

"A dream affected you like that?" Nanine asked, her smile disbelieving.

"This one did. It hasn't stopped yet. When I awoke, I found a man's hat on the bed beside me. An old campaign hat . . ."

"Brad!" Nanine exclaimed. "What a chance he must have taken. What a risk in coming here."

"I know," Virginia said. "I don't feel as though I'm quite as alone anymore."

"Wait until the baby is born," Phoebe said lightly. "You'll never be lonely again."

"Brad told me it would have to be a boy," Virginia said. "He insisted on it. And he said he'd be exactly like him."

"Is that good or bad?" Nanine asked.

"That's what worries me," Virginia replied.

"I've been thinking," Phoebe said, to stop that trend of thought, "that here we are. Three sisters. There's something else. My mother left me more than a quarter of a million dollars."

"Good Lord, you're rich. A whorehouse must be a lucrative business," Virginia said in surprise.

"The way Mama ran it, it certainly was."

Virginia made a steeple of her fingers and brought her hands close to her face. "I'm trying to think. We also have the big plantation worth at least a hundred thousand now it's in production. We have our plantation right here worth half that, I'd judge. We're owed the money we supplied to our good neighbors so they could move back.

A sum they'll repay. That would be another hundred thousand. Yes, we're wealthy."

"To me," Nanine said, "you're poor relations. Miles had Otto Mason bring a lawyer to the island and he made a will that left me . . . something just over a million!"

"We are," Virginia said in awe, "perhaps the wealthiest sisters in the United States."

They regarded this statement in wordless wonder for a while.

"But we haven't any men," Virginia said slowly. "No men."

"Shall we cry?" Nanine asked.

"Tears won't bring them back," Phoebe said. "But what in the world will we do?"

"I . . . don't know," Virginia said slowly. "I truly do not know. But don't you think we're going to find out?"

Best of Bestsellers
from WARNER BOOKS

__THE CARDINAL SINS
by Andrew Greeley   *(A90-913, $3.95)*
From the humblest parish to the inner councils of the Vatican, Father Greeley reveals the hierarchy of the Catholic Church as it really is, and its priests as the men they really are.

THE CARDINAL SINS follows the lives of two Irish boys who grow up on the West Side of Chicago and enter the priesthood. We share their triumphs as well as their tragedies and temptations.

__THY BROTHER'S WIFE
by Andrew Greeley   *(A30-055, $3.95)*
A gripping novel of political intrigue does with politics what THE CARDINAL SINS has done with the church.

This is the story of a complex, clever Irish politician whose occasional affairs cause him much guilt and worry. The story weaves together the strands of power and ambition in an informed and clear-eyed insider's novel of contemporary politics.
DON'T MISS IT!!!

__THE OFFICERS' WIVES
by Thomas Fleming   *(A90-920, $3.95)*
This is a book you will never forget. It is about the U.S. Army, the huge unwieldy organism on which much of the nation's survival depends. It is about Americans trying to live personal lives, to cling to touchstones of faith and hope in the grip of the blind, blunderous history of the last 25 years. It is about marriage, the illusions and hopes that people bring to it, the struggle to maintain and renew commitment.

DON'T MISS THESE EXCITING ROMANCES BY *VALERIE SHERWOOD*

__WILD WILLFUL LOVE
by Valerie Sherwood   *(D30-368, $3.95)*

This is the fiery sequel to RASH RECKLESS LOVE. She was once THE BUCCANEER'S LADY...but when beautiful, willful Imogene was tricked aboard ship bound for England, she vowed to forget Captain van Ryker, the dark-haired pirate who had filled her life and heart—only to banish her so cruelly. Somehow he would come to her again, and together they would soar to the heights of passion they first knew on the golden sands of a distant isle.

__BOLD BREATHLESS LOVE
by Valerie Sherwood   *(D30-702, $3.95)*

The surging saga of Imogene, a goddess of grace with riotous golden curls—and Verholst Van Rappard, her elegant idolator. They marry and he carries her off to America—not knowing that Imogene pines for a copper-haired Englishman who made her his on a distant isle and promised to return to her on the wings of love.

__RASH RECKLESS LOVE
by Valerie Sherwood   *(D90-915, $3.50)*

Valerie Sherwood's latest, the thrilling sequel to the million-copy bestseller BOLD BREATHLESS LOVE. Georgianna, the only daughter of Imogene, whom no man could gaze upon without yearning, was Fate's plaything... scorned when people thought her only a bondswoman's niece, courted as if she was a princess when Fortune made her a potential heiress.

BEST OF ROMANCE
FROM *WARNER BOOKS*

__**THE MER-LION**
by Lee Arthur   *(A90-044, $3.50)*
In Scotland, he was a noble...but in the bloody desert colosseum, he was a slave battling for the hand of a woman he hated. James Mackenzie intrigued royalty...the queen of France, the king of Scotland, the king of England, and the Amira Aisha of Tunis. But James Mackenzie was a man of destiny, a Scot whose fortune was guarded by THE MER-LION.

To order, use the coupon below. If you prefer to use your own stationery, please include complete title as well as book number and price. Allow 4 weeks for delivery.